MOON SLAUGHTER

Wolf and Gutenberg, vol. 1

A psychological thriller

ROXANN HILL
PAUL WAGLE

This novel is a work of fiction. Names, characters, businesses, places, events and incidents are either the products of the authors' imaginations or used in a fictitious manner. Any resemblance to actual persons, living or dead, or actual events is purely coincidental.

Copyright © 2024 Roxann Hill and Paul Wagle
All rights reserved.

Cover illustration by Alexios Saskalidis a.k.a 187designz.
Editors: Samantha Gordon/Invisible Ink, and Don "Yogi" Wagner.

For Sam,
whose wisdom continues to accumulate,
long after he has left us.

P.W.

"You forget that a thing is not necessarily true because a man dies for it."

Oscar Wilde, The Portrait of Mr. W.H., 1889

HE

The room in front of him is large. It seems to have no end. The moon, which shines alabastrine from outside, offers only scant light. It gives the furniture unearthly, strange contours that move and seem to come alive whenever a cloud passes over the sky.

The man waits; absolute tranquility reigns—heavy and oppressive, it announces an ominous event that will change everything. Death will come quietly, stealthily, and yet conclusively. And then, when it is all over, the moon will take on another color, lose its pale, faded glow, turn dark brown, and finally transform into a red that resembles blood.

The man is extremely tense and strangely appeased at the same time.

From far away, sounds penetrate his ear. He sits bolt upright, listens. He does not even so much as dare to breathe.

Nothing. He was mistaken.

Suddenly, the sounds come back. This time, louder.

Voices. Incoherent fragments of words are shouted. He concentrates, leans forward.

And now he hears it. Crystal clear: "You freak! You hideous monstrosity!"

Over and over and over…

He looks at the table in front of him. At the pistol he has ready to go. He grabs it, jumps up and runs…

March

21

Sunday

1

Six eternal seconds, that is how long it took to find his cell phone and halt the coffee table's glass top from its early morning knell. He had set the phone on silent the night before, but the alarm's vibration against the glass woke him.

He sat up halfway propping his elbow up on the couch while he strained to look at the display.

Too late; his mailbox was filling up.

Alex Gutenberg rubbed his face. His stubble made a faint, scratching sound as he ran his hand over his chin.

He had dreamed again. That ever-recurring dream. But the more he tried to remember the details, the faster they evaporated. And as he struggled to analyze the last images, they completely dissipated from his mind's eye.

He sat up, listened to the message on the answering machine, and furrowed his brow. He was not accustomed to being called in at this hour on a Sunday, and especially not out to Blankenese, one of Hamburg's more exclusive suburbs.

As the newly appointed Assistant District Attorney, he could not afford to appear hung over. He quickly freshened up.

Ten minutes later he was out the door, in his car, and heading across town.

Soon, he had left the apartment buildings of his middle-class neighborhood behind and reached the port. The giant cranes, which were usually busy loading containers onto the equally giant cargo ships, were standing still. A rare sight.

The unmistakable smell of the Elbe met his nose through a crack in the window as he skirted the warehouse district with its endless rows of identical red brick storehouses.

He followed the river out to the single-family dwellings of Blankenese. He passed homes stacked like an ancient fishing village, whose stucco façades were now interspersed with modern architecture. Finally, he drove into a gated community, where the yards were nearly the size of inner-city parks.

His year-old Seven Series sedan didn't stand out in this part of town, but he still did not feel like he fit in. No matter how spacious the homes were, no matter how much privacy or prestige such a place could offer, he sensed deep down he could never feel comfortable having to return to that every day.

Two gentle curves farther, and he had arrived at his destination. He pulled over, lowered his driver's side window, and showed his credentials to the uniformed police officer guarding the entrance to the property. The policeman waved him through.

Alex continued on at a snail's pace.

Two patrol cars; a dark unmarked sedan from the LKA, Hamburg's Bureau of Investigation; a VW bus from the K-

9 unit; an ambulance; and three hearses lined the curb in front of the home. Alex parked his BMW behind them.

He climbed out and took a look around. Even with the lush yard cut into the forest—and despite the evidence collection unit, who scanned the sprawling terrain with their two detection dogs—this place seemed strangely lifeless. The choir of birds that met his ears did nothing to change his opinion; amidst their cheerful chirping, the nineteenth-century villa appeared all the more faceless and dead.

He walked up the drive and was assaulted by the sun coming up over the five-car garage. The sky was bright blue, and the sun hung relatively high for this hour, seeing as daylight savings would coincide with Easter this year.

Henrik Breiter met him at the front door. "Sir," he said. And as Alex looked at him questioningly, the young detective from the LKA only shook his round head and stepped aside to make room for the Assistant District Attorney.

Alex entered. It took a bit before his eyesight adjusted to the abrupt darkness inside the house's expansive foyer. His head spun, and he told himself it was the change of light and not the alcohol he drank the night before, that was making him feel rocky.

He straightened his shoulders, ignoring the sudden nausea, and moved on.

Once he was out of the entryway, he was greeted by a gentler sunlight filling the front room via a wall of Edwardian windowpanes.

He followed a shaft back from one of countless prisms projecting rainbows on the floor. The beveled edges of those same panes refracted light around the room, dancing the spectrum off parquet wood floors, massive oriental rugs, and a stone mantel piece.

The fireplace looked fine and functional, but the lack of ashes left it uninteresting.

The drapes, the carpet, the chairs—all seemed to be in place.

He continued to peruse the far wall. The view out the windows was of a manicured English garden; he could barely see the next house through the evergreens.

He turned back to Henrik, who was leaning toward the commotion in the basement.

Without a word, the plainclothes detective swiveled around. Alex followed, and they walked through the kitchen and down the servant's stairwell into a finished subterranean parlor full of white hoods and blue gloves.

He and Henrik pulled on the requisite protective gear.

Alex suppressed the impulse to immediately enter the room. Instead, he forced himself to stop, and stood at the entrance, looking at the luxurious parlor and the scene that presented itself to him. He concentrated solely on observing, and what he saw made the aftereffects of his evening of stiff drinks dissipate in one blow.

Amid the improvised forensics lab were three corpses sitting in chairs. And blood. A lot of blood. Since it was all dry and the evidence collection unit's own body odor overpowered that of the corpses', the crime must have taken place late last night or early this morning. The corpses' temperatures and relative stiffness would attest to that.

Alex took a few steps into the room and stopped again. The first detail that caught his eye was the high, arching blood splatter that reached the ceiling. He followed the trajectory of the spray on the northern-most wall to a well-dressed man with a large piece of his scalp missing, at about the angle necessary to have left that elliptical stain on the elegant wallpaper. Presumably, the piece of his head was removed with the same sword that still ran through him, hitting some major interior vitals on its journey.

Alex lifted his eyes and filtered out the dead bodies for a moment. In the farthest corner, he discovered a broken glass vitrine displaying antique cutlasses and other edged naval weaponry; off to the right, a pool table covered with an assortment of sex toys. Along the opposite wall was a well-stocked bar. The rest of the room seemed undisturbed. He returned his focus to the group of dead men in the chairs near the broken display case.

Next to the well-dressed man with a sword sticking out of his belly was the second corpse. This man's throat was seemingly slit by a smaller yet equally sharp blade, judging by the deep, scalpel-straight incision. The victim's head was hanging over the back of the chair; the blood had swelled out of the neck and saturated his shirt. There was a dried stain on the floor below him, rigor mortis had set in, and, Alex was convinced, the body had not been moved.

He turned to the third victim and stopped a beat. Squinting, he stepped closer to get a better look. He had not been mistaken. Directly in front of him, sitting on a chair was the Reeperbahn Red-Light District Boss, *Big Karl* Marten. He had a bullet hole in his chest. His left hand was covered in blood, and there was a small knife on the ground to the right of his feet.

Henrik, who had not left Alex's side the whole time, turned to him. "So? What do you think?"

Alex exhaled slowly. Only then did he answer.

"Maybe the pimp was standing when he was shot," he said, calling Henrik's attention to a second bullet hole on the back wall above Karl's head.

"Yeah, possibly." Henrik nodded.

"Triple murder," Alex said under his breath as he looked around the room once again. His gaze stuck on a fourth chair. It was empty.

"There's another body. In the lavatory, sir," Henrik said and led the way.

The tiled room was the size of a small apartment. As soon as Alex entered, he ran into a wall of stench. He bit down hard and consciously breathed through his clenched teeth.

He spotted the fourth body beyond the pedestal sink, one hand reaching for the massage table. Distorted with pain, the dead man was lying in a pool of vomit. There was no blood.

The forensics team was waiting for the go-ahead to remove the corpse. Alex nodded almost imperceptibly, and the men spread out the plastic.

Alex watched as they bagged the body. He felt awkwardly ineffective.

"That's hideous," Henrik stated.

"Especially at this hour," Alex replied.

"Have you ever seen such a massacre?"

Alex shook his head. "Not for a long while anyway."

Henrik lowered his eyes and remained silent for a moment, and then, "There's a witness."

Alex jolted. "Really?"

"Yeah. Captain Strobelsohn brought her and her boyfriend upstairs. Our doctor is with them right now."

"The doctor? Have the woman or her boyfriend given a statement yet?"

Henrik shrugged. "No idea, but when I came in earlier the girl was completely silent and appeared to have lost her wits."

"Let's go upstairs then. We're just in the forensics team's way; they seem to have this under control."

Henrik looked around, "Is there anything special you want done down here?"

"The usual. As many photographs as possible. In case we missed something, we can review them later. And check what the neighbors caught on their surveillance systems," Alex said before he turned away and climbed the stairs two at a time.

2

The room was lined with books. Leather reading chairs were dispersed throughout, each with its own art deco floor lamp.

When Alex entered, the Bureau's doctor looked up from cleaning the cuts of an average-sized blonde woman. She was sitting on one of the leather chairs with her feet resting on throw pillows stacked on an ottoman. She had two black eyes.

Alex realized that she wasn't following the doctor's questions; she merely stared out into space, like she would not react even if he had shined a bright light directly in her face.

Captain Strobelsohn, Henrik's superior, stood at the far end of the room. As usual, the middle-aged hulk of a man seemed put off. He nodded a short recognition to Alex and turned back to the young man wearing a track suit with whom he had been speaking. The man appeared pale and extremely shocked. No wonder, after what he had found in the basement.

Henrik had now joined Alex and followed his gaze. He leaned over and whispered in Alex's ear, "That is the man who called it in. According to him, the young woman was in this confused state when he arrived. His name is Peter Westphal; he had come to pick her up for a date. And her name is Suzanne Carstens. The geezer with the sword sticking out of his gut is her grandfather."

Alex listened intently. "What did you say? Carstens?"

"Yeah, Björn Carstens. He's some kind of big shot. You know him?"

Alex hesitated almost imperceptibly. "Well not personally. He was the head of the International Chamber of Commerce when I was a cadet. If I remember right, he began his career as a diplomat, retired early, and then made a fortune in the shipping business. What was he doing with Big Karl is the question, I suppose—right after who gave Carstens his new *piercing*?"

Alex left Henrik's side and walked directly up to the doctor, inconspicuously appraising Peter, who was dwarfed when compared to Strobelsohn. Peter stood about six feet tall, with short blond hair on a head that was bent toward the floor.

Suddenly, he raised his eyes and looked directly at Alex.

Alex produced an unsuspecting smile and continued over to the two men, stretching his hand out to the young man. "Excuse me. You're Peter Westphal?"

"Yes," Peter responded.

They shook hands. Alex noticed Peter's surprisingly firm grip. And Alex noticed something else: Peter Westphal had blood stains on his jacket and sweatpants.

"I believe I need to introduce myself. I am Alex Gutenberg, from the DA's office. You were the one that called in the incident this morning?"

"Yes," Peter repeated slightly bewildered.

Alex nodded reassuringly. "What time did you arrive at the premises?"

"I suppose it was six or six fifteen."

"What were you doing here so early on a Sunday?"

"I had a date with Suzanne."

"A six o'clock date?" Alex ascertained, furrowing his brow.

Peter closed his eyes for a second. "We were going jogging."

"Who let you in?"

"I let myself in after no one came to the door." This time Peter held Alex's stare.

"Then you have your own key?"

"No." Peter shook his head. "I have not known Miss Carstens that long. When no one answered, I walked around back and found that the rear door was ajar."

"Was anything out of the ordinary?"

"Well, just that the door was open. I had never used the rear entrance before."

Alex nodded once more. "So, you walked into the house, and then… what happened?"

"At first, I didn't notice anything. After looking upstairs in Suzi's room and wandering through the house, I heard a noise and checked the basement parlor."

"And what did you find?"

Peter took a deep breath. "Suzi was sitting there on the floor of the rec room in between the chairs with the three bloody corpses. The only one I recognized was her grandfather. When I approached her, I realized she was holding a piece of his skull in her lap. She was pretty badly cut on the face, but it had long since scabbed over."

"That must have been a great shock for you to see all that," Alex noted. "Most people wouldn't have been able to think straight. But that did not seem to have bothered you."

That bewildered look appeared again. "I can't be the judge of that. It was extremely gruesome. But because of my job, I am pretty used to keeping my emotions in check. I am sure that helped."

"What do you do for work?" Alex mustered a truly sympathetic tone to his voice. "If I had to guess, I would say something that requires a bit of physical exertion. Fireman, construction, along those lines?"

"Kind of like that, I'm an underwater welder," Peter said, a bit more relaxed.

"Sounds interesting." Alex eyed the man across from him with new attention. "And dangerous."

Peter attempted a smile. "I like everything to do with the water, and I like to work alone."

Alex smiled back. "I can understand that." He got serious again. "So, this morning you were in the basement, you walked up to your girlfriend, and then what did you do?"

"I reached my hand out, and when she did not react, I moved the scalp from her lap and placed it on the table. I grabbed it by a few hairs. I know I shouldn't have touched it, but I had planned to take her in my arms." Peter paused and narrowed his eyes. "She was not responding, so I left her long enough to call the police. When I returned, she was still sitting there, and I thought I had better not move anything else, so I took a place on the floor next to her and waited for the police."

Strobelsohn, who had until this point been quiet, cleared his throat. "Sir, I've taken Mr. Westphal's statement. But I'm going to need him to come downtown and go over the details once again."

It had not escaped Alex that the police captain said the word *details* as inconspicuously as possible. Knowing

Strobelsohn, he was well aware that the captain was implying his intentions to cross-examine Peter Westphal, paying attention to any inconsistencies that might arise in his story.

"I'd rather stay with Suzanne," Peter proclaimed.

Strobelsohn wanted to answer, but Alex beat him to it. "I can understand that one hundred percent, but you can rest assured that Miss Carstens will receive the best possible care. You are presently our only witness until your girlfriend is able to give a statement. Can you appreciate our predicament?"

Peter nodded reluctantly.

"We can't waste any time," Strobelsohn hurried to add. "And maybe something will come to mind that you hadn't previously thought of, that will help us to catch the perpetrators of this horrendous crime."

Strobelsohn's reassuring words didn't seem to have an impact on Peter's reluctance. "But then I want to be taken to her immediately."

"Of course, you do," Alex offered. "As soon as the doctors release her, and all the formalities are over with. And please, don't be alarmed if forensics wants to look at your clothing or take a cast of your shoes. We can't neglect the slightest detail." As he said this, he threw Strobelsohn a willful glance. Upon receiving an affirming nod, he returned to the Bureau's doctor, who was still trying to get a response from the catatonic witness.

"When will I be able to speak with her, Hamdy?"

The doctor shrugged his shoulders. "Your guess is as good as mine, Alex. These lapses can last hours, weeks, or even months. She has obviously witnessed several brutal murders; I think you should give her a couple of days after she comes to before you interrogate her."

"That's time we don't have."

3

The elevator stopped with a jolt. The obligatory *ping* sounded.

I got out.

A normal clinic. Gray linoleum floors. The smell of antiseptic in the air. Fluorescent lights.

I oriented myself, looked around and, on the right, found the sign to the station I was searching for: *B4, Behavioral Neurology*.

A nurse appeared from one of the side corridors. She was carrying a tray of blood samples and hurried past me almost in silence, completely ignoring me. I deliberately adjusted my speed and waited until she opened the frosted station door with a key card. She stepped through, and I trailed close behind her. The heels of my pumps rattled loudly over the floor.

The hall was lined with empty, unmade hospital beds and the typical carts with bottles of water, glasses, and towels. Caregivers hurried around. Through one of the open doors to my left, I could see a patient being cared for by an orderly.

I reached the nurses' station and was just about to pass it by.

An elderly man dressed in white cotton pants and T-shirt jumped out and stood in my way. "Hello? Where do you think you're going?"

I was forced to stop.

"This is not an open station. You are surely lost." He gestured toward the entrance. "You'll have to go back."

"No," I said. "B4. That's here? Then I'm in the right place."

"But access is restricted to authorized personnel."

"I know." I turned the handbag that I wore over my shoulder, so the orderly could see my attached credentials.

He leaned forward, narrowed his eyes, and read what was written on it. Then he straightened up and smiled apologetically. "I couldn't have known that."

"No problem. You're just doing your job," I said. "I'm looking for a patient. Suzanne Carstens. Had to have been admitted about an hour ago."

"Carstens?" he said. "Room 421. If you'd like, I can show you the way."

"Thank you, that won't be necessary. I'll find it myself."

I passed him and continued on down the hall.

Framed copies of Monet and Degas paintings hung on the walls. Obviously, they were supposed to convey some sort of normality to this place. The medicinal smell seemed to grow stronger.

I took a wrong turn, went back, found the right hall, and could see a uniformed policeman standing in front of a room. He had nothing to do, so he looked at me all the more critically as I approached. He even raised his hand to stop me when I had almost reached him.

I showed my credentials once more.

He said nothing, just nodded and took a step to the side to let me pass.

I walked in without knocking.

A young woman lay catatonic on a raised hospital bed with her head propped up under pillows. Her face full of bruises, her bandaged arms stretched out powerless on the white bed sheet. IVs were attached to the back of her hand.

A doctor and a nurse were taking her vitals. When they heard me, they stopped and looked up.

"May I help you?" the doctor asked.

And again, I showed my badge. But this time, the doctor took it off my bag and studied it meticulously.

I gave him a moment and waited until he handed it back to me. In the interval, I could observe the victim. The young woman was not asleep. Her eyes were half opened; her pupils dilated. She stared lethargically into space.

"You can continue," I told the doctor. "I'll stand here on the sidelines and do my work while you do yours."

The doctor, a man of about fifty, furrowed his brow. "And your work… consists of what exactly?"

I smiled warily. "You've just read that, sir. I am Dr. Wolf, criminal psychologist for Hamburg's LKA."

The physician's expression relaxed. "Excuse me, would you like to sit down?"

I shook my head. "You don't need to worry about me."

The physician turned away from me and again devoted himself to the patient. He checked one of the drips. The nurse pulled the bedspread into place. Then they both straightened up.

"Miss Schäfer," the doctor instructed the nurse. "Pass by once an hour and change fluids as necessary. Other than that, I have given her a strong sedative. With some luck, the patient might even be able to sleep. Complications are not to be expected, but you never know."

The nurse nodded, and he turned his attention to me.

"As I said, this will take a little while," I answered his silent question.

"Yes, then…" he replied. "I'll check on my other patients. If you need me, the nurses' station can always reach me."

"Thank you," I said, watching the doctor and the nurse as they left the room.

I was alone with the patient. Suzanne Carstens was still lying motionless in bed. How old was she? Twenty-five? Probably no older.

I stepped up to her bedside. I could clearly see her chest raise and fall. She gasped softly under her breath. What did she have to go through? What had she lived to tell?

Up close, her injuries were worse than I'd first assumed. Her face had been beaten black and blue. She had obviously lost some blood. Most of it had been washed away, but I could vividly imagine how she must have looked a few hours before.

I would study the images taken at the crime scene later. But those were just photos. Here in front of me was the victim, a real person, not a piece of paper, nothing hypothetical.

"Miss Carstens?" I spoke to her—neither loud, nor aggressive, but resolutely and with emphasis. Sometimes patients in this condition respond to that.

The young woman did not move.

Sometimes the use of a surname turns out to be too impersonal for traumatized victims and arouses too few associations. I tried something else.

"Suzanne?" I said softly. "Wake up."

Childhood memories are an interesting thing. They are often able to trigger more than the most refined pharmacopoeia.

And this time, too, my words did not miss their target. But with a different outcome than I had expected. The patient began to tremble, trying to open her eyes completely. Her gaze wandered around the room helplessly. She groaned.

Either an abrupt pain or her childhood memories were not as positive as they should be. I leaned toward the latter.

Suzanne Carstens was undeniably a beautiful woman. Small, sensitive hands and a smooth, chiseled face. What stood out of place was her slightly crooked nose.

I leaned forward, stroked my fingertips over the bridge of her nose. It had clearly been broken once, long ago, and well-healed. Possibly reconstructed.

The young woman groaned again. She seemed to not like my touch.

"Do not be afraid," I consoled her. "You're safe now."

I put a hand on her forehead and gently stroked her hair. She stopped moaning; her breathing became more regular.

The door flew open. It almost hit the wall.

A man in an expensive-looking suit rushed in. He stopped suddenly when he saw me. His eyes wandered over my face, my body, my hand, the patient, and back again. He waited for me to stop stroking the victim.

Which I did not do.

We looked at each other. A tall, rather slender man. Dark, almost black hair. Temples sprinkled with the first signs of gray but cropped so short that it was hardly noticeable. Piercing, dark eyes. Five o'clock shadow. Robust, pronounced chin. Obviously strong-willed. From his attitude, he was used to bossing other people around. An ex-soldier in a tailored Italian suit.

A lot of women find such a testosterone-controlled macho type attractive. But with me, he was clearly working on the wrong keyhole.

I noticed that he studied me as intensely as I did him. Almost shamelessly, his glance wandered over me. Perhaps he believed that this was his given right.

Arrogant asshole! shot through my head.

"Who are you and what are you doing with my witness?" His voice suited him. Melodic and yet cold. And very businesslike.

I deliberately let some time pass before I answered. "And who are you?"

"*Me*?" he replied.

I began to smile. "Yes, you. Or do you see someone else in the room I might be talking to?"

One of the corners of his mouth twitched involuntarily. "You think you're a comedian?"

I did not reply.

He breathed in audibly and said, "Ah. A headshrinker."

His words were full of contempt.

"I prefer the title *Criminal Psychologist*."

The man raised an eyebrow. "And then why do I, in my role as a prosecutor, not know who you are?"

"I have only been working in Hamburg a few days now."

Again, that slight twitch around the corner of his mouth. Otherwise, he was well under control. I had to give him that.

"Dr. Evelin Wolf," he said. "I remember reading your name recently in an email."

"Yes," I confirmed. "Dr. Wolf is fine. And you must be Mr. Gutenberg."

That should have flattered him, but it did not.

"I see you've done your homework," he noted.

"But you haven't," I replied. "Otherwise, you wouldn't have barged in here." And before he could answer, I added, "Now leave this hospital room immediately."

This time I had done it. He wouldn't take that.

"You surely do not think I'm going to let you order me around like that!" He grew angry and got louder. *Well, OK then, he's no Superman!*

Before I could properly enjoy my triumph, the patient became uneasy. I had been stroking her the entire time. Now she murmured something unintelligible and moved her head back and forth.

"We should continue our conversation in the hallway," I said firmly.

Gutenberg wanted to say something, but instead threw a long glance at the wounded and nearly unconscious woman.

"Now," I interrupted his thoughts and pointed toward the hall.

He turned on his heels, stood next to the door, and held it open. I accepted his offer and steered my way past him into the corridor. He followed.

4

The uniformed officer tried to keep his stance when Gutenberg stepped into the hallway. Then he had apparently noticed the tension between us. He insecurely batted his gaze from Gutenberg to me.

The prosecutor smiled at me, and I could see how he breathed deeply; in and out. A good technique to get oneself back under control. And if you don't know about it, it goes unnoticed as well.

But I did know.

I gave him a delighted smile, and for a fraction of a second, a telltale sign flashed in his eyes. Of course, he was quick and saw what I was up to.

Sounding businesslike, he turned to the policeman, "Do you want to get a cup of coffee? You've been on duty for a long time."

"Well. Yes," said the officer. "Not that I mind. But…"

Gutenberg did not let him talk and sent him away with a corresponding head jolt. The gesture was supposed to appear succinct and self-assured, but it betrayed one thing to me: Gutenberg was still angry. About to explode.

The police officer left us. But then a few doctors appeared. They quickly stepped past us, discussing the results of an EEG. Finally, they vanished with sweeping coats into one of the rooms.

We were alone.

Gutenberg gawked at me with those dark, penetrating eyes. Otherwise, his face did not reveal any emotion. Then, he raised his right hand and showed me four outstretched fingers.

I examined his hand with a deliberate intensity before seeking to make eye contact with him again. This time he would not let go. He stared right back at me.

I did not do him the favor of looking away.

He cleared his throat. His eyelids fluttered, but just once. "Four bodies," he said. "And the only one who can tell me what happened is your Sleeping Beauty inside that room."

I acted as if what he was telling me was something immensely important. A groundbreaking discovery. I nodded openly and approvingly.

"I understand that. But even if you were able to interview Miss Carstens right now, it would serve no purpose. She is in terrible condition and has been heavily sedated. Her statement would not have cogency of proof."

That hit home. Against that, he would not have any argument… or so I thought.

"I don't give a shit about cogency of proof," he issued a clear and surprising retort. "What I need is a lead. One or more mental cases entered a house, scalped people, and cut their throats. It looked like a slaughterhouse."

He scrutinized me again.

"Wow," I whispered.

"What, *wow*?" He actually furrowed his brow.

"You think you can disturb me by describing some gruesome details, or possibly even try to intimidate me?" I moved a little closer to him. We were now so near to one another that I could have touched him if I had wanted. "I've probably been to more crime scenes than you. And I know that as an investigator you always have to keep a cool head. You can never let your emotions take over. It's called maintaining a professional distance."

He smiled. No, he grinned.

"You think I react emotionally?" His rage seemed to have been blown away. His excitement had disappeared. He came off as cool as an ice block. Perhaps I had underestimated him.

"I do not know what emotions you have," I said. "But your behavior indicates to me that you are obsessively ambitious and therefore want to solve the case immediately."

There was that grin again. I could not penetrate his ego.

"And you can tell all this? It's that easy?" he said.

Now I felt myself getting angry. So much for *professional distance.* "Besides, you are an ex-soldier. If I had to guess, an officer. And the scar on your chin suggests that you saw some combat—and got wounded. Then you landed in the legal department, and now you want to climb the ladder by hook or crook. In addition to this, you have a clearly pronounced inferiority complex."

"What?" He pretended to be stunned. But I was sure it was his shtick, which he—the thoughts rushed through my head—which he used with women to entrap them. The audacity, to try this cheap trick on me! And simply outrageous that he had almost succeeded with it.

I pointed my finger at him. "You wear an expensive suit and carry a concealed weapon. I'm sure you don't need the latter for your job."

He shrugged. "It's not my fault."

"That you have an inferiority complex?" I replied a tad too eagerly.

His smile was almost genuine. "That your relationship fell apart."

"That has nothing to do with it," I retorted.

"Yeah, it does," he replied slowly. "A new city, a new job. And if I am not mistaken, a new hair color. This dark red…" He shook his head bluntly. "As a psychologist, how would you analyze that?"

"Chestnut!" slipped out.

"Whatever," he said.

Our eyes met again. And gradually, his smile disappeared.

"No chance," I said. "You will not speak to Miss Carstens until I am of the opinion that she is prepared to do so."

He exhaled audibly. "That is your last word?"

"Definitely." This was the end of the conversation for me.

He put his hands in his pant pockets and bent back a little. "All right. We will have to work a lot of cases together in the future, and perhaps…"

"You do not want to make any silly threats now, do you?" I interrupted him.

He grimaced. "No. But it does not seem to me that this is *the beginning of a beautiful friendship*."

I lowered my eyes for a moment, finding the strength to conjure a relaxed smile across my face, with which I turned to him. "Why are most of the men I know Bogart fans? That tiny man has not been cool for a long time. Besides, he was a heavy smoker. That is an absolute dealbreaker today. You can't score with that anymore."

He looked from me to the door, behind which the victim lay. "You call me as soon as Miss Carstens can be interviewed?" This was not a question as much as it was a statement.

"Agreed," I replied.

Without saying another word, he turned around and left. His movements were fluid, he squared his shoulders. He obviously worked out a lot. When a woman gets involved with that kind of man, she has lost from the start. Guys like that only care about themselves.

Still, the way he walked down the hallway, he did not appear just alone, but very lonely.

5

Alex left his car in the empty visitor parking lot in front of the newly built six-story modern headquarters of Hamburg's LKA. He trotted up to the main entrance of the shiny gray, glass and anodized aluminum sided building, which seemed to greet visitors from every face of its round construction.

Upon seeing the new Assistant District Attorney, the front desk guard pushed a button allowing him to enter the security chamber. Alex thanked the weekend watchman, walked through the gate, and made a beeline to his usual means of exercise: the stairwell.

Five stories later, his heart rate had barely risen as he walked onto the detectives' wing of the building. It surprised him how much activity there was for a Sunday. He continued down the hall past several offices until he got to Strobelsohn's. Bumping his shoulder into the door, Alex acknowledged it was locked.

If not Strobelsohn's, then Henrik's, he thought to himself and went a few doors farther. He knocked and walked in.

The two policemen were alone at Henrik's desk in the office, drinking coffee and, presumably, comparing theories. Alex could not make out anything, since the two abruptly dropped the chatter as he approached.

"What's up?" Alex inquired.

"If it must be said, sir, Henrik was fantasizing out loud about who was going to be doing what to whom with the rubber dongs we found at the scene," Strobelsohn explained straight-faced, while Henrik grinned and raised his eyebrows suggestively.

"But honestly, we need to find out if someone was supposed to be showing up as the *entertainment*, and if they can shine some light on what went wrong," Strobelsohn continued.

Alex pulled a chair around, grabbed a coffee mug, and poured himself a cup from the pot, which was sitting conveniently on the table between the policemen. Then he took a seat by Strobelsohn and Henrik. "Let's start from the beginning: Did the alarm system record anything, or was there evidence of forced entry?"

Strobelsohn shook his head: "No. The video surveillance had been turned off before any of the guests arrived. None of the locks on the doors, or any of the windows, were pried open. But the premises are expansive, and it will take some time until we have scrutinized every nook and cranny. For now, we have to assume that the perps had access to the property."

"Or," Henrik added, "the victims knew the murderers, and let them in."

"The simplest alternative would be that they have killed one another," Alex said.

"That would accelerate our investigation considerably. We have perpetrators and victims in one room," said Strobelsohn. "But we're never that lucky. At least I'm not."

"The geezer in the toilet was probably poisoned! We should get the lab results tomorrow morning, and then we will know for certain," Henrik blurted out. He had his nose buried in a file. That is why he escaped the irritated look Strobelsohn threw him. "He is one Alistair Grauel," Henrik continued. "No record, not even a speeding ticket. Lived near the wharf in Hamburg. There is no evidence suggesting that he shot a gun, and he didn't have a speck of blood on his hands or his clothes."

"OK." Alex thought twice before asking, "Who do we have sitting between Mr. Carstens and Big Karl?"

"Dr. Hans Dietrich Schilling, a local gynecologist, who lived a few kilometers away from Björn Carstens in Nienstedten," Strobelsohn offered fresh information. "The preliminary forensics tests revealed that it's his blood on the pocketknife that was lying next to Karl and all over Karl's left hand."

"Was Karl left-handed?" Alex dug deeper.

Henrik flipped through his file and shrugged. "There is nothing about that here. But I will look into it and find out."

"Thanks," Alex said. "Let's assume our victims have actually killed each other. How would that have played out?" he pondered. "For instance, Karl cuts the gynecologist's throat. But then who shoots Karl? Carstens?"

"Possibly," grumbled Strobelsohn.

"But who gave the old man a new part?" Henrik added, again out of tempo. "There's no one left."

Henrik was a nice guy and a capable investigator. It was not his intention to show disrespect with his flippant remarks. He just wanted to fit in. Be one of the big boys. Alex was aware of that. But sometimes the young policeman shot past his goal in his quest for recognition. Alex had decided a while ago to ignore Henrik's occasional outbursts whenever possible. They would take care of themselves over time.

"Anyway, what happened down there was a real massacre," Henrik continued. "The perpetrators must have been totally freaked out." His eyes lit up. "Maybe it had something to do with the lunar eclipse last night."

"Lunar eclipse?" Strobelsohn repeated with a creased brow.

"Of course. I watched it from my balcony. Cool event. It lasted well into the morning, but I saw the moon begin to shadow over and then about half past one it started…"

"What has that got to do with our case?" Strobelsohn asked.

"Well, a lot of people freak out when the moon suddenly turns blood red…" Henrik hesitated. "One should rename manslaughter to moonslaughter."

"Superstitious drivel," Strobelsohn interrupted gruffly and the lines on his forehead deepened.

Henrik, who apparently wanted to add something more, closed his mouth, looked down with a crimson head, and said nothing.

"Let's play through our crime scenario," Alex said into the silence. "Karl must have been standing when he was shot, and then he collapsed into the chair, where he died. Whoever shot him could have commanded him to drop the knife, or it could have simply fallen when he was hit." Alex motioned to one side of Henrik's desk. "The shot came from over here. And then the murderer walks over there," he pointed to a space in between Strobelsohn and Henrik, "and slices Björn Carstens's scalp off and runs him through with a sword?"

"Well honestly Mr. Gutenberg, that is what Henrik and I really were discussing when you came in," Strobelsohn said. "It doesn't make any sense to me. Henrik reckons it was a sex party gone wrong, and possibly because of the posh address the pimp made the arrangements himself."

Alex frowned. "You expect me to believe the prostitutes turned on their boss and scalped the client for pocket money? And where does Suzanne Carstens fit into all this? She was covered in blood. And I'd bet my last cent it was not all hers… No, this looks more like a professional job to me."

"We have not found any sign, not a single track or print that they would've had to have left when exiting such a bloodbath," Strobelsohn interjected.

"What else do we have?" Alex took a sip from his coffee.

"Theoretically, it could have been our *Brunhilda*, Suzanne Carstens," Henrik speculated. "Like you said, she was covered with blood. And if the victims put up a fight, that would explain all of her injuries. I am curious to get the results from forensics. Our colleagues collected her clothing from the hospital and are in the process of analyzing the biological evidence. We'll get these results tomorrow as well."

"What about the bloody scalp she was holding when her boyfriend found her?" Strobelsohn said.

"A fragile young woman against four men, or three, if we leave the poisoned one out of it?" Alex shook his head in disbelief. "At least Big Karl certainly had a chance, time and again, to physically defend himself. And where is the weapon? We have a lot of cutlasses, and sabers, but the gun is missing."

"We're still looking. We'll leave no stone unturned."

"Anyway," Alex insisted. "A young woman kills several men, alone? I can't see that. By any stretch of the imagination." He stared out of the window and added, "But we still have this Peter Westphal, who called it in. And it is, more times than not, the guy who called it in. How did Mr. Westphal fare on his cross-examination?"

Strobelsohn raised his brows and simultaneously shrugged. "Besides some contradictory body language, his story stacked up flawlessly with what he had said at the house. I still had the opinion he knew more than he was telling us." He paused momentarily. "The evidence collection unit took his sweat jacket, his pants, and his shoes—they were also bloody, though nothing like Suzanne Carstens's."

"Forensics will have a lot to do. That will be a long report," Alex said. "How did Peter Westphal explain the blood on his clothes?"

"Well"—Strobelsohn made an ambiguous gesture with his massive hand—"he reckons that it got on his clothes when he put his arms around Suzanne Carstens. And the scalp which he took from her was literally dripping. Although he said he was careful, he cannot rule out that some had got on his clothes. As for the shoes, he suspects he accidentally stepped in one of the many pools of blood."

"Which could all be possible," Alex replied. "Have you let him go?"

"Not yet," Henrik said. "We told him he needs to sign some paperwork, once we have it ready. He is still sitting in the interrogation room if you want to have a word with him."

Alex shook his head. "No, that won't be necessary. I've already spoken with him." He looked at Strobelsohn. "You are going to have to let Westphal leave if we don't have anything on him."

Strobelsohn nodded.

Alex sat still a moment, took a drink from his coffee, and then continued, "As for me, I went to the clinic to talk with Miss Carstens."

"And?" Henrik asked.

"Unfortunately, that was a waste of time," Alex said. "There was a criminal psychologist there, and she wouldn't let me speak to the witness." He stopped short. "I was just asking myself, how this Dr. Wolf knew about the case and who sent for her."

Strobelsohn was quick to respond. "It wasn't us, but most likely our boss." He grimaced. "I had to inform Mr. Bolsen, of course. And as soon as he heard that it was Björn Carstens that was murdered in his own home, he flipped out."

Henrik grinned broadly. "Phenomenal scene."

Strobelsohn looked at Henrik soberly and back to Alex before he continued. "That's why there was such a large evidence collection unit dancing around. And in the meantime, he has already called twice to check on our progress. I would have to be greatly mistaken if Bolsen wasn't the one who invited the criminal psychologist. He more than likely intends to get us all together in a special task force."

"Ah, great, political ties, that's what's driving it. This just keeps getting better," Alex carped.

"If that damned shrink would let us talk to the granddaughter, we'd have arrested the perps already," Henrik said.

"Maybe," Alex agreed.

They pondered silently.

Alex threw Henrik a look, "Remember the slug in the wall above Karl? We know that it can't be the gynecologist; by that time, Schilling was already dead."

"Or Alistair Grauel; like I said before, there was no blood or gunfire residue found on him," Henrik added.

Strobelsohn offered his usual disgruntled opinion, "We know two people who didn't do it."

"That brings me back to Suzanne Carstens, who theoretically could have scalped the old man. But why would she kill her own grandfather? And in such a gruesome manner?" Alex said. He remained silent for a while. "The cutlass we found in Björn certainly came from the collection of nautical swords displayed in the broken glass case. If Suzanne did kill her grandfather, she would have had to be next to the smashed cabinet. From that position it wouldn't have been possible for her to shoot Karl." He deliberated again. "Let's suppose Peter was present during the murders; he could have fired the shot that killed the pimp. That's everyone accounted for at the scene; that would be the most logical explanation. But this is all speculation. We have to have hard evidence, or this will blow up in our faces."

"Yeah, we can't go on too many assumptions," Strobelsohn chimed in. "You know what they say about assuming."

And per usual Henrik sounded out too abruptly. "Speaking of asses, did you get a load of the new *shrink*? Thinking about losing my shit so I can go get my head checked out."

Strobelsohn's only response was raised eyebrows. Alex ignored Henrik's statement altogether.

Henrik's face turned red, and he bit his lower lip.

"Do you know her?" Alex asked.

"We both know who she is," Strobelsohn said. "The chief introduced her at our weekly forum. And then he pranced her around in front of every department… Imagine getting a grand tour of the premises from Harald Bolsen."

"Yeah, I could use that like a new hole in my head." Henrik backed out of his chair, "I'm going to get some fresh coffee."

Strobelsohn, no doubt, took the opportunity to see if Alex was aware with whom he was dealing. "What do you know about Björn Carstens?"

"Not much," Alex responded cautiously. "He was a big name back in the day. And once, when I was starting out in the force, a case I was assisting on gave cause to ask him some questions." Alex paused. He lowered his voice and continued, "I never really felt comfortable that I wasn't allowed to pose those questions. Let's put it that way."

Strobelsohn started to reply to that in hushed tones, only to be interrupted by the returning Henrik. "The first TV News team is at the moat. I feel sorry for anyone dumb enough to use the empty visitor parking today."

6

Alex stepped out of the LKA's headquarters, popped the collar of his jacket, and managed to avoid the throng of reporters that had gathered around Harald Bolsen, the press-happy Chief of Hamburg's Bureau of Criminal Investigations. Bolsen assured the people, the perpetrators would be brought to justice. Saying something along the lines that although it was too early to give any details, the case had taken on the highest priority.

Alex skirted the crowd, climbed into his car, and drove over the Elbchaussee en route to his office.

He turned onto Gorch-Fock-Wall and at a distance could see the dark ramparts of the building where the state prosecutors roosted. Becoming visible a little farther down was the familiar reddish-brown façade of the imposing, five-story complex itself, which dated back to the end of the century before last.

He was in luck. Because it was Sunday, he found a parking space almost directly in front of the entrance. He turned off the engine, climbed out, and hurried up the stairs to his department. Hanging his coat on a hook as soon as he had opened his door, Alex loosened his tie and got comfortable while his computer booted up.

Clicking on the local news, it did not surprise him that the first headline was already out. The words *no suspects* jumped off the page as he opened a new browser window and typed *Björn Carstens*. He waited a beat before hitting return, backspaced over this, and entered *Evelin Wolf*.

Selecting a recent picture, he was prompted to log into Facebook. He hated the fact that he had an account, but at least it would let him have a look.

However, even after signing in, he only saw limited information. This Dr. Wolf was single—that much he had figured out on his own. She was born in Hamburg, like him. And as a current city, she had Wiesbaden. The last bit was clearly outdated.

He returned to Google and looked for any articles. It did not take him long before finding a local social blog that seemed to have received the same press release, he got from the department: Dr. Wolf had eight years' experience as a criminal psychologist at the Wiesbaden Bureau of Investigation. She completed her doctorate work while at the Bureau—the title of her dissertation was *From Love to Murder: Relationship Dynamics in Crimes of Passion*.

To top it off, she had an additional degree in psychotherapy. Alex knew that continuing education ate up a lot of money. *Sponsored by daddy*—the psychologist had to have come from a well-off family.

But none of this helped Alex. If he wanted to get some real information, he was going to have to dig a little deeper.

Alex leaned back in his chair and rummaged through his jacket for his cell. He opened up his contact list and stopped. Then he put it down on his desk.

He waited three full minutes before picking the phone up again and immediately put a call through to his academy drinking buddy, who also happened to work in Wiesbaden.

"Hi, Arne, it's me Alex. How are you doing? Did I catch you at a bad time?"

"It's never a bad time to hear from you Alex. What's up?" Arne sounded happy.

"Well, I have a high-profile case that is about to hit the presses, and I need to get to a witness. Problem is, she has a watchdog of a psychologist that won't let me near her. The shrink is one of yours, and I was wondering if you couldn't help me out with what makes her tick."

"Let me guess: Dr. Evelin Wolf," Arne said in best spirits. "Forget it, man. She thwarts every attempt to pierce that armor. She dated some local loser, lounge-lizard type, forever. Never knew what she saw in him. Anyway, after that, she didn't seem that interested in any of the many, *many* men who tried to crack that case. As you've obviously already noticed, she isn't hard on the eyes."

Alex furrowed his brow. "I was talking about her but meant on a more professional level. How can I get her to release my witness?"

"Oh. She isn't going to obstruct justice or anything. She isn't some bleeding heart. She'll let you have your witness, but not before it is time." Arne laughed. "She is a lot like you; she doesn't bend the rules. And she sure as hell doesn't let anyone tell her how to do her job. I suppose that is why she has done so well for herself. And you too! Congratulations on the promotion."

"Thanks Arne," Alex said, "I'll let you get back to it."

"Is that all you called about?" Arne sounded disappointed.

"That and to hear how you were doing," Alex hurried to add.

"All right," Arne responded with some reservation, "I'll look you up next time I am in Hamburg, and we will *finally* drink *down* like we *used* to do."

7

I gently closed the door to Suzanne's hospital room. I nodded to the police officer, who was once again at his post, and went back to the nurses' station—this time, without getting lost.

Through the high glass panes, I saw the orderly who had stopped me a while before. He sat in front of a computer and tapped on the keyboard with two fingers.

It was not long before he noticed my presence. He interrupted his work, got up, and came out to me.

"Can I help you?" Judging from his gestures and his posture, he was anxious to establish a good rapport with me.

I smiled at him. "I do need your help. I have to speak with Miss Carstens's doctor again."

"Dr. Hubmann," he said, and when I nodded, he added, "Please come with me. I'll take you to him."

I followed him a short distance. He knocked and motioned that I should wait. He entered and closed the door behind him.

Staff Only read a sign on the wall. *Break Room,* I thought.

In no time, he was back. "He'll be right there."

I nodded again, and the orderly left me alone.

A minute later the doctor appeared in the corridor. The smell of fresh coffee clung to him. "Dr. Wolf? You wanted to speak with me?"

"Thank you for taking the time," I said.

"Gladly," he replied.

"Miss Carstens fell asleep a short while ago. I would be very grateful if you would inform me as soon as she wakes up." I reached into my pocket and handed him one of my business cards.

He put it in his pocket without looking at it. "She is heavily sedated. It may be that the patient first comes to, late in the evening, or in the middle of the night."

I shrugged. "That's perfectly fine."

"Good." His face indicated to me that he had to get back to his work.

"I do have another question for you," I began.

"Yes?"

"Have you noticed anything special about Miss Carstens?"

He furrowed his brow. "What should I have noticed? She has lacerations, which you have also seen. And she is seriously traumatized."

I looked directly at him and smiled. "I do not want you to tell me what everyone can see. I want you to tell me what you felt when you treated her."

"Felt?" The furrows on his forehead deepened.

"I know this is a bit unusual," I replied, letting my smile disappear. "It is important. Just try it. Try to remember how you felt."

He wanted to answer something, thought better, and took a deep breath. He shifted his gaze from me. Instead, he looked at one of the paintings that hung behind me on the wall.

"Felt," he muttered.

I remained silent.

Once again, he took a deep breath and turned his attention back to me. "A miracle that she had survived at all. It was a very close call." He paused. "Does that help?"

"Yes," I said. "Thanks a lot."

8

As soon as I pulled my Audi out of the parking garage, the sun shone directly into my face. I flipped down the visor. The weather was unusual for mid-March. Spontaneously, I pressed a button on the dashboard and the convertible roof of my cabriolet folded back automatically.

The light blast of wind that reached my face was fresh and cool, almost cold. Another flip of a switch, and the neck-level heating began to warm me. Delightful.

I started out in the direction of Bahrenfeld, to my parents' house. The term was actually inaccurate. My mother had been dead for a long time. My sister had moved with her family to London three months ago. And as for my father… He has lived in an exclusive private retirement home for several years.

The big house where I grew up had been empty since my sister's move to Great Britain. I had my belongings from Wiesbaden sent there, and it was all waiting in countless cardboard boxes for me to unpack.

I thought for a moment. No, I did not want to do that at all. Not on such a beautiful day.

I changed into the left lane at the next intersection and turned off. I used both hands to steer and let myself be carried away by the traffic.

I thought about Suzanne Carstens. How she had been lying prostrate in bed. About the bruises on her face. How her arms were anchored to the white blankets, immovable, like foreign bodies, which did not belong to her—thick bandages, the obligatory drip in the back of her hand.

Why did Dr. Hubmann believe Suzanne had been lucky to survive? Surely there were injuries. But none of the wounds were life-threatening. Where did the doctor's feeling come from? From the knowledge of what had happened in the house? I shook my head. This explanation seemed the most self-evident, but it did not convince me. So, what was it?

I remembered how I had tried to reach Suzanne Carstens. She had not responded at all to her last name. Very much so, however, to her first name. The reaction was markedly and undoubtedly negative. Moreover, for someone who was heavily sedated, extremely intense.

Perhaps this near-death experience, which Dr. Hubmann felt in Suzanne's proximity, had nothing to do with the incidents from last night, but with events that happened long before. Possibly something from her childhood.

And me? What had I felt when I had stroked my hand over Suzanne's brow? I listened to my inner self, gave it time.

Despair? No. A shattered helplessness. I had felt that until... I frowned and exhaled in a loud huff...until this Gutenberg had barged in.

I tried to pull myself together and keep my focus on Suzanne. But I could not. This arrogant Assistant District Attorney nudged himself ruthlessly to the fore. Again. Anger started burning deep inside me.

But the harder I tried, Suzanne Carstens's image faded from my inner eye. And in its place, this Gutenberg became even more present.

It took him only a few minutes to find my Achilles' heel. Of course, he was right. My relationship with Jens in Wiesbaden had failed. That's why I left everything behind. My life to this point, my friends, my work at the Bureau. Hence the fresh start in Hamburg.

With his remark, he had hurt me severely. And yet, although the fact had not escaped him that he had hit the bull's eye, he did not rub it in. Maybe this Gutenberg had something similar to a strand of decency after all?

Perhaps his coolness was simply a guise, behind which hid a sensitive, soulful person. I clicked my tongue captiously. *Yeah right, an emotional man! If he's hard on the outside, he's got a soft core...* It was exactly the same misconception that got me stuck on Jens. That would not happen again. Definitely not.

I applied the brakes and maneuvered my S3 into a parking space. I closed the convertible top, turned off the engine, and climbed out.

On the right was an endless row of old Art Nouveau buildings. But I looked in the other direction. Over the green parking, across the road, and beyond it, I could see the lead-gray belt of the Alster. The trees on her riverbanks were still bare at this time of year, dark silhouettes against the blue sky.

In the past few days, having so much to do, I had not actually realized that I was back home. I locked the Audi with the fob and walked a few steps to a four-story corner building, the first floor of which was a Greek restaurant.

Poseidon. The same old lettering on the rectangular sign above the windows, perhaps somewhat fainter, sun-bleached over the years. But still excessively ornate and kitschy. I liked it.

On the narrow sidewalk in front of the restaurant was room for some tables. One was still free. I sat down and turned my chair toward the sun.

The promenade along the river was well-traveled. Couples and families with and without carriages strolled by, joggers trotting in between. The benches were all occupied. Everyone enjoyed Sunday and the spring weather in their own way.

The white triangles of small yachts hovered over the water, accompanied by shrieking seagulls. Single sculls glided across the river, leaving a dark trail in the gentle waves. Boats were not my thing, but from firm ground, they were nice to look at.

A young waitress in a black skirt and a white blouse appeared at my table with her pad in hand. "What can I bring you?" she asked.

Before I could answer, a voice sounded, "What is going on here?"

A man in his mid-sixties stood in the entrance to the restaurant. Rather small, rotund, with a noticeable belly, which the dark vest that he wore over his shirt could not conceal. His hair was wiry and almost white. No longer tinged with gray, as I had remembered.

I eyed him as he stepped beside the waitress.

He put his hands on his hips, his face a singular, indignant accusation. "Unbelievable that you dare to sit here without first coming to see me."

I stood up. "Georgios," I said, as if that were an answer to his allegation.

He put his arms around me and hugged me. Long and firm.

At some point, he broke away from me, took a step back, and studied me thoroughly. Then he turned to the young waitress who did not know how to behave and clung to her order pad with both hands.

"Look at her," he said to her. He pointed to me. "She is emaciated. That can't be. She'll have the grill plate with lots of beans and extra tzatziki… and a still mineral water, hold the lemon."

The waitress oscillated from him to me and back again.

"And now—quickly!" He made a shooing motion with both hands.

The young waitress smiled apprehensively, turned around, and disappeared into the restaurant.

"It's a good server you have there," I said as I watched her walk away.

"She tries," Georgios said. "At her age, you were much better."

"You're exaggerating massively." I sat down, and Georgios also took a seat.

"How is the Poseidon doing?" I asked.

Georgios nodded contentedly. "Good. Very good. I cannot complain." He paused, raised his shoulder, and added softly, "I miss Victoria."

"Your wife was a spectacular person," I said.

"Sometimes I feel a bit alone, even though there are many people around." Again, he paused. A warm smile spread across his face. "But since you wrote me saying that you're back in the city and this time to stay, I'm content and happy."

"Yes," I said resolutely. "This time I'm staying."

"Of course." Georgios nodded emphatically. "Wiesbaden is not a real city. You cannot possibly live there." He leaned over to me and tapped his forefinger on the table. "Hamburg. *That* is a city! I never understood why you left in the first place."

I had to grin. "Now I am back."

Georgios pointed his thumbs over his shoulder. "And you know, Evi, you always have your home here. Whenever you need it."

It could not be true. I frowned. "Don't tell me you still haven't rented out my little attic apartment."

"Well"—Georgios looked at me mischievously—"I've tried to rent it a dozen times. But no one wants it!"

"Sure," I said straight-faced. "A small flat with a view of the Alster, you could never find a tenant."

"You got me." Georgios winked. "And besides, Victoria told me to leave the apartment free. At some point, you'd return."

"I'm staying in my parents' house."

"That's fine. But in case you need a change of scenery, or you want to have some real food, then you come see your old Georgios."

March

22

Monday

9

A wide street, rather a gravel road—lined with two- and three-story houses with flat roofs. Their brown, unadorned façades have evident bullet holes. Machine guns and grenades have left their mark.

Above him, a bright azure sky. A blue so clear that it hurts his eyes. He knows his way around here, has been here many times. But this time, it is different. A ghostly, unreal serenity hangs over the place. There is not a soul far and wide.

He walks attentively, and although it's early in the morning, it's still cold, nearly freezing. He sweats under his helmet.

The assault rifle in his hands weighs heavily on his mind. His index finger is, as he has been trained, clear of the trigger.

He reaches a corner, circling around, always ready to fire. Every fiber of his body is tense. He is waiting for the slightest hint of an ambush, but nothing happens. There is only a foreboding silence.

Suddenly, the wind stirs. Whispering, softly howling, it plunges through the ruins, and dry dust swirls in small cyclones.

A few hundred yards off in the distance is a shed. He is familiar with it from his daily patrols. He squints, cursing himself for forgetting his sunglasses in the jeep.

The shed is haphazardly made up of old boards; rusty corrugated iron serves as a roof. Something is in front of it. A person with a green jacket—leaning against the door. Motionless, head down.

He takes a deep breath, puts his finger on the trigger, and continues. Moving closer to see what's going on.

The man at the door raises his eyes slowly, looks up at him. He knows this man. But that cannot be possible! No! That should've never have happened…

Alex jolted awake. Breathing heavily, he stroked his damp forehead. The last scene of his dream hung fleetingly over his waking moment and was replaced by the sobering thought of having to talk to Suzanne Carstens.

He thought for a minute. If he knew anything about the fairer sex, it was that they had a hard time getting off the pillow. And that went double for fuzzy-headed soft-science enthusiasts like the new criminal psychologist.

He had to hurry. There was one person who could override Dr. Wolf's decision. He grabbed the phone from the bedside table and punched in Strobelsohn's number.

Thirty minutes later, he was allowed entrance into the hospital ward where Suzanne Carstens occupied a bed. Alex wandered through the halls of the fourth floor undisturbed.

He found a helpful orderly who led him directly to a room marked *Staff Only*. Alex stayed impatiently in the corridor while the young man disappeared inside.

As he waited, he felt his restlessness grow. He only had a small window of time to carry out his plan.

The door opened finally and Dr. Hubmann came out to talk to him.

"I'm Alex Gutenberg, an attorney for the city," Alex began. "Is Suzanne Carstens under your care?"

"Yes, hello—first off," Dr. Hubmann answered cautiously. "I am in charge of Miss Carstens's physical well-being. If that is what you want to know."

"Good, you're just the man I need to talk to," Alex said and tried to conjure a friendly smile, which he found difficult due to his internal strife. "As you probably know, Miss Carstens is the only witness of a quadruple homicide, and I need to speak with her immediately. The detective on the case, Captain Gert Strobelsohn, will join me any minute now and is expecting to take a preliminary statement from your patient." He looked directly at the doctor. "I hope you can understand the urgency of this situation. Your assistance is greatly appreciated."

The doctor returned his stare and did not appear impressed. "Mr. Gutenberg, is it?" He did not wait for a response and continued, "I do not think you will get very far with our patient, although there are no physical reasons that would obstruct you from questioning her. She is heavily medicated. And contrary to popular belief, the sedatives Miss Carstens is on, do not work as a truth serum." He put his hands in the pockets of his smock. "Dr. Wolf, of the Bureau of Investigation, has requested that the patient not be disturbed. And I ask for your understanding that I will leave the final word with my colleague."

Alex stood silent longer than he was used to.

"I can appreciate your professional caution, and collegial support," he said in a friendly tone, "but Dr. Wolf made this request yesterday afternoon. I am sure Miss Carstens is capable of giving a short statement by now." He took a step closer to Dr. Hubmann and added a little intrigue to his voice. "We have homicidal lunatics on the loose. We can't afford to wait for the Bureau's doctor to come around to make a new assessment. There is no telling how many cases Dr. Wolf is working on. Clearly you see how time is of the essence here?"

Dr. Hubmann nodded. "Sir, I am sure this is important. But my job differs from yours in many ways, most notably my oath not to do any harm to my patients." He looked at his watch. "Now if you would excuse me, I have several of them waiting on me at this very moment. The final decision lies with Dr. Wolf. I'd suggest you discuss it directly with her. She's drinking a cup of coffee in the break room." He stretched his hand out to Alex to bid him farewell.

Alex ignored the gesture. "Dr. Wolf is in the break room?"

The doctor let his hand drop. "Yes. She was already with Miss Carstens when I arrived this morning."

Damn, Alex thought. *It has all been in vain*. Getting up early, rushing to the hospital, trying to get Dr. Hubmann on his side. The therapist must have read his mind. She beat him to the punch.

Alex took a deep breath and swallowed his anger. It would not help matters if he lost his composure. He did not, under any circumstances, want to give the *young shrink* the satisfaction.

"Well, if that is the case, then I suggest we go right in there together"—Alex pointed toward the door—"and discuss the next steps with *our* colleague." His voice remained calm and controlled as if nothing had happened.

Dr. Hubmann hesitated. He looked indecisively at the door. Finally, he pulled on it and held it open for Alex, who walked past him, leading the way into the room. Dr. Hubmann followed after.

Dr. Wolf sat alone at a round table. Before her was the remaining half of a cup of coffee and next to it a second full cup. She did not rise, but merely watched Alex and the doctor enter.

Alex sat next to her. Dr. Hubmann remained standing.

"I didn't know how you take your coffee. So, I left it black," she said.

Alex shoved the cup aside and looked at her. "Dr. Hubmann just said there were no physical reasons that say Miss Carstens couldn't be asked a few questions."

"And that my esteemed colleague from the LKA has the final word on the matter," Dr. Hubmann immediately added.

"OK, fair enough, you did say that too," Alex addressed the doctor, without taking his eyes off of the psychologist. "What do you think, Dr. Wolf? It's been over twenty-four hours. We have killers on the loose. You can't deny me a few words with her just because she's been given a couple of sleeping pills."

Dr. Hubmann stared at his feet like he wished he were somewhere else.

Alex braced himself to hear a barrage of cogency of proof and what not. But to his great surprise she simply said, "We'll give it a shot."

"*We'll?*" Alex repeated, a bit stunned.

"Yes. I'm going to have to be present," Dr. Wolf answered succinctly.

Alex did not like that idea at all, but he was getting his way, and he decided against any further discussion.

The three started off toward Suzanne's hospital room in silence. There, a policewoman stood on duty, and next to her, Strobelsohn waited with a recorder in his hand. He put on a deliberate business-like demeanor while he greeted everyone.

"I think you can get along fine on your own from here," Dr. Hubmann said. "I need to continue. My rounds are waiting." He turned and went back in the direction from which they had come.

Strobelsohn nodded to the police officer, who opened the door and allowed them entrance. They maintained their reticence.

Suzanne lay motionless on her bed, like the day before. She was staring ahead and seemed not to acknowledge their presence.

Alex moved closer and stuck his hand out. "Hello, I'm Alex Gutenberg, a prosecutor for the city."

Suzanne did not move a muscle.

Dr. Wolf pushed past Alex, stood next to Suzanne's bed, and caressed her shoulder without saying a word.

Suzanne did not respond to the touch.

Alex pulled his arm slowly back and tried again. "Miss Carstens, Captain Strobelsohn and I would like to ask you a few questions about the night before last."

Suzanne rolled her eyes up into her head and seemed to be looking in Dr. Wolf's general direction. Her shoulders started to tremble. The psychologist stroked them, but this did not seem to help matters. Suzanne began to moan, her shaking intensified.

Strobelsohn stepped forward and spoke softly, "Miss Carstens, please, we only have one or two questions. Do you know who is responsible for your grandfather's murder?"

Suzanne riled up as if she were having an epileptic seizure. Her entire body was shuddering. With her neck arched back into her pillow, she stared at Dr. Wolf.

The numbers on one of the monitors started climbing and the machine began to beep.

Dr. Hubmann rushed into the room. "I think that is just about enough, gentlemen."

Dr. Wolf threw her head, motioning that Alex and Strobelsohn should get out. She was stroking Miss Carstens's hand when the two men took their leave.

As soon as they were out of the room, Alex looked at Strobelsohn. "It doesn't appear we're going to get any statement out of her today. Why don't you head back to your office, and I'll try to smooth things over here. We need these people on our side."

Strobelsohn shook his head. "I've never seen a witness react like that. She must have really gone through a lot that night."

"Yeah." Alex nodded. "But it doesn't do us any good unless we can get her to talk about it."

"I'll see you back at my office. Surely the lab results will give us something to go on." At that Strobelsohn turned around and left Alex alone.

As the thought of the forthcoming discussion passed through Alex's head, Dr. Wolf quietly stepped into the hall.

"Well, are you convinced now?" She asked so unobtrusively that Alex was put off his guard.

"I see she is not ready to speak to me, or Captain Strobelsohn for that matter. We'll send a woman tomorrow; she might feel more comfortable then."

"If you think that would help," the psychologist responded curtly.

Alex could tell she wanted to say more, but she held her tongue. This infuriated him, but he did his best to not let her see it. "Do you have a better idea?"

Dr. Wolf merely shook her head.

Alex could feel the blood rushing to his ears as the phone in his breast pocket began to vibrate. Stepping away from her he took the call.

"Hello Captain Strobelsohn, do you have some news for me? … Yeah? … Okay, I'll be right behind you."

Alex put his phone in his pocket again and turned back to her as calmly as he could.

"The lab results are in?" Dr. Wolf surmised.

"Mhmm," Alex mumbled.

"Then I shouldn't keep you any longer."

10

Alex pulled out onto the street with two women on his mind. One would not speak with him at all and when the other did, he was not sure he liked what she said. He was so lost in thought, he missed his turn on Deelböge and followed the traffic and his GPS's suggestion up the 433. What had gotten into him? He was never that inattentive.

Arriving at the LKA headquarters, Alex parked in front of the modern building and made his way through the security door and up the back stairwell.

Detective Henrik Breiter sat in front of Strobelsohn's desk when Alex let himself in after a short announcing knock. Henrik stood upright and then grabbed one of the chairs along the rear wall for the Assistant District Attorney.

Alex took the seat from him and placed it next to the young detective's.

Strobelsohn, who sat enthroned in his swivel chair, twisted his mouth. "That didn't go so well at the hospital. How did you manage to appease her?"

Alex sighed quietly. "I didn't. I didn't even admit that it was too soon to question the witness and just said that we would send a woman tomorrow. Maybe that wasn't right. What would you have done in my place?"

"To tell you the truth, Mr. Gutenberg, I don't think that girl will talk to anyone." Strobelsohn said frankly. "I don't know what I would have suggested. Hypnotism?"

Henrik nearly jumped out of his chair. "She'll probably start speaking after we arrest her boyfriend."

Alex raised one eyebrow. "Oh yeah? What do we have on him?"

Dramatically opening the file in front of him, Henrik started in. "First and foremost, besides the blood stains he said must have come from trying to move Suzanne, there are traces of Björn's blood sprayed on his jacket. These splatters are not smeared. He has Big Karl's blood as well as that of the gynecologist, Dr. Schilling, on his pant leg and shoe."

Henrik really was giving it his best.

"Thank you, Mr. Breiter," Alex said with an appreciative nod.

Strobelsohn cleared his throat. "The spatter pattern might indicate that he was present when the act occurred. But they could have just as easily come about when he took the blood-soaked scalp from Suzanne Carstens. Both are possible. As for the blood on his pants and shoe—that could have come from his sitting next to Miss Carstens. And Big Karl's blood... maybe he grazed a bloody object."

"Everything is still unclear," Alex stated. "That doesn't prove anything."

"Like when I took Westphal's statement, I felt as if he was hiding something from me," Strobelsohn said.

"You want to request a warrant for his arrest to make Westphal talk?" Alex double-checked.

Strobelsohn nodded. "We do not have many other options."

Alex thought for a moment. "Good. Let's try it. With a little luck, the magistrate will play along. What else do you have?"

Henrik eagerly dug through his file. "Suzanne Carstens had blood from two of the victims in the parlor on her, from her grandfather and Big Karl, and was presumably there when the murders took place. And just as we had assumed, the gynecologist's blood is all over Big Karl's left hand. The pimp's fingerprints are on the knife, which he had by all appearances cut the doctor's throat with. I will still ask, but I think we can take this as evidence that Big Karl was left-handed." Henrik flipped to the next page. "And as we had guessed, Big Karl was standing when he was shot. We still haven't found the gun."

"That leaves the sword which killed Björn Carstens." Alex said. "Did the forensic specialists find anything on the cutlass besides the blood?"

"Unfortunately, not," Henrik replied.

"Not even a fingerprint?" Alex ascertained.

Henrik shook his head. "None. According to the lab report, the handle was wiped down."

Strobelsohn butted in. "Tell him about the poison."

"Oh yeah, get this," Henrik continued. "They were all on opiates, Fentanyl. Sixteen something-or-others per milliliter. Now, opiates don't seem to fit in with a sex party but what do I know?"

Alex shook his head. "Maybe they didn't realize they were taking it."

"Well, I doubt they imagined they were consuming near lethal amounts of nicotine!" Henrik piped in. "Fentanyl was not the only substance the lab found. Alistair Grauel, the old guy in the bathroom, who, by the by, died from an apparent heart attack, had the highest concentrations in his system. Of both Fentanyl and nicotine."

"Nicotine!?" Alex repeated in wonderment.

"It takes a lot of nicotine to kill a person," Strobelsohn pondered. "How do you get someone to take that amount without noticing?"

"Alcohol," Alex offered. "Were their drinks spiked?"

Henrik shook his head. "Well, there was nothing found in them. The men were all having different cocktails: two Long Island iced teas, a gin and tonic, and one Scotch. However, there is no evidence that the glasses had been drunk from."

"No?" Alex asked puzzled.

"No," Henrik confirmed.

"Was there alcohol in their stomachs?"

"Yes." This time Henrik nodded. "All of them. But there were no lip prints on the glasses. And the only fingerprints on Karl's tumbler were from his right hand." Henrik looked at Alex. "Maybe Carstens wanted to poison the attendees? Or, Schilling, the gynecologist? He could have gotten the nicotine."

"And then he took it by mistake? I doubt that. Where else could you get that poison?" Alex contemplated for a moment. "What about an e-cigarette? Don't those have lethal amounts?"

"Funny you should ask, Mr. Gutenberg, because that was my first thought too." Henrik continued, "But the forensics guy told me that in Europe, the liquid nicotine in e-cigs has less than two percent concentration in it. He did say something like, it isn't unheard of to get pure nicotine by the liter in other parts of the world, or that a good cigar soaked in water could have enough nicotine to kill an adult man."

"So, what do we have? Four men drugged, poisoned, and then slaughtered. We can exclude all of them from being the mastermind. Someone took their time to cover their tracks. If it isn't our star-crossed lover, then they are still out on the run, and until Suzanne Carstens starts to speak, we don't have anything else to go on." Alex turned to Strobelsohn. "How soon will we have the warrant for Peter's arrest?"

Strobelsohn opened his mouth to respond. At that moment his boss, Harald Bolsen, barged in the door. "Arrest? Do you have a suspect on the Carstens's murders?"

"Good morning, sir," Strobelsohn mumbled a little surprised. "We only have the boy who called it in. Our eyewitness is still not capable of making a statement."

"Not capable, or she doesn't want to incriminate her money-hungry lover?" Bolsen let out. "I need to be able to tell the people their homes are safe. You get me a killer even if you have to invent one."

Turning to leave, his gaze fell on Alex. "Oh hello, Mr. Gutenberg, of course I didn't mean anything with that. We'll get the man who did this and supply you with the evidence needed to convict him. Good day." Without waiting for a reply, the chief of the LKA let himself out of his subordinate's office.

Stretching his eyes as wide as he could, Alex nodded to Strobelsohn. "Well, I guess you have your orders."

"I've got to go arrest some poor underwater welder while the real killers are running high stakes on the Reeperbahn." Strobelsohn sighed.

"I know what you mean. I don't think that kid could have done it, but like you said, he witnessed more than he has told us. Let's get him back in here. He shouldn't be too hard to find. Wasn't he asking to be granted visitation rights yesterday?"

"I'm sorry to interrupt, Mr. Gutenberg," Henrik broke in. "I've been waiting for an appropriate moment, I was about to tell you, and then Chief Bolsen came in and I nearly forgot."

"What is it Henrik?" Strobelsohn replied, a little more dour than necessary.

Henrik had a guilty face. "I forgot to mention this to you too, Captain Strobelsohn. The evidence collection unit found a cufflink in Björn's right hand. It's probably nothing, but he had a different pair on and no one else in the room was wearing any."

"This just keeps getting stranger." Alex furrowed his brow. "No one drinks from their glasses and old man Carstens is changing his jewelry. Was there anything special about them?"

"No, only that it was a bit tarnished and incomplete," Henrik answered.

"Incomplete?"

"There was only one single cufflink. It appears to be made of gold, with an inset diamond. Here is a picture of it. Have a look for yourself."

Alex took the folder from Henrik and after a short gander said, "We'll have to search his belongings and find the other one. And we still need the gun. You guys get to work on that warrant, and I'll see if Peter Westphal was offered any visitation from our friendly Bureau psychologist."

Strobelsohn reached his hand across the table. "All right then, I'll call you as soon as we have the warrant. And good luck getting anything from that icy shrink."

"Oh, she is not all that icy," Alex admitted. "She is only doing her job. And Mr. Strobelsohn, you and I both saw Suzanne Carstens today. I hope she snaps out of it soon, or she might actually be seeing her boyfriend up on trial for this."

Strobelsohn stood as Alex walked himself to the door. "Icy or not, good luck all the same."

11

I sat in a guest chair in a broad, tiled hallway, waiting. The lower third of the wall was also tiled. The rest, along with the vaulted high ceiling, had been painted with white, slightly yellowed tempera. Historically protected building.

It was peaceful. Only the occasional muffled ringing of a telephone or the murmur of voices penetrated through the closed doors of the numerous offices. By comparison, the LKA bubbled with life. There was always someone in the hallways or stairs, talking to colleagues, visitors coming and going. But here at the Hamburg prosecutor's office: a burgeoning oasis of tranquility.

I sat up straight in my chair.

Waiting is an art. Once you have mastered it, it is very relaxing. It helps you to focus on what's about to happen and provides loads of serenity and confidence.

After another ten minutes, I heard footsteps, and at the same time a tall, slender man in an elegant suit came around the corner. He walked briskly in my direction. Then his posture indicated that he had recognized me. For a tiny, traitorous moment, his movements fell out of rhythm. Really only briefly, and you would only be aware of it if you consciously concentrated on it.

A blink of the eye later and Gutenberg had rebounded.

Suddenly I felt strangely uncomfortable. I had to force myself to remain sitting still without taking my eyes off him.

He stopped in front of me and looked down. "Dr. Wolf?"

My restlessness grew stronger. I slowly rose to my feet. "Mr. Gutenberg," I responded.

We stood face-to-face... close, like the day before in the corridor of the hospital. And we both remained silent.

Actually, I wanted him to be the first to speak. He won.

"Our conversation this morning, in the clinic, got interrupted," I said as his dark eyes ogled me. They even flashed for a fraction of a second.

"Then we'll pick it up in my office," he said.

He did not give me an opportunity to reply. Instead, he turned to the door next to me, opened it, and asked me to enter with a silent gesture.

We went through a reception area, where one woman worked on a computer. Again, he held a door open, and we were in his office.

I looked around. Light gray, unadorned filing cabinets, light gray shelves full of legal books, a light gray desk with matching chair. A light gray meeting corner with four chairs. They were black for a change. And a similar light gray chest of drawers, on which two photos stood: a group shot of soldiers and a picture of policemen. Both photographs seemed to be older.

He reached in my direction, and at first, I did not know what he wanted. Then he helped me out of my coat. This was absolutely old-fashioned, on the other hand pleasantly unexpected. I suppose that's why I liked it.

He hung my jacket on the coat rack, slipped out of his own, and placed it beside mine. He looked at me and pointed to the conference table.

"Please, make yourself comfortable."

I sat down, and he chose a spot opposite me.

"Would you like something to drink?" he asked.

"No, thank you," I declined.

Silence descended upon us. And this time, I was determined to leave the initiative to him.

A small, irritated crease appeared on his forehead. His mouth twitched, and then he started. "Miss Carstens is my most important and sole witness. She must have seen the perpetrators. I urgently need her statement."

I waited a moment before I replied. Finally, I said, "You can keep trying to question Miss Carstens. Either you do it yourself, or you send Captain Strobelsohn. For all I care, go ahead and assign a younger or alternatively a more senior female officer. The result will always be the same. Miss Carstens will not speak to any of you."

He rocked back on two legs of the chair and folded his arms in front of his chest. "Really?"

I nodded and leaned forward. "Miss Carstens is displaying all the symptoms of a post-traumatic anxiety disorder. This is usually accompanied with a catatonic demeanor and, in most cases, causes retrograde amnesia."

The fold on his forehead deepened. "In layman's terms that means she can't remember anything at all and is completely worthless to me as a witness?"

He wanted to continue, but I interrupted him by shaking my head. "On the contrary. All the experiences, everything she has seen, have been burned into her memory in every detail. The episode was so terrible that her body activated a protective mechanism that prevents her from recalling it."

He sat up straight and let his arms sink. "That's the same thing."

"No, it is not," I said firmly.

"No!?" He exclaimed. "How do you figure?"

"I am a trained psychotherapist. I could work with her over a longer period, if you would agree, and Miss Carstens wants it. Then, in time, she would open up, step by step."

Now, he leaned forward as well. He had come almost too close to me, but I did not budge.

"What do you mean by *longer period*?" he asked.

I raised my eyebrows. "I can't answer that. A couple of days, a few weeks, several months. It will take as long as it takes."

"You've got to be kidding me." He backed up slightly, putting more distance between us.

"That is the only option we have," I said. "And if you do not want me to work with Miss Carstens, go ahead and get another therapist. It won't bother me. I have just explained to you the only way that I could imagine getting through to her; you've got to decide." I paused. "But this I will tell you right now: If you want me to work with Miss Carstens, it means that you must involve me in the ongoing investigation. I would need to know about every detail, no matter how unimportant."

He did not like that. It could not have been clearer. He drew his eyes together. His lips narrowed. "How come?"

"Don't get me wrong. I will not interrupt your work. But Miss Carstens will present me with images, associations, and metaphors. And I can only decode them if I can compare them with the results of your investigation."

He abruptly stood up, spun away from me, and went to look out one of the windows. After a minute, he turned back to me and walked up to the table. He sat down. "Good. Let's say I agree and put you in the loop. Can I rely on you to keep me posted? About *all* the insights you gain?"

"Of course," I responded earnestly. "Otherwise, it doesn't make any sense."

"What you have suggested to me is absolutely out of the ordinary."

I nodded. "It is also an absolutely unusual case. And if it reassures you any, I've done it before."

"At the Bureau in Wiesbaden?"

He had researched me. Exactly like I had him.

I could hardly suppress my smile. And I was sure that he picked up on it.

"Exactly," I said. "In Wiesbaden."

"We should discuss the parameters of our cooperation more closely," he said.

He was right about that.

"You've got a good point," I confessed frankly. "That would be important and helpful for everyone involved—especially for Captain Strobelsohn and his team."

Gutenberg looked at his watch and cleared his throat. "What would you think if I invited you to lunch and we went over the details?"

"Lunch?" I did not expect that, after he had refused my cup of coffee in the break room.

He looked at me in anticipation.

"Do you know the Poseidon on the Alster?" I asked.

"No. Where is it?"

This time I did not hold my smile back. "I'll give you the address. It is not far from here. Ten minutes by car."

"Good," he said. "Then we'll meet in half an hour."

12

Gutenberg actually held the door for me when we entered Poseidon. He followed me, but stopped frozen in his steps.

The place sometimes had this astonishing effect on guests on their first visit. The large bar was decorated with white, Ionic columns, which bore an oversized frieze, like on ancient temples. The elegantly painted plaster walls gave the impression of being made of solid marble. And replicas of ancient Greek statues of every size stood in several corners.

There were not too many tables in the front room. From having worked there, I knew that there were exactly twenty-two. Each was covered with a blue-and-white checked tablecloth and a white overlay. At this hour, shortly before noon, Georgios's restaurant was almost full. A mixed crowd had arrived: men and women in business suits, guests in casual attire, a scattering of students, one or two families. There was the usual, intimate sound of a mixture of muted voices, laughter, the clinking of glass and porcelain, and soft background music playing a typical

Bouzouki band. And you could not escape the scent. This wonderful fragrance of good food.

My stomach growled.

Just then, a table for four in a corner became free. I turned to Gutenberg and gestured with a sidelong hand. He tried to smile, but his attempt came off a bit uneasy.

Arriving at our table, he helped me out of my coat like he had earlier and carried it to the cloakroom. Now, I was really interested. I waited for his return, and Gutenberg pulled out my chair like it was normal, remained standing until I sat down, and then took the seat opposite.

As if out of thin air, Georgios appeared next to us, in his white shirt with the tight-fitting dark vest over it. He held two menus in his hand. And he shone.

"Evi, my love. What can I bring you to drink?" he said as he gazed intently at Gutenberg.

"I'll have the usual," I replied. "And the state prosecutor would like?" I looked at Gutenberg invitingly.

His eyelids flickered slightly irritated. Then he said, "A nonalcoholic beer."

Georgios's smile grew wider. He turned to Gutenberg. "Would you like the menu, or may I suggest something for you?"

Gutenberg looked at me enquiringly.

Before I could answer, Georgios said, "All right then. I would recommend Shrimp Saganaki as a starter. And as a main course, I suggest a Greek-style Dorado, and for dessert yogurt with honey and pistachios."

Gutenberg's eyelids twitched again. "Is that fine, Dr. Wolf?"

"Yes," I said. "Wonderful."

"A good choice," Georgios confirmed. "The waitress will bring everything in a moment." He beamed once again in my direction and left us alone.

Gutenberg cleared his throat. "A relative of yours?"

"Better," I said. "A friend."

He nodded as if he understood what I meant.

The waitress came with our drinks—for me a large, plain water without lemon and for Gutenberg, an alcohol-free beer.

We toasted and drank.

Gutenberg sat his glass down. "If I understood you correctly, you intend to treat Miss Carstens."

No small talk, he got straight to the point.

"First and foremost, I have to coax the patient out of her catatonic state," I explained. "Then Miss Carstens must agree to enter therapy and release me from my professional confidentiality in the event the information I receive from her is relevant to the case." I paused. "Then the real work begins."

He frowned. "How is that supposed to happen?"

"It will be anything but easy. It would help if she was in a normal environment and not in custody." I hesitated again. "Do you think Miss Carstens is guilty?"

Our waitress came to our table and delivered two bowls brimming with fried shrimp.

We tried it.

"That's good," he said visibly surprised.

"The Poseidon is the best Greek restaurant far and wide," I said. "A hidden jewel."

"Mhmm," he murmured, taking another bite.

"So? Do you think Miss Carstens is guilty?" I repeated my question.

He continued to chew and then swallowed. "I don't believe she did it single-handedly. But she could have something to do with the murders—together with her boyfriend."

"Mr. Westphal?"

"Precisely. Based on laboratory results, which your colleagues at the Bureau received today, a warrant for his arrest has been requested. And at this moment, Captain Strobelsohn is in the judge's chambers. We're asking for it to be fast-tracked."

"Because of the negative publicity that comes with the case." I said.

"As well," he said. "I personally do not care. As soon as we have the warrant, Mr. Westphal will be arrested, we'll confront him with the laboratory results and interrogate him meticulously."

We ate in silence.

I put the cutlery in my empty bowl and dabbed my mouth with a napkin. "Do you think the two of them did it?"

Gutenberg was also finished with his appetizer. "I can't exclude it. There are still too many unknowns." He paused. "You said something about several therapy sessions. Can that somehow be stepped up?"

"Hardly," I said. "Miss Carstens's present state was obviously caused by trauma. In theory, exposing her to another shock might snap her back to reality. But such radical methods are dubious at best. I am not going to do that. I know softer, more effective means to help traumatized patients. The initial phase is the most difficult."

"I understand," he said.

This time, our waitress was accompanied by Georgios. The young woman took our used dishes and Georgios presented two large plates. "There you go," he said. "Dorado with tomatoes, feta, olives, and rosemary."

Gutenberg bowed his head as a sign of his appreciation. Georgios stayed at the table.

"Are you a state prosecutor?" he asked Gutenberg.

"Assistant District Attorney," I answered for him.

Georgios was not deterred by this. "And not married," he stated unapologetically, while he studied Gutenberg's ring finger.

This promised to be interesting. I put down the cutlery I had just picked up and leaned back in my chair.

"No. Not married," Gutenberg confirmed.

Georgios bent down a bit. "No children?" he said in a clandestine tone.

Gutenberg hesitated indiscernibly. "No children either."

Georgios turned to me. "Did you hear that, Evi?"

"I did," I said.

Georgios opened his mouth to add something, but decided otherwise and stroked his white, wiry hair. "Enjoy," he said, and left.

Gutenberg smiled. Sincerely. The first time in my presence. He had pleasant laugh lines. "A natural interrogator, your friend."

"He is. And an excellent chef."

We concentrated on the fish. It melted on my tongue.

"Back to our collaboration," he said after a while. "What is important to you?"

"Well," I said. "Regular meetings. With you, but also with Captain Strobelsohn. I need an insight into the investigations and in return you can benefit from what I learn from Miss Carstens. Teamwork."

"Teamwork," he repeated.

We remained silent for a while. In no time, our food disappeared. He had been as hungry as I.

He set his fork and knife aside. "And now I'm curious about the dessert."

"Me too," I said.

His cell phone rang. He made an apologetic gesture, pulled it out of his jacket, and held it to his ear. "Gutenberg." He frowned. "*Where* is he? … Hold on a second!"

He covered the phone with his left hand and looked at me penetratingly. "Did you give Mr. Westphal permission to visit Miss Carstens?"

I shook my head. "No. I haven't spoken to Mr. Westphal at all."

Gutenberg nodded, taking his hand off the receiver. His gaze lingered on me as he continued the call. "Tell him, he can visit her in half an hour. … Yes, of course, … I'll be there, and then you can arrest him."

He finished the conversation.

"And?" I asked.

"Peter Westphal is standing in front of Miss Carstens's hospital room," he said. "Somehow, he managed to get in there unnoticed. The policewoman has stopped him. And Mr. Strobelsohn has arrived with the warrant for Peter Westphal."

"You want to be present when they make the arrest," I determined.

"You as well?"

"Yes," I admitted frankly.

He rose. "Then come with me."

13

In front of the hospital room where Suzanne Carstens lay, were three people: the uniformed policewoman from this morning, standing next to her Captain Strobelsohn, and in the middle a young, blond man. They were having a lively conversation, or rather, aggressively conversing, when Gutenberg and I approached.

I directed my attention to the blond. *This must be Peter Westphal*, I thought. A little taller than me, somewhere just over six-foot, casual wear and a brown leather jacket. Wiry figure and hectic movements.

Like the day before, Strobelsohn was trapped in one of those suits that can be found in every department store. The pattern of the carefully knotted tie glared at me; it was, to put it mildly, adventurous. We reached the small group. And the conversation stopped.

Peter Westphal turned to Gutenberg: "Mr. Prosecutor," he began, "I want to see Miss Carstens immediately. You told me that I could visit her as soon as the police took my statement. I have cooperated, but now I am continually stopped from going in, and pushed off to a later date."

Westphal was more than excited. When he talked, the muscles in his face twitched, the gestures seemed harsh and convulsive. His stiff posture demonstrated to me that he was at a point where he had to employ a lot of energy to maintain his cool. Maybe I could help defuse the situation.

"Hello, Mr. Westphal." I hastened to preempt Gutenberg. "Evelin Wolf, psychologist." I reached my hand out. He ignored it.

"I am taking care of Miss Carstens," I continued in a quiet yet articulate tone. "And I fully understand your desires. I would want the same if I were in your situation. But please bear in mind that Miss Carstens does not recognize her environment. Visiting her now makes little sense and would possibly be detrimental for her condition. You do not want that, do you?"

"Detrimental?" He turned pale. "How could that be?" I had succeeded in connecting briefly with him. But then his eyes flashed. "I don't care. I want to see her! Now!"

"We can't go on like this," Gutenberg interrupted. "Mr. Strobelsohn, please inform Mr. Westphal."

Abruptly, Westphal turned to the officer, "About what?" He hissed.

Strobelsohn was the picture of tranquility. "A warrant for your arrest has been issued in connection with the murders in the Carstens's villa."

"Mr. Strobelsohn will carry this order out now," Gutenberg added.

"But..." Westphal started.

"No *but*s," Gutenberg broke him off. He made an imploring gesture. "Mr. Strobelsohn, please..."

The captain pushed the tail of his jacket slightly aside and reached for his belt. With proficient fingers, he opened the belt clip and pulled out the handcuffs.

"Mr. Westphal?" he said.

The young policewoman, who had hitherto closely followed, took a step toward Strobelsohn, presumably to assist him if necessary.

To my surprise, Westphal obeyed. Without hesitation, he stretched out his arms to Strobelsohn. Apparently, he had accepted his fate. No more danger.

Mistake.

The violence that Westphal had long suppressed, burst out of him explosively. Without the least sign of forewarning, he side-stepped Strobelsohn's knee with full force, then kicked him in the stomach. The policeman writhed in pain, groaned, and fell silent, when Westphal's elbow slammed down on his head.

The giant collapsed. In doing so, he obstructed the policewoman, who had hurried to assist him. Westphal landed a fist on her jaw. She was thrust against the wall. He then jumped on her, tore her gun out of its holster, whirled around, and pointed the pistol at Gutenberg.

All the while, I had been practically paralyzed. Like a frightened spectator in the cinema, I just observed what was happening around me. Powerless, without the slightest opportunity to intervene or to alter the situation.

In the meantime, Gutenberg reached his right hand to his back waistline, where he carried his weapon. But he froze. Without blinking, he looked down the muzzle of the pistol held in front of his head.

Silence.

The heavy, rattling breathing from Strobelsohn. The policewoman's wheezing.

"I am going to her now," said Westphal. A statement delivered matter-of-factly. "And you, Mr. Prosecutor, are coming with me."

I snapped out of my trance. "Mr. Westphal," I said, wondering how convincing my voice sounded. "Are you aware of what you are doing? This is hostage-taking, above and beyond the assault and battery from before."

He continued to stare at Gutenberg. "It doesn't matter," he replied. "I have to see Suzi. And he's coming with me."

Nobody moved.

"If you insist," I said. "But you're not going without me. I will not leave Miss Carstens alone."

It sounded pathetic, but I had deliberately chosen these words so that he would understand them in his excited state.

Strobelsohn came back to himself. He made a move to get up and grab his service weapon.

"No," Gutenberg said sharply. "Leave it!"

Without turning around, Westphal felt behind him and opened the door to Suzanne's room. He walked in backward, the gun in his outstretched arm.

"Come on," he ordered.

Gutenberg entered too, and I followed.

"Close the door," said Westphal, when all three of us were in the room.

I obeyed.

"Place a chair under the latch!"

Again, I obeyed.

Westphal took another step back. His head twitched toward the bed, stopped for a second, and then returned to Gutenberg and me.

"Suzanne," he said over his shoulder.

The patient in the bed kept her eyes closed. She did not react.

Again, he risked a quick glance. "Suzi, it's me! Peter!"

No reaction.

"Say something!"

She remained silent.

I cleared my throat. "I wasn't lying to you outside. She does not grasp what is happening around her. She has retreated into her own world."

The first time I had observed Westphal I had recognized the symptoms. The change in his facial features, the pallor of the skin. And it started again.

He shouted at me, his voice building a crescendo. "This can't be true! You're doctors! Two days! The whole thing happened two days ago! She had to have come to! You haven't even tried! You pigs have only sedated her!"

"Mr. Westphal," said Gutenberg. "You can see for yourself; this isn't achieving anything."

"Shut your trap!" Westphal moved a step closer.

"Do not make this worse than it already is," said Gutenberg. "Give me the gun, or…"

"*Or* what?" Westphal pressed the muzzle of the gun to Gutenberg's forehead.

Everything happened at once.

Earlier, Westphal had acted quickly. This time, Gutenberg was even faster. His right hand swung up, grabbed Westphal's pistol by the barrel and wrenched it sideways. Away from the body. A shot was fired. An earsplitting explosion.

Gutenberg came with his left and landed a punch on Westphal's windpipe. The suspect collapsed as if he had been struck by lightning. Gutenberg jumped on him and hit him. Again, and again.

A frantic pounding at the door. Somebody tried to force their way in, presumably Strobelsohn.

And then the scream. A shrill, all-penetrating tone—animalistic, savage. Suzanne Carstens was no longer lying down. She had bolted upright. Her eyes, wide open, nearly bulging out of their sockets. She looked around the room, confused, glanced at her bandaged arms and the hoses attached to them. She pulled them out, blood squirted on the white blanket.

I jumped to her side, clutched her upper body, and held her tight.

With tremendous power, she tried to rip herself free. I tightened my grip.

She did not stop screaming; she stomped and threw herself back and forth. I did not let go.

The chair, which I had stuck under the handle, fell. The door flew open and Strobelsohn and the policewoman stormed into the room. Together they helped Gutenberg pick Westphal up. The young man staggered, half stunned. His face began to swell.

They twisted Westphal's arms behind his back, and I heard the handcuffs ratchet shut.

Gutenberg bent down and picked up the pistol, which Westphal had lost in the scuffle.

"Take him away," he shouted, breathing heavily, to be heard over Suzanne Carstens's shrieking.

Westphal struggled to free himself from the police officers' grasp and turned his head desperately to have another look at Suzanne.

"Fucking pigs," he yelled. "You have no idea! Let me go! We haven't done anything wrong!"

He shouted this over and over again as the police officers dragged him out of the room.

As soon as he disappeared, I could feel a twitch running through Suzanne's body. She reared up one last time, became stiff, and toppled back. Her scream fell silent.

Gutenberg looked at me. "Is everything OK?"

The question was admittedly ludicrous. But at that moment it did me good. "Yes. I am fine." I brushed the hair out of my eyes.

Dr. Hubmann and two nurses appeared in the doorway. "Is anyone hurt?" the doctor asked.

"No," I replied. "But your patient needs your attention."

I looked back to Gutenberg and tried to smile but failed miserably. "Go ahead. I will stay behind and let you know later."

March

23

Tuesday

14

The typically sober office was vibrant for a Tuesday morning. Alex checked his inbox. Several documents to sign, memos from the meetings he missed the previous day. He had to appear in court on Thursday and considered delegating it to a junior member of his team. Then he thought better. It would require just as much time to brief a substitute; he would show up at the scheduled appointment and take care of that himself.

Alex had a lot on his mind.

He somehow doubted Dr. Wolf would be able to get Suzanne to talk any time soon. Peter Westphal would be processed by now and, after a night behind bars, more willing to discuss what really happened in the basement of Carstens's villa. If Alex couldn't get Suzanne to speak to him, he would have to settle for questioning his current prime suspect.

Statistically, the odds of solving the case were already against him. And if a week should pass without any substantial leads, those odds tended toward zero. Evidence disappears at an exponential rate, alibis are acquired, people fall off the face of the Earth.

Peter Westphal was at the scene; in view of the blood splatters forensics found on his clothing, he could have been present when Björn Carstens was murdered. His claim that he was picking Suzanne Carstens up for a six o'clock jog on a Sunday morning was more than a little dubious. And his highly aggressive behavior yesterday at the hospital, when he forced his way into Suzanne's room at gunpoint, made him even more suspicious.

So, what was Peter Westphal concealing? And why was he concealing it?

The phone vibrated against his chest. It was Strobelsohn.

"Gutenberg."

"Mr. Gutenberg, I hate to bother you so soon after breakfast, but we've got a new case. Another tragedy. You're going to need to have a look before we scrape up this mess. We're at the Burchardkai Container Terminal, in the port's yard for unclaimed deliveries."

Alex exhaled audibly. "I'm on my way."

Hustling out of the office, he stopped at his secretary's desk. "Julia, I'm going to have to delegate Thursday's hearing after all. Get Mrs. Buchholz to oversee it. She'll need the least amount of briefing. Have her call me if there is anything she does not understand from my notes."

Less than a half hour later, he was rolling onto the expansive terminal. The Burchardkai yard was business as usual; a ship with thousands of containers was being unloaded. Men in orange vests and hard hats were climbing up and down, unlashing the steel boxes, gesticulating with gloved hands to be understood over the noise. Having the appearance of a choreographed dance sequence, giant straddle lifts, so-called van carriers, and loading cranes collaborated to put a small dent in the ship's payload.

Alex parked and, as he climbed out of his car, was met with a melee of rank smells. The stench of exhaust and oil overpowered the distinct aroma of the Elbe, which always reminded him of his childhood.

It did not take him long to find a man with a walkie-talkie, who appeared to be some sort of shift supervisor. He pointed Alex in the direction of the container-holding depot.

The commotion seemed to be concentrated on a stack of three steel boxes. As Alex approached the holding yard at the backside of the terminal, he was met by Henrik and Strobelsohn.

Alex greeted both men simultaneously, "What do we have?"

Strobelsohn stared in silence at his feet for a moment and Henrik shook his head, like he always did, when the crime scene was particularly gruesome. His face was on the whiter side of the pale spectrum.

Finally, Strobelsohn glanced up and made eye contact with Alex. "I can't describe it, and I don't want to look at it again."

Henrik cleared his throat and pointed at the doctor standing by the short stack of containers. "Hamdy, I mean, Dr. Moustafa, can give you the particulars."

Alex continued on around the end of the open container and acknowledged the doctor with a nod. He looked inside and stopped short. Overcoming his immediate horror, he proceeded into the confined cavity.

Bodies were flung every which way across the interior. Two, four, six, too many to count, most of them clustered together near the entrance. They had all surely once been beautiful, young women, but that was no longer the case. Distorted blue faces, gnarled fingers, chests exposed bearing scratches from where they had clawed at their skin.

Alex took a deep breath. It required a certain amount of ambivalence, his job. He had worked through these feelings long ago; if he didn't want to miss anything, he had to keep his eyes open and not turn away with repulsion, yet if he let it get too commonplace, he risked losing the fire that drove him.

Cordless space heaters and battery-powered lanterns stood near a cluster of camping toilets in one corner. Mostly emptied bottles of water discarded together with light weight blankets in the other, beyond a row of mattresses. A few corpses lay there in the fetal position, having not woken from a bad dream.

Alex crooked his neck and examined the ceiling: air vents had been cut into the top of the container, reminiscent of a little boy puncturing the lid of a jar full of insects. What kind of psychopaths were they dealing with?

"Appalling, isn't it?" The doctor was standing right behind him. "The women experienced a protracted and painful death by suffocation. Look at the skin coloration: a univocal sign of oxygen deficiency." He paused and squatted next to one of the women. Gently lifting her hand, he showed Alex her bloody fingers and broken nails, and then pointed to scrapes on the inside of the gate. "They were trying to escape."

"They scratched their breasts because of the lack of oxygen?" Alex ascertained in disbelief.

"A final desperate attempt to get air," Hamdy answered, while he rose.

As they slowly walked out of the container and headed toward the police officers and witnesses, Hamdy added, "There is a survivor. We just sent her in an ambulance to the university clinic. She is in critical condition, and I fear she won't make it. Dr. Jakobsen is accompanying the transport."

They had reached the others standing at a considerable distance from the opening.

"Did the survivor say anything before they took her?" Alex asked.

Hamdy shook his head. "She was unconscious when I arrived."

Strobelsohn joined the conversation. "The dock workers said she was shouting and banging on the gate of the container, but fell silent before they could get her out. These things have strong seals that take some doing to get off." He gave an acknowledging nod to the taller of the two longshoremen, who appeared to have something to add.

"My colleague, Sven," the large man began and motioned to his younger co-worker, "and I were the ones who heard the shouting. We did need a bit of time to find a tool to cut the seal. We even discussed if we shouldn't get a customs agent first, but when she suddenly stopped yelling, we ran to get a bolt cutter. Like I told the doctor, it probably took us two or three minutes to open the container."

"That is the problem." Hamdy clarified. "If it was a matter of minutes, we have reason to fear permanent brain damage, due to this lack of oxygen—that is, if she ever wakes up from her coma. The other women had all suffocated. She was lucky to escape, but there is no promise she will survive."

Alex turned back to Strobelsohn. "Did she have any documents on her?"

"No. she didn't, and by all appearances, none of the others did either. The container was loaded in Kaliningrad and the dockworkers think the woman was yelling in Russian or Ukrainian. But they could hardly hear anything at all and might be mistaken."

Henrik pointed at the middle box. "When the shipping container was not collected, it was stacked with this mismatched one that sealed the air slits sometime early this morning. If you look closely, this middle container is a newer model made from composites. It is lighter and has different flooring than the older steel containers. It appears that this difference is the reason the air holes in the roof panel were blocked."

Alex nodded slowly.

"These holes had been made at the far edge of the clefts in the top, presumably so the driver of the straddle carrier wouldn't see them from above. I suppose they did not add any vents to the sides for fear of being pulled out in inspection."

"This happens all the time, that shipments are forgotten about," the younger dockworker said. "When containers are not collected on the first day, they are brought to this yard during the graveyard shift and kept here until they are picked up."

"*Tragically mismatched?*" Alex furrowed his brow. "And the driver didn't hear the screaming. Who is the recipient of the *shipment?*"

Strobelsohn spoke up. "*Stardaenz-Spedition* is on the paperwork; they are a generic shipping company that could have been contracted by anyone. The company has one owner-operator, Wilhelm Hugenot, and the business is registered to his home address. An apartment in St. Georg."

"And?" Raising both arms and shoulders, Alex needed more.

"We've got an officer there now, but no one came to the door," Henrik interjected.

"Thanks Henrik," Alex said with his head cocked. "I need you to organize a Russian and Ukrainian translator to meet me and Captain Strobelsohn at the university clinic in half an hour. And then check with the logistics coordinator; find out everything you can about this *Star Dance company*, how often they receive shipments and from where and whom."

"Yes, sir," the young detective answered attentively.

"Captain Strobelsohn, I'll meet you on the third floor," Alex continued. "If we can't locate Wilhelm Hugenot, then we can at least try to speak to the only other person we have that might know who was smuggling those women into the country."

"Did you say Hugenot?" the taller of the two dockers spoke up. He looked at his co-worker. "Isn't Hugo's family name Hugenot? Sven?"

"Who?" Sven seemed to be somewhere else with his thoughts.

"The pretty boy who pilots a van carrier on second shift. Hugo."

The younger worker thought a minute. "Yeah, that's his name, Wilhelm Hugenot."

Alex turned to Henrik and raised his brows in a 'who knew' gesture. "Henrik, you follow up with the yard foreman, after you have arranged for a translator. Captain Strobelsohn and I will be at the university clinic."

15

No one was with Suzanne Carstens when I went to see her in the morning. On the way, I had stopped in and bought a fruit smoothie. I placed the paper cup with its fat straw sticking out on her hospital table and swung the tray around, so that she could reach the drink effortlessly. She watched me the whole time, but her expression remained vacant.

I pulled up one of the visitor's chairs and sat down beside her. I took the chance to examine her more closely. Her wounds were gradually healing. The color of the bruises had changed. No longer purely purple and red, they were now washed over with a yellowish green. The swelling in her face had gone down. The IVs had also disappeared.

She looked exhausted, as if she had been subjected to severe physical exertion. But she was breathing calmly. No visible trace of excitement.

I waited. We remained silent.

After a few minutes, she glanced down at the smoothie. She stretched out her arm, grabbed the juice, and drank from it. Then she placed the cup back on the table.

Moving as slowly as possible, I took my notepad out of my handbag, opened it, and pulled a ballpoint pen out of its sheath. I clicked it into the writing position and tried to make eye contact with my client.

"How are you?" I asked.

She answered without hesitating. "Good."

"I am Dr. Evelin Wolf, a criminal psychologist with the LKA and a psychotherapist," I continued.

She made a slight smile—as if out of courtesy.

"Do you know who you are?" I asked.

She lowered her eyes. "Suzanne Carstens."

"And how old are you?"

"Twenty-four," she responded promptly.

I took down my first note.

"Can you tell me what month we're in now?"

She looked up, slightly confused, and turned her head toward the window. "Spring," she said. "March or April."

I gave her time again to return her attention to me. "Miss Carstens, where do you live?"

"Hamburg." She accompanied her statement with a confident nod.

"Hamburg is big," I said. "Can you be a little more specific?"

She remained silent for a long time; her eyelids fluttered. "In Blankenese," she said, and added the exact address.

I deliberately noted her response slowly to provide her an opportunity to relax.

Finally, I attempted a friendly smile. "Do you have any idea where you are?"

She looked around the room as if she were seeing it for the first time. "In a hospital. I'm in a hospital," she said firmly. The fact did not seem to bother her.

"Do you know why you are here?"

She kind of shrugged her shoulders. "I'm sick?"

"No," I said.

"I had an accident." Again, unperturbed, as if it did not concern her in the least.

"Something like that," I confirmed, ensuring I came off as objective as possible. "A few days ago, some people died in your grandfather's house. You were injured during the incident."

Her body twitched once; she folded her arms in front of her chest. I could hear her breathing.

Again, I waited—until she loosened her arms and lifted her gaze.

"Can, or do you want to, tell me something about it?" I inquired.

Her answer consisted of the hint of a headshake.

"Your grandfather, Björn Carstens, is one of the dead."

The trembling returned. Her lips quivered, she stared at the window. But she did not close her eyes.

"You were present when these people died. Can you remember anything?"

She turned to me abruptly. "No!"

We remained silent. I did not ask any more questions, because she was obviously determined not to answer me anymore.

She grabbed the smoothie again and sucked it until the air and the residual liquid she drew through the straw made slurping sounds. She put the cup down but kept her hands on it. She spun it around and read the inscription.

Suddenly she paused. "Why are you here?" she asked me.

"I can help you remember everything."

"Everything that happened at home? Regarding the death of Mr. Carstens?" She called him neither *Grandfather* nor *Grandpa*, not even *Björn*. For her, he was *Mr. Carstens*.

I nodded. "Exactly."

"Why would I want that?"

"Someone will have to be held accountable. Four people were murdered. The authorities will not simply ignore this."

She pursed her lips. "That is of no importance to me."

"That may be," I said. "But the police and I need to find out. The perpetrators may have been friends, complete strangers, or—" I broke off intentionally.

"Or?"

"Or you," I added.

"I do not care." No notable reaction on her face.

I pretended to write something. Then I said, "Or it could have been Mr. Westphal."

She removed one hand from the cup, drew it over her cheeks, and rubbed her eyes.

"Peter Westphal. You know him," I probed deeper.

She exhaled audibly, pressing her thumb and forefinger against closed eyelids. "I can't remember," she finally replied. "But the name sounds familiar to me."

It took a long time before she lowered her arm.

I retracted my ballpoint with a click. "You must decide. If you want us to work together to find out what happened, who committed the crimes, whether Mr. Westphal is guilty or not… you must cooperate with me."

The window seemed to fascinate her. "There is no other possibility?"

"Not really."

Her chest raised and fell before she returned her attention to me. "All right. And what we discuss, you'll keep to yourself?"

"The details that are important to catch the perpetrator will be passed on to Mr. Gutenberg."

A first sign of interest slipped across her face. "Who is that? Am I supposed to know him as well?"

"Mr. Gutenberg is the prosecutor responsible for your case."

Her mouth narrowed. "And if I refuse?"

"If you refuse?" I gestured uncertainly with my hand. "Then there is no guarantee that the real culprit will be caught. But that's not everything." I had her full attention. "You had suggested before that you were ill. And I said you weren't. That was not completely accurate. Your body has almost recovered entirely. But only when you remember can your soul begin to heal."

She snorted. Loud and unabashed. "What do you know about my soul?"

I stuck the notepad in my purse. The silence that spread between us weighed heavily.

"And?" I said after a longer while. "What have you decided?"

"I'll do it."

I rose to my feet.

"Why are you getting up?" she asked, irritated.

"I'll leave you alone now. On my next visit, we will arrange the details of our cooperation—the place, the time, and how we will proceed."

"Then we're doing this here, in the hospital," she said with conviction.

"Definitely not," I replied.

Her hand squeezed the empty cup. The waxed cardboard cracked, and the plastic lid popped off. "I can't go to Blankenese." Her cheeks grew pale, the shuddering returned—with increased severity.

I stepped closer and touched her upper arm. "No one is going to force you to stay in Blankenese. Trust me. We'll find another solution that suits you and works for me."

"You promise?" she whispered, and the expression in her eyes resembled that of a frightened child.

"Yes," I said with a gentle smile. "I promise."

I turned around and left.

16

Alex sat for a moment after finding a space for his sedan in the hospital's underground parking garage. Running over his objectives for his hopeful forthcoming interview with the survivor from Burchardkai, he conceded that the container full of dead women affected him more than he would have liked to admit. Who could have penned up such young creatures in a steel box as if they were common livestock—not caring in the least if they reached their destination alive or not?

Undoubtedly, arriving alive would not have resulted in their well-being. He pulled himself together. His best chance to find out anything about the people responsible for this appalling human trafficking lay unconscious in the critical care facility of this hospital.

He left the parking garage and made his way to the adjacent emergency room.

The admitting nurse was very young; he would not think she was a day older than twenty-five, yet the expression on her face told him she had experienced a lot in her short life. She directed him to continue through to the intensive care unit.

Alex quickly found Hamdy's assistant, Dr. Jakobsen, standing in front of an open door to a room full of orderlies. Alex could imagine how the doctor's premature gray garnered him a bit of respect, but he could not hold a candle to the admitting nurse when it came to his poker face. His full set of eyebrows raised over his puppy dog blue eyes betrayed how much it had moved him.

After shaking the young doctor's hand, Alex immediately looked beyond the crowd and saw a blonde woman; she appeared to be unconscious. A tube under her nose fed her oxygen, and machines measured her vitals through cables that seemed to be attached to every extremity.

"Her O^2-Sat is stable. Keep an eye on that. And we can slowly start to hope that she will pull through. The paramedics gave her two amps of Bicarb. Run the arterial blood gases and determine the state of acidosis," the physician assistant explained to the orderlies as they filed past Alex and Dr. Jakobsen.

Alex knew better than to ask to speak with the patient. He had his ass sent back to him in a cart the last time he tried that. Instead, he spun around to Hamdy's assistant.

"Dr. Jakobsen, did she ever come to?"

Jakobsen nodded his head noncommittally. "I accompanied her in the ambulance. She sort of came in and out of consciousness before she aspirated on her own vomit and passed out once again when we got here; that has been over thirty minutes now. And from what he just said, she is still in critical condition."

Captain Strobelsohn, accompanied by a woman Alex presumed was the interpreter, walked into the intensive care unit.

Alex raised his hand to call attention to his whereabouts and waited for them to approach. After formally introducing the Ukrainian translator, Strobelsohn looked furtively over his shoulder, bent his head down, and spoke covertly to the state prosecutor. "Do you think we're going to need her services at all?"

Alex pursed his lips and offered the hint of a headshake. "Your guess is as good as mine. Let's hope for the best."

Alex led the way as the trio left Dr. Jakobsen in the hall and cautiously approached the motionless witness. Alex could see how beautiful she was, once, not long ago. The dark rings encompassing her eyes concealed the fact that she was still a child. Late teens, twenty at most. She had an innocent, plain look about her; eyebrows were not plucked, and she wore her hair in an outdated style. A small-town girl swept away with promises of adventure, travel, and fortune. Now her only movement consisted of her chest rising and falling with every breath.

Alex ensured that Strobelsohn and the translator were standing behind him with a sidelong glance. Then he turned back to the young woman. "Hello," he said to her, making an effort to give his voice a soft, gentle tone.

She remained unresponsive.

Alex waited a short while, and then he tried a second time. He bent a little closer to the patient. "Hello, can you tell me your name?"

While he spoke, he searched the young lady's face for a telltale sign that she acknowledged his presence.

Nothing but this inhaling and exhaling.

Alex thought about what Dr. Wolf would do. He remembered how she had caressed Suzanne Carstens. He imagined the psychologist would do the same in this situation.

He deliberated for a moment. It was worth a try.

He stretched his hand out and stroked the unconscious woman's forearm. "Hello," he said a third time.

Nothing happened. There was no change in the patient.

Alex straightened up. *That would have been too easy*, he thought as he turned to the translator and Strobelsohn, who was filming with his cellular phone.

He shrugged his shoulders. "Well, it didn't seem to go the…"

Alex saw Strobelsohn's expression change. The massive detective raised his eyebrows in astonishment while his vision trained on something just beyond Alex. At the same time, Alex felt cold fingers wrap around his wrist. Nails dug deep into his skin.

Alex spun on his axis.

The young woman had opened her eyelids. Her one hand still clung onto him. With the other she scratched at the empty air. She stared at him, her hollow eyes desperate, and panicked. Her lips moved.

At first, Alex could not make out what she was saying in a near whisper. He bent down closer.

"What did you say?" he asked.

Her lips moved again and this time he heard her terrified moan. "Dmitri Ivanov."

He looked into her sunken eyes. "Who is that? Did he do this to you?"

Without looking away, he made an impatient hand gesture toward Strobelsohn and the interpreter, to get them to hurry closer.

At that moment, the young woman began to scream at the top of her lungs. "Dmitri Ivanov! Dmitri Ivanov! Wi dolschni pomotsch nam! Pomotsch!"

Alex instinctively flinched a bit. And when he looked back, her eyes rolled into an eerie white. "Ivanov… Dmitri Ivanov," she muttered.

Her tight grip around his wrist loosened. Her arm fell limp on the bed.

The machines started beeping and Alex and the others quickly clung to the back wall as the code team flowed into the room.

"PH is at 7.21, Carbon dioxide is 53, O2 is 79. She is in acute respiratory distress. We're losing her. She is having a pulmonary embolism. Get a chest X-ray, STAT."

Alex led Strobelsohn and the translator into the hall while the staff tried to resuscitate the young lady.

He watched how the doctors ardently fought to save the woman's life; he saw it, and any chance he could have hoped to retrieve information disappear in the echo of the EKG. And with the last drawn-out tone, he knew they were both gone forever.

17

Strobelsohn clicked on a wireless mouse, and a shaky image appeared on the screen of his laptop: medical equipment, a white wall, the back of a man's head, and then a patient in a hospital bed.

I had seen more than a few dead bodies over the years. And the young woman reminded me of them. With her sunken cheeks, the pale, almost waxy skin, and the exceedingly sharp contours of her nose, she seemed more dead than alive. Only the rising and falling of her chest proved that she was still breathing.

I repressed the emotions that welled up in me; instead, I focused solely on the footage.

The video wobbled again, and then a close-up of her face. The woman opened her eyes. Her pupils were alarmingly dilated. Her mouth moved. She seemed to whisper something that could not be heard due to the rhythmic sounds of the oscilloscope and other monitoring equipment.

"What did you say?" echoed a man's voice. It was Gutenberg's. He spoke softly and thoughtfully, and yet he strove to establish his authority.

The woman in the bed groaned. Again, her lips moved. This time, she clearly said something, but I could still not understand what it was.

"Who is that? Did he do this to you?"—Gutenberg.

The woman's expression changed. Her mouth opened once more. Her eyes, which had been deep set a moment before, threatened to pop out of their sockets. Suddenly she screamed, "Dmitri Ivanov! Dmitri Ivanov!" And then she added something else. Three, four words—I suspected Russian or a related language.

The recording wobbled heavily. Briefly, a close-up. I caught the profile of Gutenberg, then the face of the patient, the face of a dying woman.

The life support devices in the room sounded an alarm. Loud, piercing beeps, atonal whistling. The focus of the camera hopped around wildly. The floor, the ceiling, the floor again, and then several people dressed in white rushed to the bedside. Voices…

The screen went black.

Strobelsohn's office filled with a deafening silence.

I leaned back in my chair. The cheap plastic squeaked under my weight. I forced myself to look away from the laptop and glanced at Gutenberg, who sat seemingly unmoved across the table from me. Either he was as callous as he let on, or he had incredible control over himself. I could not decide which rang truer.

Strobelsohn, on the other hand, demonstrated deep concern. He nervously rubbed his chin. And Henrik Breiter, the young policeman, was so upset that he did not know what to do with himself other than twist his mouth into a grin. The grimace resembled a caricature. It came across empty and expressionless.

Gutenberg cleared his throat. "Mr. Strobelsohn had the presence of mind to film with his smartphone while I spoke with the patient. What do you make of it?"

The question was meant for me.

"Excuse me," I groped for clarity. "What did the young woman say? I only heard a name."

"Play it again," Gutenberg ordered Breiter.

The young policeman nodded, clicked twice, and the recording started. The images returned with a tangible coldness. They displayed the death of a woman, captured her last words.

When the short film had ended, the room went quiet.

Strobelsohn flipped through the file in front of him, tapped his index finger on one of the papers, and finally said, "The deceased cried out a name: Dmitri Ivanov. And then she cried out in Ukrainian. *You must help us.*"

All eyes were on me.

"And?" Gutenberg asked.

"What happened to the young woman before her death must have been terrible." I tried to put into words what I had observed. "She was more afraid of this Dmitri than she was of dying."

Strobelsohn puckered his mouth. "Is that possible?"

"What do you mean?" I turned my head in his direction.

"That someone can be more afraid of a person than of death itself—does that actually happen?"

I looked the captain straight on. "Death is something abstract. But this Dmitri is painfully concrete."

Henrik Breiter coughed. "We suspect Dmitri Ivanov is in Russia. That is why we have contacted Interpol and the German Embassy there. We should hear back from them soon and then hopefully we will know who Dmitri Ivanov is. At the same time, we are following up on who shipped the container from Kaliningrad."

Breiter rose, went out to the coffee machine, and came back with a fresh, full pot. He stopped beside me and looked at me quizzically. I reached out and picked up one of the mugs stacked in the middle of the table. He poured me a cup.

I smiled. "Many thanks." Something warm would do me good now.

"You're welcome," he replied. A slight blush passed over his cheeks.

"What else are you doing on the case?" Gutenberg inquired a bit too brusquely.

Oops! I looked at Gutenberg. Judging from his knitted eyebrows, something seemed to annoy him. Maybe the whole situation. No. It was young Henrik, who was still rooted beside me, pot in hand, eyes shining.

Men, I thought, and said aloud, "Milk and sugar I'll get myself. Thank you."

Breiter nodded hastily. He poured Strobelsohn a cup, although he had not requested it, then placed the jug awkwardly on the table and plopped down boorishly in his seat.

"So? What else are you doing?" Gutenberg asked him a second time.

"We are trying to clarify the identities of the dead women, but I am skeptical about whether or not we will succeed," the young police officer said frankly. "And we are checking the freight papers to find out who exactly was responsible for the container. But also, there, I'm rather pessimistic."

Gutenberg pointed at the dark screen. "It is evidently clear that we are looking at human trafficking. No one is going to come forward and say that a container full of young women has not shown up."

"We will also be questioning this Hugenot, and we are waiting for the results from forensics," added Henrik, who had apparently caught himself again. "We can't do much more at the moment."

"Mr. Hugenot is the van carrier driver who should have picked up the container from the port," Strobelsohn answered my inquisitive look. He seemed depressed.

I could understand him all too well. "You now have two major cases to deal with. That is certainly no easy task."

"Definitely not," Strobelsohn responded like a bolt of lightning. "In order to perform proper police work, you need resources, time, and personnel. But no one is interested in my opinion. And Bolsen… Our boss simply does not care. Staffing is not exactly his cup of tea. Other things are much more important to him."

"Everyone has their own priorities," added Gutenberg. "And I can imagine that Mr. Bolsen has his." He slid down in his chair and stretched out his legs. "At the moment, however, it does not do us any good to complain about our working conditions. We have to get on with what we have."

Everyone was silent. Breiter stirred his coffee. The spoon knocked dully against the porcelain.

Of course, what Gutenberg had said was right. It was a moot point to get upset with things like staffing if you could not do anything about them. Still, he could have shown a little more empathy. Strobelsohn and Breiter were under considerable stress.

"Actually, I came today because of the murders in the Carstens's villa." I changed the subject to lighten the gloomy mood that threatened to spread. "At least in that case, I can help you a little by working with Suzanne Carstens."

Gutenberg nodded. "I have informed them about our arrangement."

"And you are all in agreement?" I asked.

Breiter nodded hastily and Strobelsohn shrugged his shoulders. "For all I care," he muttered, "it can't do any harm. But do you really believe that this will work?"

I took a drink from my coffee. "I am firmly convinced of it. I have done this many times in the past. However, it is necessary that all the investigators—and I am including myself in that—meet regularly to report on their progress. Exchange information, so that nothing is overlooked."

"What about client confidentiality?" Strobelsohn ascertained.

"A very important point." I nodded affirmatively. "Miss Carstens has agreed to the therapy and consented to my request to inform you of relevant facts from our discussions."

"Sounds great," Breiter said. And again, Gutenberg's eyebrows contracted.

With his subconscious reaction, Gutenberg revealed more to me than he wanted. I found myself liking his behavior. For a second, I was self-critical, but then curiosity gained the upper hand. Now let's see how long I can pull this off.

"I have one more request," I said. "You all have your work and I have mine. I will not be able to be part of the investigation all the time. If one of you could occasionally send me a completely informal, written update whenever something important happens, that would be helpful."

"I'll take care of that," Breiter hurried to say. "I'd be happy to do it."

I looked at him but watched Gutenberg out of the corner of my eye. He twisted his mouth in disapproval, but only shortly before a knowing smile spread across his face.

Damn it, I thought. *He's on to me.*

"You will supply Dr. Wolf with the requested information," Gutenberg said to Breiter. "Good." He moved to the front of his seat in preparation to rise.

A knock sounded, the door opened, and a uniformed officer walked into the room.

"What's up?" Strobelsohn asked.

"Mr. Kirchner is here," the officer replied.

"Kirchner?" Gutenberg repeated.

"The head of Carstens's domestic staff," the officer explained.

Breiter leaned forward in disbelief. "The *what?*"

"That would be the butler," Strobelsohn grumbled. "Fat cats have butlers."

"Very well," Gutenberg said. "Then we should chat with him." He stood up and reached his hand out to bid me farewell.

I did not respond. I remained seated and looked at him.

He understood immediately. "You want to join us?"

"At the interview?" I furrowed my brow, as if I had to think. "Yes, I probably should. That would make sense."

"Then come along," Gutenberg said.

18

The Landeskriminalamt always seemed so alive. The corridors breathed a peculiar urgency; everyone appeared to be passionately resolving something. Alex felt a little jealous about this when he looked around; in comparison his office resembled a monastery.

He returned his thoughts to the impending interview.

"…though my suggestion may sound a bit unorthodox, I would be thankful to you all for playing your part," Dr. Wolf had just said, oscillating her glance from Strobelsohn to Henrik. "It could be useful in my work with Suzanne Carstens if we could get the butler to give us a deeper insight into the Carstens family."

Henrik instantly nodded in his own slightly over-zealous manner. Immediately afterward, he threw a furtive glance at Strobelsohn, presumably to make sure the police captain was not angry with him for his hasty consent.

Strobelsohn was the picture of tranquility. He shrugged. "If that is acceptable to Mr. Gutenberg."

Dr. Wolf turned to Alex and looked at him intently. She had dark blue eyes, which he noticed for the first time.

"All right," he said. "Why not."

The foursome set off and moved along in tempo; they were swept up in the verve of the hallway.

The gaunt man that awaited them in the interview room was a small-scale version of a storybook mortician. Strobelsohn introduced himself and his colleagues to Michael Kirchner, Björn Carstens's head of staff, who rose from his seat and shook everyone's hand in turn.

The butler had to be around fifty, Alex surmised. He had sags below his markedly drooping eyes. With such a face, Alex had expected him to carry himself more slowly. But the man's gesticulations, reactions, and movements in general were surprisingly agile, succinct, and all together stealth-like.

Alex began by offering Kirchner a fresh cup of coffee. When the butler accepted, Henrik threw Dr. Wolf an inconspicuous look and then said, "I'll get the coffee and bring another stool. We're short one." Without waiting for an answer, he left.

Alex, Dr. Wolf, and Strobelsohn pulled up the three chairs, aligning them to face the interviewee. Out of habit, Alex waited for everyone to take their seat before he sat down himself. He looked at his notes. "Mr. Kirchner let's get straight to it, shall we? How long have you been working for Björn Carstens?"

The butler thought for a moment. "Just over eighteen years," he answered deferentially.

"All that time in the same position?"

The butler corrected his posture, almost imperceptibly. "Yes, sir. I am a valet by trade."

"Were you working at the Carstens's villa this past Saturday?"

"Yes, sir."

"At what time did you leave?"

"I and the rest of the staff were sent home at five p.m.," Kirchner replied succinctly.

Dr. Wolf's conjecture was right, Alex thought. The butler behaved distant and tight-lipped. It would not be easy to coax the information they needed from him. There was a reason he emphasized being a valet by trade. He acquiesced in his occupation and the obligation to discretion that came with it.

Alex leaned back a little and Strobelsohn took over. "Five p.m. Is that when your shift usually ends?" he inquired with piqued interest.

Kirchner hesitated once again. "No, sir. We are generally completing our day at seven p.m."

"So, five p.m. was an exception?" Strobelsohn inquired further.

"Mr. Carstens would dismiss us early once or twice a month." The butler straightened up in his chair. "Usually on a Saturday," he added.

Strobelsohn scratched the side of his head just above his left ear. "He would let you go home early on these nights as a means of rewarding you for work well done?"

"Oh, no sir. Mr. Carstens paid us dearly, and he knew this. He did not think it was necessary to give us perks of any sort."

"Why did he let you off early then?" the captain asked.

"I believe on these nights Mr. Carstens desired… privacy."

The butler avoided Strobelsohn's gaze. Alex noticed how uncomfortable Kirchner had become when the man blushed awkwardly.

Alex leaned forward, resting his wrists on the edge of the table. "What makes you so sure he wanted his privacy?" he asked. Returning to an upright position, he caught Strobelsohn's intrigued eye contact.

The butler owed Alex an answer. But he remained reticent and lowered his gaze.

Dr. Wolf cleared her throat. "I am sure this is very difficult for you, Mr. Kirchner. You have worked for the man for nearly two decades."

The butler looked up and nodded silently.

Dr. Wolf nodded as well—once. Then she tilted her head slightly and stared attentively at the butler without saying a thing.

After a short hesitation, the butler took a deep breath. "Mr. Carstens was not the ideal employer. I do not mean to disrespect him, but I remained in his service because he paid more than most, not out of any personal loyalty you might have gathered from fictional accounts of valets. I would just like to do a service to his memory and help you in any way I possibly can, to find whoever is responsible for this."

"That is fine; we appreciate your candidness," Dr. Wolf said. "I did not mean to paint you with some stereotypical characterization, but I could not help but notice that you felt uncomfortable when you spoke about these evenings. If it wasn't out of remorse for losing your employer, might it be that you are worried you could implicate yourself by telling us about some of his orders you have carried out?"

Kirchner bit his lip. He remained silent.

Everyone's attention was drawn to the doorway. Henrik walked in, holding the door open with one foot. With the help of the other he was moving the heavy chair into the room, while trying not to upturn the tray with the coffee pot and cups, which he held with the same arm that cradled his notepad at the elbow. The tail of his coat got caught by the door handle, and his notepad fell to the floor. The full tray nearly slipped out of his hands. He tried to catch his balance and the cups rattled alarmingly.

"Could you take something from me?" He looked imploringly at the butler, who sat closest to him.

Kirchner eagerly jumped to his feet, relieved the young police officer of the chair and carried it to the table.

"Thank you very much. That was a close call." Henrik smiled gratefully.

The butler smiled back. "My pleasure," he said, visibly more relaxed.

Henrik poured coffee for everyone, picked his notepad up, and plopped down in his chair in an exhausted explosion. "Well, what did I miss?" He took his cup and drank a sip.

Strobelsohn enlightened him. "Mr. Kirchner was just informing us how Björn Carstens would often send the staff home early because he wanted privacy."

"Privacy?" Henrik looked at everyone in turn.

The young detective plays his part really well and convincingly, you have to give him that, Alex thought. Aloud he said, "That's exactly what we had asked Mr. Kirchner before you came in, Mr. Breiter."

"And?" Henrik turned to the butler and took another sip of coffee, before he continued. "We found certain *objects* in the basement. This *privacy* you have been alluding to—might I assume has something to do with these?"

The butler clasped his hands together and began kneading the pads of his fingers with his thumbs. After a while, he paused. "Mr. Carstens would ask us to turn off the exterior lighting and surveillance cameras, as well as leave the back door ajar, when we would go for the night," he answered, visibly agitated. "I was just doing my job, and all of Mr. Carstens's staff will tell you that they too have been asked to turn off the cameras for one of these evening soirées."

"And that bothers you." Dr. Wolf took the floor. "That is more than understandable."

"No, ma'am," the butler hastened to say. "My embarrassment is solely due to the fact that Mr. Carstens was not always…" He cleared his throat and lowered his eyes. "Well, he was not always discreet."

Alex leaned forward. "What do you mean by *soirée* and *not always discreet*?"

The butler directed his undivided attention to him. "I can't tell you who would be in attendance, but there were clearly more than a few guests, and occasionally Mr. Carstens would leave things lying around. Things some members of my staff would refuse to touch and then bring to my attention. I'd gather these things and throw them away."

"Björn Carstens asked you to turn off the security system and leave the doors unlocked so he could be undisturbed during his debauched parties," Strobelsohn said. "Is that an accurate assessment, Mr. Kirchner?"

"Yes, Captain, that sums it up. Except maybe to be clear that we were not present. We could only infer about the… orgies from the mess that accompanied these evenings."

"Who is this *we*?" Strobelsohn probed.

"The three employees that were on duty Saturday, myself included, and the two part-time staff."

"Did any other outsiders know about these *soirées*?"

"I unfortunately cannot answer that for you."

Strobelsohn smiled and offered a nod of his head in recognition. "And the men that were found dead next to him? Karl Marten, Alistair Grauel, Hans Schilling—did you know any of them?"

The butler smiled, albeit briefly. Then he became serious again. "Yes, all three of them were constant fixtures at Mr. Carstens's side. Not usually together, but if Mr. Carstens spent any time that wasn't a formal affair, one of these men or a combination of the three were present. Only Dr. Schilling would attend Mr. Carstens's respectable parties." He hesitated. "I might venture to say the four men were good friends, but I had the odd chance to hear them speak negatively about one another in different situations. Conspiring against one another, as if they were business associates. But I cannot comment on that because I never knew what they did. They would usually not discuss specifics when I was around. Again, I can only infer from pieces of broken-off sentences over the years."

"Did any other people take part in these conversations?" Alex asked.

"No, to be honest, Mr. Carstens hardly spent time with anyone else," the butler answered staring down to his left. A sign that he was telling the truth, or at least making a concerted effort to remember from his experiences.

"What about Suzanne Carstens?" Dr. Wolf obviously tried to use the butler's pause for breath to possibly catch him off-guard. Alex was genuinely interested in how she took charge of the interview. He mused to himself that that was indeed their agreement. Between remembering Henrik climbing into the room and the thoughts of Dr. Wolf's interrogation style, Alex had to suppress a sudden urge to smile. With one eye closed, and teeth breaking through the blanket of his lips, he quickly turned away from the butler and focused on Dr. Wolf as she formulated her question.

"Björn Carstens and his granddaughter... How did they get along?"

"You want to know about their relationship?" The butler frowned. "I would say that there was not much love lost between them or any rapport at all. They didn't take their meals together, living alongside one another more than with each other."

"Was that always the case?" Dr. Wolf inquired further. "Or did they have a good relationship that, for whatever reason, changed over the years?"

"No. Ever since I have worked for them, they have not had a close connection, not like you would usually expect between a grandfather and his granddaughter. Even after her mother passed away. Nothing changed. That always seemed odd to me."

The air cleared over a pregnant pause when Dr. Wolf asked, "In your heart of hearts, do you think Suzanne Carstens was afraid of her grandfather, or Mr. Carstens maybe feared her somehow?"

Michael Kirchner shook his head in silence. "If you ask it that way, I think she was the one who avoided him. I cannot say if that bothered him. On the surface, Björn Carstens showed no quarter. And he was always extremely strict toward her; as a child she was very careful to follow his rules."

"Thank you, Mr. Kirchner." Dr. Wolf looked at the others. "That is all the questions I have. If my colleagues don't have any more, you are free to go."

The psychologist is giving the impression that this is her interrogation. It is getting out of control. Alex held himself back from a sharp remark and exhaled audibly. "I believe we are finished for today. We have your statement, and you have Captain Strobelsohn's card. In case you think of anything else, please don't hesitate to call us. Thank you for coming in."

"I am pleased if I could be of assistance," the angular man said.

He moved out of the room with noticeable agility. The door fell into its latch.

"I want to thank you for letting me take part in the interview," Dr. Wolf said. "After Mr. Breiter provided that wonderful distraction, the butler seemed to no longer fear sharing his emotions in an open and honest manner."

Alex was not sure if she meant that sarcastically or not. "Kirchner seemed to be contrived to me. I think he is hiding something."

"Maybe," she said, "but he was not lying. He implicated himself in the crime. I tend to believe everything he told us. It sure backs up my theory on Suzanne's childhood. He has been in Carstens's service since she was a little girl. And no matter how you paint it, she did not have a nice childhood."

"You got that from what he just said?" Alex asked skeptically.

"From that, and the fact that Suzanne called her grandfather *Mr. Carstens* when I spoke with her," she asserted. "We can be assured Björn Carstens and his granddaughter did not have a close relationship. We also know that Carstens had something to hide. Not least because he had his staff go home; none of them lived in the villa. And not only because he had the lights and surveillance system turned off. He would interrupt his conversations whenever his butler would approach."

"At least the lights being out on the night of the murders is consistent with the neighbor's security camera. And then the lights came back on around half past eight," Henrik said. "There was a black Mercedes Vito that arrived about nine p.m. and, by the looks of it, left with the same occupants after shortly pausing in front of the gate. We have part of the tag number and should have a match later today."

"Well, we need to see if his story holds up to the evidence on the surveillance system from previous weeks. Henrik, can you check on that today too," Alex more stated than asked, before adding, "And kindly ask the neighbors to adjust their camera to not be filming off of their own property, or we will be liable to prosecute."

Dr. Wolf was obviously not finished leading the investigation. "Someone has to find out what business activities these four men were involved in."

"I think this is something my office can look into," Alex offered.

"That will be helpful," she said, "but maybe we should speak with Peter Westphal first."

Alex's gut reaction was to fire off a harsh comeback that would put Dr. Wolf in her place. But the candid expression on her face exhibited to him that she was just as affected by the case as he. It was not her intention to challenge his authority. He reined in his anger and concocted a smile.

She looked at him with puzzled nearly inquiring eyes, then returned his smile.

19

Peter Westphal was bombarded with questions: date of birth, place of birth, address, telephone number, cell phone number, and lots of other insignificant things that had been asked long ago and were already on file.

Gutenberg seemed to have an inexhaustible arsenal. He acknowledged each of Westphal's answers with urbane interest, as if one of them could hold the key to solving the murders.

Of course, that was not the case. All of that had the sole purpose of breaking down the suspect's reserve. To lure him into an unguarded statement.

So far, however, Gutenberg had not had any success with this strategy.

I leaned back in my chair, arms crossed over my chest, letting the scene here in the barren interrogation room of the prison take effect on me.

Gutenberg behaved in a manner which I had come to know from him: deliberate, factual, and self-confident. He chose his words and formed his sentences without any show of emotion. The suspect, on the other hand, behaved quite differently than I had remembered from the day before. In the hospital, Peter Westphal had seethed, threatened to blow up, and finally lost complete control. Now he showed another facet of his character. He was self-restrained, courteous, calm, and patient.

Exactly that was the crux of the situation. After all, anyone would be upset if he became the suspect of a murder investigation, no matter how convinced he is of his innocence.

In addition, Westphal hardly paid any attention to me; he kept his eyes trained on the prosecutor the entire time. He even went so far as to barely blink. He put a lot of energy into appearing dependable and honest. He hid his true feelings, most likely his real intentions.

He lied to us. Deliberately.

And how did Gutenberg react to this *performance*? Well, he pretended to buy Westphal's guise. This, in turn, reduced the suspect's anxiety, which he hoped he had artfully concealed from us.

Gutenberg demonstrated endurance. He dangled freedom in front of the suspect, waiting for the right moment to strike. But I wondered when Gutenberg would get to it, when he would corner Westphal. Because that is exactly what he intended to do; the posture of the state prosecutor had evinced this to me. He sat more on the front half of his chair, his feet planted firmly on the ground.

Westphal had not necessarily detected this from his vantage point at the far end of the table, nor did he have the appropriate experience and knowledge to pay attention to these small, non-verbal tips.

Earlier, Gutenberg had invited me to take part in Westphal's interrogation. He had even offered to give me a lift in his car. The latter I had declined, because… Why actually? Well, I honestly could not say. Maybe because I wanted to drive to Georgios's afterward for dinner… No, that was not the reason.

So, what was it then?

Distance. It was okay to conduct interviews together, to ponder concertedly in an office about motives and suspects. A lunch in a public restaurant was okay. But a long drive, just the two of us confined in a car—that was, at least for the time being, too personal.

Comfortable distance is always a good idea.

Overall, the cooperation with Gutenberg was quite successful. He had included me in the interview with the butler. He even agreed to my suggestion of utilizing young Breiter as a diversionary tactic to get Kirchner talking. That had worked well.

Right now, Strobelsohn and Breiter were busy with the container case. The poor guys really did not have an easy job. Our boss, Bolsen, was only concerned about his career—his team was insignificant. The important thing was that he came out smelling like a rose.

Westphal's words washed over me. I had been distracted for a moment.

"I am very sorry," he was saying. "I really do not know what got into me. Usually, I'm not like that at all."

He was probably talking about yesterday's incident at the hospital.

"I simply had to see Suzi. And you had promised me, Mr. Gutenberg. I was terribly worried—" He broke off.

Gutenberg acknowledged this statement with a vacant smile and leaned back. "Let's come to the night of the murders."

"Gladly." Westphal's Adam's apple bobbed up and down. He swallowed.

"Has anything crossed your mind that you forgot to tell us about?"

Westphal furrowed his brow before opening his clasped hands to reveal his palms. The gesture should signal a disarming helplessness. But it did not pan out; it transpired a tad too late. "I've told you everything I know about it. Admittedly, it is not much. I arrived early in the morning."

"You have already said that." Gutenberg replied. "Then let's change the subject and you tell us a little about yourself instead."

"About me?" Westphal showed the first sign of uncertainty in this interview. He sat up, to some degree, in his chair.

"Yes. Please," Gutenberg responded.

"Well, there's nothing really noteworthy." He thought for a moment. "My mother died young." A short pause. "My father as well."

"From what?" I interjected.

"Of what?" Westphal was visibly startled. "Which one?"

"Your father," I said bluntly. "Your mother died from natural causes. But what about your father?"

He blinked. "How do you know that?"

"Please answer Dr. Wolf's question." Gutenberg seized the reins.

Westphal lowered his head and bit his lip. Then he looked up again. "My mother had cancer. And my father…"

Gutenberg and I waited.

"My father committed suicide."

"Hmm," I said. "How old were you then? We need it for our record."

Westphal's face was pale, and his eyelids fluttered. His restraint crumbled. "Seventeen. I was seventeen."

"You were still in school at the time," Gutenberg noted.

"Senior year."

"So," Gutenberg said, "you graduated from high school."

"Yes. Shortly thereafter."

"And then?"

"Then I got an endowment and studied marine biology. First in Hamburg and later in Sydney. It was a very interesting time."

He intended to win points and distract. But I did not do him the favor of taking the bait. "You received an endowment? From where?"

He hesitated again. Longer this time. "From a private citizen."

"He surely has a name," said Gutenberg dryly.

"Carstens."

Gutenberg leaned forward in his chair. "Björn Carstens financed your studies?"

"Yes," replied Westphal, giving Gutenberg a defiant look. "He knew my father."

"From where?" I prodded.

"My father… worked for him."

"That is a coincidence," Gutenberg said. "You are dating his granddaughter, your father was an employee of the deceased, and you reported the murder…"

"So many coincidences," I said. "Now you're going to tell us that you worked as a marine biologist for Mr. Carstens…"

"No." That came swiftly and unmistakably. "I have a job as an underwater welder in a shipyard, but you already know that."

"I don't understand." Gutenberg raised his eyebrows in an exaggerated arch. "You studied marine biology; you were even educated in Sydney. Why aren't you working as a marine biologist? Did you interrupt your studies?"

Westphal grunted. "I have a degree. But first of all, there are few jobs in my field. And secondly, they are usually very poorly paid. As an underwater welder, I earn a lot and can work alone. That suits me. I really can't complain."

"But your work is not without hazards, is it?" I threw in.

He shrugged his shoulders. "If you remain focused and pay attention…"

A brief silence fell over the room.

Westphal looked at me. His eyes expressed a sense of urgency, nearly pleading. I could not tell whether he was just pretending. "How is Suzi?"

"Given the circumstances," I replied curtly.

"Has she come to?"

"She will be released tomorrow."

"And then?"

"I'll start working with her, so she'll remember."

"Remember." Westphal displayed a subconscious tell when he wiped the back of his hand across his lips. "And where will she live?"

"She'll be accommodated accordingly," Gutenberg said in an evasive manner, before turning to me. "Do you have any further questions, Dr. Wolf?"

I shook my head. "No, thanks. That's it from my side for the time being."

"All right." Gutenberg grabbed his file and stood up.

I got up as well.

"You'll tell me if there is any news from Suzi, won't you?" Westphal asked.

He probably intended the question for me.

Gutenberg answered. "Within limits."

20

Peter Westphal was taken away by two uniformed police officers. With his head hanging, he walked in between them, footsteps echoing down the hall, until finally the three disappeared around a corner.

Gutenberg leaned against the wall, crossed his arms in front of his chest, and looked at me.

"He's hiding something," he said.

"Patently," I confirmed.

"The question is what."

"Let's remember what he did tell us," I said. "Because that was a lot."

"Really?" That came as somewhat of a surprise to me. It sounded sarcastic.

I was taken aback. Was he making fun of me?

I studied him more closely. No. On the contrary, it seemed important to him to talk to me about the interrogation, to exchange our opinions. However, he did not necessarily want to divulge this to me. That was the reason for his guarded posture and this slightly provocative undertone. But the sparkle in his dark eyes betrayed him.

It revealed that he was genuinely interested in my point of view.

Eyes do not lie.

I ignored his last question. Instead, I said, "His father's suicide must have shaken him to the core. He did not want to go into that. But unconsciously he did just that by bringing it up as the first thing when you asked him to tell us something about himself."

"That's self-contradictory." Gutenberg's face appeared skeptical.

I shook my head. "Not at all. He has never processed his father's suicide. That still bothers him. And earlier"—I gestured over my shoulder to the interrogation room we just came out of—"he exerted a lot of energy to show us his sweet side. He had to remain so focused on this that he couldn't avoid the slip-up from happening."

"Hmm," Gutenberg said. "If you think so…" He dropped his arms. "Maybe I should…"

"Yes," I agreed. "Absolutely. Let's find out what we can about the suicide. Why it came to that. The exact circumstances. And, if possible, how Peter found out. Maybe he even witnessed it."

"All right," said Gutenberg. "I'll ask Strobelsohn to look into it." He stopped, apparently thinking. "How do you assess Westphal yourself?"

I made a vague gesture with my hand. "He divulged that to us as well. He can work systematically. And he tackles tasks head on, with a focused and meticulous diligence."

"True." Gutenberg nodded.

"At the same time, he carries out an activity that is far below his qualification."

Gutenberg raised his eyebrows. "You think that matters? I find it completely understandable. He earns more money as an underwater welder."

"At least that's how he painted it for us. But if we take a closer look, there is a very different picture." I counted on my outstretched fingers. "He studied for years. He was even abroad for a while. He was committed to something. He had been working toward a goal. And then, in one fell swoop, he puts everything he had achieved in jeopardy." I made a dismissive gesture. "He gives it up."

"What do you conclude from this?"

"That is a sign of a frayed personality, and, in most cases, that is caused by an extremely stressful, life-changing experience. Or else…"

"Or else?" Gutenberg repeated.

"There are reasons that loom over all of it. Compelling reasons that Westphal cannot control and that he is not telling us about… That with the money," I added, "he just said that so we would stop putting him through the ringer."

"He told us that he likes to work alone."

"That's exactly what you would expect from a sociopath."

"Sociopath?" Gutenberg twisted his face in disbelief. "Are you not being a little too extreme? Sometimes I like to work alone, for example, and sometimes I'm happy when I don't have to see anyone at all."

"I don't mean that," I said. "That is normal."

"Well, that's good."

His spontaneous answer made me smile. Then I forced my thoughts once again back to Westphal. "Remember when he went crazy yesterday? He was overcome by emotion. That in the hospital with Suzanne Carstens was a purely authentic reaction. Today he put on an act for us: the reliable worker, the innocent victim, the worried friend."

"And you think that's just a guise?"

"Guise, façade, no matter what you call it. In order to clear up the killings, we have to look beyond the protective barrier Westphal is hiding behind."

Gutenberg pursed his lips. "You believe that he harbors romantic feelings for Miss Carstens?"

I had to laugh. *Harbors romantic feelings...* I did not expect such an expression from Gutenberg.

He looked at me, irritated.

"Sorry," I hurried to say. "How you put it... that sounded, somehow..."

A few rooms down from us, a door opened, and a police officer stepped into the hallway. I waited until he disappeared in the direction of the elevators.

I cleared my throat. "I'm not sure how Westphal feels about Miss Carstens. But from what I observed, he has a problem with the idea that her memories from the night of the murders might come back."

"I noticed that too. His reaction was poignant."

I nodded. "He could be afraid she might fall back into the catatonic state when she remembers the terrible experiences from that night. Or he wants to protect himself or her, because he or she or both carried out the murders."

Gutenberg pushed away from the wall he had been leaning against. "You think it might well be that these two are responsible for the massacre?"

I hesitated with my answer. "Conceivably," I finally admitted. "On the other hand, we don't have a motive. What reason do Peter Westphal and Suzanne Carstens have to kill these four men?" I stopped again. "Overall, I have the feeling that behind the massacre in the basement of the villa lies much more than meets the eye. This was not just a bloodbath of some old, horny men who were planning to have an orgy."

"*Feeling*," Gutenberg repeated, and the tone of his voice made me prick up my ears.

"Do you have a problem with that?"

"In this context, yes."

"Really? Why?"

His mouth twisted mockingly. "You do not want to psychoanalyze me right now, do you?"

I forced myself to smile. "Small occupational hazard."

He remained serious. "I prefer relying on facts, evidence, and logic." He took a deep breath. "But I came to the same conclusion as you."

"Good," I said. "Then we agree."

He stared at me, and for some reason I sensed an urgent need to avert my eyes. I looked to the nearby window that faced the courtyard of the jail. For the first time since we had been standing in the corridor, I noticed that dark clouds had formed outside. I heard the patter of fine raindrops against the glass.

"Where will you keep Suzanne Carstens?" I asked after a while, as I slowly turned back to him.

Gutenberg's demeanor was unpretentious, almost neutral. And, yet I had the distinct impression that my brief uneasiness had not escaped him.

"In a hotel," he answered. "In a suite. She's got enough money. So, that won't be an issue."

"Do you think she will be safe there?" I asked.

"At least for the time being, I'll post a police officer at her door just in case."

"That calms me down. And a hotel is great. A neutral setting, somewhere I can work well with her."

"Have you developed a strategy?"

"I have indeed," I affirmed. "However, it depends on her reaction. If, and how much, she gets involved. I have to stay flexible and respond to her. Not the other way around."

"I'm curious what you will discover," he said.

"Me too," I admitted. "That's the interesting part about our professions. You never know what you'll find in another person."

He did not reply.

21

The evening was cold and wet. The unremitting rain pelted the roof of the car and ran down in streams over the windshield. The wipers rhythmically swept back and forth. Their intermittent squeal, mixed with the interminable hum of the heater, produced a monotonous and overall wistful melody.

The heavy clouds had ensured a premature darkness. Tail- and streetlights reflected off the countless puddles as Alex made his way home, more exhausted and morose by the minute.

In all actuality, the afternoon had started out rather well. The interrogation of Peter Westphal had given him new clues that would help with the case, which was most definitely due to Dr. Wolf. She had shed light on things and situations from a completely different angle. Sure, her approach took some getting used to. He still had a hard time sizing her up, and sometimes her manner made him livid. But even though he did not care much for psychologists in general, he could not help but realize that she knew what she was doing. She definitely did not belong to that headshrinker ilk who was constantly spouting out some watered-down pseudo-wisdom. She had professional competence. And not a small amount. He had to give her that.

With these thoughts, and an overall satisfaction with the course of the day, he had spontaneously decided to stop by the LKA again. He wanted to inform Strobelsohn and Henrik about the interrogation in the jail and to find out if there was anything new with the two ongoing investigations.

In retrospect, he should have left well enough alone.

Strobelsohn and Henrik were not the only ones in the office. Hamdy had also been there. He had brought over the first lab results for the case of the suffocated women on the Burchardkai dock. And while Alex listened to Hamdy's detailed report, his good mood immediately disappeared. The water in the half-empty bottles they had found in the container had a dangerous mixture of sedatives. All of the women had puncture wounds in the crooks of their arms. Obviously, they had been drugged, dumped into the container, and then sent on their way.

They must have come to during the journey. Being thirsty, they drank the water, only to be knocked unconscious again.

Whoever had smuggled the women in the container had acted intentionally. They wanted to make sure that the girls went undetected during the trip from Kaliningrad to Hamburg. They had to prevent them from attracting attention by shouting or beating against the steel walls.

This revealed to Alex that the women had not voluntarily embarked on the journey. They had been kidnapped. And this was certainly not the first time the culprits had done this. They were positively unscrupulous, accepting that some of the girls might die of an overdose during the long voyage.

The women were merely livestock for the perpetrators. Common freight. Nothing more. Alex and his colleagues were clearly dealing with large-scale human trafficking.

He had hoped to catch up on some much-needed sleep; however, as soon as he parked his car in its spot under his house, he got the unusual urge to have a drink with his fellow man. He did not feel like telling anyone about the horrors he had witnessed. But maybe just seeing people still alive with their own set of miseries might help him get some rest.

At least the rain had eased off. Alex pulled the lapel up on his jacket and marched into the wind five houses down to the corner bar, complete with the prerequisite lace curtains, brass rails, and three tables of regulars trying to forget their day's drudgeries. He hoped he too could find solace here. One neat Irish whiskey would surely do the trick.

The double went down almost automatically; he thought about leaving to have a smoke but ordered another drink instead.

Nobody said a word to him, not even the bartender. Maybe they had seen the news. Berndt was usually quick-witted, but all he offered today was the rise and fall of his brow in a consolatory nod as he poured the whiskey.

Alex drained his second and started for the door. After two steps, his swimming head reminded him he had not eaten much besides a couple rolls with cold cuts earlier in the day. He needed to remedy that situation, and his thoughts quickly went to the untouched second portion he had carried out of the Chinese restaurant the night before. Better than the bar food this place had to offer.

His luck was changing. The rain had stopped completely. He headed toward home, a bite, and his bed.

He unlocked his door, got out of his wet overcoat, and hung it in the closet, and grabbed the Szechuan Chili Chicken and a cold seltzer out of the fridge. He set it all out on the coffee table, turned on the news channel and proceeded to eat the leftovers with the included disposable chopsticks.

He nodded off before the news loop started at the top of the hour.

Alex woke up in a cold sweat. He had been dreaming. He could vaguely remember scurrying through a grid of dark back alleys, with steep vertical plumbs that served as an open sewer and horizontal axes that appeared to be unused market stalls.

He *must* have been running; his feet, which were still stuck in shoes, were tangled up in the cushions of his sofa.

He could not remember the dream, but that was irrelevant. He knew all too well why he had been running.

Alex sat up and brushed the hair from his brow. What he needed was another stiff drink.

He walked over to his makeshift bar at the far end of his bookshelf. The decanter had maybe one shot left in it. He emptied it in a glass and thought of the conversation he had as a kid with his uncle. They had been remodeling a kitchen for some distant relatives he hardly knew. He recalled telling his uncle how these people must be alcoholics because they had a bar stocked with every imaginable libation. His uncle corrected him, saying that it was a sure sign they were not alcoholics. Alcoholics would only have the one bottle they were working on, aware somewhere in the back of their mind just how soon they would have to get another.

Alex could not understand why he kept worrying about being a lush. He did drink often, but rarely more than his personal limit of three beverages. It never seemed to affect him as quickly as it did others, who he was sure were alcoholics.

Or maybe he was lying to himself…

He looked at the glass in his hand, thought about the two doubles he had bought at the bar and had to confess that technically this was really his fifth and not his third drink of the day. And in the back of *his* mind, he was aware it would not be his last. It looked like this was going to turn out to be one of those nights.

He changed into something a little less conspicuous, swapping his suit and dress shoes for urban street wear and trainers. He decided he would walk a good ten blocks from his house; he did not want to see anyone he knew. Plus, the neighboring district offered more action.

The Chinese carryout had hit the spot. Even cold and straight out of the box: party stamina. He grabbed an old parka out of the closet and set off to find the bottom of a bottle.

He filed past his corner bar, took a left, and let the wind push him forward. He must have gone more than fifteen blocks. Half an hour had passed before he spotted an out-of-the-way hole to crawl into.

The bar had seen some life, years before; that is when the walls were decorated by a local cartoonist from a popular scene magazine. The scene had long since left this place; it was a survivor of the gentrification that had pushed most of the establishments out of business. *Patsy's* appeared to have enough local pull to afford the rising rent.

Alex found a seat that stood on its own, in a room just beyond the bar, where most of the action seemed to be around the pool table. He sat, slowly nursing his Jameson.

Some wiseass was giving the bartendress a hard time. *None of my business.* Alex decided to ignore it.

When the drunk wandered past him to smoke a cigarette in the courtyard, he left the door wide open. Cold wind squalled and blew up the back of Alex's jacket. Alex bit down hard on his molars, got to his feet, and shut the door. He returned to his whiskey.

The jerk reappeared. And of course, once more he acted like he grew up in a barn. Alex had to get up and pull the door closed.

The muppet started up with that same crap again at the bar.

Alex was slowly getting tired of this guy's MO as he mumbled his muddled come-on lines with drunken delivery to every female customer that ordered a drink.

After the fifth time of suggesting the sultry maiden behind the bar accompany him home when her shift ended, Alex approached the jerk. "I think you've said enough for tonight."

To his amazement, the fire-head beauty came to the drunk's defense. "He isn't hurting anybody. Leave him alone."

The drunk just snorted and threw Alex an inordinately contemptuous sneer.

"What are you looking at?" Alex squawked at the unbathed man.

The guy's mouth twisted into an insolent grin.

Alex balled his fists and forced himself to return to the isolated island of his table. He ordered another drink and hoped the whiskey would help curb his aggression.

Two doubles later, his tickling tonsils told him he had reached his limit; that and the fact that the alcohol had done nothing to calm him down. It seemed to have the opposite effect.

Time to go home.

When he stood up, his knees nearly buckled under him. He gained control and walked upright out of the bar.

As soon as he stepped outside, the bitterly cold Baltic air hit him like a ton of bricks. Alex rubbed his shoulders and had to stop for a second to catch his breath. He stretched his arms over his head and then immediately dropped his hands to his knees. He was not going to vomit, but stretching his frame was not helping either.

Alex lifted his eyes from their vocal point between his shoes just as his drunken friend fell out of *Patsy's* front entrance.

The inebriated man gawked at Alex and with an astonishing coherency said. "Hey, you fuckwit…" Then he spun on his heels and started to walk in the opposite direction.

Enough of this! Alex's blood boiled over. He set out in full strides behind the drunk. Clutching the man's jacket high and low, Alex swung him around and smashed the jerk's face into the brick wall of the house they were passing.

With a formidable satisfaction Alex realized that the fool actually wanted to fight. The idiot came at Alex, face badly bruised, and grabbed him around the neck, apparently trying to wrestle.

Alex plunged both arms above his head sweeping like a swimmer's breaststroke, breaking free of the man's grasp. Alex slammed two hands down hard on his opponent's shoulders and simultaneously brought his knee up to the man's face. He heard a resounding thud when the bridge of the drunk's nose snapped.

Blood and crazed maniac were now all over Alex.

Alex did his best to block the multitude of blows the lunatic wildly delivered. He managed to grab the man's lapels and slammed his body back and forth between two parked cars.

The crazed drunk did not give up; he had gotten ahold of Alex's head and was able to land two upper cuts before Alex could wrest himself free. The man threw a wild right hook, which Alex easily deflected with a rolling block and used his opponent's momentum to lay him out on the patch of grass in the parking where the dogs relieved themselves. Alex delivered two quick punches from a squatted position.

Breathing heavily, Alex rose to his feet, turned, and stumbled away. Double vision and bright flashes of light told him he had not escaped unscathed. But he kept walking.

An hour later, soaked from the continual drizzle, he found himself standing in front of Dr. Wolf's stately single-family dwelling, staring at the windows. The lights were out. Surely, she had long gone to bed.

He stretched out his arm until his finger was merely an inch away from her doorbell.

He froze. How had he gotten here? And more importantly: What did he think he wanted?

Had the bar and the fight all been a bad dream? Was he sleepwalking?

He took a deep breath. Then he took another one. His throbbing head and sore jaw assured him he had not imagined the entire evening.

He quietly lowered his arm, stepped away from his colleague's stoop, and decided to walk home.

March

24

Wednesday

22

Outside, the sun was shining. There was no sign of yesterday's downpour. Alex kept his head slightly lowered and slid down in his seat to keep his face in the shadows. His eyes were overly sensitive to the light today.

Henrik had stuck a cup of coffee in his hand as soon as he had set foot in Strobelsohn's office. Alex stirred it. The spoon slapped against the side of the porcelain and made a nerve-racking clang. It seemed to resonate inordinately loudly in the quiet room.

He carefully guided the cup to his lips and took a sip. The strong black brew was just what he needed to get the signs of life to return. His jaw ached from his early-morning brawl. Although he had slapped a Band-Aid over the cut on his chin before coming in, the iridescent bruise seeping out from under it removed any chance of it looking like a shaving accident.

Alex took another sip and glanced up. Strobelsohn and Henrik gawked at him intently. It seemed to have not been lost on them that he had a hangover. They were not dumb. And the way they looked at the Band-Aid divulged that they were wondering what had happened in the last fourteen hours.

He had to get on with it. Alex pulled himself together, smiled, and said, "What's up?"

"We're preparing for Bolsen's weekly tongue-lashing," Strobelsohn grumbled. His sullen facial expression spoke volumes.

The corner of Alex's mouth hinted at a smile. "What does Bolsen need to know? Let's start with the Carstens case. What do we have so far?"

"We are still going through the videos from Carstens's neighbors," Henrik eagerly began. "We concentrated on Saturdays at first, which did not take long, because the system only captures two months of footage before it gets overwritten."

"Then there is nothing older?" Alex asked.

"Unfortunately, not," Henrik replied. "I was told by the neighbor it did not make sense to keep it."

Alex shifted uncomfortably in his chair and averted his eyes from the two officers. "Please don't forget to get them to change the angle of that camera."

"I haven't," Strobelsohn hastened to assure. "We will, of course, inform the neighbor accordingly, but for now, we should feel lucky that they weren't careful when they installed it."

Alex nodded and concentrated on the young detective. "So, what did you see?" Henrik sat up from his slouched position and moved to the front of his chair. "On three of the Saturdays, the same black Mercedes Vito arrived around nine p.m. after Alistair Grauel, Dr. Schilling, and Karl Martens. I think we can believe what the butler told us; the van would usually leave sometime between three and four-thirty on Sunday morning. Also substantiating

Mr. Kirchner's statement, by all appearances the exterior lights were only turned off on these nights."

"However, last Saturday, the lights came on around eight-thirty, only to be turned off again after eleven p.m.," Strobelsohn spoke up. "And if you remember, the van did not drive onto the property."

Alex placed his right thumb under his lower lip and concealed his chin behind cupped fingers. "The lights being out must have been the signal for the Mercedes that the coast was clear. Do we know who owns the van?"

Henrik flipped the top page of his file. "It is registered to Karl Martens, and belongs to one of the pimp's establishments. The Pink Playhouse on Herbertstraße."

"Henrik and I will accompany a colleague from the Davidwache this afternoon to see what the manager can tell us," Strobelsohn quickly added.

Alex acknowledged his colleagues' initiative with a short, pained smile. "Did anyone else come or go on Saturday or Sunday? What about Peter Westphal? Did you see him arrive, as he said, at six in the morning?"

"No," Henrik answered.

Alex raised his eyebrows and simultaneously twisted his head in a slow, forward-sloping nod. "Have you watched the entire video from Saturday?"

"We looked at some of it sped up, showing every tenth frame," Henrik admitted, "but we did not see anyone else."

"That means we can neither confirm nor refute Westphal's statement that he arrived at the villa early Sunday morning. But no matter when he came, somehow he must have gotten on the property?"

"There is another entrance," Strobelsohn said.

"A second entrance? Well, when were you going to tell me?"

Strobelsohn's jaw tightened visibly. "Our people did not discover it right away. It is a rusty gate, hidden behind a tall hedge of evergreens. It leads to a barely used, narrow path. We presume it once served as the garden waste disposal for the properties that butt against it. The alley opens onto the adjacent street."

"That may explain why he is not on the video," Alex said. "Peter must have entered through this gate. You need to…"

"I plan to go to the prison afterward and check that with him," Henrik interrupted him.

"Maybe it would be better if Captain Strobelsohn did this." Alex looked from Henrik to Strobelsohn. "That way you could cross-examine his initial statement and play around with his memory. Ask him if he saw any cars in front of the house; get him to tell you he accessed the property from a different direction."

"Of course, but anyone else who was familiar with the grounds could have come in this way, undetected," Strobelsohn said. "Neighbors, friends, acquaintances, employees…"

"Or anyone looking for a back way in," Alex added. "Did the evidence collection team find anything there? Footprints, fingerprints, tracks?"

"Not yet."

Alex cleared his throat. "That is not exactly a lot. We don't have anything else?"

"Unfortunately, not. So far," Strobelsohn confirmed, and Henrik made a guilty face.

Alex took a drink from his coffee. "That won't be enough for Bolsen. What about the multiple murders at the Burchardkai Terminal?"

"Henrik was finally able to locate Wilhelm Hugenot," Strobelsohn said. "He'd been tending to his boat. He was getting it ready for the new season. That is why he was not home."

Alex's attention was piqued. "What was he like? What kind of an impression did he make?"

"He seemed to be a typical blue-collar worker," Henrik said as he leaned forward to refill Alex's coffee without being asked. "Medium to smallish stature, I would say around five foot eight, missing three digits on his left hand. He did know a thing or two about boats."

"How many people work for his transport company?" Alex asked, "What was it called again? Stardust?"

"Stardaenz. S-T-A-R-D-A-E-N-Z," Henrik spelled it out. "It is a one-man operation. It is just him and his old tractor trailer. His main source of income comes from his job as a van carrier driver on the dock; the transport company is his side gig." He nodded as if to agree with this last statement.

Alex raised an eyebrow. "Well, did he know anything about the container?"

"He denied any knowledge of it. He said had never been contacted regarding the shipment either."

"Has he ever worked for this company before?"

"He said he had often been contracted by the same company; he would usually get a short notice, pick up a container, and deliver it to the outskirts of town to an abandoned farm."

"And I presume he did not know who he was working for," Alex said.

"I am afraid not." Henrik twisted his mouth into a frown. "He was always paid-up front, and he never met anyone in person. Payments came from a corporation: Russian Folk Artisans LLC."

"An LLC? Well, a corporation has to be registered to someone."

Strobelsohn puffed out his cheeks and let the air escape noisily. "An old widow who died six months after the corporation was formed; the bank account is in another company's name, which appears to be a daughter corporation of yet another company. The account only ever has enough money to cover these shipments."

"We are getting a warrant to see who made payments on the account," Henrik added.

"Besides that, I have asked Henrik to question the customs agent." Strobelsohn took over. "It might be a coincidence, but every shipment to the Russian Folk Artisans was handled by the same official: Mathilde Hauke. She is scheduled to work the second shift this evening."

"That is a good lead," Alex said, "though how likely would it be that a woman is involved in the trafficking of sex slaves?" He thought for a moment. "What about this farm?" he asked Strobelsohn.

"The farm is owned by the same deceased widow's estate as the Russian Folk Artisans LLC but was purchased six months after her death. That has been nearly fifteen years now. It has been on the market ever since," Strobelsohn replied. "However, the selling price is so high that one would expect a working dairy." He leaned forward in his seat and looked Alex straight on. "The old woman was in hospice when the Russian Folk Artisans Corporation was formed, died six months later, and six months after her death she *literally* buys a farm. If you ask me, the whole thing stinks of identity theft."

"It certainly does," Alex agreed.

They fell silent.

"Have you heard from Interpol or the German Embassy in Moscow?" Alex asked after a while.

"Interpol has something on Dmitri Ivanov; they are sending us a file by courier, but it hasn't arrived yet,"

Strobelsohn said. "And there has been no response from the German Embassy either. But they always take longer. Let's call it typical... diplomacy."

Henrik leaned on his elbow. "And what are we going to tell Bolsen? He will read us the riot act if we don't show him some results."

"Well, at the moment, we don't have much to offer him." Alex narrowed his eyes and considered their options. "Bolsen is addicted to notoriety. So, you tell him we're on the right path, we have a suspect in custody. We're following a couple good leads. And you extend cordial greetings to him from the German ambassador in Russia."

"But that's not true." Henrik rattled off dumbfounded. "The ambassador did not send any…"

Strobelsohn grinned sardonically. "That does not matter. The main thing is Bolsen thinks that some dignitary takes him seriously. And we can continue investigating in peace, without him getting too much under our skin."

23

Alex had busied himself with his schedule and mail while his two colleagues defended their efforts to their boss in solving one case deprived of evidence, and the other carried out far away.

He acknowledged his rising guilt, not just for leaving the two to stand up for themselves, but he had relinquished his entire caseload on his assistants at the state prosecutors' office.

Despite how much notoriety would accompany these cases, he seldom felt such a burning desire to catch the perpetrators. He would gladly deflect the credit to Bolsen in exchange for putting the psychopaths responsible for these deaths behind bars.

Less than fifteen minutes had passed when Henrik held the door for the captain, and the two rolled into Strobelsohn's office. Alex could not help but notice their good mood. He packed his mobile phone away. "I take it that went well?"

Strobelsohn brandished a rare grin. "He bought it lock, stock, and barrel. As soon as Henrik extended greetings from the ambassador, Bolsen seemed to forget about reprimanding us. I think he was more interested in getting us out of his office as soon as possible so he could brag to his wife or golf buddy. I'm not sure who he was going to call, but he promptly dismissed us. As we were leaving, I saw him reach for his breast pocket; that's where he keeps his smartphone."

"That's good to hear. One less problem. For a little while, anyway." Alex smiled and stood up to go.

Strobelsohn's telephone rang. "Hello, Captain Strobelsohn, LKA. How may I help you?"

"I'm headed to my office; there is a mountain of work awaiting my attention." Alex then addressed Henrik quietly. "If there is anything new, let me know." He nodded to Henrik and Strobelsohn and opened the door.

Strobelsohn stopped him with an urgent wave of the hand. He covered the mouthpiece. "I have the Federal Intelligence Agency on the phone," he said in a low voice.

"The BND?" Alex responded just as quietly, furrowed his brow, and pulled the door shut. Then he turned completely back to the police captain.

"I am presently in a meeting with Detective Henrik Breiter, and Assistant District Attorney Alex Gutenberg," Strobelsohn spoke in the receiver again while he looked Alex in the eyes. "They are both working on the case. If it is all right with you, I will put you on speaker." Strobelsohn remained quiet for a second. "Okay." He pressed a button and set the phone in the cradle. Lowering his head closer, he said, "Hello, can you hear me?"

"Yes, hello gentlemen," announced a soft voice. "My name is Myra Steinhagen. I am a case worker for the BND in Berlin. A colleague from Interpol called me this morning and asked me to contact you regarding Dmitri Ivanov, in connection with human trafficking."

"Good morning, Ms. Steinhagen. This is Assistant District Attorney Gutenberg." Alex took the floor. "What can you tell us about Mr. Ivanov?"

There was a long, knowing pause. "Mr. Gutenberg, we have a pretty extensive file on Dmitri Ivanov, and to be honest, trafficking in sex slaves seems right up his alley. In a country run by criminals, he is an exception; we are fairly sure he made his start in the transport of drugs in Asia, but he quickly diversified."

"What exactly do you mean?" Alex asked.

Myra Steinhagen continued, "Amongst other things, Dmitri Ivanov allegedly runs the world of counterfeit groceries in Russia, the former Soviet States in the Caucasus, and Central Asia. And he would need the government's blessings to do something like this. He is similarly involved in gun trafficking. We have some intelligence that suggests he worked both sides of the Chechen War. But as with all of our leads, they run dry; we do not even have so much as a photo of him."

"How is that possible?" Alex asked.

"He operates through a network of emissaries, and the higher up the ranks, the more clandestine they become. Ivanov is not your typical Russian billionaire oligarch who likes to be seen in public. Being an ex-KGB agent, his background also proves difficult to research since you cannot stop what you cannot see."

"That means, in other words, we can't get our hands on him?" Strobelsohn asked.

Myra Steinhagen seemed to hold her breath. "Well, not as long as he remains in Russia. As I have said, what we know about Ivanov is only hearsay. We are not even sure Dmitri is his given name. So, it is no surprise to obtain information that Dmitri Ivanov is once again working beyond the borders of the former Soviet Union."

Alex stepped closer to Strobelsohn's desk. "Can we speak with an agent or someone in the field in Russia?"

"For now, I will be your formal contact with the BND," Mrs. Steinhagen hurried to respond. "I can either arrange a supervised viewing of Mr. Ivanov's file here in Berlin or we can send someone to you, but the sensitive material within may not be photographed or copied in any way. Leaked information is the biggest threat for the men and women who collect it."

"I can appreciate that," Alex said. "If you have the resources, we would not say no to your offer of delivering Dmitri Ivanov's file to the offices of the LKA in Hamburg."

"That would be no problem for us. We could have someone there tomorrow afternoon."

"Shall we have a driver meet your colleague at the airport?" Strobelsohn offered.

"That won't be necessary. We'll use our own driver."

"Thank you, Mrs. Steinhagen." Strobelsohn picked up the receiver. "I assume you have my email address. Could you send me your contact details?" After a longer pause he said thank you again and hung up the phone.

Alex rubbed a hand over his sore jaw. "Well maybe you'll have something for Bolsen, after all."

24

I unlocked the adjoining room of the hotel suite, which until now had been sealed off. Then I turned to Suzanne Carstens and beckoned her with a wave of the hand. We entered together.

A bright room with three large windows, whose furnishings were kept emphatically simple at my request: a black leather loveseat in front of a coffee table with a box of tissues, two bottles of mineral water, and some glasses. Opposite the couch was an armchair, also covered in black leather, and within its reach, one of those typical gray, rolling file carts.

Suzanne Carstens hesitated. She remained indecisive and looked around.

"You should take the sofa," I said. "The chair is for me."

We sat down.

I had the furniture arranged in such a way that I had the light at my back so as not to miss any of my client's emotions. I looked at her. She was agitated. That was understandable. A new environment, a new situation. She did not know what to expect.

Her bruises had subsided. But she herself was still far too sallow. A pretty woman, young and attractive. An expressive face. Natural blonde hair, strikingly dark eyes, high cheekbones. A petite nose grabbed my attention. The swelling had almost completely disappeared. As a result, the spot where her nose had once been broken became more pronounced.

I smiled. "The other rooms are your living quarters. We shouldn't be distracted here."

She looked around for a moment and said, "I like it."

I leaned toward the file cart and shook the middle drawer. It did not give. I took the key chain from my pocket again and unlocked the drawer. In the compartment lay a pad of paper. I took it out along with some colorful fineliners.

Suzanne Carstens closely followed my every move.

"This cabinet contains my personal things," I said. "Writing material and medication—in case you might need some."

"I'm not sick," she said. "I don't need any pills."

"They're only here as a precaution." I leaned back. "So? Did you sleep well?"

She nodded. "Yes. I did."

"How are you being treated in the hotel? Are you satisfied with the service?"

"I had my breakfast brought to my suite. But maybe I'll take supper in the dining hall."

"Nice," I said.

She smiled insecurely.

I started. "The room here, and the time we spend together, belong solely to us."

A slight blush spread across her cheeks.

"You already know my name," I went on. "I am Doctor Evelin Wolf. I was born and raised in Hamburg. I completed my psychology degree here, then moved away for a while and am glad that I'm back in my hometown." I paused. "And you?"

"I was born in Hamburg too," she said.

"We have something in common," I said.

That was not enough to allay her uncertainty.

"My job is to help you restore your memory. That's my objective, but that's what you want too, isn't it?"

"Yeah," she agreed, but only after some hesitation.

"Good. We will work toward that."

"Will it be difficult, or take a long time?"

I shrugged. "Let's wait and see. As a first step, I would like to get to know you better."

She furrowed her brow. "How can we do that, if I have forgotten almost everything?"

"Little by little," I said. "Let's start with what you do remember." I pushed the pad and the set of colorful felt-tip pens over to her.

She looked skeptically at the art supplies.

"I would like you to sketch your house for me."

"You want a picture? I can't draw very well."

"Maybe that didn't come off right," I said. "I meant more of a floor plan, like an architect would make. An outline of your house in Blankenese."

She crossed her arms in front of her chest. "No. I can't, nor do I want to do that."

"That's fine. You don't have to do anything you don't want to. But my request is not about accuracy. I would just like to get a general idea of where you grew up. An approximate layout of the rooms, how the furniture is arranged in them, things like that. Do you think you can do that for me?"

She bit her lip. "A rough draft, I guess."

"And after you have drawn a general plan, you could mark the spots where you felt most comfortable as a child."

"The house has three floors," she said.

"Mhmm."

"And a basement."

"Mhmm."

"I do not want to draw the basement."

"Whatever you like," I said.

"Then I'll start on the first floor."

"Perfect." I nodded encouragingly.

She sat on the edge of the couch, picked out a blue felt-tip, and opened the sketch pad. Her chest rose and fell. Then she began to work in long, clear lines. In no time, she had drawn an outline. She put her pen down, grabbed a brown one, and began concentrating on the furniture. She drew circles, squares and rectangles. After a while, she stopped.

"This is the first floor?" I asked.

"Yes." She nodded.

"All right. Now could you explain it a bit to me?"

She looked at me with huge, dusky eyes.

"I've never been to your home," I told her. "I can see the rooms, but I do not know what they are. And even though I can see the outlines of the furniture, I am not sure if they are tables, sofas or cabinets."

"Should I label them for you?"

"What would you think about pointing to each and telling me what it is? That would be enough for me."

"OK." She thought for a moment, and then tapped the page with her finger. "So, that's the kitchen."

I leaned forward. "Aha. Pretty big."

"Yes. Two stoves. A commercial-sized fridge. And here is the breakfast nook table with six chairs."

"Where did you usually sit?"

She pointed to a circle beside the door. "There. This is where I sat and watched the cook when she baked cakes. She would always let me nibble on the dough."

"Your own cook?"

"Yes. Mrs. Jensen. Her marble cake is the best." She smiled, and I could see the tension ease a bit from her face.

"Super," I said. "What's this next to it? The dining room?"

"That's over here." She pointed to another part of the drawing.

We meticulously worked our way through the floor plan. She explained each room to me, pointing out where she sat in front of the TV, a large fireplace, which was never used, and the patio door. Occasionally she gave longer explanations, told me about small incidents, trivialities and peculiarities that she associated with each spot.

She never mentioned her grandfather. Not once.

Then she was finished.

"What about your bedroom?" I asked.

A dark shadow came over her eyes. "That is on the second floor."

"Of course," I said. "How silly of me."

All at once, she became strangely withdrawn, on the border of being hostile.

I picked the sheet up and looked at it appreciatively. "Now I have a good idea of where you grew up. Thank you for taking so much time with it."

I put the drawing right in the middle of the coffee table, between us. "Now, if I asked you what your favorite spot on this floor was, what would your spontaneous answer be?"

Without hesitation, she tapped her finger on the paper.

"And what is that?" I asked.

"The stairs." She emphasized the word as if it were self-evident, as if I had to realize why she liked this spot in particular.

I raised an eyebrow and nodded reassuringly. "The stairs."

She exhaled serenely and leaned back.

I looked at my watch. "We're done with this for today."

"That's it?" she asked, surprised.

"That was a lot," I replied. "And you did very well." I paused. "Do you have any questions for me?"

"Yes." She lowered her eyes. "Yesterday, you mentioned a name. Peter... Peter Westphal."

"That's right."

"I've been thinking a lot about it. The name sounds familiar to me."

"That's excellent," I said. "Your memory is slowly coming back. When you think of the name, how do you feel?"

"Feel?"

I looked at her expectantly.

"Good," she replied resolutely after a bit. "I have a nice feeling about the name. I like it."

I got up. "Good memories always return first."

"Really?"

"Really."

"Then I'm looking forward to our next session," she said.

March

25

Thursday

25

The basement rec room of the Carstens's villa, where the killings had taken place. The chairs in which the deceased had sat. On the walls and on the floor, I could see the blood stains, the markings from the evidence collection team, reminiscent of every other homicide scene.

"So?" Gutenberg asked from behind me.

I turned to him. "Just like the photos." I pointed to the group of chairs. "Suzanne Carstens was sitting right in the middle of those? Between the bodies all night?"

"That's correct. Right there."

His face remained unaffected. I looked at him. In the artificial light, the bruise, which the Band-Aid, on his chin barely covered, became even more pronounced. The blotch shimmered almost unnaturally down here, and I secretly wondered how Gutenberg got his injury. Judging from the dark rings under his eyes, he had not slept at all last night, and perhaps had a bit too much to drink. Something seemed to be bothering him.

I concentrated on my work again and looked to the left. A large wooden countertop, shelves covered the wall behind it, displaying a multitude of brightly colored bottles.

I went over. "An impressive bar. This has seen a lot of parties."

"That's right," he replied curtly.

I hesitated. "Should I put on gloves?"

"That won't be necessary." He said with a wave of his hand. "The evidence collection team has been through here. Twice. It doesn't matter if you touch anything now."

I opened one of the cupboard doors under the bar: cases of alcohol.

"Somebody wanted to make sure his guests would not get dehydrated," Gutenberg remarked.

In the next cabinet was a whole hodgepodge of sex toys. "Oh," slipped out of me.

"Intriguing?" he asked.

I looked at him. His question was clearly meant to be serious—professional, not provocative or sexist.

"It seems fitting," I said.

The third door was a built-in dishwasher, partially filled. Glasses and the like. Not remarkably interesting. I closed it again.

"The bar is well-equipped," I commented.

"Björn Carstens had money to burn. He could afford that."

I looked around again. "I think that's enough for me."

Silently we returned via the servant's staircase and kitchen back to the front living room on the first floor. I took a seat in one of the armchairs. Gutenberg settled down opposite me.

I looked from the open fireplace to the big lattice windows and out into the garden. The lawn glistened lush green in the sunlight.

"What do you think of it all?" Gutenberg asked me.

I turned to him. "The atmosphere in the basement is depressing."

"No wonder." He grimaced. "Blood on the walls, on the floor, actually everywhere. And we both know what happened down there."

I shook my head. "That's not what I mean. The basement on the whole is depressing. No windows, only artificial light."

He knitted his eyebrows for a moment while he looked at me. "Like what happens down there should stay down there."

I did not expect that answer. He always pretended that he had no feelings, as if he were governed by logic alone. And then he immediately understood how I felt.

"The basement furnishings were intentionally designed and planned to the last detail. Up here, you can't see or even hear anything that's going on down there. As though it were two different worlds." I paused. "Other horrible things have happened in that cellar."

"I got the same impression."

I reached into my pocket and pulled out the folded sketch that Suzanne Carstens had drawn for me in the morning. I put it on the table in front of me and smoothed it out.

"What's that?" Gutenberg leaned over.

"This is from Miss Carstens. I asked her to draw a floor plan of the villa earlier today."

"She actually did it?"

I smiled. "Well, with a little persuasion from me. But after her initial hesitation, she seemed to even enjoy doing it. However," I pointed at the intricate parquet below my feet, "She did not want to draw the basement, or her bedroom for that matter. Only the first floor—that was her condition."

"Hmm," Gutenberg said. "What's the purpose of the drawing? We have the floor plan. You could have gotten the furniture layout right off the bat from Strobelsohn or me. We have forensics' sketch in our file."

"Of course," I agreed. "But I have to connect with her somewhere. That's why I asked her where she felt most comfortable when she was a child. She told me the kitchen, and in the other sitting room." I pointed beyond Gutenberg. "That would have to be over there, the couch where she always watched TV." I looked at the sketch. "What surprised me the most? When I asked her to show me her absolute favorite spot, she immediately pointed at the stairs."

"I do not understand." Gutenberg frowned in disbelief. "Or does that have a symbolic meaning? The stairs… An archetypal representation for…" He trailed off, pursing his lips and shrugging his shoulders.

"The stairs as a symbol? I don't think she meant that," I replied. "In the context of our conversation, she was specifically indicating a location."

"Then we should take a closer look at those stairs."

"It couldn't hurt," I agreed.

I grabbed the picture and kept it in my hand. We got up and went to the foyer. A wide mahogany staircase, elegantly lined with wooden wainscots and crown molding, led up to the second floor.

Side by side, we climbed the stairs. On the walls hung gold-framed pictures of sailing ships, the Port of Hamburg, and the warehouse district. Nothing that would have any significance for a child.

At the top, a large landing and a hallway to several rooms.

Gutenberg stood at the railing and peered down. "The staircase is wider than a lot of townhouses," he said. "But why would that appeal to her?" He glanced up at me.

"Since we're up here, do you care to see Miss Carstens's bedroom?"

I shook my head. "I don't want to do that. I'll save it for later. I would first like to see what she has to say. If I don't know the room, I'll be unbiased and hear things that I might otherwise ignore."

He nodded, and we made our way back to the first floor.

Out of the corner of my eye, I noticed that he was watching me.

"You're disappointed," he noted.

I shrugged my shoulders. "Somehow I expected more."

We had arrived back at the foyer. I studied Suzanne's drawing and spun around once on my axis. "I'm not wrong. The stairs must have some significance."

Gutenberg took a few steps until he stood by the wall paneling. "There is a cavity under each staircase," he mumbled more to himself.

He began to push against the wainscoting. The third panel opened with a squeak.

Gutenberg whistled softly through his teeth. "What do we have here?"

"Forensics didn't discover that?" I made sure.

"No." He shook his head. "Strobelsohn or Henrik Breiter would have told me."

We peeked inside.

Darkness. It reeked of stale air.

Gutenberg felt around the inside of the paneling. I heard the click of an ancient light switch. Nothing happened.

"Seems to be broken," he said.

He reached into his jacket, pulled out his cell phone and turned on its flashlight function. He used it to shine inside.

A small room, maybe nine square feet, with the ceiling sloping upward in unison with the steps it followed. A barren wood bench and a plaid wool blanket.

"Can I go in?" I asked him.

"Nobody has been in here for a long time," he said, pointing to the untouched layer of dust on the floor. "So yes."

I squeezed past him. I had to stoop; the room was not high enough to stand upright. Not for an adult anyway, maybe for a little girl.

Gutenberg handed me his cell phone. I shined the light around. Nothing. No drawings or any other items.

I reached for the blanket and lifted it cautiously. Underneath was an old doll. Without any clothes. The body was made out of yellowed fabric, the arms, legs, and head of porcelain. The limbs were strangely twisted. Her translucent eyes stared back at me.

I bent down and picked up the toy.

"You find something?" Gutenberg asked from the entrance.

"Yes." I gave him his phone.

He took it and switched it off as I stepped through the opening, back into the foyer.

"Here." I showed him the doll.

"Kind of ugly," he said. "Worn out. Do you think it belonged to Miss Carstens?"

"Why not?"

"With all that money, it seems that Björn Carstens would've given his granddaughter something a little…" He hesitated. "…something nicer to play with."

"Maybe he did," I replied. "But children do not care that much about appearances. It may well be that she had the doll since she was a little girl and that it has some importance for her."

"Will that help you? Can you use it in your sessions with Miss Carstens?"

I glanced back into the darkness under the stairs. "Possibly." I turned to him. "May I take it with me?"

He puffed out his cheeks. "If it helps… I think I could justify that." He closed the wooden panel. "Can you explain to me why children would voluntarily play in a hole like this when they have an entire house and a huge garden at their disposal to blow off steam?"

"Whoever sat in there was not playing," I said. "That was a hiding place."

"From what?" Gutenberg eyed me intently.

"That's the question," I replied.

We left the villa. Gutenberg carefully locked up the house, and we walked side by side down the drive.

About halfway, I stopped and looked around warily.

"What is it?" he asked.

"Nothing." I tried to smile. "I just had an eerie feeling we were being watched."

"Watched?" He also looked around. "There's nobody here." He put his hands in the pockets of his jacket. "It sounds strange, especially coming from me, but sometimes crime scenes have that effect. Something seems to linger, after… the incident, the murder." He stopped and made eye contact with me. "Maybe you think that is funny."

"I understand quite well what you mean," I replied. "Why would I think that was funny?"

We had both parked on the curb in front of the property and walked the rest of the way to our cars without a word. But our silence was pleasant, almost intimate.

26

Alex climbed behind the wheel. Since he was already late for the viewing of the BND file, he jumped on the B 431. Though it was a couple kilometers farther, the 4.4-liter motor under the hood would make it up in time.

He entered the LKA and looked at his watch. The meeting had begun nearly an hour before. He decided to take the elevator to the fifth floor.

Alex quickly found Henrik and Strobelsohn from the note left on Strobelsohn's office door. Conference Room 5J. When he entered, his eyes fell on an elderly man, well over sixty, wearing outmoded, heavy-framed glasses and had rather unkempt, thinning hair. He was sitting at the corner of the table. Presumably, the courier from the BND.

Strobelsohn raised the folder he was holding and used it to point, "Mr. Gutenberg, the Assistant District Attorney, who will be prosecuting the case. Sir, this is Mr. Schlesinger from the BND."

"Please excuse my tardiness," Alex said as he walked over to Schlesinger.

The courier rose. Alex offered a firm hand and held the elderly man's eye for a polite moment. "Nice to make your acquaintance."

Schlesinger bowed his head slightly. "I'm happy to be at your service."

Strobelsohn broke the ensuing silence. "Mr. Gutenberg, as you can see, Henrik and I are completely engrossed in the files."

"Of course." Alex nodded and took a seat.

"It really is true," Strobelsohn continued, shaking his head in disbelief. "The BND does not have a single image, not even a sketch of Dmitri Ivanov. He makes the Cosa Nostra and Camorra crime families look like amateurs."

"It's repeated time and again in these reports that he operates behind an impenetrable network of functionaries. So much so that the field agents question whether Ivanov even exists," Henrik said and then returned to the document he had open in front of him.

Alex reached for the stack of files in the middle of the table.

"May I?" He acknowledged the BND courier, who nodded, and Alex helped himself to the uppermost file folder.

"If Dmitri is as resourceful and accomplished as you say he is, it is quite possible that he is not in hiding at all, but simply sitting in broad daylight," Alex said and dug into the briefs. Utilizing his speed reading skills, he glanced over the first sentence and the center line of each paragraph, scanning for something that might help him learn more about the psychopath they were dealing with.

After he pored over the hefty BND file, he too began to see the common theme. None of the field agents who made investigating him their job could document anything tangible on Ivanov.

Disappointed, he exhaled audibly.

Schlesinger, who had returned to sitting silently in the corner, cleared his throat.

Alex glanced over at the crotchety old BND man from behind his manila folder. "Yes?"

"Captain Strobelsohn and Detective Breiter have told me about the ghastly discovery in the container on the Burchardkai docks," Schlesinger said. "I don't mean to meddle in your investigation, but it would interest me why you're so convinced Dmitri Ivanov is behind this."

Alex took note that the courier was indeed meddling, although he had attested to not mean to. Despite the fact that this initially brought a smile to Alex's face, he concentrated on what the weathered man might have to offer.

"Why do we believe Ivanov is responsible for this?" he repeated the question. "Our only witness screamed his name several times with her dying breath."

The courier nodded slowly in a knowing manner. "I was afraid of that."

"What do you mean?"

"When I was a younger man, in the field in Russia, nearly every unsolved transgression was accredited to Dmitri Ivanov and his organization, even though there was rarely any evidence that linked his crew to the crimes."

Suddenly, the man's unassuming appearance garnered more attention from Alex. "Are you implying that he couldn't have anything to do with the death of these young women?"

"That's not what I mean to say either." The courier hastened to make a point. "You just can't be so sure. That is exactly the problem with Dmitri Ivanov."

Strobelsohn could barely contain his agitation. He ran a hand over his chin. "Could you be a little more specific? Which is it? Is Ivanov behind the activities on Burchardkai, or isn't he?"

Schlesinger was the picture of calm. He took a drink from his cup and went on. "I'm afraid that is not so easy to answer. Some people like to adorn themselves with borrowed plumes. I'm sure you'd agree."

Strobelsohn nodded. "Certainly."

"It is not unheard of in the underworld either."

"You mean a third party is pretending to be acting on Ivanov's behalf?"

"Ivanov is very powerful; he has his fingers in every imaginable enterprise. Everyone wants to belong to his crew. And there are braggarts and impostors everywhere."

"Well, I think if Ivanov's empire is actually as large as you describe it, one might confidently foresee him expanding his business to include human trafficking," Alex remarked.

Schlesinger made a vague gesture with his hand. "Presumably." He adjusted himself in his seat, as if he had suddenly become uncomfortable.

Strobelsohn looked at him briefly and seemed to deliberate. Then he leaned over and spoke in a confidential tone. "Between colleagues, we know how the shop is run."

Schlesinger looked at him questioningly. "What do you mean?"

"Well," Strobelsohn spoke even more quietly, the sound of his voice even more clandestine, "those of us from the old guard don't always include everything in our reports for good reason, do we?"

The courier's face changed. From one second to the next, the disillusioned office worker disappeared, and the seasoned undercover agent resurfaced. His eyes sparkled.

He hesitated, but only briefly. "If you ask me that way… According to the Russian government Dmitri Ivanov is no longer amongst the living. And that has been the case for more than thirty years."

"How could he be dead for three decades and still have such an active file with the BND?" Strobelsohn scoffed in disbelief.

The operative seemed to enjoy the attention he was getting. He smiled broadly. "That's the question, isn't it?" Without waiting for an answer, he continued, "Maybe I should start with what we do know about Dmitri Ivanov. He was a member of an elite KGB unit and gained quite a reputation amongst the Mujahideen of Afghanistan because of the interrogation methods he employed in the province of Nangarhar."

"I'm guessing his investigation techniques were exceedingly brutal?" Alex inquired.

Schlesinger nodded. "They were indeed inordinately brutal, some say he was single- handedly responsible for the mass killings of 1980. If you want to know more, in regard to why others have compared him to the Butcher of Prague himself, the *Über-Nazi*, Reinhard Heydrich, you can read about it in his file. But beware: most, if not all of that was written much later." Schlesinger paused for a moment. "While working for the KGB, Ivanov apparently got his start in the drug business. By the middle of the eighties, he was supporting himself solely through his smuggling activities. But at the time, he did not even appear on our radar." Schlesinger sat up straight. "We did not have anything on him before he turned up dead."

"How'd that happen?" Henrik asked.

"Ivanov's criminal activities grew rapidly. He expanded considerably. Not everyone was happy to see this. Above all, some well-established mafia clans eyed his machinations with suspicion. And when he grew too big for their liking, they acted."

"They wanted to stop him," Henrik said.

"Either that, or get their share," Schlesinger confirmed. "According to the Russian authorities, Ivanov had a twin sister. One day, she and her two girls, his two nieces, were kidnapped…" Schlesinger licked his lower lip. "You should know, Ivanov was married at the time and possibly simultaneously having an affair with a diplomat in our embassy, but there is reasonable evidence that the relationship with his sister was unnaturally close. Presumably why the kidnappers chose her and not Ivanov's wife. Anyway… Dmitri Ivanov supposedly made a deal for their exchange near Volgodonsk, in the St. Antimo Orthodox Church during midnight mass on Christmas Eve. What happened is not completely confirmed, but sometime during, before, or after that exchange, the church went up in an explosion. Counted amongst the more than one hundred and twenty dead were Dmitri Ivanov, his sister, and her two daughters."

"Hold on," Alex interrupted. "The authorities were sure that Ivanov was one of the victims?"

"Apparently." Schlesinger nodded. "His widow received a military pension for him. In the time around the fall of the Soviet Union, the government did not simply pay on pensions without a clearly identifiable body. That much I can assure you. But"—Schlesinger raised his forefinger in the air—"his wife only got the pension for a short while."

"Why only for a short time? Were her widow's benefits revoked?"

"No." Schlesinger shook his head. "She, too, tragically died in an unexplained apartment-house explosion."

"Quite a coincidence," Henrik remarked dryly.

"Yes, isn't it?" Schlesinger gave him a quick glance of approval. "Shortly after the big explosion in the church, we saw the emergence of a new violent crime element in Russia, which differed significantly from the underground organizations we had seen before. They were becoming increasingly more active outside the Soviet Union. Again, and again, one name would rise to the top of the scum…"

"Let me guess," Henrik interjected. "Dmitri Ivanov."

"Exactly."

"But, if Ivanov is dead, who have you been chasing all these years?" Strobelsohn seemed more confused than ever.

Schlesinger took his time to answer. "What I have just told you was the official story," he said finally.

"That implies that there is also an unofficial version." Strobelsohn looked directly at him.

"In a manner of speaking. But more of a legend. A ghost story told to children who misbehave…" Schlesinger broke off.

"If I had been in your position"—Alex took the floor—"I wouldn't have listened to all this official nonsense and investigated it myself."

Schlesinger looked at him. "That's what you would have done?"

"And *that* is exactly what you did," Alex said.

"But what I learned… I can't vouch for as the truth."

"All right, now you've sparked our curiosity," Strobelsohn said.

The old BND agent reached for his coffee. Henrik topped it off.

"Thank you," Schlesinger said, took a sip, and placed the cup back on the table. "Well. Over twenty years ago, I was working near Volgodonsk. I was younger and still rather curious then, and I wanted to see the place I'd heard so much about."

"You visited the village where Dimitri Ivanov was killed?" Strobelsohn asked.

"That's right," Schlesinger confirmed with a smile. "When I went, it was the middle of summer, and it can be unbearably hot there at that time of year. It's a big village, almost a town. There had once been a large Russian Orthodox church in its center. It looked like it had been quite old and pretty impressive. When I arrived, the streets were deserted and there were only ruins left of the church, most of the onion-domed bell tower meagerly held up by wooden scaffolding, the sanctuary, and remnants of the walls. It didn't take much imagination to see that there must have been a large explosion, followed by a fire."

Silence fell over the room. Alex and the two policemen listened intently to the words of the BND agent.

"I finally found someone who would talk to me," Schlesinger continued. "An old man, who for a bottle of vodka, told me under the shade of a walnut tree what really happened: Members of the Kudryeva Mafia had kidnapped Ivanov's sister and two nieces. Ivanov had agreed to pay a terrific ransom. Since the exchange was to take place in public, they chose the completely packed St. Antimo Church during midnight mass on Christmas Eve. Ivanov appeared in a black Mercedes sedan. He dragged two large suitcases with him into the church…" Schlesinger broke off and leaned forward.

He started again in a lower voice. "You have to imagine. A bitter cold winter night, the town is covered in snow, the church filled to capacity. The parishioners singing… The door swings open, Dmitri Ivanov enters. He hands the two suitcases over and leaves St. Antimo's with his sister and her two young daughters. Nearly everyone in the village is present… When Ivanov gets outside, he places his relatives in the car and drives away. But not far. Maybe five or six hundred meters to the top of a small hill, where he stops and watches the church go up in flames. You see, he had hidden explosives in the suitcases, under the fat wads of money. Enough dynamite to kill all the kidnappers and more than a hundred of the faithful. The pastor had been ripped to shreds on the altar."

"And then what happened?" Henrik asked wide-eyed.

"The survivors ran into the open. And what they saw there made their blood run cold: Dmitri Ivanov forced his sister and both of his nieces out of the car. They knelt in the snow… The old man told me he saw it with his own eyes. They even folded their hands in prayer. Ivanov walked behind and shot each of them in the back of the neck. Their bodies fell forward, and blood stained the snow red."

"Wow," Henrik whispered. "What a maniac."

"Ivanov stood there for a minute. Then he picked up the bodies, heaved them into the trunk, and drove away slowly. And that… is the legend of Dmitri Ivanov." The BND agent fell silent.

Strobelsohn furrowed his brow. "That doesn't sound right. He first pays a stack of money to free his relatives. And earlier you said he had a close relationship with his sister, if not more… Why would he shoot her?"

"That doesn't make any sense to me either," Alex said.

"No, it doesn't," Schlesinger agreed. "But in the weeks that followed, all the people behind the abduction were murdered, together with their families and anyone who had ever done business with them." He made a pregnant pause. "That is why nobody dares to take on Dmitri Ivanov."

27

Shortly after seven, the Poseidon was packed. The waiters, the kitchen—everyone was busy. Except for Georgios. He stood by my side at my tiny table for two. He wanted to keep me company.

"It's simply not healthful to eat alone," he said. "But I am here."

I smiled at him. "Exactly, Georgios. And it's good for me to have some peace."

"I can imagine that. As a psychologist…" He fell silent and looked at the door. Three men wearing suits entered. They stopped and craned their necks, searching. Presumably, searching for an empty table.

"Uh," Georgios said to me without taking his eyes off the newcomers. "Isn't that Mr. …"

"Gutenberg," I completed his sentence straight-faced.

"The chief prosecutor, right?" Georgios did not wait for my answer. Instead, he stood on his tiptoes, waved the large menu he held in his hand, and exclaimed loudly, "Yoo-hoo!"

The entire restaurant and of course Gutenberg, Strobelsohn, and Breiter stared in our direction.

Actually, I am pretty robust, nothing upsets me that easily. But at that moment, I felt like climbing under the table.

Gutenberg and the two policemen shuffled through the restaurant and came to a stand-still in front of us.

I took a sip from my water and nodded to them.

"Good evening, Dr. Wolf," Gutenberg said.

"Good evening, gentlemen," I replied. And addressing the two policemen, "May I introduce you to Georgios Papadopoulos? The owner of the Poseidon. This is Mr. Strobelsohn, and his colleague Mr. Breiter from the Hamburg LKA."

The men shook hands.

"What a pleasant surprise to meet you here, Dr. Wolf," Gutenberg said. "We didn't mean to disturb you. We just wanted to grab a bite…"

"Fiddlesticks," Georgios interrupted him gently, yet equally persistent. "You're not disturbing Evi. You can see. She is all alone. Right, Evi?"

I did not even try to reply. If Georgios was on a run, it did not make any sense to try and stop him.

"Of course, you will dine together," he stated.

"Um…" Gutenberg replied, not very cleverly.

Georgios raised a finger. "Don't argue. This is my place. I know my way around here. As you can see, Evi's table is too small for four people. All the other seats are taken. And you surely require a certain amount of privacy and some …" he grinned tellingly, "intimacy. I know what such important dignitaries like you need." He leaned over to me. "Evi, what do you think? The side room, wouldn't that be more appropriate?"

I furrowed my brow. "Didn't you rent that out to the Shanty Choir?"

"Ach." Georgios waved the menu around in the air. "That was years ago." He pointed at a white door on the opposite wall. "If you would please follow me." Although he said *please*, it was more of an order.

I got up, and we snaked through the packed dining room together.

Georgios grappled inside his black, tight-fitting vest and fished out a massive bundle of keys. He opened the door, flipped the light switch, and the side room was illuminated.

I was well familiar with it. So I was able to concentrate on the reaction that the daring interior design, and especially the numerous adornments, would elicit from my colleagues. In the middle of the approximately three-hundred-square-foot parlor was a table with six chairs. Two spare chairs stood in the corner. The room itself was even more bombastic than the restaurant: crammed with Greek statues, the walls adorned with pictures of temples and ancient gods, interspersed with framed sailor knots tied out of short pieces of thick, coarse rope. And nets were stretched across the ceiling, with a catch of plastic fish, shells, and starfish trying to outdo one another in the glitter stakes. Two or three colorful lighthouses tastefully rounded off the ambiance.

"Wow," Breiter muttered, and Strobelsohn had obviously been rendered speechless.

Gutenberg was the first to recover. "A shanty choir actually rehearsed in here?" he asked in disbelief. "Isn't it a little… too…" He started to finish his sentence two times. Finally, he cleared his throat and said, "narrow?"

Georgios put an arm around his shoulders. To do this he had to stand on his tiptoes again. "The singers were all a little older," he said. "Recently they lost a few. It would be more accurate to say, every year the choir got smaller."

He urged Gutenberg forward to the left side of the table and waited for him to sit down. Then he corralled me into the spot next to him. Strobelsohn and Breiter took the chairs opposite us.

"There. That's that," Georgios said, visibly satisfied.

The men ordered their drinks, and Georgios said, "For your dinner, I could show you the menu, but I suggest the yellow perch."

"Perch?" Strobelsohn grumbled skeptically. "Sounds interesting, but I'd rather have a look at the menu first." He glanced at the leather-bound bill of fare that Georgios was still holding in his hand.

Georgios pressed it to his stomach. Tightly. "I bought the perch fresh from the port this morning. I can highly recommend it."

"Perch sounds good, I…" was all Strobelsohn managed to get out.

"Wonderful!" Georgios exclaimed. "Perch for the chief of police."

"Chief inspector," Strobelsohn corrected him, completely distracted.

"Of course!" Georgios made a dismissive gesture. He turned to Breiter.

"I would like gyros," the young policeman said courageously.

Georgios stared at him with a piercing gaze.

"… or rather, perch," Breiter hurried to amend.

"An excellent choice," Georgios commented. "And Mr. Presiding Judge of the Courts?" He looked at Gutenberg.

Gutenberg's mouth rippled slightly. "Perch, I understand, is a good choice."

Georgios let out a relaxed breath and beamed into the circle. "Evi's already ordered the perch. She always takes my advice."

The first statement was true, the second not.

"Just a few minutes, and then you can have dinner. A waiter will bring your drinks. I must go into the kitchen. When I have such distinguished guests, I do the cooking myself."

Georgios left us alone, and after a surprisingly short time, the drinks were brought to the table.

"Let's toast our cooperation," Gutenberg said.

We all took a sip.

I looked at the three men. All at once, they appeared exhausted.

"You had an eventful day, didn't you?" I addressed the two policemen. "Are there any new discoveries on the Carstens case?"

Strobelsohn wiped the beer froth from his upper lip. "By every measure. We've evaluated the recordings from the neighbor's surveillance camera to verify Westphal's statement."

"Did you find anything on the tapes that will help you?"

"Not really. On Saturday night, nobody came to the gate except a van that stopped and left after less than five minutes. The same goes for Sunday."

"But we have discovered another entrance," Breiter added eagerly, "in the back of the property, hidden behind a hedge."

"Exactly," Strobelsohn said with a nod. "I covertly asked Peter Westphal about it, and he confirmed that he knew of this gate and always used it when he visited Miss Carstens."

"Then we can't prove Westphal's testimony, that he arrived at the villa at six in the morning," I ascertained.

"Exactly," Strobelsohn grumbled.

"But that also means," Gutenberg took over, "that the murderer or murderers could have entered this way as well. So, we know as much as we did before."

"We have identified the owner of the van," Breiter said.

"And?" I asked.

"It belongs to one of Big Karl's brothels. The Pink Playhouse."

Gutenberg bent over. "You wanted to check that out today. Did you manage to do that?"

"We did," Strobelsohn confirmed. "We questioned the ladies who were present. And we spoke to the so-called manager."

"What did you find out?"

"The ladies were nice." Breiter grinned and raised his eyebrows, which garnered him a berating look from Strobelsohn. The young policeman's ears turned slightly red. He went on with an emphasis on objectivity. "The women were not exactly communicative. They were clearly afraid of possible ramifications."

"And the manager?" Gutenberg enquired.

"He had the outwardly appearance of a typical boring accountant. He also seemed tongue-tied," said Strobelsohn. "But at the same time, he repeatedly assured us that he intends to cooperate. He will come to the LKA tomorrow with his lawyer."

Gutenberg pricked up his ears. "Oh! When?"

"We thought you'd want to be there," Strobelsohn replied. "The appointment's at eleven. Your secretary said you didn't have anything scheduled then."

"Perfect." Gutenberg turned to me. "I think it would be good if you could join us in the interview. I realize this is a little short notice…"

"No problem," I assured him. "I do not want to miss that."

Georgios appeared with a long wooden slat on which stood a row of shot glasses. He held it out to us. "Compliments of the house."

We helped ourselves.

Gutenberg smelled his aperitif. "That's not ouzo," he said bewildered.

"Ouzo, Ouzo!" Georgios shook his head reproachfully "We are not in Athens. We are in Hamburg. We drink *Helbing Kümmel* schnapps here. Cheers!" He left our room as quickly as he had entered.

I sipped at my caraway liquor and put down the glass. "Mr. Gutenberg was kind enough to accompany me to the Carstens's villa. Until now, I only knew the property from photos, and it was important that I could experience it in person."

"The place is rather depressing, isn't it?" Strobelsohn said.

"Yes," I confirmed. "That it is."

"Dr. Wolf discovered a secret room there within a very short time," Gutenberg said.

Breiter looked at me, his expression a mixture of disbelief and admiration. "But we've searched every corner of the villa. That is incredible! How did you do that?"

The young policeman was disarmingly honest; you had no choice but to like him.

"I had a meeting with Miss Carstens today. She gave me a hint," I replied. I didn't want to go into more detail. At this juncture, the other information I had received from Suzanne was not relevant for the case.

"That so-called *hint* was pretty cryptic," Gutenberg took over. "But Dr. Wolf was able to solve the mystery."

That wasn't entirely true. Strictly speaking, Gutenberg had found the entrance. He had done it, not me. And I was going to put that right. Give credit where credit is due. But when I wanted to start protesting, he smiled at me. A warm, open smile that reached his eyes. I couldn't help it, I had to return it. Then I looked away.

"Where is this room?" Strobelsohn asked, and I was very relieved to hear this question.

"Under the stairs," I hurried to answer. "I believe Miss Carstens hid there often as a child, but I can't prove it."

"I told you the house is depressing," Strobelsohn said.

The door opened again. Georgios reappeared. Across his hands and elbows, he balanced four large plates of fish and placed one in front of each of us. Then he folded his arms over his stomach and waited.

Gutenberg was the first to try. "Outstanding," he praised.

Strobelsohn also took a bite: "Exquisite!"

Breiter seemed to be hungry. He did not even stop to comment on the perch. While chewing, he nodded to Georgios, winked, and raised a thumb.

Georgios smiled broadly. "If you need me, I'll be right outside." He left us alone.

We remained quiet for a while. All one occasionally heard was the soft clattering of cutlery on porcelain, accompanied by restrained moans, which always occurred subconsciously when a meal tasted particularly good.

Strobelsohn wiped his mouth with a napkin and drank a sip of his beer. He put down the glass. "Apart from that, we were busy with the case of the container at Burchardkai. Does that interest you as well, Dr. Wolf?"

I was forced to remember the blurry footage Strobelsohn had taken with his cell phone. "Ever since I've seen the film of the dying woman, I can't get it out of my head," I said frankly. "So, yes, I'm interested."

"I can understand that," Breiter said. "The steel box where the dead girls were…" He cleared his throat. "We've checked on it. Every shipment from this company seems to have been processed by the same customs officer."

"And you suppose…?" I started.

"We believe," Gutenberg said, "that this treacherous company regularly smuggled women in the containers."

I finished my fish and set the cutlery aside. "That would be human trafficking on a massive scale."

"Exactly," Strobelsohn confirmed. "We've found at least twenty-five of these shipments in the cargo roster just in the past two years. And that's far from the end of it."

"Did you get a chance to talk to the customs officer?" Gutenberg asked. He had finished his meal as well.

"Her name is Mathilde Hauke," Strobelsohn said. "However, we couldn't talk to her because she didn't show up for her afternoon shift. She did not call in to report her absence. We sent an officer to her apartment, but he found no one there either."

Gutenberg furrowed his brow. "Strange," he muttered.

"But we took the customs documents with us," Breiter eagerly interjected. "Colleagues of ours who regularly handle such inquiries are going through the paperwork."

The door opened a third time. Now Georgios carried a tray with four huge ice cream sundaes with whipped topping and several wafer-thin waffle cakes. And he didn't come alone. The same waiter from before accompanied him, cleared our empty plates away, and provided us with fresh drinks.

Georgios began to serve us dessert.

Strobelsohn gave his sundae a wistful glimpse. Then he sighed and pushed it decisively to the side. "No dessert for me, thank you. I have to watch my calories."

"*Calories?*" Georgios repeated with a disapproving undertone. "Calories are completely overrated. A man of your stature," he patted him benevolently on the shoulder, "who has so much to do, he has to eat something!"

Strobelsohn looked up at Georgios, then down at the sundae, and finally pulled it back in front of him. He held his spoon like a preschooler holds a crayon.

"There you are!" Georgios nodded to all of us, and again we were on our own.

I grabbed one of the waffles, dipped it in the luscious cream topping, took a bite, and chewed. "Is this Dmitri Ivanov really behind the human trafficking?" I asked.

"No idea," came Strobelsohn's curt reply, and he shoved a heaping spoonful of ice cream into his mouth. "Today we had a courier from the BND in the office. They sent him all the way from Berlin to bring us records, on the man, in person."

"And did you find anything interesting?"

Breiter shrugged his shoulders. "It is difficult to say. This Ivanov guy was probably in the KGB once. He seems to be involved in a lot of large-scale criminal activities. But the BND does not even have a picture of him on file."

"Really?"

"Really," Gutenberg confirmed. "As if Ivanov were a phantom… However, this BND man told us a horrific story."

"About Ivanov?"

"He must be a complete lunatic," Breiter took over. "A real freak."

"What makes you say that?"

Breiter pushed his half-eaten sundae aside and leaned toward me. "The courier told us that a rival gang of criminals had kidnapped Ivanov's twin sister and her children and wanted a ransom. The exchange took place in a completely full church. Dmitri Ivanov got his relatives out of there and blew everyone else up." He made a dramatic pause. "And after that, what do you think he did?"

I shrugged my shoulders. "It's hard to say. What did he do?"

"Instead of just leaving with his sister and nieces, he killed all three of them with shots to the head. Just like that." Breiter raised his right hand with fingers formed into a pistol. He pulled the imaginary trigger. "Bang!" He paused again for effect. "If this isn't a lunatic, I don't know who is."

I remained silent. Three pairs of eyes looked at me.

"You're not of the same opinion?" Gutenberg finally asked me.

"That Ivanov is insane?" I replied.

"Yeah."

I pursed my lips. "There is a school of thought that says that anyone who kills another person is in a state of mental confusion."

Gutenberg studied me. "But you do not think that applies to this Ivanov."

"Not at all. If this story is true, Ivanov acted with cold-blooded intention. He sacrificed what he loved most for his business, because his sister and her children made him vulnerable. From that moment on, everyone knew there was nothing more important for Dmitri Ivanov than his criminal activities, and that he would stop at nothing; absolutely nothing at all could hold him back." I reclined in my seat. "From the logic of a businessman, his actions were extremely coherent."

The three men fell silent.

After a while, Strobelsohn said, "Doctor, you're offering us some strong medicine tonight."

I shrugged my shoulders. "You asked."

28

Half past ten in the evening. The rush hour in Poseidon was over; only a few guests were still sitting in the main room of the restaurant. Strobelsohn and Breiter had said goodbye. Gutenberg and I were alone.

Georgios poked his head through the door of our adjoining room. "Was everything all right, Evi?"

"Wonderful, like always," I replied, and Gutenberg nodded in agreement.

"Great." Georgios remained undecided for a short time, and then he entered. He was carrying a round tray in his hand. There were a few glasses and a bottle with a yellowish gold liquid. Its label was colorful, almost kitschy, with a ship in the middle whose white sails were blowing in the wind.

He put the tray down in front of us. "I wanted to invite you to a little farewell drink."

Gutenberg leaned forward to take a closer look at the liquor. "Oh!" he said, surprised. "A *Linie Aquavit*."

"Yes!" A broad grin spread across Georgios's face. "It has traveled once around the world, crossing the equator twice. This is something special."

I inflated my cheeks and let the air flow out noisily. "If I take one now, I'll have to leave my car and call a cab."

But that was not what bothered me. I was not sure if I wanted to spend time alone with Gutenberg when it was not necessary for official business reasons. Principally… What was so bad about it? Actually, nothing spoke against…

And un-principled? the internal psychologist immediately fired back.

"I wouldn't be able to drive anymore either. But it's worth it, don't you think, Dr. Wolf?" Gutenberg looked at me intently.

While I was still debating whether he meant by *it's worth it,* the special Aquavit or the fact that we would be sitting here alone, Gutenberg turned to Georgios. "Would you like to join us?"

I had not expected that. That was just… awfully nice.

"I'd be delighted to join you," Georgios hastened to say. He looked at me. "If I'm not bothering you."

"Of course not," I replied. "You're not interrupting anything."

Georgios pulled one of the chairs out and sat down noisily. Then he leaned forward and distributed the glasses. Gutenberg grabbed the bottle, removed the cap, and poured us a drink.

"In mine, feel free to add a little more." Georgios made a small gesture of encouragement with his forefinger, and Gutenberg added some more schnapps to the glass.

Georgios lifted his Aquavit. "Skol," he said convincingly, as if he did not come from the Peloponnesian peninsula, but was raised by wild Vikings.

I strenuously suppressed a grin. We toasted one another.

I took a small sip. "Tastes great," I said to Georgios. "And your perch was simply over the top."

"We certainly would have missed out if we hadn't heeded your advice and chosen something else," Gutenberg added. "Wouldn't you agree, Dr. Wolf?"

"Oh," Georgios waved it away, but I could see that he felt flattered. He paused momentarily. Looking from Gutenberg to me and back again, he finally said. "Mr. Presiding Judge of the Courts, I don't know how this is done nowadays. But before, in my time… when you worked with someone… and then you would have a drink together… after this, you would be on a first name basis. That always made a lot of things easier."

"So?" The corners of Gutenberg's mouth curled upward. He turned to me. Apparently, he wanted me to decide.

I hesitated. "My name is Evelin," I finally said.

"Alex," Gutenberg brandished that rare, warm smile.

"And me," Georgios said, "I am Georgios. I don't work with you, but I hope that from now on I won't just see Evi here more often."

"As far as I'm concerned," Alex replied, "if it's all right with Evelin."

Again, I was incapable of answering immediately. I was too busy analyzing what was going on inside me.

A sudden pain to my shin. Georgios had actually kicked me under the table. Pretty hard.

I pulled myself together. "Why wouldn't it be okay with me?" I replied truthfully.

"There you go," Georgios exclaimed and poured us another. "So that the taxi is really necessary!"

He raised his shot glass again. "To the two of you, that you quickly solve the difficult case you're working on and bring the criminals to justice."

We drank.

"Actually, there are two cases," Alex remarked.

"Really?" Georgios asked, surprised.

"Yeah, really," I confirmed.

"So, it's all the more important that this be sorted out. Hamburg is a beautiful city. And that's the way I want you to keep it."

My schnapps was empty. "Could you order us those taxis?" I asked Georgios.

"Two?" he made sure.

"Yes," I replied.

My gaze caught Alex. A strange expression scurried across his face. For a second, I had the distinct impression he would have preferred to share a cab with me. And I too had a feeling for a tiny moment that came close to a type of disappointment. I guess I should not have, we should not have, drunk the second aquavit.

"Two taxis." Georgios rose. "I'll do it right away. As soon as you put your coats on, they'll be here."

Alex also got up. "Nice to meet you," he said to Georgios, reaching his hand out to him.

Georgios grabbed it. "Me too, Alex," he said.

29

Alex closed the car door behind Evelin and watched her cab drive away.

He took one sweeping look over the sleeping Alster. The dark river was encircled by a halo of city lights, which danced back and forth across the soft tide, as if they were alive.

With effort, he could hear the water lap onto the shore over the droning engine of the second taxi that had in the meantime pulled forward to wait on him.

Time to go. He drew in a fresh breath of air, climbed into the backseat, told the driver his address, and the taxi rambled over the cobblestones and around the next street corner, in the direction of Alex's home.

Evelin's parting words kept replaying, over and over, in his thoughts. 'It was nice to finally meet you.' Or something of the sort. He had repeated it so often, he was sure he had changed the words or the syntax or whatever. Was she referring to that nonsense Georgios conjured up to try to get them together, or did they actually cross a barrier of sorts?

"I must confess, I don't even try to understand them," the cab driver mumbled rhythmically, and Alex looked up inquisitively. Their eyes met for a moment in the rear-view mirror.

The back of the driver's hair was combed upward, a clear sign of premature balding; as he turned his head to respond to Alex's silent question, the tell-tale peach patch shone through the sparse hair's efforts to conceal it.

"Sorry, just an old song going through my head," the driver explained.

Alex wondered if the man used the line often, if it were part of the man's repertoire. He did remember the song. It was not a mainstream hit, but popular with the cool set when he was still a kid and too young to think about being cool.

Alex turned his eyes away from the driver and looked out the window. They were still following the river. A couple was walking along the Alster. But it did not appear to be the pleasant evening stroll of two lovers. Quite the contrary. The woman was clearly giving the man an earful. Whatever the man did or did not do, he was getting chewed out for it now.

Alex had to think about his ex. Though this woman appeared to be even more animated than he could honestly remember Vanessa to be, her gesticulations reminded him of how Vanessa had continually emasculated him for some shortcoming or failure to perform at his best.

Vanessa. He snickered to himself, and his lips turned up into a bitter smile. She never gave him the benefit of the doubt. She never really seemed to be on his team. No, she was more of the naysayer, who continually reminded him of his position in society and that it was not one that would impress her family or friends.

Alex pushed the thought of her out of his head. He could still see the quarreling couple in his short-term, iconic memory: the man sauntering calmly along the river beside the woman, his hands in his pockets, not even attempting to defend himself. Who knows? Maybe he was guilty. But by all outward appearances, the defense had already rested its case. The verdict was made before he had ever taken the stand.

Just like when Vanessa delivered the death sentence to their marriage. No consideration for the council, no pre-trial disclosure. Only the crude delivery of the sentence. No arguments were heard from either side. She simply finished it and selfishly took it all into her own hands, *and* in the bed they had bought together. Signed and delivered: guilty of all these charges.

Were all women like this? At least in his experience. If they did not outright ghost you, they would remove themselves from the equation, mental stalemate, a complete impasse. No longer there, emotionally and above all physically. Driving the beast that lies below the surface of every man to its limits.

What about Evelin? he asked himself.

No matter how patient Evelin came across, or how interested and at the same time interesting she could be, there was someone, somewhere that she had driven up the wall. This Leisure Suit Larry from Wiesbaden that she had ended it with, he was probably ridiculed to the point of not seeing straight. Maybe the schmuck had no other choice than to break her heart. Probably the only way he could get her to listen.

Either that, or maybe the guy never really gave her a chance in the first place.

The taxicab turned into Alex's neighborhood. Through the windshield, he could see the welcoming lights of small neon advertisements. He asked the driver to let him out there, and the cab rolled to a stop, directly in front of his corner bar. Alex paid the fare and added a generous tip; he never forgot where he came from and how fortunate he was, least of all for shedding himself of Vanessa.

Alex climbed out onto the curb. He looked through the lace curtains at the nearly empty bar and thought about his father. He wondered if, like his old man, he was preordained to be a drunk, and walked in anyway. *One shot and then it is off to bed.*

A woman was sitting alone at the bar, half standing, half straddling her bar stool, like a bicyclist waiting at a traffic light. Not a bad chassis, and even after she flashed him her broken smile, he was finding it hard to escape the temptation.

He quickly downed his whiskey and made his way for the exit before he did something he might regret. He picked up his pace, walked through the door he had barely just entered, and forced himself to not look back.

Home was less than two minutes away. He'd brush his teeth and climb immediately into the bed he had left in admirable condition eighteen hours before.

He unlocked the door to his empty apartment, turned on the light, and hung his jacket on the coat rack. He paid a quick visit to the restroom and then headed directly to his bed.

The red display of his alarm clock read 12:42. He got between the sheets, switched the lights out, and turned onto his side, simultaneously pulling the covers over his bare shoulder. The contours of the furniture, which first appeared in the dark, began to swim. He closed his eyes and fell asleep.

A protracted and penetrating tone. A siren. No, it's the howling of the wind.

He can't see anything. Then there is this blue: the wonderful, pure blue of a cloudless sky in the early morning.

He is standing in the middle of the dusty street again between the demolished homes. All he has in terms of security is the weapon he is holding in his hands.

He concentrates. In the near distance, he can make out the shed. And without wanting to, without being able to resist, he approaches it, irresistibly attracted by a force he cannot overcome.

A person is leaning against the wide entrance gate of the barrack. A man. He slowly raises his head and looks toward him.

Impossible! That can't be!

The man at the gate has his arms spread out. He seems to be waving at him. But he is not moving. Not an inch. He is not able to, because in the center of the man's palms are big, rust-colored nails. Somebody had tacked him to the wood with them. That couldn't have been long ago. Blood is still running out of the wounds.

"Alex," he hears the man whisper hoarsely. "Alex…"

And then the wind returns. Whining, howling, getting ever louder, penetrating through his head, reaching deep in his heart, freezing everything in its path…

Alex jolted bolt upright in his bed. There was sweat on his brow and his breath was a high-pitched wheeze. He felt around for the switch of his bedside lamp and twisted it on. The sudden brightness made him squint.

His eyes fell on the alarm clock. 2:11.

It took a long time before he lay down again. And it took him even longer to fall back asleep.

March

26

Friday

30

The taxi pounded over the cobblestones. With every jolt, Alex felt the flash of an aerial shell exploding high in the sky at a Port Anniversary fireworks display. He had a hangover and a head full of conflicting topics: his dream, Evelin, and oddly even Vanessa, interlaced with questions from his upcoming interview with the attorney and his client, the manager from the Pink Playhouse. He was thinking he needed a day off when the cab rolled to a standstill in front of the Poseidon.

Alex climbed out and noticed Evelin's car parked along the waterfront. This time he had arrived earlier than she. What was she doing right now? Was she sitting in a taxi this very moment on her way there? If he waited a little, he might be able to catch her and...

And, what? he thought to himself. *Say hello?*

The phone in his breast pocket began to vibrate. He took it out.

"Gutenberg."

"Good morning, Mr. Gutenberg. Captain Strobelsohn speaking."

"Good morning, Captain." Alex reached his BMW. With his free hand, he fished the keys out of his jacket and pressed one of the buttons on the fob. "I was about to head over to the Bureau. What's up?"

"There has been a break-in at the Carstens's."

"What?" Alex, who was about to open the door of his car, stopped with his hand awkwardly suspended in midair.

"Yeah," Strobelsohn carped. "I'm at the scene with the evidence collection unit. It must have happened sometime after you and Dr. Wolf were here yesterday."

Alex lifted the handle and climbed in. "I'm on my way."

He started the car, activated the hands-free system, and pulled off the curb.

"Thank you, sir," Strobelsohn said.

"Wait a minute." The pitch of Alex's voice dropped an octave. "What about the interview with the manager of the Pink Playhouse and his attorney?"

"Henrik can handle it; I discussed the details with him this morning. He'll ask them the usual questions."

"Good. I'll be there in half an hour."

Alex threaded through the traffic. As he accelerated to enter the passing lane, new thoughts rolled into his head, all spiraling around the break-in. Who would have risked crossing police tape? Was it the assassins coming back for something they had missed? If so, what were they looking for? And more importantly, did they find it? Or could it just be some opportunist who read about the murders in the paper and then robbed the vacant house?

Whoever it was, Alex hoped they were sloppier this time, and more generous with damning evidence, because this case was turning cold. He and his colleagues were not getting anywhere. It seemed like they were running in circles.

The light in front of him turned red. He came to a stop and impatiently drummed on his steering wheel with his forefingers. Yesterday, when he was with Evelin in the villa, she had a curious feeling that they were being watched as they left the murder scene. Could someone have been casing the place while they were in there?

Twenty minutes later, he exited the highway and drove nearly directly into the plush carpeted yards of Blankenese. Alex had to admit this was another level. An echelon he would never be able to enter. It did not really matter if he felt he could be comfortable there or not.

As a secret misanthrope, he had always appreciated Groucho's sentiments with his wisecrack about never belonging to a club that would have him as a member.

Was that the truth? Did Alex even find it necessary to be accepted by these people? Or was it sour grapes that came from a childhood of standing on the sidelines when being asked to join was never an option? He shook his head and snorted quietly, almost contemptuously.

The road made a sweeping curve, and he got a good glimpse of the back side of the Carstens's villa. All of a sudden, he was sure there were a lot of people in this neighborhood he would not want to trade places with.

On second thought, that went for the lot of them.

He pulled up to the same scene he had arrived at just four days prior. This time, although there were half as many squad cars, the place seemed twice as eerie as on that first occasion. As if some of the evil that had occurred here oozed out of the residence and penetrated the grounds.

Strobelsohn met him on the street. As soon as Alex shut his door, the captain was at his elbow.

"Good morning, sir," Strobelsohn said.

They shook hands.

"What happened?" Alex asked as they made their way up to the villa.

"Someone broke in through the backdoor and, by all appearances, went directly to a safe which we had missed in the front sitting room."

Alex stopped and looked Strobelsohn square on, "A safe? Where?"

"In the fireplace."

"Strange place for a safe. No wonder the chimney appeared unused. Did the perpetrators get it opened?"

They started walking again, climbed the steps to the front door, and entered the foyer.

"Yeah," Strobelsohn replied. "And our thief spent little time trying to crack the lock. Instead, he immediately smashed the steel box out of its hiding place in the side of the mantle. They used a brand-new sledgehammer that they brought with them and left leaning against the wall."

They cut across the expansive yet gloomy entryway. A member of the evidence collection team approached them, only to hurry past to the front yard.

"Maybe we can track that purchase," Alex said.

Strobelsohn shrugged his shoulders dubiously. "I was thinking the same thing. If the receipt was also there, I would be convinced this was all planted to throw us off our nonexistent scent."

"It sounds like they knew where they should look, so we should count out a curious stranger."

"And... the burglars didn't care how much noise they made either. After smashing the chimney to bits, they used presumably loud explosives as jam shots on the hinges to get to the contents."

The veteran police captain led Alex into the front sitting room. Alex stopped for a moment and looked around. Plaster and chunks of dark-red bricks covered the white oak with maple inlay parquet. The erstwhile polished hardwood floors had deep scratches and dents where the bricks had landed. The battered door of the safe was leaning on one of the Edwardian windowsills. And above the fireplace was a new gaping hole about where an old stove would have been built into the mantle.

A crime scene photographer was taking countless pictures. Every time he touched the digital camera, a stylized click resounded, imitating the closing of a mechanical shutter. Two of Strobelsohn's colleagues from the evidence collection unit were carefully scouring every inch of the room for fingerprints.

"I suppose there is no saying what was stolen?" Alex asked.

"No, not what was stolen, but…"

"…what was left behind was interesting?" Alex completed the sentence with a rhetorical question.

"You could say that." Strobelsohn indicated with a nod that Alex only needed to do an about-face. Alex turned in that direction and there, spread over a sideboard, lay an array of things which had been found in the vault.

Together they walked over to get a closer look.

Strobelsohn picked up a stack of manila file folders, with a single name on each tab. He showed Alex three with the murder victims: Alistair Grauel, Dr. Hans Dietrich Schilling, and Karl Marten, then more, labeled with the names of local celebrities and prominent regional politicians.

"What do they contain?" Alex asked and added automatically, "Have you already checked?"

"Just briefly flipped through them. It appears that Björn Carstens kept incriminating information on each of them."

"Really?" Alex's curiosity had been piqued. Out of the corner of his eye, a reflective twinkle made him bend over.

He spotted two transparent crystals lying next to a black velvet pouch. They seemed to be of an exquisite cut and color due to the way they sparkled and refracted the light that fell on them.

"Those two gems. Are they diamonds?" he asked Strobelsohn.

"Yes. There were probably more in the pouch and the burglar missed these two in his haste."

"That is certainly a possibility."

Strobelsohn handled another small, labelled bag with kid gloves. "And do you know what that is?" He did not wait for Alex's answer but continued on without taking a breath, "Inside is the match to the cufflink that was found in Björn Carstens's hand."

"Oh?" Alex inspected the evidence. "This just keeps getting stranger."

He reached for a wood box with tarnished brass latches. "And what do we have here?" he asked. Taking a ballpoint pen out of the breast pocket of his jacket, he worked the latches and lifted the case open with the help of his pen. "It's empty. Do we know what was in there?"

Strobelsohn gawked at Alex. "Everyone here thinks it was a Walther P38. If you look closely, you can see the unique filigree shape of the Walther in the gun oil stains on the velvet, which rules out most other imaginable pistols."

Alex knitted his eyes. "A 9mm. That could be our missing murder weapon."

"Again. My first thought," Strobelsohn replied, kvetching.

There was an awkward silence for a minute. Alex looked around the room. The photographer seemed to have finished with his work and was in the process of putting his camera away.

"Did anyone see what happened?" Alex asked.

"No, at least not the neighbors we have been able to contact. No one saw or heard a thing."

"What about the neighbor's surveillance system?"

Strobelsohn shook his head. "That was the first place I checked this morning. To our great misfortune, they have followed our advice and changed the angle of the cameras."

"Shit," Alex muttered to himself and then to Strobelsohn, "We can't get a break on this case. Do the right thing, and it turns out to be wrong."

31

Strobelsohn led Alex to the back end of the villa.

"The first thing they did was disable the alarm," he said and pointed at a hole in the wall next to the back entrance. A ganglion of disconnected wires protruded. The copper tips shimmered in the morning sunlight. "Then they simply pried the door open." He gestured with his head toward the visible damage to the wood.

Alex examined the clear signs of breaking and entering. "Whoever did this wasn't doing it for the first time."

"I agree. This does not look like the work of an amateur."

"Have the evidence collection team found anything?" Alex asked.

Strobelsohn grimaced. "Unfortunately, nothing really useful."

"So, a dead end here as well?"

Strobelsohn nodded his head silently.

Alex put his hands in his pockets and his eyes wandered over the garden for a moment. The buds on the bushes and trees were more swollen than the week before. It would not take long until they would burst, and tender green leaves would make their way into the open air.

He turned his attention to Strobelsohn again. "Was there any indication that the burglar or burglars were in other parts of the house, besides the living room?"

"No."

"What about the party room in the cellar?"

"Nothing suggests that anyone has been down there either."

"Just to be on the safe side, let's have another look around." Without waiting for Strobelsohn's reply, Alex spun on his heels and walked into the house.

The basement appeared untouched. The air was cold, stale, and smelled of death.

Alex stared across the parlor at Strobelsohn. "Do you suppose Björn Carstens could have cleverly hidden cameras that we might have missed as well?"

Strobelsohn returned a half-shrug. "Now you're reaching for the improbable. And besides, do you really think the old man had enough of his wits about him to capture his own slaughter on film? I believe he was more concerned with the edge of that sword than snapping blackmail shots. Though we might best answer that question by examining the photos in the files upstairs. They would tell us whether any of the photographs were taken here or not. And if so, we'll have this place pulled apart."

"OK, I hear you. But please entertain me for another minute, and then we'll get out of this horrific space," Alex said as he hovered near the shattered display case. "Let's see what we have. One of our weapons, the cutlass, came from here, and was used to slice Björn Carstens's scalp off. A second weapon, a knife, was lying at the foot of Karl Marten's corpse. The third weapon, the firearm which shot him, is still unidentified, as is the fourth."

"The fourth?" Strobelsohn tried to get a grasp of Alex's conclusion.

"Yes, or rather the first. They were all drugged with a cocktail of nicotine and opiates, and it was indeed the cause of Alistair Grauel's death. We have not discovered the drugs' delivery system. Or has the lab come back with a new report I don't know about?"

"No," Strobelsohn grunted. His entire posture betrayed that he felt just as uncomfortable in the basement as Alex. "There was no evidence of the drugs anywhere on the property. As far as the nicotine is concerned, the forensics experts have suggested the murderer used the liquid for refilling electric cigarettes. But even that, in the end, is merely hypothesis."

"Hmm." Alex pursed his lips. "The stuff was discovered in the victims' stomachs and in Alistair Grauel's vomit. Their drinking glasses bore no trace of the drugs. That leaves only one conclusion, namely…"

Strobelsohn's eyes lit up. "All of the glasses weren't just wiped clean… they must have been replaced!"

"Exactly. When I was here with Dr. Wolf the day before yesterday, she opened a dishwasher behind one of the cabinet doors. It was full."

"You mean…"

Alex nodded. "We need to ask your colleagues from forensics to examine the glasses in there."

"If the dishes were washed, I doubt our people will find anything we could use," Strobelsohn said. "But I will commission it anyway. It can't hurt."

Strobelsohn's cell phone rang, Alex watched the lumbering officer fishing around in his oversized pocket, visibly frustrated as he turned his back to give himself some perceived privacy, or maybe it was an attempt at better reception. He ripped the phone out and left to take the call in the restroom where Alistair Grauel had died.

A half beat later, the police captain stepped back into the light of the underground parlor. "Henrik is finished interviewing the manager of the Pink Playhouse and is on his way here."

Alex nodded mechanically. "Well then that will give us some time to have a short peek around. Let's go back upstairs."

"Good," Strobelsohn muttered, apparently relieved.

Having returned to the first floor, the two men went to the main staircase. Alex was marveling at the simplicity of the door to the secret cubbyhole under the stairwell; besides the sunken antique hinges, there was no other mechanism. The well-fitted panel was held snuggly in place solely by its adroit craftsmanship.

Strobelsohn cleared his throat, and Alex stepped away to let the captain have a glimpse at the dusty bench inside the hidden broom closet.

"This was constructed so as not be seen," Alex said as he pointed out the skillfully embedded brass fittings.

"That could be reasonably assumed." Strobelsohn straightened himself up and gently pulled the panel shut. "Is there something in particular you wanted to have a closer look at?"

Alex thought for a moment. "Perhaps on the second floor. I know your crew has searched it thoroughly, but I haven't had the chance yet. We could go through Suzanne and Björn Carstens's bedroom suites once again. When I was here two days ago with Dr. Wolf, she turned down the opportunity. She feared that she would not be able to approach her client in an unbiased manner if she had seen her sleeping quarters. I can understand that. But we're not criminal psychologists; we've got other objectives."

Gert Strobelsohn led the way up the steps and along the banister to Suzanne's room. Entering, he immediately turned to the first piece of furniture he encountered: a chest of drawers. He tilted it to ensure it was not attached to the wall, cloaking a similar secret hiding space like they had found under the stairs. The few utilitarian objects on top of it, a bottle of mousse, hair clips, and elastic bands, jostled in place when he tipped the cabinet.

Alex glanced around the relatively barren room. A bed, a chest of drawers, and a row of shelves sparsely populated with the only personal items in view. A portrait of a younger version of Suzanne on a sailboat, albeit the dated frame and clothing made Alex suspect it was her mother. A display of keepsake necklaces that looked as if they were rarely moved. And on the bottom shelf, a stack of three paperback books and a few pieces of costume jewelry made of leather and glass. Nothing of significant value. As a matter of fact, there was not a personal belonging in the room that looked like it cost more than ten euro.

Nothing that revealed anything about Suzanne Carstens. No affiliations, no pinups, and hardly any childhood memories save the picture of her mother and her inherited baubles.

The art on the wall, though nicely matted prints of typical images, could have been picked out by Björn's executive assistant for a short-term rental. The staid images were suitable to anyone's taste and preferences. That was just it; the whole place seemed to Alex as if someone *stayed* there, more than they lived there.

Strobelsohn pushed Suzanne's mousse back to its place in the center of the chest of drawers. "She doesn't have many possessions. Not what you'd think for an heiress."

Alex inspected Suzanne's walk-in closet. "She makes me appear the slob," he called out, "She has all of her blouses together, followed by her pants and then skirts, and they're all organized by color. It borders on compulsive behavior."

He stepped back into the room. The furniture was simple but well-built. Combined with the color-coordinated carpet, bedspread, and curtains, it all gave the impression of a hotel suite.

Even the attached bath struck Alex as less used than a single-night stay. There was nothing on the counter, save a brush. And the lack of hair in it made it appear like a prop. The drawers contained a stack of towels. The medicine cabinet over the sink: one compact, a lipstick, tampons, toothbrush, and toothpaste.

Strobelsohn had followed him into the restroom.

Alex pointed to the opposite wall. "There is a door here." He went over and pushed the handle tentatively down.

"It's not locked," he said with a surprised voice.

Another bathroom. Both men walked in. Alex switched on the light.

"That is strange, sir." Strobelsohn grumbled: "Two bathrooms with a connecting door that cannot be locked."

In contrast to Suzanne's, Björn's quarters appeared much more lived-in. The bathroom cabinet was full of prescription bottles and cologne. An electric razor sat in its charging station on the edge of the sink, the battery light pulsating green.

Alex pulled the plug out of the charger. "Were all of the meds cataloged?"

"Yeah," Strobelsohn replied. "What I can remember without the file, he was taking beta-blockers for high blood pressure. That and three different types of erectile dysfunction pills: Viagra, Cialis and another one, which I can't recall."

The two men stepped through to Björn's chambers and immediately sank into the plush carpet. The dead man's furniture was over-stylized: a dark wood canopy bed with matching bedside tables and a writing desk, and walls covered with what appeared to be original German expressionist artwork.

Farther to the left, a chest of drawers with a few belongings: a pair of sunglasses, a cigar cutter, a humidor filled with Montecristo No. 2 cigars, and an opened velvet lined case containing a collection of gold cufflinks.

"That's interesting," Strobelsohn said. "This is where he usually took off his pretentious buttons." He pointed at the box. "Strange that he kept one in the vault. And in an extra bag. The thing must have had a special meaning for him."

"Most likely," Alex agreed with him. "And holding the second one in his dying hand should have a reason, too. That's not a coincidence."

Strobelsohn nodded. "I'll ask forensics to examine the cufflink from the vault, and have another look at the other one."

The bedside table nearest the lavatory had a remote control and an ashtray on top of it. Alex pulled open the top drawer to find a box of condoms and various sex toys.

"Safe sex was obviously important to the guy," Alex said.

"And that is not all," Strobelsohn pointed nonchalantly at an assortment of penis rings.

Then he paused and glanced at his watch. "I think we've seen everything we need to see. We should intercept the files that were found in the safe before they get packed off to the Bureau."

32

"Why do you think Suzanne's room lacks all character?" Strobelsohn asked, while they made their way to the main floor. "Most kids her age, and especially with that kind of money, would go crazy sprucing up their surroundings, if you know what I mean."

"You're right," Alex said. "Those aren't really the trappings of a millionaire's granddaughter—although Björn's suite appears to be furnished by the same decorator, even when it effuses a more lived-in impression. But her quarters have the uniformity of a department store display window."

"Not a lot of personality in the whole house. The living space on the first floor looked like it was ordered from the same catalog: The Scotch and Soda Guide to Mansion Decoration," Strobelsohn aped. "And Suzanne Carstens seems to only wear the cheapest costume jewelry. Maybe she does not put any value in expensive chains and rings."

"Possibly," Alex said.

"Or else it's her style, expressing rejection of her place in society," Strobelsohn continued. "She does not find it necessary to head some non-profit. She is fine staying out of the limelight… Mixing in with her peers could be more important to her."

"That is plausible," Alex said.

The two men landed at the foyer, and Strobelsohn stopped in his tracks.

"What's the matter?" Alex asked.

Strobelsohn scratched his head. "That connecting door is bothering me. I know the villa is old. Back then they built passages everywhere. But one would think Suzanne Carstens would want to lock her bathroom. Especially when I remember how the butler described her and her grandfather's relationship as distant."

A young lady from the evidence collection team walked past them, nodding in their direction. She was carrying a carton containing the files from the safe.

"Hold on, wait a second." Alex stopped her.

She looked at him quizzically.

"Alex Gutenberg, Assistant District Attorney," he introduced himself. "Do you need to take these files to the lab immediately, or could you leave them with us, so we could start processing them?"

She hesitated, but only momentarily. Then she smiled and held the carton out to him. "Here you are. An hour or I'll get in trouble. We've taken fingerprints, but please, wear gloves anyway, and I'm going to need them back before I leave."

"An hour," Alex repeated. "Thank you." He smiled in return and took the container.

Arriving in the library, he dropped the box on a table. Strobelsohn reached into his coat pocket and pulled out two pairs of latex gloves. He and Alex stretched them up to their wrists.

Strobelsohn picked up the top folder. "Let's see if they contain any clues."

"I'm curious." Alex searched out the file bearing the deceased gynecologist's name: Hans Schilling.

He began to read, then paused and frowned before plunging back into the folder. Hastily, he leafed through. "Wow," he finally mumbled.

Strobelsohn looked up from his documents.

Alex tapped the papers in front of him. "Incredible! These records suggest that Hans Schilling was not Hans Schilling at all."

"Rather?"

"Assuming these copies are not fake, Schilling is supposed to have used an alias. It says here, his real name is *Eberhard Schindel*. And he supposedly lost his license to practice as a physician about twenty-five years ago."

"He was not allowed to practice anymore?" Strobelsohn repeated. "Then something really serious must have happened."

"He's purported to have carried out back-alley operations. One of the women, a young prostitute, almost bled to death. That was in…" Alex leaned over the file again. "Exactly, it says here… That was in Leverkusen. On the surface, he had a successful gynecology practice there, but was secretly performing abortions."

"Was he prosecuted?"

"Yes." Alex nodded. "He was sentenced to fourteen months imprisonment."

"Eberhard Schindel from Leverkusen." Strobelsohn pulled out his smartphone and typed in the name. "I'll look into that later."

"Absolutely," Alex replied. "Schilling, or Schindel, is said not to have started serving his sentence, because he went into hiding before. And a short time later, he opened a gynecologist's office here as Dr. Hans Schilling. He only saw private patients."

Strobelsohn snorted. "And let me guess: He continued doing what he did before."

"That's right. In addition to his private practice, he was apparently the personal physician for Big Karl's prostitutes. I mustn't go on with all that. You can well imagine."

"I do not want to imagine that!" Strobelsohn's face had turned red.

"But that's not all." Alex's expression became somber. He held up a photo for Strobelsohn to see. "Apparently, he liked noticeably young girls. There are about ten more similarly disgusting shots in here."

"What a pig!" Strobelsohn exclaimed. "She is just a child." He pressed his lips together into a thin, furious line, released his eyes from the photograph, and took several deep breaths. Only then did he focus on Alex again.

He cleared his throat. "Were any of the photos shot in the basement of the villa?"

Alex looked at the pictures again. "No. Definitely not. They seem to have been taken in different places. At least two of them appear to be from a long time ago."

"Maybe from when he was in Leverkusen," Strobelsohn replied. "Before they caught him." He paused. "Schilling must have had remarkably close and well-connected contacts. It is not easy to get all the necessary documents, exams, and ID cards to open a gynecologist's office. It takes more than your common counterfeiter."

"Much more." Alex closed the file, placed it on the table, and leaned back. "And I would be very surprised if our well-respected Björn Carstens did not have something to do with it."

The men were silent for a while. Then Alex asked, "What have you found?"

Strobelsohn pulled the dossier he was poring through wide open and turned it for Alex to see the photographs held in place by paperclips.

Alex could not decipher the first image immediately, and then realized he was looking at a much younger Karl Marten bending over a frail woman, who stared up at him with terrified eyes. He held her upper arm in his left hand. Rings flashed from his raised right hand. He was about to hit the already excessively beaten girl. The picture pinned below was a zoomed-in image of the damage done to her face. Her eyes were both swollen shut, and there was a deep gash running from her left temple down to her jaw.

The police captain turned the page to where a newspaper article showed a black and white image of what appeared to be the same woman. She was dead. Though her face had been cleaned and made up for the photograph, it had been impossible to completely conceal her injuries. The headline read: *Police ask for help identifying woman found on the banks of the Elbe last month.*

"Holy shit," Alex muttered. "She is probably not the only one that this sick sadist tortured and killed. If you ask me, he died too easily."

It took Alex some effort before he could grab the next folder. *Alistair Grauel* was typed in bold letters across the tab. He was poring over the contents when suddenly he felt a presence behind him. He lifted his head. A blue latex hand was holding a paper cup out for him to grab. The hand belonged to the young lady from the evidence collection team. She had obviously gone to a coffee shop to buy him and Captain Strobelsohn real mugs of java. While hardly noticing the captain, she studied Alex with a lingering smile.

"Thanks." Alex exhaled audibly and then took a big sip of the bitter black contents before returning her smile.

Her dark eyes lit up. She beamed at him.

Out of nowhere, Alex had to think of Evelin. He wondered if she would want to hear from him. Should he contact her and tell her about the break-in? They had, after all, agreed to keep each other updated. Or shouldn't he wait until she was finished with her appointment with Suzanne Carstens? There was really no reason to interrupt her, Suzanne couldn't possibly know anything about the break-in. It was more important for Evelin to discuss the night of the murders…

He realized the young officer was still standing in front of him, leaving little doubt of her expectations.

He inclined his head at her affectionately but with definitive brevity. "We're going to need another half hour with these."

She understood immediately and slight disappointment slid across her face. Nodding a silent farewell, she walked stiffly out of the library.

Alex turned to Strobelsohn. "According to Björn Carstens's notes, Alistair Grauel was running legitimate businesses."

Strobelsohn reached into the box of files and picked up the back half. Sitting across from Alex, he quickly flipped through the papers. "In all likelihood, Grauel was moving funds using those private firms. Or why do you think Björn Carstens kept this stack of receipts? All of them between eight and ten thousand euro?"

Alex put his paper cup down. "The connection is slowly becoming more evident."

"Yes," Strobelsohn agreed. "Big Karl was the pimp, Schilling, or Schindel, was the personal physician of the prostitutes, and Alistair Grauel handled the finances, making good money out of bad." He chewed on his lower lip. "The only question is, what role did Björn Carstens play?"

"Thanks to these files, we might be able to find out," Alex said. "This break-in, which at first seemed to be another dead end, is turning out to be our greatest source of evidence. I hope I get a chance to thank the burglar."

33

Henrik burst into the library where Alex and Strobelsohn were seated. "I wish you could have seen how guilty these guys looked!" He appeared animated and quite full of himself.

Alex suppressed a smile. The young officer did not get to lead often, so when it came to sharing new information with his colleagues, he noticeably cherished the moment.

He let Henrik enjoy the attention. It somehow reminded him of himself before—he bit down hard on his back teeth—before life taught him how unflattering such self-ingratiating antics really were.

Alex pondered whether he was being oversensitive about it because he himself was still guilty of grandstanding. He silently wondered how someone kept themselves from traipsing around like a complete dumbass in such situations. No immediate answer entered his head.

Instead, he asked Henrik a typical Evelin question. She had been dominating his thoughts and somehow rubbing off on him. "What was your initial hunch when the manager of the whorehouse spoke? Not his attorney, but the manager himself: what did your intuition tell you?"

Henrik looked side to side at two empty reading chairs, chose the one on his right and flopped down into it. "Well, I feel the same way I did yesterday when me and Captain Strobelsohn visited the Pink Playhouse. This guy is holding something back."

"What exactly did he say?"

"He said that Big Karl did not *broadcast his business*. He claims Karl Marten never spoke to people on his mobile phone, but always made plans face-to-face."

Alex raised his brow. "Seriously? Big Karl was that paranoid?"

Henrik nodded. "Apparently. A search of his logs by our friends in the Bureau shows he really only ever dialed one number on the cell phone found in his pocket—his mother's." He hesitated. "Apart from that, the bordello manager gave me some details, like what arrangements Big Karl had made with the prostitutes. Even if all that might be good and true, I still had the distinct feeling that he was hiding something."

Meanwhile, Strobelsohn had finished his coffee. Lost in thought, he crushed the cup in his massive hand and formed it into a ball. "I came to the same conclusion when we questioned some of the women yesterday. We're not getting the entire story. Maybe we should ask Dr. Wolf to visit the ladies and see what she can find out. The girls might be more willing to speak to a woman, especially one who isn't a police officer."

"That would be worth a try," Alex said and turned to Henrik. "What else did the two say about the night of the murders?"

The young detective spread his fingers and pressed their tips together. "Not a lot. Just what I was explaining to you.

The fact that Karl Marten did not call, or that the girls came back without hearing anything, was not out of the ordinary for the manager. According to him, that is how Karl worked. He was either where he said he was going to be, or you had to expect something more important came up, and you wouldn't be surprised that he did not show."

Alex smiled broadly. "So, if I understand you correctly, the manager did admit to dispatching a carload of prostitutes to Björn Carstens's villa Saturday night?"

"That he did not say. But he did say he personally bought them a drink when they returned. He maintained, somewhat sincerely, that he knew nothing about Big Karl and his affairs, that he was responsible solely for the operations on the premises of the Pink Playhouse."

"My understanding of Big Karl's enterprises is exactly that," Strobelsohn clarified. "He hires autonomous managers who are one hundred percent accountable for their own business and have no knowledge of anything outside of that. Karl pays them dearly. But it is each of them individually who has one foot in prison, while Karl simply shares in the rewards, risk-free."

Alex shook his broad grin to and fro. "All things considered, with a special light on why we are even talking about Big Karl, right now... There appears to have been some risk in it after all, wouldn't you agree?"

Strobelsohn raised his eyebrows. "Oh yeah. And when you have friends like Björn keeping all your secrets on file, you never know what evidence might crop up against you."

"Would you mind telling me what files you are talking about?" Henrik had ostensibly climbed off his high horse.

"The burglars left these in the vault." Alex pointed at the stack of folders on the table. "Along with a few diamonds, the display case of a 9mm pistol, and of all things, the match to Björn Carstens's missing cufflink."

34

"Thank you for agreeing to see me," I began.

"Where is the most honorable Mr. Gutenberg?" Peter Westphal asked, and the corner of his mouth curled up contemptuously. Like during our last talk, he sat across from me in the jail's interrogation room. But this morning, we were alone.

"I wanted to speak with you one on one," I replied. "Mr. Gutenberg and I go about things differently."

"Of course." A barely suppressed snort. "You're a *psychologist*."

"You make that sound like something bad." I paid attention to his every move. He appeared to be in control, concentrated, and not exactly cooperative.

"You consult a psychologist when you're sick," Westphal responded.

"Sometimes that is the reason," I agreed. "Right now, my main objective is to look after Miss Carstens." He winced ever so slightly when I mentioned Suzanne's name. I continued, "I want to support her with processing her trauma, so she can remember, among other things, the night of the murders."

Westphal held his tongue. His gaze froze on me—a bit too intensely for my liking. The thought of Suzanne Carstens overcoming her amnesia seemed to make him uncomfortable for some reason, just like on our first encounter. And he didn't want me to notice. That's why he was giving me this fifty-yard stare.

"Miss Carstens's present condition is not good for her," I said. "You want to do your part, so she gets well, don't you?"

He ran his tongue across his lower lip once. His pupils dilated. "Of course."

His reaction could not have been any clearer. On the one hand, Suzanne Carstens's welfare was of the utmost importance to him, yet on the other… He was afraid. Really, afraid. But of what?

"Fine." I smiled.

"But how is my talking to you going to benefit Suzi?" he asked.

"To be completely honest with you," I said, "I am not making any real progress reaching her."

He furrowed his brow, a weary expression spread across his face. "That doesn't answer my question. How am I supposed to be of any use to you? I'm in prison. Nobody is letting me see her. She can't visit me…" he paused.

Maybe, in hindsight, this morning's spontaneous idea to drop in on him was not such a good one. I had hoped he would open up, at least a little to me, if Gutenberg… if Alex wasn't present. After the incident in the hospital, Westphal could not have the best association with Alex. But maybe I had been wrong and Westphal would not cooperate, regardless of the circumstances.

"In the hospital," he started as if he was reading my thoughts, "I had the impression Suzi did not recognize me at all. I would have expected her condition to have improved at least a little since the night of the murders. But she seemed completely out of it, before she… until… until she let out that hellish scream. I was as much of a stranger to her as you were."

The first real signs of emotion out of him: defiance and desperation.

"That is not entirely correct," I countered.

"No?" A spark of hope flashed in his eyes.

"No," I repeated myself adamantly. "In the meantime, the situation has changed. As soon as I mention your name to Miss Carstens, she is by all appearances better. Even if she cannot consciously assign you, her response is undoubtedly positive."

He visibly restrained himself, but still I had the impression that he was happy and relieved.

"Are you going to help me?" I asked again.

He hesitated and began to nod. At first barely noticeable, then more articulately. "I will do what I can."

"Thank you." I leaned back a bit in my seat. "Where did you and Miss Carstens meet?"

"Me? And… Suzi? Meet?" He repeated my question. Not a good sign. He was trying to buy some time, probably in order to come up with a story. I had to be on my guard.

I remained quiet.

"Well," he slowly started. "When I had visited my father in his office, I had seen her once or twice."

"I recall you telling Mr. Gutenberg and me that your father had worked for Björn Carstens."

"Yes." Very curt. He pushed his thumbs into the flesh of his palms. And then he stopped suddenly.

"Did you and Miss Carstens talk then?"

"No." That came quickly and without deliberation.

"And later? I have the feeling your present relationship is quite close. Am I right in thinking that?"

His shoulders lifted and fell slightly. His expression softened. He opened his mouth several times just to close it again. Finally, he said, "I have a work colleague. He has a Laser. It's docked in Blankenese." He pointed his finger needlessly at the barred window. "Something was broken on the helm, and he asked me to help him weld it. I did that for him." He fell silent.

I also remained quiet and waited. Nothing is as effective in getting someone to talk. The longer the silence lasts, the more intense the urge to express oneself becomes.

Westphal took a deep breath. "Suzi has a sailboat there. A small yacht, nearly twenty feet long. Nothing special. The boat is rather old. It belonged to her mother... *Ad Astra*."

"Ad Astra?"

"That's the name of the boat." He smiled.

I returned his smile.

He sat up; his eyes went past me. "The Ad Astra was next to my friend's boat. Suzi struggled to hitch the jib..." He looked at me. "Uh, hang the little sail onto the main stay."

I nodded. "I was born in Hamburg. I'm familiar with nautical terms."

"You sail as well?" He looked at me in a new light.

I tilted my head from side to side. "I took a course when I was a little girl. As it quickly turned out, it's not my cup of tea. I prefer to watch from the shore."

His smile widened. He loosened up.

"Miss Carstens was having trouble hitching her jib?" I picked up the thread.

"Yeah, the stay rings were jamming after the long winter."

"Did you recognize Miss Carstens right away?"

"Not really." He made an inadvertent hand gesture. "Only after she mentioned her last name."

"And the other way around? Did she recognize you?"

"No."

Once more, he fell silent.

"The yacht," I started again. "You said Miss Carstens got it from her mother?"

"Yes. They always used to go out together. Down the river, past the Elbe islands. Sometimes out on the open sea for days. The boat has two bunks and a galley."

"Miss Carstens enjoyed that?"

"And how! That was, and still is, her favorite thing in the whole world. The water, the waves, the wind… she simply loves it."

"Like you."

Westphal didn't answer.

"You have a lot in common," I said, encouraging him to continue.

A muscle in Westphal's neck twitched. That comment must have hit a nerve.

"Then you started seeing each other regularly?" I asked as if I had not noticed.

"Yes," he said after a while. "She took me on the Ad Astra. In all conditions, Suzi is a very good sailor. And I… I taught her how to dive." The shadows disappeared from his face.

Now or never. "So, you weren't in the house in Blankenese very often?"

"Every once and a while." A fine coat of sweat formed on his brow. "I don't want to discuss this anymore."

"You could greatly improve your own situation if you talked about it with me. And it would probably do you some good too… It would help Miss Carstens, in any case."

Wrinkles formed around his eyes. "Do you think I'm stupid? This stuff with Suzi is only an excuse. You're just trying to interrogate me!"

"Are you hiding something?" I asked.

He jumped up, almost knocking over his chair. "I think we're finished."

35

Midday in Hamburg. I was stuck in a traffic jam. Whenever the light turned green at the distant intersection, the line of cars moved forward a few yards. Then it came to a standstill. Patience was the motto of the hour. I sighed.

Peter Westphal... I could still hear his voice: deep at the beginning of a sentence, toward the middle the pitch rose higher, and finally it lowered again. It was almost a natural sound wave, as is the case when you tell the truth. Or if you're a good liar. Clever liars can control that to the utmost.

To which group did Westphal belong? I could not conclusively decide. Not yet. I did not know him well enough for that. But, when I recalled his telltale facial expressions and gestures, I tipped more toward the latter. In any case, he had something to hide.

And Suzanne Carstens? How did he feel about her? Westphal liked her a lot, and he was afraid for her. That was real. I was sure of that. He loved Suzanne Carstens.

Ringing, my hands-free system frightened me out of my thoughts. I read *Gutenberg* on the screen.

"Yes?" I answered. Not very revealing, and not at all original. But the formal *Wolf* seemed inappropriate to me.

"Evelin? This is Alex."

Damn! shot through my head. *The first name basis was perhaps not such a good idea from Georgios after all. Professional distance functions differently.*

Nevertheless, this new familiarity did not feel wrong, but rather very good. *Double damn*!

"Evelin? Hello?"

"Yes?" I pulled myself together. "What's up?"

"Where are you?"

"In my car. I'm stuck in traffic."

"Is someone with you?"

"No. I am alone. You can talk."

"Have you had your therapy session with Suzanne Carstens?"

"No. I am just on my way to her now. This morning, I decided to spontaneously drop in on Peter Westphal again."

"So?" That sounded pompous. And not exactly pleased. "Did you get anything out of it?" Markedly slower, but still irritated.

Although I did not have to justify myself to him, he was entitled to an explanation. We had agreed to cooperate. For that to work, each of us had to play with open cards.

"I was hoping to learn something from Westphal that I could use to reach Suzanne Carstens," I said.

"And? Were you successful?" Now much calmer.

"Well. Maybe, maybe not. We'll see later. I am cautiously optimistic."

A relieved exhalation. "Why… Why I'm calling. There was a break-in at the Carstens."

"Come again?" The traffic light turned green, and I started at a walking pace. "In their house?"

"Exactly."

"Do you have any clues? Do you know who it was?"

"No. Not yet. But the thieves broke into a safe hidden in the fireplace. They were obviously looking for something. Whether they found it… we're not sure. Anyway, they left behind some rather interesting items."

"What?" Red. I stepped a bit too hard on the brakes.

"It's too much to go into now. I'll tell you later in detail. But we have found a few files that were apparently created by old man Carstens."

"Files?" That came unexpectedly. "On whom?"

"On VIPs, politicians, and the three deceased. All extremely racy material. I suppose it was for blackmail."

"Or maybe for reassurance," I replied.

"Reassurance? What do you mean by that?"

"If you want to get things done, it's never a bad policy to know which skeletons your partners have in their closets."

"Yes. Of course." He exhaled loudly. "This break-in fundamentally changes the situation. The murders may take on a completely different dimension." He paused. "It's more important than ever that Suzanne Carstens remembers. We need her statement. Urgently."

I could see his point. "Well," I said, "that will be difficult. She has to want it too."

"Nevertheless. I'm not a psychologist… but, if you could possibly…"

"Good," I said. "I'll think of something. However, I cannot make any promises."

36

On the small coffee table between the leather sofa and the armchair stood several full bottles of mineral water and clean glasses. Suzanne Carstens did not look much different than at our last meeting. During our greeting, however, I had the impression that her extreme tension had eased a bit. Our discussions had gradually become kind of a routine for her. She knew, or believed she knew, what to expect. And she could handle that—at least in a way, because she was still reserved and careful.

"Is there anything new with you?" I asked her.

"No," she replied, lowering her eyelids and saying nothing else.

"Last time, you drew a plan of your house for me. I would like to express my gratitude to you once again for that," I continued.

A quick look. "Why?"

"I want to understand, so that I can help you. That's why I drove to your house. And I was happy that I had your plan with me. I did not feel like a stranger in the villa, but was able to get my bearings quickly… It is huge."

Her mouth twitched slightly. Her expression changed, closed. If I was not careful, I would lose the little rapport I had built with her. I had to alter my approach to build some common ground.

"I was in the kitchen," I said. "I sat down where you always sat. That's a nice spot." I smiled at her. "Then I explored a bit around the downstairs."

"You did not go upstairs?"

"No," I said firmly. "Maybe there will be a chance later. I did not think it was appropriate. I would not want anyone looking around my room without asking me."

She gave me a shaky but grateful smile.

"When I walked through the living room and den, I took a closer look at the stairs you called to my attention."

A brief flash of her eyes. "You discovered the little broom closet, didn't you?"

"Yes," I confirmed calmly. "Rather by accident. And inside was an object." I rifled through my bag, which was sitting beside me on the ground, and took out the old doll. I smoothed her hair and laid it gently and without further ado on the coffee table within Suzanne Carstens's reach.

She glanced away for a moment before returning her attention to me.

"Maybe later"—I felt my way closer—"we can go to the villa together, and you can explain the importance of the hiding spot."

Alex had urged me earlier on the phone to speed things up. And that was my plan: getting Suzanne Carstens to return with me to her grandfather's estate. And then she could not block the memories that would inevitably encroach on her. Granted, a risky venture, but the only one that seemed reasonably promising to me.

"To the villa?" She repeated hesitantly, "Perhaps."

She would not make it easy for me. I changed the subject.

"I saw Peter Westphal this morning."

She blinked several times in a row.

"You are starting to recognize names more?" I dug deeper.

"Hmm." She shrugged. "Not really." She unconsciously ran her fingertips over her throat. A clear sign that she was hiding the truth. Presumably, at least in that point, her memory had returned, but she did not want to tell me for whatever reason.

"Peter Westphal is your boyfriend," I said. "And he is nice."

This time she did not pretend. Her smile was genuine. "Really?"

"Yes. He told me how you met. Can you still remember that?"

"No." She took a deep breath and exhaled audibly.

"In the Blankenese Sailing Club. Peter Westphal was helping a colleague weld on his helm there."

No reaction.

"Your boat was next to it,"

Her dark eyes lit up. "Exactly! I had trouble with the sail!" Came flowing out of her. "The stay rings had corroded over the winter. And…"

I heard a door fall into its lock in the adjoining living room of the hotel suite. The sound of a vacuum cleaner came closer to us. Housekeeping.

Suzanne Carstens resumed her sentence. "I could not get the damn things…"

The vacuum cleaner stopped. Someone started whistling a song, out of tune and quite loud.

Suddenly Suzanne changed. All the color disappeared from her face. Unconsciously, she took hold of her doll, pressed it against her breast, and stared past me at the wall.

I leaned over to her. "Miss Carstens? Is everything OK?"

She paid no heed to me at all.

"Suzanne?"

Nothing. Instead, she began to pant, breathing heavily. Her eyes became vacant.

I got up, opened the sliding door, and stepped into the hotel suite. An elderly man was leaning over the built-in refrigerator and was refilling the drinks in the minibar. The whistling came from him.

"Excuse me," I said.

He looked up startled. "Oh! I thought there was nobody here."

"It's all right," I replied. "I'm sorry, but we need absolute silence right now. Could you please come back in an hour?"

He hastily straightened up. "Of course."

"Thank you very much," I said. "That would be nice of you."

I waited until he had left the suite. Then I returned to our consultation chamber. I stopped in my tracks. The chair where Suzanne Carstens had been sitting was empty. She was gone.

My eyes wandered around the room. The windows were closed. Thank God. But where was she?

In the corner behind the couch, I spotted some blonde hair. I stepped closer. Suzanne crouched low to the ground, the doll pressed against her.

Slowly, so as not to frighten her any further, I sat down on the carpet next to her. And I waited. When nothing happened, I put my hand on her forearm. Her muscles were tense, rigid.

It took several minutes, then she began to tremble. I strengthened my grip.

After a while, she moved and finally turned her head to me.

I just looked at her.

She twisted her mouth in agony. Her eyes were wet.

"We do not have to continue today," I said.

Tears ran down her cheeks. During all my years as a psychologist, I had never seen such utterly hopeless desperation.

"Maybe we should think about going out," I suggested, "to get some fresh air."

She took a deep breath. "That would be great," she replied nearly inaudibly. "I have not been outside for days."

"Where do you want to go?" I hurried to ask.

"On the Ad Astra," came back like a shot from a pistol.

Naturally. She wanted to get on her boat. Escape everything.

"I'd love to take Ad Astra out for a sail," she continued. "Not far. Only a bit up the river."

Shit, I thought. Me and boats—not a good combination. I did not like being on the open water. And if I was honest with myself, I was scared of it.

Suzanne Carstens looked at me with feverish expectation. The psychologist in me knew that I had a unique opportunity to get in touch with her. On top of that, I did not have the heart to disappoint her and deny her vehement wish.

"Good," I said. "You'll take me with you?"

"On the Ad Astra?" she replied. "Yes. With pleasure."

37

Another day destroyed by cloud cover. This was a permanent dilemma in Hamburg: enjoy the clouds or quickly go crazy. *If the gray overcast gets you down, wait, and the sun will come in its own time*—that is how one survives a life in this city.

Alex didn't think more than that about the weather. At least it wasn't raining.

He pulled into his parking spot at the sleepy DA's office, slipped in just as he slipped through the gate, unnoticed. He had a lot of catching up to do, and unnecessary chatter about new developments wasn't going to help him with his backlog. There was the review from the preliminary hearing that Mrs. Buchholz had taken over for him, and of course, a mound of unopened mail.

His reception room was empty. As he passed through, he noticed that the screen saver on his secretary's desk had not engaged. He imagined she had just stepped away. Alex entered his office, flipped on the lights, and threw his coat carelessly over one of the conference chairs. He sat down to work at his own desk for a change.

After signing the last deposition, he fished into his pocket for his cell to give Evelin a call. He was anxious to find out how it went with Björn Carsten's granddaughter.

Four rings later, he was hanging up. *She is still with her client*, he thought. That was a good sign. Evelin could have finally made progress with the young woman. Perhaps Suzanne had started to remember the night of the murders and could give them the clues they desperately needed to solve the case.

He would wait a little while and try to call Evelin again later. He had plenty to do in the meantime.

From the neighboring room, he could hear muffled sounds. It appeared that his secretary had returned to her desk. Alex pressed the button on his speaker. "Hello, Julia. I hope I didn't frighten you. I came in while you were indisposed."

"I must admit you did startle me a bit. What may I do for you, Alex?" his secretary replied.

"Could you please ask Mrs. Buchholz to come see me as soon as she has a spare minute?"

"Of course, and welcome back."

Alex realized he hadn't been in the office for two days, but did not think it was that traumatic. Apparently, these guys did not have enough to do when he wasn't around.

He grabbed his phone and checked to see if Evelin had tried to reach him. No message. He thought it was too soon to call again and decided to wait another half an hour.

A few minutes later, Mrs. Buchholz walked in without knocking. Alex quickly stood up and tried to get to the door or shake a hand, or… nothing. She was already in the seat that faced his desk. Feeling oddly ineffective, he dropped into his chair.

"Hello, Mr. Gutenberg. I understand you have been made part of a special task force," the young prosecutor stated.

"You do?" As far as Alex knew, there had not been any mention of an official unit. Maybe Julia said as much to cover for his absence. "Who did you hear that from?"

"It was announced this morning in the departmental email." She went on talking, and Alex could only think of one culprit: *Bolsen*. He unconsciously pressed his lips together in a thin line.

She glanced at him quizzically. "You look a little confused. Am I giving you news you didn't already know yourself?"

"Actually yes," Alex admitted. "I hadn't realized there was an official task force; we are working on a high-profile murder case. I suppose you have heard."

"I had seen something about it on the news Tuesday, and assumed that is why you asked me to cover for you at the preliminary hearing," Mrs. Buchholz added politely.

"Yes, and that is why I have asked you in this morning. How did it go?"

"Nothing out of the ordinary; the defense has not offered any evidence to their man's whereabouts. But they did submit two new character witnesses."

"Do you feel comfortable looking further into the case?" Alex asked. "I may need you to try it for me."

The young state prosecutor smiled, and a faint red washed over her face. "Of course, Mr. Gutenberg. I'd be honored. Thank you for thinking of me."

"No need for that. There isn't anyone here I'd trust more. *Thank you*." He uttered these last two words with such emphasis to sign off as much as show his gratitude.

The young district attorney collected her papers and parted with a quiet smile.

Alex did not hesitate. As soon as Mrs. Buchholz closed the door behind her, he fished out his cell and hit redial. He let it ring seven times before hanging up.

He glanced at his watch. Could a therapy session take three hours? Wasn't that a bit long?

He scrolled down his list of recent calls and pressed another button.

"Hello, Captain Strobelsohn. What's this I hear about a task force?" Alex got straight to the point.

"Well, you've heard right. I just found out about it half an hour ago," the captain's surly reply resounded. "It was announced before we were even told."

"I don't suppose Bolsen had anything to do with that."

Strobelsohn laughed grimly. "Where would you get that idea?"

"Is Dr. Wolf also on it?"

"Yes, sir. Henrik as well. It is official. We're on one team now."

"I'm happy about that," Alex said truthfully. He took a short break before he finally got to the real purpose of his call. "Well speaking of the team, you haven't heard from Ev... Dr. Wolf, have you?"

"Can't you get ahold of her?" came the quick counter-question.

"No," Alex said, and noticed at the same moment that he sounded more worried than he had intended.

"Detective Breiter said she was interviewing Suzanne Carstens today," replied Strobelsohn. "You might want to check at the hotel if she is not picking up her calls."

"All right, I will. Thanks." He hung up, only to type in Evelin's number again. This time there was no ring. Instead, her voicemail answered.

Alex stood up, grabbed his coat, and pulled it on while walking. He hardly had his arm popped through the sleeve when his hand met the door handle.

"Julia, I'll be out for the rest of the afternoon," he let his secretary know over his shoulder and slipped back into the solemn halls of Hamburg's prosecutor's office. His were the only footfalls as his heels clattered over the marble tiles.

Once more in his car, he said in a clear voice, "Call Dr. Wolf." Like before, he was greeted by her answering message.

"Come on, Evelin, where are you?" he said to himself as he unintentionally left a skid mark when he pulled out of his parking spot.

The drive seemed like an eternity to him. Then, he admitted to himself, it must be due to the rain that he had not noticed until now. It was coming down pretty good for a spring thunderstorm, and that translated into slow-moving traffic. Alex tried to ignore his growing anxiety. He turned on the radio to distract himself, only to switch it off a few minutes later.

Finally arriving at the hotel, Alex pulled into the first parking spot next to the handicap stall, ran through the downpour to the front desk, and marched past the receptionist. He took the elevator to the top floor.

There was a uniformed police officer standing in the hall. Alex wanted to walk past him, but the policeman stopped him. "May I be of assistance?"

Alex spun around. "Where is *the patient?*"

"I'm sorry, you are?"

He is doing his job, Alex reminded himself, and said, "Gutenberg, Assistant District Attorney, and now partner with Dr. Wolf on this case."

The policeman did not move an inch. "One moment," Swiveling around, he spoke into his radio inaudibly. He was probably checking Alex's information.

Alex took a deep breath and forced himself to stay calm.

Finally, the policeman turned back to him. "Yes sir, the patient has left the premises with Dr. Wolf."

An alarm set off in Alex's head. "And where exactly did they go?"

"I am sorry, sir. Dr. Wolf did not say."

38

The water shimmered leaden gray. The waves were powerful, reaching about two feet in height and carrying caps of white foam. It wasn't at all like being on a river. The Elbe was wide enough to be mistaken for a sea, if it weren't for those pale green patches of shoreline stretching to the left and right into the distance.

I sat in the aft deck of the Ad Astra—the cockpit; it was situated at the rear of the boat as it is with most small yachts. A lowered area in the open, with two opposing wooden benches and a corridor in the middle that led to the cabin.

I had barely noticed the strong, cutting wind while we were still in the city. But now, it filled the sails of the yacht, and the Ad Astra flew over the waves as quickly as lightning.

Before we headed out, Suzanne Carstens had insisted I take a fleece jacket and hooded windbreaker, as well as a wool scarf, stocking cap, and gloves, all of which she had pulled out of a storage compartment in the cabin. I was glad that she had done so. Without the warm clothes, I would not have lasted more than five minutes.

We came upon a huge cargo ship, loaded to the brim with colorful containers, on its way to the port. At twenty feet, the Ad Astra was not exactly tiny, but shadowed by the giant ocean liner, it felt like we were in a nutshell. This comparison failed miserably to soothe my need for security, or to increase my sense of well-being.

Occasionally, I discovered white, fretful spots that I could not clearly identify due to the great distance. They were other sailboats. All in all, only the foolhardiest sailors dared to leave the harbor in their Lasers and yachts in weather conditions as rough as these.

From time to time, a fine mist of spray mixed with larger drops hit me. I had the feeling that my face was freezing, slowly but surely. Additionally, the yacht lurched from side to side, and my stomach didn't exactly appreciate that. This was clearly not my sport, though I felt overall better than I had anticipated.

Suzanne Carstens was at home. She sat opposite me. In one hand, she adeptly steered the ship with the so-called tiller, a rod that served as an extension of the rudder. While in her other hand, she pulled on a rope, and inexplicably to me, controlled the position of the huge sail.

Ever since we placed foot on the Ad Astra, my client seemed transformed. She was lively, her eyes sparkled, she appeared to know exactly what she was doing. Extremely competent and concentrated, she was altogether a different person.

I had been hoping to have a chance to talk to her, but that proved impossible. The wind howled, and we had to practically scream to communicate. I decided to make the most of the situation and get this trip over with as quickly as possible. In any case, when this was past, at least

Suzanne Carstens and I would have something that connected us. I could build on that.

Suddenly, a gust of wind hit us. And then another. The boat lurched and tilted sharply to the port side. I clung to one of the lines running behind my head and forced myself to breathe in a controlled manner.

"Yippee!" Suzanne yelled, giddily. She was in a great mood.

I hid my fear and my burgeoning nausea as best I could behind a forced smile.

She turned to me. "Would you please take the tiller? I have to go to the bow to lower the jib."

"Sure," I shouted out loud. "What do you need me to do?"

"Just hold the rudder the way it is now. Continue straight ahead."

I grabbed the stick. Suzanne stood up, climbed smoothly onto the edge of the boat, and moved with the care of a tightrope walker to the front tip. It was beyond my comprehension how she could do that. She did not so much as touch the handrail or support herself even once.

When she reached the bow, she leaned down, took a rope, and pulled it hard. Eventually, she lifted her head up and shouted something in my direction, which I didn't get due to the strong wind.

She yelled again and waved at me to come to her. Then she pointed to the lock for the tiller next to me.

"Hook in," I could make out now. And once more she made that inviting gesture to me.

I had no choice. I secured the rudder and carefully got up. With my legs akimbo, I stood there, trying not to lose my balance. Then I grabbed the railing with both hands and climbed onto the gunwale. I avoided looking down at the water. Instead, I kept my gaze fixed on the bow.

One step, then a second and a third…

Suzanne opened her mouth and shouted something at me.

"Be…"

I didn't hear the rest.

The boom, which is attached to the mast and holds the mainsail, swung furiously in my direction, hit me across the shoulders, and swept me off the boat.

Impact. Water.

I went under, not feeling anything at first. Then suddenly, shockingly, freezing cold. I kicked my legs instinctively and my head popped above the waves. Filled with panic, I gasped for air.

The tail of the Ad Astra swung past me.

I had lost my stocking cap. My hair and my face were wet, and the merciless wind hurt unbearably. At the same time, I felt my clothes soaking up water. I began to sink.

I kicked harder, spread my arms, tried to swim. I only managed a few strokes. The water of the Elbe was around forty degrees, maybe less. My muscles began to stiffen, and it became more difficult for me to move.

The yacht, with Suzanne Carstens on board, travelled farther and farther away from me.

I panicked, fought wildly, panted, and immediately coughed up the water that had gotten into my lungs. And suddenly, I knew Suzanne Carstens was crazy. In her madness, she had murdered her grandfather and his friends, for whatever reason. Now, it was my turn. She had been playing me the whole time, lured me onto this damn yacht, and now, she would let me die a horrible death.

"A tragic accident," she'd say afterward, opening her dark eyes like a deer caught in headlights. No one would be able to prove otherwise.

I had a hard time keeping my head above water. The Ad Astra was almost out of sight. No other boats nearby. I wasn't going to make it…

The white sails of the small yacht started to flutter, then the Ad Astra began to turn, and I could not believe it: She came back.

39

There was not much more Alex could do. He had called Evelin's office, her home, then, the LKA. He spoke with Henrik Breiter as well as Strobelsohn. And in between each attempt, he had tried to reach Evelin again on her cell. Without success.

He figured she had her reasons to not pick up her phone.

Suzanne Carstens was, in his opinion, incompetent. Most likely, even dangerous. More than dangerous. Damn, maybe she had even killed her own grandfather.

Evelin was alone with this madwoman. Somewhere. And he could not help.

He decided to wait at home.

Arriving at his apartment, he had to admit that he was worried about Evelin. Now, with all the distractions missing, he became even more aware of it.

He poured himself a whiskey, sat down in his chair, and drank. Half the city knew he was anxious to speak with Evelin. Once they saw or heard from her, they would surely tell her to reach out to him.

The alcohol burned on his palate, but he did not notice it, nor did it seem to calm him down. Alex emptied his glass, put it on the coffee table in front of him, and poured himself another.

After a while, he realized that he was getting tired. The excitement of the day had taken its toll. He looked out the window to his balcony. The storm had increased in strength. Streams of water ran down the glass.

He put his head back slightly and closed his eyes.

Just for a moment, he told himself. *Only for a tiny little moment…*

He fell asleep.

The dream begins differently than usual. Alex is out on his own balcony, and the rain has suddenly disappeared. He is looking back into the room and at the armchair he had just been sitting in.

All at once, the door opens, and a stranger enters.

Who is this intruder? Alex asks himself.

He sort of remembers the Gore-Tex jacket the stranger is wearing. He'll have a chance to find out who it is, since the stranger is coming out to join him.

And then Alex recognizes the intruder: it is himself, a younger version of him. Together, they turn and walk to the edge of the balcony and look out over the city. But what he sees is no longer Hamburg. And the vantage point has changed into something he knows ever so well.

Nothing else in the dream changed: the same longitudinal drainage canals and the latitudinal row of shops. It is easy to see from the rooftops, and there are clear-cut passages that one can use to traverse from here to there.

No one looks up at a bazaar. No one pays you any mind. You can move stealthily by, like a sleight of hand. Until you don't…

The wind wails and howls. Loudly. And even louder still. Alex is no longer on his lookout, but in the middle of the dusty street. He is alone. And the sky is blue. Not a single cloud.

The surrounding houses are ruins. They rise, ghostly, above him. No visible signs of life anywhere, and yet he knows that he is being watched. Out of the darkness, eyes are directed at him.

His hand tightens around the handle of the assault rifle. He can no longer put it off. He has to look. At the dilapidated shed. At the door. At the man standing there, nailed through his hands and ankles.

The man's green uniform has long rips in many places. The fabric is soaked with dark liquid. It is blood from the countless wounds that the knife stabs have left in the man's body.

The man raises his head. This can only be done slowly and laboriously. He has bright eyes. Gray, like the stones of the surrounding houses. And his hair, which is black at first, shines red in the sunlight. It is also saturated with blood, so much so that drops run steadily over the man's forehead and sore, swollen face.

Alex knows the man.

That shouldn't have ever happened! Never!

"Alex," the man whispers hoarsely. "Alex. Please!"

The man's chapped lips form more words. But Alex can't understand them any longer. The wind sets in again. Howls and whines and screams.

He cannot stand that! Nobody could!

Alex bolted upright. Panting, he sat bent over in his armchair.

40

Outside the windows of the small yacht, night had already fallen. Sometimes, when the boat swayed from side to side in the swell, I recognized a band of glowing dots on the distant mainland. The fierce wind had gained strength; it passed over the Ad Astra, howling. The constant beating of the waves, the rattling of metal on metal and the creaking of the boat orchestrated into a strange background noise. I felt as if I was outside of space and time.

After Suzanne Carstens had managed, with great difficulty, to fish me out of the water and had nursed me back to health, we had initially planned to return to Blankenese, but the rapidly worsening weather put a stop to that. Additionally, our daylight was fading fast. Suzanne therefore headed for the nearby, hidden bay of *Hanskalbsand*—one of the uninhabited small islands which lie in the middle of the Elbe—and dropped anchor. We would stay here until morning.

The boat's cabin was almost six feet deep and so low that you could only stand bent over in it. In the middle ran a long table. On it sat my cellphone, wrapped up in a towel. It got wet when I fell in the river and it was not working, at least for the time being. I was sitting on a bench that also served as a bunk, wearing an old tracksuit, and had a woolen blanket over my shoulders. My hair was still damp.

Meanwhile, my client skillfully worked a hotplate, made tea, and put the pot and two cups on the table. She took a seat next to me, leaned behind us reaching at an angle, and unearthed a dusty bottle of rum with its seal already broken. Without being asked, I held my cup out to her. She poured a lot for me, helped herself, and then filled the cups with hot tea.

I clutched the steaming mug with both hands. I was cold from the outside in. Carefully, I sipped the brew.

"Thank you," I said.

She raised her cup to me, and we both drank a sip.

"I'm so sorry you fell overboard," she said.

"Me too." I pulled the edges of my mouth into a painful grin. "It was horrific."

"It happens all the time," she said. "It's usually not so bad. But today the water is quite cold, and the waves are high…" She fell silent.

"It wasn't that," I said. "I didn't think you were coming back."

I watched her reaction. Her eyes widened for a moment. She looked frightened.

"Why wouldn't I?"

I chose my next words with care. "I was seriously afraid you were trying to kill me."

A pregnant pause lowered on the room.

In the dim light of the only lamp in the cabin I could see how she struggled to come up with an answer. She stared into her tea for a long time. Finally, she glanced up.

"Then you are convinced that I had something to do with my grandfather's death."

"You didn't?"

She shrugged her shoulders hesitantly. "I can't remember. But I think that I… didn't do it."

She was lying. I had no doubt. But I was unable to determine whether she lied about not remembering, or the murders in the basement of her house. Or both.

I let a minute pass before I said, "Maybe you can explain something else to me."

"What?"

"This afternoon, in the hotel, when the cleaner started whistling, you completely froze. You squeezed your old doll against your chest." I pointed to my bag, amongst my things. The doll's head stuck out as if it was trying to eavesdrop.

"That must have scared you," she said.

"Yes," I admitted. "I hadn't expected that."

She tried to smile. She could not. "I'm sure you had thought about giving me one of your tranquilizers that you keep in the drawer of your wheeled container."

"Not necessarily," I replied. "But what was that about?"

"It's important to you, isn't it?" she asked tonelessly. She was trying to buy some time.

"Yes," I said.

"You probably would like me to explain the broom closet, right?"

"You pointed the stairs out because you *want* to talk to me about it. Because you *have* to tell someone. Otherwise, you would have kept it to yourself."

She listened up. "It's that simple?"

I smiled at her. "Most of the time, anyway."

"Okay." She nodded, more to herself, as though she tried to build up her courage. "My mother…" She stopped.

I waited, listening to the storm raging outside.

"He used to whistle when he'd beckon her. Sometimes she would scream. Then he'd hit her until she was quiet. And he made her… I hid until it was over."

"Your grandfather abused your mother," I said calmly.

She nodded again. "Yes." Tears swelled up in her eyes. "There was nothing I could do about it. I was just a child, after all."

"That is horrible. I'm so sorry to hear that," I replied quietly.

We remained silent for a long while.

"What was with your father?" I eventually asked. "He didn't intervene at all?"

"My father?" She curled a corner of her mouth upwards. An undeniable sign of contempt. "He left my mother before I was born."

"You've never met him?"

"No. My mother mentioned him a few times. He was her one true love." She snorted. "A fantastically great *love…*"

"Do you know his name?"

She shook her head. "My mother never told me. And on my birth certificate, it says *unknown*."

My cup was empty. I refilled both of ours with tea and rum.

"You and your mother had a very close relationship," I stated.

"Yes." An expression appeared on her face. A mixture of pride and melancholy. "She was a beautiful woman. She never scolded me." She hesitated. "Would you care to see her?"

"Yes, I would like that," I said.

She leaned way back again, opened another compartment of the built-in chest of drawers, reached in purposefully, and pulled out a picture frame. Gently she wiped it clean with her sleeve and handed it to me. "Here you go."

A slim woman in a summer dress. The resemblance to Suzanne Carstens was uncanny. Blonde hair, dark eyes. The same, otherworldly melancholic expression in the face.

The woman looked directly into the camera. She did not smile. Around her shoulder lay the arm of a man. The rest of him was missing. Judging by the slightly uneven edge, someone had cut him out.

"Your mother certainly was a beauty," I said. "How old was she when the picture was taken?"

"Maybe in her mid-twenties?"

"About the same age as you are now."

"Yes." She stared reverently at the photograph.

"And the man next to her, who is that?"

Her shrug was extremely vague. "I guess that must've been my grandfather."

She lied to me again. She knew exactly who had been standing next to her mother because she had cut him out herself. She didn't want to see him. Especially not together with her mother. I could understand that very well.

"What happened to your mother?" I asked her.

"She died when I was still rather little." And before I could reply, she quickly added, "She went to the hospital. In an ambulance. She never came back."

March

27

Saturday

41

During the night, the storm had worked itself out, and the rain had stopped. Getting on 11 a.m., it was still very windy, and dark clouds passed over a lead gray sky.

Suzanne Carstens and I were on our way again. High waves were constantly beating against the bow of the Ad Astra, making her dance across the water and swing back and forth in an alarming way.

Strangely, it didn't bother me anymore.

The distant stretches of land on both sides gradually moved closer to us. Soon we would reach the marina in Blankenese.

I sat in the cockpit with Suzanne, holding the tiller while she took care of the sails, which were inflated to the point of bursting. We shot over the water like an arrow—most of the time in silence. Not because Suzanne had fallen back into her old listlessness, but because we could hardly understand our own words.

This morning my mobile phone was miraculously functioning again. On the display I saw that Alex had called me many times the day before until late in the evening. Although my battery was almost empty, I tried my luck to reach him shortly before we started out. He answered after several rings. I told him that I was with my client on her boat, that we were on our way back to Hamburg, and that we would arrive around noon.

Alex's responses were compendious and monosyllabic. Maybe it was due to the bad connection, but his voice left me with the distinct feeling that he had just woken up. He sounded like he had overslept; his words were labored and intentionally articulated. I had the underlying impression of his tongue sticking to the roof of his mouth. He had been drinking. And not just a little.

Then my cell phone beeped, and the call broke off abruptly. But that was immaterial. I had been able to convey everything he needed to know.

While we were fighting our way up the river on the Ad Astra, I thought about Alex. About the day I first met him. How we immediately got on each other's nerves and how gradually a kind of professional respect had developed between the two of us. And then… Was there more? More than the usual sympathy among colleagues? Perhaps. I recalled a few situations in which he had smiled at me. Didn't I sense, or read in his eyes, that his interest in me went beyond the purely professional?

I contorted my mouth. I was probably just wishing for that.

Sometimes, however, when I was with him, I could feel something completely different. And it was starkly evident. There were things that burdened him. Experiences, possibly a heavy loss. He did not talk about it, did not even admit it to himself. But shadows of the past were present, gnawing at him and pressing him down.

On the right bank, I noticed a strange structure. As we approached, I realized that it was a high pile of tree trunks, branches, pallets, and similar flammable material. This evening, Easter bonfires would be burning everywhere. That it had rained heavily, and the wood got soaking wet, did not matter. The strong wind would dry a lot of it. And as for the rest, North Germans knew how to help. A little good, old gasoline, and you have a blazing fire. I grinned.

The Blankenese Marina came in sight. On the pier, which jutted out far into the water, stood a lone man. Arms and legs akimbo, hands in his pockets, he braced himself against the hard breeze. His half-opened coat was fluttering in the wind.

He did not move, staring incessantly in our direction. Alex.

I waved to him. And he returned my greeting.

Suzanne took the tiller now. With a skill that only comes from many years of practice and experience, she steered our small yacht to its slip.

Alex appeared on our jetty. He gave Suzanne a sign, she threw him the rope, and he expertly lashed it to a cleat. He helped us climb ashore. Suzanne first, then me.

He held my hand a heartbeat longer than necessary. Our eyes met. I let go.

"How was it out there?" he asked, trying to convey an innocuous facial expression.

He was a lousy actor. I could clearly tell how much he had worried. Deep lines were dug into the sides of his mouth. He had dark circles around his eyes and hadn't shaved.

"How was your trip?" he asked again, and I realized that I hadn't answered him the first time.

"Oh," I said. "Great."

He looked at me in the way that I had just scrutinized him. Apparently, I too was a pitiful actress. Because judging from his body language, he noticed that something had happened, something that I did not want to talk about now.

"I'm happy for you," he said and smiled. "It was quite stormy. Especially yesterday."

Suzanne wiped a strand of hair from her forehead and held on to it unnecessarily.

"May I introduce you to Mr. Gutenberg?" I said to her. "You've met before, but you probably don't remember him. You were not feeling very well at the time."

"Mr. Gutenberg?" she repeated, nodding his way guardedly.

"Miss Carstens is a talented sailor," I hurried to explain to Alex. "It wouldn't be my chosen profession. But I felt very secure with her." And to Suzanne, "Thanks again for the wonderful time, Miss Carstens."

"You're welcome." She smiled apprehensively. "I love it out on the water." She spoke quiet, but unwavering. "In all conditions. You're just away from it all. Every now and then I need that."

"Who doesn't?" Alex replied. "I can understand that all too well."

We fell silent. The wind tugged on the boats and on us.

Alex looked down at the tips of his shoes and up again. "I came in a taxi. My car… went on strike and just didn't want to start this morning."

He was lying. I could see his oversized BMW parked right next to my Audi in the adjacent lot. He did not want to leave me alone with Suzanne Carstens. Not even for the duration of a short drive.

"Cars. When you really need them, they break down." I sighed. "Then I suggest you go with me. We'd better take Miss Carstens to her hotel first, and after I'll drive you home."

"That works for me," Alex said.

Suzanne remained silent.

I pulled my key out of my purse and dangled it in front of Alex. "When I think about it… actually, Miss Carstens and I are both quite beat. It would be great if we could sit in the back while you play chauffeur for us." Then looking at Suzanne, I asked, "What do you think about that, Miss Carstens?"

"Good. Really good," was her prompt reply.

"Well, then let's go," Alex said, taking the key out of my hand.

42

Alex moved the driver's seat all the way back and asked Evelin and Suzanne Carstens if they still had enough space. As he took his place behind the wheel, he was surprised how much leg room the Audi had. He slid his weight forward two clicks and glanced up at Evelin in the rearview mirror. She smiled shortly and then said, "Onward James, to the Hotel Atlantic Kempinski."

Alex pulled out of the parking lot and took the opportunity to use the mirror again. He thought he caught Evelin at the same time her eyes darted out of view. She seemed relaxed and Suzanne Carstens was too. Maybe Evelin had made some progress and there would soon be a statement. Anyway, the witness seemed to be comfortable enough to sit side by side with her therapist.

Arriving at the hotel, Alex started to get out of the car with Evelin and her patient. But Evelin laid a hand on his shoulder, and he immediately understood. She did not want him to accompany them.

Alex reluctantly stayed put and waited impatiently as Evelin brought Suzanne Carstens up to her hotel suite. He knew there was something his colleague was concealing, and he wanted to find out what really happened on that boat.

Evelin finally returned. Climbing in the passenger seat, she asked, "Should we go back and get your BMW? I saw it parked outside of the marina."

"I came with the intention of driving you. To allow you a moment to get your things together," he hesitated, "or catch up on missed calls. I might have caused a bit of a worry asking around for you last night."

"*You* were worried," she stated plainly.

He did not want to admit that. What he did or did not think was none of her business. But her gaze was calm and accepting. His answer seemed important to her.

"Yes," he heard himself say.

"I'm sorry," she said quietly.

Neither spoke for a while.

She was the first one to break the silence. "That's a great idea of yours to drive. Thanks."

Happy that she had changed the topic, Alex started the Audi and backed out of the parking space.

Reticence again.

He cleared his throat without being able to hide his agitation. "Very well. Now tell me what the hell happened."

"The long and the short of it," she began. "Peter Westphal had disclosed to me yesterday morning that he had first met Suzanne on the Ad Astra and that she was an outstanding sailor."

Alex nodded. "And?"

"I brought up her boat and a flood of memories came back. She asked if we couldn't go out on a short sail. I thought it would build a bond between us, and as you have witnessed, it did."

Alex waited to see if she would continue to talk. When she did not, he said, "But something else transpired that you haven't informed me about yet."

"I fell overboard, and I thought she was going to leave me to die. She proved me wrong by turning the Ad Astra around and pulling me out of the water."

"Good heavens." He shot her an alarmed look, before returning his eyes to the road. "You're lucky you didn't catch pneumonia." He shifted gears and gave more gas than he needed.

He forced himself to remove his foot from the accelerator.

"Her boat was well stocked with warm clothes and warmer rum. I think I will be fine," she added.

Alex realized he was entitled to a more detailed explanation. His first impulse was to castigate Evelin for acting so irresponsibly. But then he had to admit that he was partly to blame. He had told Evelin the day before to push things along and move to get Suzanne Carstens to remember and talk. And in all actuality, he did not just ask. If he was honest with himself, he had implored her. Evelin was only doing what he had demanded from her.

He decided not to question her judgement of taking the witness away from her protected environment. Instead, he tried to concentrate on the benefits of the outing.

"So?" he exhaled audibly. "Did you get anything out of her?"

If Evelin had noticed his internal turmoil, she did not let on. "I was hoping that I could build more trust from Suzanne," she said. "As far as that goes, I think I was very successful. The experience has created some form of harmony and mutual appreciation. Can you understand that?"

"Yes," Alex replied, somewhat calmer.

"More specifically, Suzanne confided in me that her grandfather abused her mother. That she shared this information with me is an enormous expression of trust."

"Wow!" Alex exhaled audibly. "But to tell you the truth, that does not surprise me. I have not learned much about Björn Carstens that leaves a particularly good taste in my mouth."

"He would whistle for her mother, like he was calling his dog," Evelin said from the passenger seat. "Suzanne falls apart whenever she hears whistling. She was a little girl and felt helpless and terrified because she couldn't prevent the sexual abuse."

"That must have been terrible for her," Alex said. He forced himself to stop thinking about it and concentrate on the case at hand. "Anyway, job well done. We now have a probable cause."

She suddenly spun her head and eyeballed him steadily. "Alex? Do you really think she could have killed those men?"

He made a noncommittal gesture with his hand. "No. Not really. But the nicotine we found in the corpses leads me to believe that someone in the house was in on it, and if it did not go to plan, it could have turned into the blood bath we found."

"I just can't imagine her as the murderer," Evelin replied. "She is such a fragile creature." She hesitated. "She is lying about something, though. Whether about what she remembers or how much she has forgotten."

"I suppose you might be surprised what some people we think we know are capable of doing without affecting our opinion of them. They are just really good about hiding the skeletons in their closet."

"That's true," she agreed. "But then again…" She fell silent suddenly and looked at her watch. "Almost two," she mumbled more to herself. And turning to him, she said, "Listen, I need to pay my father a visit. I have been putting it off all week. But I'm famished. What do you think about having an early dinner at Georgios with me first?"

He had not expected that. Suddenly, he noticed he was also hungry. "Sounds good," he hurried to say. "What if I invited Henrik and Strobelsohn along? I haven't told you, but we've been formed into a special task force until we clarify the deaths in Blankenese."

"Really?" She laughed quietly but heartily. "From the first day I got called in, Bolsen seemed overeager to present the press with a murderer." She stopped short. "Let's do it. I'll reserve a table."

Alex fished his cell phone out of his breast pocket. Without taking his eyes off the road, he pressed a button.

"Call Strobelsohn on speaker."

It rang a couple times.

"Strobelsohn."

"Captain Strobelsohn, I am with Dr. Wolf, and we are going to have a late lunch at Georgios's. Do you think you and Henrik could meet us there in… around three?" Alex looked over questioningly at Evelin.

"Two hours," Evelin mouthed and additionally raised two fingers in the air.

"Or maybe four o'clock would be better," Alex added.

"Four o'clock. Yes. Of course," Strobelsohn replied loudly. "That will give us a chance to discuss the new developments and set up next steps. We'll be there."

Alex slipped his phone back into his pocket. "Will that give you enough time to get your things together?"

"Yes. I'll just jump into the shower and wear something casual, meaning five minutes later, and we can get back on the road." She paused. "What about your car?"

"I think I can pick it up afterward; you want to go see your father, and I have nothing better to do," he said, a bit befuddled.

"Good," she smiled. "If you take the next exit, it would be the quickest way to my place."

43

Alex let Evelin explain the way to her house. He did not want to tell her he knew where she lived. Because—then she probably would have asked about that. And what should he have answered? That he had walked there a few days before in the heavy rain after a drunken brawl, and was within the width of a hair of ringing her doorbell at two or three in the morning? No, that was out of the question. So, he pretended not to know her address. That simplified things—for him, and ultimately, for her.

They had arrived. She pointed to a stately half-hipped dwelling.

Funny. He had not noticed the striking shape of the roof at night, or the wrought iron fence. How could he forget there was a metal gate he had to have walked through?

He contorted his face. *Step one: admit that you have a problem,* he thought to himself while he parked.

As he followed Evelin to the front stoop, he noticed her home looked different in daylight. Stone gray and a hedge around the yard, the only trees were in the parking along the street. It surprised him how welcoming the monocultured lawn seemed; he wouldn't have anticipated that.

Evelin unlocked the door and led the way in.

She stopped, her eyes wandered around the living room, and she said with an apologetic smile, "I've only been able to unpack the bare necessities. I haven't had time for more." She turned to him. "Regardless, make yourself comfortable. I'll be right back."

With those words, she left him alone.

She had not exaggerated. The place was scattered with boxes. Mostly closed, with two large initials written on each: LR. A few around the mantelpiece had been opened. They contained framed photographs.

She started with her cherished memories, he thought. No wonder: the walls were bare. There was little sign of life besides a blanket and pillow on the couch. Where she most likely lay when watching the tube.

A squeal from the plumbing, followed by the rush of water. Encouraged, he stepped farther into the house. Walking through a small corridor, he came to a well-lit kitchen. Even in the overcast day, the freshly painted, ivory-colored room was filled with light. Typical cabinetry, brilliant white, simple yet elegant. On the counter, a used mug and an open box of cereal. Crunchy nuggets of oats and dried fruit. Next to it, a bowl with spoon sitting in a pool of milk. Alex placed it in the sink and ran some water in it.

He grabbed the empty mug of coffee and rinsed it out as well. The pot was still on the burner. He dumped the contents and cleaned the sides of the glass with the sponge and dishwashing liquid sitting on the edge of the sink. Opening the cabinet above, he found filters and a canister of coffee. He filled the machine to six cups, added four heaping scoops of fresh grounds, and flipped the switch. Not sure about Evelin, but he was feeling the effects from the night before and caffeine would remedy that.

She was still in the shower, so he returned to her photos on the mantel. Face up in the box was a picture of about an eighteen-year-old Evelin. He raised it up to take a closer look. Wow! No, he was mistaken. Not eighteen. But a much younger Evelin, nonetheless. She could not have been older than her early to mid-twenties. Clearly, no longer a high school graduate.

And he recognized the imposing pavilion-like building with the baroque columns and the domed roof in front of which she stood. It was the main building of the University of Hamburg on Edmund-Siemers-Allee. Evelin was dressed up. He suspected that the shot had been taken on the occasion of her graduation ceremony.

What happened to that young lady? His mouth contorted. *Ten years of service will harden the softest skin. Evelin had not escaped time leaving its mark.*

Alex placed the picture on the fireplace and picked up the one already standing there. Evelin and a distinguished elderly man. Well-tailored three-piece suit, under a waft of gray hair. Dad.

Alex carried the framed picture with him back into the kitchen. He set it down next to the coffee machine and poured himself a cup. Looking for the sugar, he heard the hair dryer spark up and filled Evelin's cup as well. He tried to remember, but could not think of how she took hers.

Milk. He splashed a healthy slug and returned his attention to the photo. She was smiling happily in it. She apparently got along well with her father.

That was quick. She was walking down the stairs, hair dried. Slacks, shirt, no visible makeup.

Why doesn't she go like that every day? shot through his head. Out loud he said, "Do you take it black and bitter or light and sweet?"

"I could smell that from upstairs," she said, as she bounded down the last step into the kitchen. "At this point, I'd drink it anyway it came, but yes, milk and one sugar."

Alex met her halfway with the mug he had poured for himself and avoided her eyes by finding it necessary to search out the sugar for the second one. He did notice she was looking past him. The picture.

"Your dad?" he asked and hoped she wouldn't be upset that he took it off the mantel.

He spooned the sugar into the cup and stirred it as he turned to her.

She smiled. He had worried for no reason.

"Yeah, at least fifteen years ago," she said, and her smile changed, almost melancholy. "Time flies by."

"He looks serious. Was he strict?" he asked and immediately regretted it. "I'm sorry, that is none of my business."

"No, that's fine," she said with a slight nod. She sipped at her coffee. "He had an important position. He was a head doctor. A neurosurgeon, specializing in facial reconstruction." Answering his silent question, she continued, "Not like plastic surgery, but like plastic surgery… for an accident victim… so their facial expressions still work. More or less. He was always serious; I can count the times I saw him laugh, maybe because he was constantly ready to be called in. For him, his work was his everything."

"You seem to be very proud of him," Alex said and then hurried to add, "in the photo."

"I had just returned from traipsing around, as kids do on summer breaks. I think I realized while travelling, how many things he had told me when I was growing up were conspicuously true. He was special in his own way." She stopped suddenly.

"*Was*? How is he doing now?"

"Good, good." She stared into her cup and then glanced up again. "He is living off his pension in a retirement community."

Alex stopped short. *Old folks home?* But Evelin was burning a hole in the back of his head with that stare, so he said, "That's great."

"He is comfortable there. And now that I live in town, I can visit him more often… I'm visiting him after dinner."

"Nice." He was feeling awkward and tried to convey an inconspicuous expression. "We need to think about Captain Strobelsohn and Henrik. We should slowly get going."

She nodded a bit too eagerly. Apparently, she too was relieved for the change of topic.

"Yeah" she said. "But this time I'm driving. I just need to grab my coat."

Alex returned the photograph of Evelin and her father back to its spot on the mantel.

She hadn't been speaking straight to him. Obviously, she had her own secrets.

44

Alex realized he couldn't collect his BMW right now; his internal obsessive-compulsive time manager reassured him he would not forget and went as far as scheduling an appointment directly after dinner. He did not care how it would look for Henrik and Strobelsohn that he and Evelin had arrived in one car.

Ever since he brought up her father, Evelin had been somewhat distant, and that suited Alex just fine. Instead of speaking, he pretended to concentrate on the car stereo. He shuffled through her pre-programmed radio selections and stopped on some old trumpet-filled jazz song. The cool notes outweighed the thick air.

They were the first to get to the restaurant. Georgios greeted them at the door and exclaimed, "I have your private room ready. No one will bother you there. Not even me."

"Oh, you are too good to us, Georgios. Though to tell you the truth, that is very attentive," Alex said with an indebted smile. "We do have a lot to talk about and it really is not public information."

Georgios led them to the adornment-crammed, ex-shanty choir room. Pulling the door shut, he said over his shoulder, "I'll be right back with your drinks."

Evelin took the initiative and chose the far side of the table. Alex hesitated briefly and decided to sit across from her; it seemed more natural.

He was about to thank her for inviting him into her life but was thinking that was a categorically odd thing to say. And besides, now she had indicated that she needed distance. So instead, he started in about the food.

"Did you notice if he had a special menu advertised? He didn't make any suggestions this time."

"My fallback is always the number two: Souvlaki, pork or chicken skewers served with tomatoes and onions, pita, and of course, tzatziki," she was saying as the door opened. "Well, hello, Captain Strobelsohn. We were just discussing dinner. Come right in."

Gert Strobelsohn blocked the view of most of the statues as he squeezed past Alex to take a seat. "Henrik called. He will be a little late. He had to run to the forensics lab but said we should order whatever Georgios suggests for him."

Alex folded his menu shut. "That is a good idea. I think I will put my fate in Georgios's hands as well."

"I heard you had gone missing since we last saw each other. Or was that just Mr. Gutenberg's imagination getting the better of him?" Captain Strobelsohn said to Evelin, with an oversized grin. "It's good to have you back in one piece all the same."

"Well actually I *was* lost at sea," Evelin answered. "Suzanne Carstens and I had unwittingly decided to go sailing yesterday afternoon. The storm rolled in, and the boat made an unexpected turn. The boom knocked me overboard. I was convinced she was going to let me drown. But she proved me wrong by coming back to fetch me out of the water. The storm grew in strength, and we took cover in the bay of an island until morning."

"That sounds like a hell of an experience," Strobelsohn said.

"Well, I wouldn't have gone so crazy if they weren't out of cell range. I could hardly sleep for worry," Alex admitted.

"That was sweet of you," Evelin said sincerely. "I'm glad there was really no danger, and to be honest, my spontaneous dip in the Elbe was worth it. Suzanne Carstens has started to open up to me."

Georgios bumped through the doorway with a fully loaded tray.

"I have Evi's still water, and both plain and sparkling for the gentlemen," he said, placing the large bottles on the end of the table. He pulled the now-empty tray in front of his black vest. "Is there anything I can bring while we wait for your young friend?"

Evelin started. "I think we are going to order for Henrik. I'll take my number two, unless you have a recommendation."

"You need protein. You should have the big grill plate instead of a small dinner," Georgios said with eyebrows raised in a query.

"Ok fine, the big grill plate it is," Evelin said and looked at Strobelsohn.

"Four times," the police captain took over. "We'll all eat our weights in spicy meats. Right, Mr. Gutenberg?"

"Right," Alex confirmed.

Georgios chuckled shortly. "OK then, would the gentlemen care for something else to drink?"

Alex said, "Water is fine with me."

"Me too," Strobelsohn said, handing the menus across Alex to Georgios. "You could bring a large Pilsner for the detective. He'll be here any minute."

"Very well, I'll leave you to your business. One beer and four grill plates coming up." Georgios shuffled his feet together like a matador seeking praise, spun on his axis, and left the room.

Strobelsohn turned to Evelin. "Back to Suzanne Carstens. You were saying that she has started to open up to you?"

"Yes," Evelin responded with a nod.

"Dr. Wolf has made progress with our eyewitness. I picked them up at Blankenese Marina earlier, and I must say Suzanne Carstens looked like she was ready to talk to us," Alex hastened to add, because he was thinking what Suzanne Carstens had shared with her therapist was not really everyone's business.

Evelin shrugged. "Even with the progress, I have the feeling we aren't going to get anything out of her anytime soon. She has remembered the events of the night of her grandfather's murder, but refuses to speak about it."

Strobelsohn opened his mouth to reply at the very moment Henrik came in. He was carrying a mug of beer, which Georgios had evidently handed to the young police officer immediately upon entering the Poseidon.

Henrik smiled conspicuously longer than necessary when he realized he should sit next to Evelin.

Taking a seat, he picked up his beer and said, "Prost" and made a healthy dent in the drink. Setting his glass down, he exclaimed, "I've got some forensics results."

Alex leaned forward. "And?"

"They checked the glasses in the dishwasher for traces of nicotine. But they couldn't detect anything."

"Dead end, as we had figured," Alex muttered.

"Yes. Unfortunately." Henrik frowned with evident regret. Then his eyes lit up. "But get this. There *is* dried blood residue."

Strobelsohn gawked. "Traces of blood on what?"

Henrik turned and looked everyone in the eye shortly before continuing. "On the cuff link that Björn Carstens held in his hand. Just a little below the stone on the base of the setting."

"What about the other cufflink that was found in the vault?" Strobelsohn wanted to know.

Henrik shrugged his shoulders. "Nothing."

"Do they have a match for the blood?" Alex asked.

"Yes and no." Henrik shook his head. "What they could tell me is that it is a near match to Peter Westphal's DNA. It must have come from a close male relative of one degree."

"That means either from a brother or a father, theoretically a son?" Evelin reassured herself.

"That's right!" Henrik beamed at her. "They're looking at it more closely now, but this is the preliminary result."

"Usually, the final results come out the same," Alex said. He paused momentarily. "The father is out of the question, he committed suicide several years ago. Westphal's son—that would be unlikely. Peter Westphal is young, any son would still be a child… Does Peter have any brothers, or a son for that matter?"

"As far as we know, he doesn't," Strobelsohn replied. "But I'll definitely have a look into it. First thing in the morning."

"Good work, Henrik," Alex said. "This could turn out to be important evidence."

There was a knock and Georgios came in. Four plates, brimming with grilled meat, skillfully carried between hands and elbows, immediately found a spot in front of each of them.

Henrik had forgotten his beer and sat with knife and fork looking at his plate hungrily. "What do we have here?" he asked with a broad smile. "It smells absolutely wonderful."

"We have mixed grill of pork and chicken skewers, lamb chops, and white fava beans cooked with caramelized onions, the way Evi likes them," Georgios gleefully announced.

"This is a ton of food. Good thing I brought my appetite," Henrik said as the door swung shut behind Georgios.

Nobody said another word, devoting their attention to dinner. Alex was the first to break the silence.

"In our case with the container at Burchardkai, is there any news about the owner of the freight company or the missing customs agent? Their disappearance directly after the young women were discovered dead in the container does not speak well for their innocence."

"Yes, that is very suspect." Strobelsohn put down his fork and rubbed a napkin across his mouth. "We assume they are on the run. There were no bookings under their names out of the airport, but that does not stop them from boarding a train. I believe both of their cars have been located, right Henrik?"

Henrik washed his food down with a big gulp of beer. "That is correct, sir. Neither of their homes has any sign of flight or disruption. And no one has collected the mail for either of them. They have both, by all appearances, vanished into thin air. There is an all-points bulletin out on them."

"With all consideration, Mr. Gutenberg," Strobelsohn said, "they had two days on us. The dragnet cannot be set wide enough to expect to catch them."

Alex glanced over to Evelin for her opinion. She seemed even more aloof than when they had been en route to Georgios. Her old man must be bothering her; maybe it was time to call the meeting short.

Alex decided to give it a try anyway. "What's on your mind?" he asked.

She seemed to return from far away. She looked at him and raised one shoulder. "Oh, it's probably nothing…" She concentrated on Strobelsohn. "Did you get a chance to pull up the archive file on the Westphal suicide?"

Gert Strobelsohn swung his head and ricocheted the question to Henrik with a nod.

"No… not yet," Henrik stammered in response.

Evelin smiled. "Could you please do it tomorrow? I would be very grateful."

Alex couldn't hold his curiosity back. "May I ask why?"

Evelin shrugged again. "Just a hunch."

45

At seventy-one, my father was still a handsome man. Thick, gray hair that was slowly turning white. Neatly combed, freshly shaved. He wore a casual jacket over a pastel shirt. The way he sat, he looked content and full of energy.

The window behind him offered an unobstructed view of a carefully landscaped garden. The trees did not have any leaves yet, but spring was already making its presence felt. The lawn was dotted with small purple crocuses. In the dying light of day, they glowed almost dreamlike.

"I'm under a little pressure right now, Evi," he said. "I have a lot to do."

"Oh, yeah?" I asked.

He made a serious nod. "In two weeks, I will take part in this big, international convention in New York. *Challenges of today's facial plastic surgery—A new approach*. I will present the accumulation of my work there."

"That sounds interesting," I said. "How far along are you with your preparations?"

"I have already organized all my patients' photographs. Before and after. The statistics have been checked and updated by my two assistants." He paused. "You know, I want to design my presentation in such a way that it can also be used as a handout. That is extremely important to me. I hate it when the printed material doesn't match the lecture."

"That I can understand very well."

He smiled and patted my hand. "You're a perfectionist just like me, Evi." He sighed and became serious. "With all the built-up anticipation around my trip, I mustn't forget my patients. They are relying on me. They need me. That is why I am always available. The hospital can get ahold of me anytime." He fished into the inside pocket of his jacket. "I have my pager. It's always on. Day and night." He pulled out the box and placed it within his reach on the table.

"Be careful not to overwork yourself," I said.

He raised a hand defensively. "Evi, don't worry. If I ever start to overdo it, Rosie stops me. You know her, she always watches out for me."

I swallowed hard when he voiced my mother's name. Still, I forced myself to smile. "It will surely be a very successful convention."

"Yes." He put the pager back in his pocket. "I think it will be. This international exchange is very important." He blinked, looked around, and stared at me again. "Who are you?"

"I'm Evi," I said. "Your daughter."

"Evi! Of course! I know that!" His blue eyes sparkled. "Nice of you to drop by! Unfortunately, I'm awfully busy right now."

"If I'm disturbing you…"

"No, no," he interrupted me. "Please stay here."

He grew silent.

"What are you doing now?" I asked him after a while.

"I… am preparing for a convention. In New York. I will be giving a lecture on…" Wrinkles appeared on his forehead. "Facial reconstructions and my surgical methods. They are proving to be extremely innovative."

"The presentation at the conference sounds very exciting," I said.

"It is indeed. It means a lot of work alongside my patients, of course. Nevertheless, I make sure that I am always available. I have to be, in my position. My beeper…" He broke off, stared blankly at the table. "Where is it? Where's my pager?" He looked around, leaned forward to gander at the ground. He raised his head again, his breath sped up. Frantically, he began to search his sport coat.

"Try the inside pocket of your jacket," I hurried to say. "That's where you usually keep your beeper."

"What are you talking about?" His voice acquired a cutting tone. "Never!"

"Yes," I insisted gently.

Reluctantly, he reached into his jacket and pulled out the beeper. "There it is. Thank God. You know, my patients, the staff, they all need me. They can't get along without me." He put the beeper back on the table.

An irritated expression flitted across his face. "Now, who are you again?"

"I am Evi, your daughter."

He drew his mouth into a thin, angry line. "You don't have to tell me that! I'm not demented…" He smiled. "Evi, nice of you to visit me! How did you get in?"

"With my key."

"Of course! Your key." He hesitated and added quietly, "It's good you have a key. It is always cordoned off here. It's not easy to get in or out. I've started locking my office.

Mostly, for the peace and quiet. But also because of my work and the convention. It's in…" He deliberated. "Amsterdam. It's about… about my work… with the patients. About…" His expression grew impatient. "About…"

"It's about your facial reconstructions on accident victims."

He pointed a finger at me and merrily wiggled his eyebrows up and down. "Exactly!" He peered around and rose halfway up out of his chair. "Where's Rosie?"

After all these years, I have never gotten used to him talking about my dead mother, his wife, as if she was still alive and would be standing in front of us at any moment.

"Mom is down in the kitchen," I replied.

"That's my Rosie!" With a smile, he let himself sink back. "She makes sure I don't work too hard. She ensures I take regular breaks and eat something." He reached for his beeper and meticulously stowed it away in his jacket.

Afterward, he turned his attention to me. "Mrs. Schoenhofer, that will be all for now. Please listen to my dictation right away and type the letters. This is important."

"I'll do it immediately," I said, but remained seated.

"Do you need something else?" He sat up alerted. "Where's my beeper?" Once again, his search began.

"You put it in your inside pocket, Professor," I said.

"Yes! Of course!" He pulled out the case and put the old, broken remote control on the table.

"Mrs…" he started to say.

"Schoenhofer," I said.

"Please call my daughter, Evi. Send her my best regards. The day after tomorrow is the twenty-ninth of July, my sixtieth birthday. Rosie and I expect her and her sister Frederike for dinner. Do that immediately after the dictation. I must… uh"—he stroked his forehead—"I have to work. I have to prepare for a conference in London."

I got up. "I'll take care of everything, Professor. You can count on me."

He didn't answer me. He stared blindly out of the window.

After a while I bent down to him and stroked his hair. "See you soon, Daddy," I said.

He might have even heard me.

I left him alone at the window with the view of the garden and its countless purple crocuses.

A woman walked past me. She was wearing a hoodie, with the top up and pulled down low to conceal her face. She was barefoot. Her hands were stuck inside blue latex gloves. I watched her for a moment. Her jeans were hanging halfway down to her knees and a diaper was sticking out.

I kept going. In the back of the large common room, two women sat at a table playing Parcheesi. The board and the pieces were oversized. They had to be. A precaution against accidental swallowing.

I reached the corridor that led past the patients' rooms to the exit. I avoided being run over by a woman who appeared to be about eighty years old. Someone had put her in a cross between a shower stool and bumper-car walker, a construction of light metal tubes with castors on the floor and an integrated seat. This trolley provided all-round protection against falls and enabled its pilot to move around safely.

As the old woman passed me by, she screamed, "Yes, yes, yes, Auntie!"

I went around the corner. Two orderlies were busy picking up a man from the floor, who had apparently fallen asleep there.

Then I met a man in a wheelchair. He wasn't old, forty tops. His hair was long, as was his beard. He was wearing a sweater and diapers. No pants, no socks, no shoes. I knew him from previous visits.

Then I had reached the exit. To the left of it was the chart room. I knocked.

A young doctor, perhaps twenty-five, opened the door. "Ah, Dr Wolf," she said. "Do you need to go?"

"Yes, soon," I said. "I just wanted to ask about my father's current medication."

"Come in for a second." The doctor took a step to the side and let me enter.

She picked up a file and opened it. Without looking at me, she said while reading, "I'm afraid we've had to increase the dose of Haloperidol again two weeks ago. Besides that, he's still taking Pipamperone and Risperidone, but the latter in relatively small amounts."

She lowered the file and glanced up. "He became very aggressive because he couldn't find the remote control. We did not have another option."

"The remote control is his beeper," I said. "It is extremely important to him. You can take everything away from him, do anything to him, and he'll remain peaceful. But if he doesn't have his beeper…"

"We are well aware of this," she interrupted me. "The beeper had disappeared. Gone. The thing resurfaced days later in another resident's room. In the meantime, it became very difficult with your father. He wouldn't tolerate any other remote control and even attacked one of my colleagues."

"I'm sorry," I said. "I noticed he had a bandage on his left arm. An injury?"

She nodded. "It is almost healed. Three of us had to hold him down when the beeper disappeared. He wouldn't swallow the sedative and became violent. He is old and has paper-thin skin, and it just…" She broke off.

"Tore," I completed her sentence. "It must have bled a lot."

"Yes." She shrugged her shoulders. "We really did our best."

"You do your job very well." I hastened to offer praise. "I know he can be unruly at times." I paused. "I am back, living in Hamburg. Now I'll be able to visit him more often."

The doctor smiled. "That will make your father happy. He has his enlightened moments."

"That's right," I replied and continued in my thoughts: *Unfortunately, the lucid phases are happening less and less. And one day there will be nothing left of my dad except his empty, wheezing body—exactly like the purple crocuses fading in the dying light of the day, and then night comes and plunges everything into impenetrable darkness.*

46

Everyone going his own way. Strobelsohn to the wife, Evelin to see her never-spoken-of father. Hell, even Henrik had plans. He was attending the Easter bonfires at the Hamburg Horn Racetrack.

Alex thought long and hard. Besides the failed marriage, he did not have any semblance of a family since his uncle passed away. And even he, could not have lent any solace.

The taxi had pulled up to the Blankenese Marina. Alex climbed behind his own wheel and started back in the direction from which he had just come.

He pondered the rest of his evening and realized he had no one to share it with.

Why could he never make it with the women he had been set up with? There was a problem of sorts, a mismatch. And when it came down to it, he was clearly the common denominator. He was the obstacle.

What could he say? He did not fit in modern society. That was it; he was no longer *fit* for a relationship.

There were plenty of reasons. For one, he couldn't share intimacies. Was he supposed to tell every woman he met what he had done? They wouldn't be able to understand.

But what about Evelin? She sounded levelheaded enough, for a soft science aficionado anyway. But Arne was right. She had set her ramparts high. She did not appear to let anyone get beyond those defenses.

Arne? Maybe Alex should run over to Wiesbaden. He shook his head… No. Right now, there was too much going on in Hamburg. He had no choice but to stay in the city.

A drink seemed ill-advised. There must have been a time when he was so exhausted and drained from work, he fell straight into his bed without a single drop. But that was long ago. Alex could not remember an evening in an eternity that he had not had at least one alcoholic beverage. And if he really was honest with himself, it never stopped after the first.

Okay, flitted through his head. *Let's test it. Sit at the bar and order only one.* Then he laughed at himself. Too late, there were those two shots at Georgios's. Evelin had declined hers, and in the guise of a true alcoholic Alex could not risk the precious aquavit going to waste.

Test failed. A drink it is. Alex opened his peripheral vision to scan for the warm promise of alcohol advertised through hot colored neon lights.

Funny that he thought of his late Uncle Frank and alcohol simultaneously. And then again, not. Frank had taught him a lot about drinking. For instance, that you could give in to its velvet allure and not let it rule you like it had his father.

Frank could knock them back with the best of them, including Alex's father, but it never struck him that he let the liquor get the upper hand. It was more than just being able to hold his own. His uncle gave into the abandonment of the elixir but remained in control.

When you start surrounding your life with it, Alex could hear his uncle's deep voice. *When you are singularly identified by it. Then it has assimilated you.*

That was another thing Alex remembered about his uncle. He always used words in ways that seemed to stretch their meaning a bit. And though he usually made a mental note to, Alex never got around to looking them up.

An ostensibly empty cocktail bar caught his eye. There was even an available parking space right out front. Alex backed into the spot and leaned forward to get a look at the clientele. One table of two girlfriends interested only in chatting with each other. Alex knew that, because no one was trying to hook up in an empty bar. The neatly aligned bottles and the elegantly written sign, *Surreptitious,* said finely poured cocktails and expensive whiskeys.

It sounds like rye and bitters will be on the menu this evening. Alex climbed out of his car eager to give in to his favorite vice.

He headed to a corner booth. "I'll have to research the card." He smiled and answered the bartender's silent question.

Backs against the wall. Was that his uncle's advice too? He truthfully couldn't recall. It sounded like one of those typical lines from a gangster movie he had seen when he was too little to comprehend.

With your back against the wall, you could tell when your enemy—or the opposite sex—would be making a frontal assault. But Alex was right. The two girls did not even notice the barman come over to get his order.

Alex let his eyes run quickly down the list of cocktails. "What's in an *Irish*?" he asked.

"Rye, Grand Marnier, and bitters," the barman rattled off emotionlessly.

"No. I believe I'll stick with an *Old Fashioned*."

The bartender made a short swelling of his cheeks that was supposed to represent a smile and a response of confirmation in one. He took the word *speakeasy* literally.

Alex lost count after the two girlfriends left. Before that, he had polished off three. Finally, he felt the place couldn't really afford to stay open just on his behalf, so he thought he would do the bartender a favor and head home so the man could too.

Alex lifted his right foot which tingled strangely like it had fallen asleep. He stood up and put his weight on the leg and immediately tipped over on his side. He was lucky enough to catch hold of the low couch he had been sitting on in the last second so that nothing was really hurt but his pride. And he wasn't so drunk to not know that it was irrelevant to the man he was about to settle with for the evening.

Alex dropped two bills on the table and stupidly gestured that it was for the bartender, but simultaneously raised an eyebrow asking if it was indeed enough to pay for the damages.

The barman, as quietly as he had said hello, shook his head in a way to assure Alex his check had been covered sufficiently and that he could continue on his way.

"With that, I'll bid you a good night," Alex stammered and shuffled to the front door.

"Well. Maybe, maybe not. We'll see later. I am cautiously optimistic," the barman said.

That was the weirdest damn thing Alex had ever heard anyone say, and then, for some reason or other, he had to think about Evelin. She had gone to see her father; she probably had a lot to talk about.

Without considering the late hour or his insobriety, Alex climbed behind the wheel of his oversized sedan. What he did consider was the next time he bought a car, he'd get a number smaller. He pulled away from the curb.

The time it took to travel the short distance passed obliviously in two forgotten, unrequited love songs. Alex turned up the volume, straightened his back, locked his elbows with both hands on the steering wheel, diligently made the last curve, and came to a standstill in front of Evelin's house.

All the lights are out but somebody's home, Alex thought and haphazardly shut the heavy car door harder than required.

He didn't remember climbing the stairs or pressing the bell, but he stood there ready to own the moment.

The outside light came on and the door opened a crack.

"Hi, I felt like I had to tell someone," he started.

Evelin opened the door wider. "What are you talking about?"

"Well, 'cause there's no one around."

"I don't get what you mean." She eyed him attentively.

"I tried. I really did. You give me the feeling that you'd understand…"

Her gaze grew more concerned. "What's the matter and why are you on my front step at one in the morning?"

"I just feel like such an ass. I wanted you to tell me I was an ass."

47

Evelin let him come in without a word. She led the way into the living room and switched on the light.

The room had not changed since his last visit: all the moving boxes still scattered, some half unpacked, others taped shut. A few pictures on the mantelpiece. She had neatly folded the blanket and placed it together with the throw pillow on the edge of the sofa. Alex sat down beside them.

She tightened the belt of her bathrobe and disappeared into the kitchen. The typical sound of cupboards opening and closing. She returned with a glass of sparkling water and handed it to him.

He took a sip. And then another. He was thirsty, he only realized that now.

She sat opposite him. He looked at her. Her hair disheveled, no makeup. She seemed vulnerable, albeit calm and in control. Without a trace of nervousness. As if it was nothing special for her to be roused out of bed in the middle of the night by a guy who, drunk and full of self-pity, was spouting some nonsense.

He put the glass down, twisted his mouth in embarrassment. "Oh," he said. "I don't know what got into me. I have no idea why I came here. I'm sorry, it was stupid of me."

She stayed somber. "Really?"

"It's probably the stress. I'm just a bit overworked." He laughed. That sounded affected, and phony even to him. "I have seen and experienced many things in my career. Albeit… The two cases we are working on… That doesn't justify my behavior…"

"So?" she said. Nothing further. She held her tongue again.

The silence dragged on. Alex picked up his glass and took a drink. He put it down.

She remained reticent. She just looked at him. With those blue eyes.

The sofa was uncomfortable. He shifted restlessly back and forth.

"Are you all right?" she asked.

What should he answer?

"Yeah," he said. "It's just my back… It's pressing me there."

He reached behind. "May I?"

She nodded.

He pulled his pistol out of its holster and put it on the coffee table next to the glass. The light reflected off the dark metal and the black plastic handle.

He leaned forward and pushed the gun farther away.

She looked at it briefly before she turned her attention back to him.

Silence creeped in again. Nearly unbearable.

"I'm terribly sorry I came and woke you up," he said. "I'll drink my water and then I'll go."

Her face did not change. "If that's what you want…"

"Yes, of course," he asserted.

She looked at him intently. "Or you could tell me what you came here to tell me."

"Me?" He acted surprised. He wanted to jump up and run out the door. But he didn't move.

"Sometimes," she said, "it takes courage."

"I am courageous," he replied.

"I don't doubt that," she said.

He reached out for the water glass, pulled back halfway, and looked at the gun instead. He took a deep breath, raised his gaze, and stared straight into the blue of her eyes.

"I was in the army for a while," he began.

"Mhmm." She didn't seem surprised.

"Foreign deployments. Two in Afghanistan."

She nodded.

"Peacekeeping, actually." He shrugged. "It sounds easy, but it's a lot more complicated. We always made sure that we kept the best possible interaction with the nationals."

"Mhmm."

"I had a local interpreter who spoke German. Ehsan. He had studied in Munich before returning home."

Ehsan… Alex fell silent. He shouldn't have even started. Anything else, but not this.

She waited a while. Then she said, "This interpreter, Ehsan, he helped you make contact with the public?"

"Yes," he heard himself say. "Ehsan was recognized and appreciated. He was with us a lot. Over time he became a real friend. He often stayed late into the evenings at our camp. Would watch movies with us. He liked romcoms."

Her eyes were merciless.

"One night," he continued, "Ehsan was on his way home, and the Taliban caught him. They tortured him badly." Alex paused. "I found him the next morning."

"Dead?"

"Of course," he hurried to reply.

Evelin looked at the gun. The muzzle pointed at her...

The howling of the wind. The pristine blue sky. The assault rifle in his hands. The brown houses with their flat roofs—their façade shot up, damaged, or destroyed by mortars. Not a soul in sight. But Alex knows that they are there, watching him from their hiding places.

Right in front of him is the dilapidated hut. A man nailed to the shed. Rusty iron spikes piercing his hands and ankles.

Alex places his finger on the trigger of his rifle and approaches carefully. The man raises his head strenuously. And only now Alex recognizes him: Ehsan, or what is left of him.

Ehsan is bleeding from a multitude of wounds.

This should never have happened! Not under any condition!

"Alex," Ehsan whispers hoarsely. "Please!"

Alex forcefully ripped himself out of the past. Evelin was still sitting opposite him. She didn't seem to have moved an inch.

"He wasn't dead when you found him, was he?" she said quietly, yet firmly.

He wanted to go wild. He wanted to argue. Tell her she was wrong... The memories came back. Insuppressible...

Ehsan's lips are swollen and chapped. His face barely recognizable. He mumbles more words that Alex cannot understand.

Alex leans his rifle against the hut. He gets close to his friend. Iridescent green flies ascend buzzing. Alex shoos them away, but they hover nearby. He can still hear them. They are just waiting to land on his friend anew.

Ehsan's clothes are torn and drenched in blood. There, where the knife has been rammed through the fabric.

Gently Alex unbuttons Ehsan's green jacket. Ehsan gasps and mumbles. Alex pulls up his friend's T-shirt a little and looks underneath it. Ehsan's belly is slit from the bottom left to the top right. His intestines spilling out pink and sinewy. Alex quickly drops the shirt and tries to close the jacket once more.

"Please, Alex," Ehsan moans. "Please."

Alex's gaze falls on Ehsan's crotch. This area is also red, and the pants are soaked in blood. They have mutilated his abdomen.

"Please," Ehsan murmurs again. "Please…"

Alex freezes. "No," he forces out feverishly. "I'll bring you back. To our doctor. He will…"

"Please, Alex… Look at me…"

Alex doesn't budge.

"Please…"

Alex's hand gropes for the pistol in the holster. He pulls it out, cocks it, and presses the muzzle of the gun against the bottom of Ehsan's chin.

"Please, Alex, please. You're my best friend. I… I can't take this anymore. I won't…"

Alex pulls the trigger. A deafening blast. The sound ricochets multiple times off the stone walls of the houses.

Alex closed his eyes briefly and opened them again. He took a deep breath.

Evelin examined him without emotion. "You shot him."

"There was nothing else I could do." His voice sounded rough.

"Ehsan would have died anyway?"

He had to clear his throat repeatedly. "The injuries were too severe. The pain, the awful pain. He couldn't bear it. No one could."

She pointed at the pistol. "You used that gun."

How did she know that? He nodded.

"And that's why you always carry it with you."

"Yeah. I don't want to forget."

She shook her head. "You're lying."

"Excuse me?" Anger flared up inside him. Where did she get the nerve to say he…

"You kept the gun for another reason as well," she persisted, undeterred.

Alex had to blink.

"When you can't stand it anymore, you plan to use it on yourself," she said.

That was it: the naked, unadorned truth. He had been afraid to say it out of fear of what this admission would do to himself. But now… Strangely enough, it felt different than he had feared. How? Lighter? Better.

"It's true," she said. "That gun is intended for you."

"Is it that obvious?" he asked.

"It is." She raised her eyebrows briefly. "That's why you drink every night. That's why you get into fights. You are trying with all of your might to destroy yourself."

She had gone too far!

"Bullshit!" he hissed. "Why should I do that? Do you think I'm crazy?"

"Crazy?" The shake of her head came promptly and clearly. "Not at all. You're punishing yourself because you cannot forgive yourself that you survived, and Ehsan did not."

Alex noticed that he was sitting on the very edge of the sofa. He leaned back.

"If you'd like, you can stay here tonight," she said. "On the couch."

"I don't want to be a bother," he replied automatically, although at that moment he would have rather done anything than go back out into the darkness alone.

She smiled. For the first time that evening. A warm, open smile. "It's no problem between friends."

She rose, took the blanket off the pillow, went to him and gently but firmly pushed him to the side. He let her do it. He lay down, and she spread the blanket over him.

"Good night." She made a move to step away.

"You have nothing to worry about," he said.

She looked at him.

He pointed at the pistol and repeated, "You have nothing to worry about."

"I'm not worried," she said. "Sleep tight."

She turned around, walked to the door, and switched off the light.

"See you in the morning," she remarked.

"See you in the morning," he replied.

March

28

Easter Sunday

48

In the dining room stood a lonesome table, made of simply adorned dark oak. It belonged to my grandmother. My sister had left it behind when she moved out. Probably because it was too heavy or too old-fashioned for her. I liked it.

In the one-room apartment in Wiesbaden, I had not had much space for furniture. And I had not yet been able to implement my plan of buying matching chairs and some chests of drawers or a display case for the house. Subsequently, the room looked as if I was currently using it as a warehouse, with most of my boxes stacked along the south wall. They were waiting to be unpacked. I had not even begun to get around to it.

I fetched two stools from the kitchen, dug out the lacy, white tablecloth and the good china—an indigo blue strawflower pattern—from one of the boxes and set everything out. I had bought rolls and croissants. I put them in a bowl and placed it on the table together with butter, jam, honey, muesli, and milk. Finally, the tea pot warmer and the coffee pot. Done.

I took a step back and appraised my work. An oasis in the midst of my chaos—not perfect, but the best that was possible under the circumstances.

When was the last time I made breakfast for someone other than myself? It had been long ago.

I heard a door close on the second floor, and shortly thereafter, Alex on the steps. His hair was damp from the shower. There was a bluish-black shadow covering his cheeks. I had been able to give him a fresh toothbrush, but I couldn't supply him with a razor. He looked good with the beginning of a stubbly beard. It gave him an adventurous appearance, especially when coupled with the open white shirt that he buttoned up while coming down the stairs.

I forced my thoughts elsewhere.

"Good morning," he greeted me and smiled, somewhat embarrassed.

"Good morning," I replied with a welcoming gesture. "Please have a seat."

Was that too much? Flitted through my mind.

But then he said, "I'd love to," as he sat down.

I took the chair across from him.

As if we had done this a hundred times before, Alex grabbed the pot and poured me coffee without my asking, handed me the cup and pushed milk and sugar in my direction. Then he served himself.

"Thanks for the shirt, by the by," he said. "Miraculously freshly washed."

That made me smile. "You're welcome. My washing machine has a fifteen-minute express cycle, and the dryer didn't need much longer."

I pointed to the bowl with the rolls. "I didn't know exactly what you like for breakfast."

"Buns are great," he said.

We remained silent for a while and ate.

He raised his eyes and looked around. "It's nice here," he observed staidly.

"It will be one day, if I ever finish unpacking," I replied.

"All the same." He glanced down at the table. "The room seems very… personal."

"There's no avoiding that," I said. "When you stay somewhere long enough, you inevitably take over the space, give it your own touch."

He seemed to be paying attention. "Always? I used to have my own four walls, but that is another story. Ever since I lost my house in the divorce I have been, more or less, a single-room dweller."

I didn't know what he was getting at. "Yes, of course, that's always the case. I feel that way even in hotels. After the first half hour I have arranged my things, where I need them, and how I like them. An imprint of my own personality, so to speak… Why do you ask?"

"Why? I was looking at Suzanne Carstens's room with Gert Strobelsohn."

"The one in the villa?"

"Right. You deliberately didn't want to see it."

I nodded. "Otherwise, I would have had a preconceived opinion of her."

"Well, in the end, you hadn't missed much." He took another bun and cut it open.

"How come?"

He spread butter on both halves. "Because it was practically empty. It came off… barren, like in a furniture store. You know, where they put cardboard dummies of books, usually Goethe, to make it look homey." He grabbed the honey. "It puzzled Strobelsohn and me somewhat."

"Really? It doesn't surprise me at all."

"No?"

"No," I asserted. "Think about it. She witnessed her mother's abuse in the villa for years. She must have hated it there. She was forced to stay in that house. But she never really lived in Blankenese, let alone made a *home* there."

Alex's mouth turned up. "I don't mean it badly… Maybe she is just a psycho. A hot mess. Disturbed and unable to give her surroundings her own touch."

"That's not true." I shook my head. "You're forgetting the Ad Astra. Her yacht. Every square inch breathes her personality. The boat is distinctively furnished. With her own belongings… things that have meaning to her. That's where she lives, in the moments she is on the Ad Astra." I hesitated. "Her mother probably had it like that, and she kept it the same way."

"Hmm." Alex stared into space.

"What are you thinking about?" I asked him.

His eyes focused on me. "I'd love to take a closer look at that boat."

"What's stopping you?"

"Well… I don't think it is a good idea to ask Suzanne Carstens to do it. Or to have a snoop about. I could never get a search warrant."

"You don't need one," I said. "I know where she keeps the key to the cabin."

He frowned. "But I can't…"

"But I can," I interrupted him. "I'm not a prosecutor. And as I just happened to remember, I must have forgotten my favorite pen there. Down in the cabin. I absolutely need it." I smiled.

Alex's expression clearly showed me that he was not convinced.

"Just come with me."

He nibbled at his lower lip briefly. "What if someone sees us? What then?"

I grinned wider. "In the morning after the Easter fires? The few boats on that little dock? Everyone will be sleeping off last night's drunk."

49

I unlocked the hatch to the cabin and peeked down into the small, squat room. I could not see much; it was too dark. I felt around for the switch with my fingers and flipped on the light. Then I descended the few steps, turned and motioned for Alex to join me.

He followed with his head ducked low. He looked around. "Pretty cramped."

"But very functional. Everything you need is here," I said, pointing toward the bow. "There is another bunk there. And stowed underneath it are the blankets." I touched one of the built-in drawers. "There are some provisions in here. Cans, cookies, things like that."

"You spent the night in this tiny room, you and Suzanne Carstens?" he inquired incredulously.

"Went surprisingly well," I confirmed. "It was actually quite comfortable."

"And this is where she told you about her mother and grandfather?"

"That's right," I said. "Then she even showed me a photo of her mother."

"Can I see it?"

"Sure. I don't think she would mind." I opened a drawer. Playing cards, a few CDs. Two paperbacks, detective stories, dog-eared. No photos. I found what I was searching for in the next drawer. I grabbed the framed picture and held it out to Alex. He leaned closer.

"Suzanne Carstens and her mother look exactly alike."

"That was my first impression as well," I said.

"And the man next to her?"

"Suzanne cut him out. I suspect it was her grandfather."

"May I?" Alex took the photo out of my hand, narrowed his eyes, and examined it more closely. "Uh-huh, Björn Carstens."

"You seem to be pretty sure of that," I said.

He tapped his finger on the wrist of the arm wrapped around Suzanne's mother. "Look here. The cufflink."

"Oh yeah," I said. "Is that one of the cufflinks... which was found in Carstens's grip and its match in that blasted open safe?"

"Exactly."

I frowned. "Strange. It..."

That was as far as I got. Alex's phone rang.

He made an apologetic gesture, took it out of his pocket, and held it to his ear. In doing so, he straightened up and hit his head against the low ceiling of the cabin. He cursed under his breath and then said, "Gutenberg... Aha... Oh! Where's that?" He looked at me. "Of course. I'm in the neighborhood right now with Dr. Wolf. We'll probably get there before you. Yes. I'll see you soon." He lowered his cell phone.

"What is it?" I asked him.

"That was Captain Strobelsohn. Hamdy had called him from a crime scene."

"Where exactly?" I inquired.

"At one of the Easter fires. Just a few minutes from here. Hamdy had strongly suggested that we come check it out."

50

Alex climbed behind the wheel and looked irritably at his dashboard's display. It had only been six months, so he remembered where to go in the menu to change the clock. Daylight savings: An hour of life passed in the flip of the dial.

Evelin's eyes met his from the passenger seat. "I had nearly forgotten. That is why I am so tired."

"You think you are suffering." Alex closed his eyes and rubbed his temples to accentuate his misery. "I felt as if a semi-truck ran through my head when you came down the stairs this morning."

He pushed the start button, the engine came to life, and he drove the car off the small parking lot of the deserted Blankenese Yacht Club. Heading directly through town, he could see the former fishing village. Today the streets were nearly bare, and he was able to better observe the traditional stucco homes built on the inclines of the old center.

Two right turns, and he was back on the banks of the Elbe. Relatively desolate this morning, several blackened spots on the ground with towering vestiges of charred timber revealed where bonfires had burned the night before.

Around a high pile of scorched wood was a ring of police cars, two ambulances and one long fire truck. A red and white tape barrier was lined with a half dozen people trying to get a better look at what had been found in their neighborhood.

More specifically, what they were gawking at was the evidence collection team painstakingly dismantling the pile of burnt wood and pallets, piece by piece. A female officer in uniform ensured none of the on-lookers crossed the barrier.

Alex parked his BMW. He and Evelin climbed out. Together, they made their way around the spectators.

Hamdy appeared out of the midst of the crew, wearing a hood and gloves of a matching royal blue. He approached Alex and Evelin and gave a sign to the policewoman to let them enter. The officer nodded and lifted the plastic tape. Alex and Evelin ducked under it.

Alex made a short shrug in the guise of a greeting. "Hi Hamdy. Has Captain Strobelsohn already arrived?"

Hamdy stopped a good two yards in front of them and waved a gloved hand. "Not yet."

"What do you have for us?"

"There has been a lot of precipitation in the last week, and to get the Easter fires going"—Hamdy displayed the area with the swing of an arm—"whoever was in charge here used gasoline."

"That usually does the trick," Evelin stated.

"Yes, it worked this time too." Hamdy frowned. "The pile was blazing. But then, the wind kicked in. The fire grew out of control."

"Did someone get hurt during that?" Evelin asked.

"*During* that, luckily not. The fire department came in time. They put out the flames."

Alex raised an eyebrow. "You said *during*."

"Around an hour ago, a group of kids were here cleaning up the mess from the bonfires. A young girl discovered a foot sticking out of the heap. They said she flipped out. Her boyfriend immediately dialed the police, and our colleagues called me in."

"You found a body?" Evelin inquired.

"Two victims, a male and a female. The evidence collection team have extracted the remains. They did not have an easy time with it. But because the bonfire had been extinguished after only burning a few minutes the corpses were not completely mutilated. And as soon as I saw one had three fingers missing… I remembered the van carrier operator from the Burchardkai docks you were searching for. That's when I called Captain Strobelsohn."

Alex nodded slowly. "Thank you, Hamdy. Is it the dock worker, then? Were you able to identify him?"

Hamdy shook his head. "We'll have to request dental records. Today is Sunday. Tomorrow, Easter Monday. It will take some time before we have a definitive answer. But the age seems to match the description of the van carrier pilot, as does the build. Then there are the three missing fingers… I think we can assume with some degree of certainty that this is the man you're looking for."

"What about the woman?" Evelin asked.

"She could be your vanished customs agent, but the same applies here; the corpse matches the description, but even then, only the dental records can verify our suspicion," Hamdy qualified.

Out of the corner of his eye, Alex noticed two men approaching. Strobelsohn and Henrik. He turned in their direction.

"Hello captain. Hello Henrik," he said as they arrived, pointing at the burnt debris from the bonfire. "Two corpses have been found in there. Hamdy seems to think these are our missing dock workers."

"The van carrier pilot and the customs lady?" Henrik asked.

Hamdy nodded.

"That would explain why they both disappeared without a trace" Strobelsohn groused.

They shook hands.

"Nice, that you could join us," Strobelsohn said to Evelin, and Henrik grinned affably.

Evelin smiled before she turned back to Hamdy. "Have you put together what happened? The man and woman weren't burned alive, were they?"

"No. Hamdy responded quietly. "I must surmise they were already dead when they were placed under the makings of the Easter bonfire."

Alex looked at him. "Are you sure?"

"I'm positive. And you'll be too, after you've seen the victims. Let me show you…"

"Will that be necessary?" Strobelsohn interrupted.

"I think so," Hamdy said. "The nature of the injuries could be important for your investigation."

Hamdy led the way behind the fire trucks where a high-walled tent had been erected. Inside, hidden from prying eyes of the onlookers, two gurneys bore body bags.

Slowly, he unzipped the gray plastic sack containing the dead man. Strobelsohn and Henrik immediately raised their hands. Alex could not be certain if their sudden reaction was to block the view or ward off the cloying smell of burned flesh. Obviously, it had gotten to Strobelsohn in such a manner that he left the tent in search of air.

The body reminded Alex of victims of suicide bombers he had witnessed in the Middle East. The carbonized corpse before him had most of its skin removed by the fire. A mosaic of cracked puzzle pieces loosely organized to form a blackened bark of what was left.

Captain Strobelsohn returned to stand next to Alex on the edge of the gurney.

"You see this here?" Hamdy said as he gently moved the corpse a little to the side, pointing at the wrists. "These are traces of a zip tie. The plastic has been melted into the tissue by the heat of the fire." He indicated two hollows on either side of the spine. "And their shoulders have been dislocated."

Alex's face hardened. "I know what that is. The KGB called it *the swan*: bound hands raised behind the back. All their weight hung on their wrists, and when the joints give in it looks like an aquatic bird batting its wings." He paused. "I heard about it when I was in Afghanistan. I had a friend, Ehsan, who told me about the ways the Russians would torture the Mujahideen they had captured."

"They also had suction scars on their faces." Hamdy pointed at triangular bruises around the nose that despite the severe burns could be derived.

Alex cleared his throat. "They connect a vacuum to a gas mask, which nearly suffocates the victim. It is called *the elephant*, another method the KGB used to torture."

In contrast to Strobelsohn, Henrik did not seem to be fazed by the site of the burned corpse. "You said they were dead when they were buried under the wood. When were these bonfires built?"

Hamdy shrugged his shoulders. "Well, the victims seem to have succumbed sometime Friday night. I will be able to give you more accurate answers after the autopsy."

Evelin waited until he had finished. "A lot of the bonfires were already erected when Suzanne Carstens and I returned yesterday morning from our… sailing trip." She glanced down at the corpses once again. "They must have suffered a lot."

Alex clapped his hands together. "I'm sure they did. These are cruel torture techniques. That's why they are so effective."

As Hamdy nodded in agreement, Strobelsohn grew pale and breathed loudly through his mouth.

"Did they die from the torture?" Evelin looked equally moved.

"No," Hamdy answered. "They have both been shot in the back of the neck."

Alex pricked up his ears. "You mean, they were *executed*?"

Hamdy nodded quietly.

"This was not a murder of passion. The perpetrator or perpetrators proceeded calmly, calculated and with efficiency," Evelin said.

Strobelsohn seemed to have shaken his discomfort. He narrowed his eyes. "But there is just one thing I don't understand. Why didn't they simply dump the bodies into the river or bury them somewhere in the woods?"

"What do you mean?" Alex did not follow.

"That's crystal clear," Henrik interjected. "It would have been much easier and faster to sink them in the Elbe or drop the stiffs in the woods. In order to hide the bodies under the Easter bonfire, the perps had to at least partly dismantle and rebuild the pyramid of branches and pallets. This was a feat that took time and considerable effort."

"You're right," Alex agreed, and noticed a slight blush of pride come over Henrik's face.

Strobelsohn smirked in his peculiar, disgruntled way. "So why did the perps take the unnecessary risk of getting caught?"

"There's a logical explanation," Evelin said.

"And what is it?" Henrik asked.

"They hid the bodies on purpose in the bonfire. Because it was a message. An unequivocal threat."

"A threat?" Alex asked. "For whom?"

"I don't know." Evelin shook her head back and forth. She stood still for a moment. "It appears as if they had been trying to get some information out of our suspects."

"OK, I agree," Alex said.

"And you seem to be convinced that these are KGB torture techniques."

"That's right."

Evelin stared into space. "The victims most likely worked at Burchardkai." She looked Alex straight on. "Is it possible… do you think Dimitri could be behind this?"

"It's not completely out of the question," Alex said as he gnawed on his lower lip.

"Yeah, it *has* to be related to our ghastly discovery in the container on the docks and the human trafficking," Strobelsohn said. "There's no other plausible explanation."

Henrik fidgeted his fingers through his hair and shifted his weight from one foot to the other. "We had better get a move on it. This happened more than twenty-four hours ago. We need to get an APB out on them."

"On whom?" Alex snorted. "We have no idea what these people look like. We have no names, no descriptions. This is the biggest dead end of a week full of dead ends."

51

Strobelsohn had gone to the office with Henrik to file witness testimonies. Neither of them had appeared particularly enthusiastic. I could understand that. They had been looking forward to their first day off in over a week, and now that was not going to happen.

Hamdy accompanied the remains of the victims to the pathology ward. He intended to carry out the autopsies immediately.

It was just after one. Alex and I could not do anything for the time being. I hesitated, then I simply asked him if he would like to go to Georgios's with me. He said yes without hesitation. Apparently, he did not want to be alone on Easter Sunday either. Or did he want to spend time with me off the clock?

What nonsense! I dismissed these childish thoughts, which would lead to nothing anyway. Instead, I leaned back in the passenger seat, let the moment rule me, and enjoyed the ride. Alex knew how to handle a car. We glided smoothly along.

Neither he nor I felt the need to speak. The calm did me good.

We were not the only ones who had the idea of eating out on the holiday. The street in front of the Poseidon was full. Eventually, Alex found a space three blocks away. He parked the BMW, and we got out. It was cool, but it smelled like spring. Together we strolled along the Alster Riverwalk.

I stopped and watched a small paddle boat in which a family of four was sitting. The children were still young. They all wore bright orange life jackets. Laughing, they passed us by, leaving a fading white trail of froth in the dark water.

"Dreadful," I said more to myself.

"Huh?" Alex gave me a look.

"What people can do to other people."

He nodded. "Torture is always terrible."

I looked at the river and the happy people, trying to quash the dismal images from the Easter fire. I did not succeed.

"What's wrong?" Alex asked me after a while.

Only then did I realize that he had most likely been eyeing me the whole time. Strangely, I did not mind.

"When someone tortures somebody," I said, "they need space and seclusion. They do not want to be disturbed. They have to be able to concentrate on their work."

"That's right," Alex confirmed.

I turned to him. "The question remains… Where do you find that in Hamburg?"

"There are a thousand places." He shrugged his shoulders. "The city is huge."

"Yes, but if you're from out of town? If we assume that the interrogation methods are techniques of the former KGB, the person who used them is not necessarily from here. Then he doesn't know his way around very well. Where would someone like that go?"

Alex took his time with an answer. "He would choose a place he knew."

We fell silent.

"And suppose," I started again, "that the victims from the Easter fire and the container full of suffocated women are related. Would that help us narrow it down?"

Alex inflated his cheeks and let the air flow out audibly. "I don't know. All the brothels… The women have been temporarily relocated…" He paused and furrowed his brow.

"Are you thinking of something in particular?"

"The only place that spontaneously comes to mind that's secluded… on the outskirts, but not too far away, would be the farmhouse on that property."

"Which property?"

"The old farm where this van carrier driver said he always transported and deposited the other containers from Burchardkai."

My heart started pounding with excitement. "Do you have the address?"

"Not here. In the office, in my files." He drew his eyes together. "But I remember. The house is near the Mellingburg lock."

"I know the area from way back," I replied. "The lock is north of the city. A nature reserve… There aren't many buildings there."

"Besides, the farmhouse has been vacant for years," Alex said. "It should be easy to find."

I looked at him in anticipation.

"Do you want to go there?" he asked.

I nodded.

"Now?"

"Why not. Or do you have something better to do?"

"No." He hesitated. "We just shouldn't expect too much from this. Even if that's where the torture took place… These were professionals. They did it on Thursday or possibly Wednesday. Most likely on Friday night, they buried the bodies in the Easter fire. Today is Sunday. They're probably long gone by now."

"Presumably," I agreed with him. "But at least we would have identified the scene of the crime."

He smiled slightly. "That would help us."

"So?" I said. "What if we take a short trip?"

"What about lunch?"

I could not help from laughing. "Suggestion: We'll have Georgios pack us some snacks, and we'll eat them on the way."

52

Stairway to Heaven resonated quietly over the sound system. Alex began to hum along, at first cautiously, then unabashedly, while we crept over the country lane in his BMW. Suddenly, he broke off and gave me a sheepish glance. "Sorry."

"Hmm?" I said.

"The singing. I'm not used to having a passenger."

"Doesn't bother me at all," I replied. "I like Led Zeppelin."

"Nevertheless." He narrowed his eyes and stared outside. "I had thought the search would be easier. Now where is this damn shack?"

"Let's call Strobelsohn," I suggested. "Henrik will have the address within a minute. He'd grab the file and… voilà."

"*Voilà*," he muttered.

I hesitated. "Why didn't we think to call the LKA right off?"

Alex smiled briefly. "It was nice for a change. Just the two of us." He did not look at me but pretended to focus on the surroundings.

I acted as if his remark was nothing special, although I had to admit to myself that it pleased me.

"True. Pretty nice," I said as casually as possible.

He drove around a gentle curve, which branched off onto an unmarked dirt road pocked with potholes.

"*Klabautermann Stieg*," I read from the GPS.

Alex braked and tapped on the steering wheel with two fingers. "That's it! We're in the right place. How could I have forgotten that? Good old Klabautermann!" He turned onto the narrow dirt drive and slowed down further. Even moving along at a crawl, and considering his luxury car was certainly equipped with excellent shock absorbers, we were shaken up.

"Klabautermann," I repeated. "That is a ghost."

"A *ship's goblin*," he corrected me with a jokingly raised forefinger. "Lives aboard and warns the captain of imminent danger."

I turned to him. "You don't seriously believe in those old wives' tales?"

"I'm a real Hamburger. Like you. We are the progeny of seafaring men." He smiled. "Do not deny your roots!"

We passed a dense, natural deciduous forest with undergrowth. In front of us sat a lone farmhouse with an ancient stable attached. Lush moss grew on the partly sunken thatched roof. In the back of the property stood a brick barn with a rusted corrugated steel roof.

The whole estate seemed desolate and abandoned. Weeds sprouted all over the gray rock, covering the driveway.

"This must be it," Alex said.

53

The gravel crunched under the wheels of the BMW. Alex let the car roll far into the yard. Then he came to a stop and turned off the engine.

We climbed out.

I looked around. A real wasteland. No neighbors, not a soul in sight. I could make out the sound of water in the distance. That must be the locks.

"No one's been here for ages," I said. "I think we could have saved ourselves the trip."

"You're probably right," Alex replied. "But while we're here, it wouldn't hurt to explore a bit."

Without waiting for my answer, he set off and walked single-mindedly toward the farmhouse. I followed him.

He tried the door. To my great astonishment, it was unlocked. Alex put his shoulder into it, and it sprang open. The rusted hinges protested with a piercing squeak.

A sound, similar to an angry hissing, and something jumped at us. I involuntarily leaped backward. A brown ball of fur shot between Alex and me and disappeared in the nearby undergrowth.

"Feral cat," Alex remarked.

"Oh, really?" I replied snappishly.

He grinned.

We peered inside the building. An empty hallway, full of cobwebs. Thick dust all over the floor with distinct paw prints. In one of the corners lay a dead bird. A narrow staircase led up to the upper level.

We stepped in. Alex turned right, toward the first room.

"Wait," I said, holding him by the sleeve.

He spun back around to me. "What is it?"

"Your coat. It's dirty."

"Oh, damn," he said, squinting at his shoulder. "I bet that's the paint from the door. It must have flaked off."

"Stand still." I tried my best to clop the spot clean.

"Thanks," he said. He removed his trench coat, shook it off, and put it over his arm. "That's the other option."

Together, we explored the first floor. Several small rooms, all empty. Some of the blinds were broken.

"What a dump," he remarked.

"I don't know what you see," I said. "With a little imagination, you could make a showcase out of this."

"*Showcase*." He twisted his mouth mockingly. "Imagination alone won't get you far. You'll have to have a pile of money."

"Yeah, so? Hamburg is expensive. And a single-family dwelling in the city and still out in nature… I think it has something."

We were back in the hallway.

Alex looked thoughtfully at the stairs. He grabbed the shaky handrail and climbed two steps. The planks under his feet creaked and snapped alarmingly.

"Do you really want to go up there?" I asked him.

"Why not?"

"Why? Because the stairs might collapse under you?"

"Nonsense." He shook his head and turned away.

"Okay," I said to his back. "I warned you. I'm going to stay down here and snoop around for a while."

"See you soon," he said and disappeared from my field of vision.

I heard his footsteps above me as I inspected the rooms once more. I reached the kitchen. There was a door on the opposite wall.

"It's just a bunch of swallows' nests up here!" shouted Alex from above. "And bird shit."

"Your own fault! You're the one who absolutely had to go up," I said out loud.

I opened the door.

The stable. Of course. I had seen it on the way in. It was attached to the house. Practical. And it smelled the way stables usually smell. Of hay and straw and something else that I could not place.

The windows were boarded up. I peered into the darkness, but could not make out much.

Flashlight. I felt inside my jacket and took out my mobile phone. I lowered my head and looked for the app…

I was seized by the upper arms—an iron grip. Someone dragged me forward. I stumbled, felt a blow on my temple. The pain exploded in my head, the phone slipped away from me, and I sank to the ground, powerless.

Unconsciousness threatened to engulf me. I fought against it, felt my arms being ripped backward. Fiery clamps cut deep into my wrists. I was bound, probably with a wire or cable tie. A piece of cloth muzzled my mouth. It stank, I choked, I could hardly breathe.

My assailant dragged me like a wet sack farther into the room, away from the entrance. He just left me there.

The fainting returned in waves. But I did not give in to it.

The dull sound of footsteps muffled through to me. They were directly above. It had to be Alex.

"An old chest of drawers has been abandoned by the previous occupants," he shouted. "Chew marks. Looks like animals have been gnawing on it. I'd better not open it, or a rat might jump at me too!"

In the meantime, my eyes had gotten used to the darkness. Traces of daylight crept between the cracks in the boarded-up windows, a little filtered through the open door into the stable. Every time Alex moved on the second floor, dust and sand trickled down. The small particles danced through the air of the luminous slats before disappearing into the darkness.

Now I could see my assailant. A tall, brawny guy. Pressed against the wall, he lurked just to the left of the entrance. He held a pistol in his hand.

An ambush, I thought. *He is going to clobber Alex.*

My heart started beating like crazy and my gaze raced around. It stopped on the ceiling. There, some heavy metal hooks had been screwed into the black wooden beams. On the floor below, dark liquid. Dried blood. Next to it… I concentrated… gas masks. Two of them.

Alex's words came to mind. What had he said earlier? By the remnants of the Easter fire when Hamdy showed us the corpses?

In Afghanistan, they connected a vacuum cleaner or a suction device to a gas mask. This nearly suffocates the victims. They called it the elephant, another favorite from the KGB's extensive catalog of torture.

Paralyzing, icy-cold panic spread through me. I would die here. This was where Alex and I would end. Like those two dockworkers. They had been tortured in this stable.

A rumble above me. "I opened the chest of drawers. You haven't missed anything up here. It's empty."

His strides drew away. He came down the stairs.

I had to warn him. It was our only chance. Our *last* chance.

I tried to set myself free, I was squirming back and forth. The pain in my joints became unbearable. I almost swallowed the stinking gag. I choked again. No sound, not even a squeak, could escape my throat.

"Evelin, it's going to require some serious cash to fix this up," Alex kept talking out loud. "But I agree with you. The view from up there… it could be incredibly attractive and worthwhile."

He took a few more steps down. My fear became immeasurable.

And then… I could not believe it. He started half humming, half singing. *Stairway to Heaven.*

That stupid, stupid song! Why was he humming it now? Didn't he realize what was happening to me? Why didn't he notice that I had not answered forever?

Again, I coiled up in an effort to spit out the rag. Unsuccessfully.

Alex's shadow fell into the room. Then he stepped through the open door. He was still singing. Somewhat off-key. Quietly. He had not noticed the slightest thing that had happened to me. He had no idea of the danger he was in.

Alex, I cried out to him in desperation in my thoughts. *Please! Watch out!*

My assailant raised his arm and pressed the muzzle of his weapon against the back of Alex's head.

Alex's humming suddenly broke off. He stopped.

"You," said the stranger. "Kneel." He spoke with a heavy Russian accent.

Now, I understood. He was planning to shoot Alex in the neck. Clean and neat, like the victims from the Easter fire. And then it was my turn.

Alex did not look at me. Instead, he spun to the Russian without any haste, his coat still casually thrown over his arm. As if nothing was wrong.

The two men stared at one another.

"You." The Russian made one quick motion with his pistol. "Down. Kneel."

Alex nodded once.

A shot rang out. And a second one.

The Russian was hit in the torso. He stumbled backward into the wall which he had been previously leaning against, firing a single round from his gun. I felt the bullet fly right past my cheek.

The Russian collapsed.

Alex dropped his coat. Some smoke rose from the fabric. In his hand, which now came into view, was his gun.

54

The shots echoed in my ears. Immobilized, I kept my eye on Alex. He stepped straight up to the dead man and kicked the weapon out of his lifeless fingers. The pistol slid across the wooden floor with a whir.

Alex bent down and groped with his free hand for the carotid artery of the Russian. His firearm was pointed at the Russian's head the whole time.

A few seconds later, which felt more like an eternity, he rose and hurried over to me.

He crouched down beside me. He boorishly pulled the gag out of my mouth while simultaneously concentrating his attention on the entrance. He still held his gun in his hand.

I choked, almost had to throw up.

"Are you all right?" he asked, after I was more or less back to my senses. He did not let the door out of his sight. He appeared calm, but I could feel that he was extremely tense.

I took several deep breaths and finally cleared my throat. "I'm fine," I said. "As well as can be expected."

"Your wrists," he said. "Come closer."

I slid a little bit in his direction and turned my back to him.

He felt my wrists and tried to loosen the cable ties with his left hand. He did not succeed.

A noise. And then a loud crash. Outside, not far from us.

Alex raised his pistol and aimed at the entrance.

"What was that?" I whispered.

"Quiet!" he replied voicelessly.

I understood. The Russian had not been alone. He had at least one partner. And he or they were about to storm the room to finish what their friend had failed to do.

Fear rose inside me. My pulse pounded painfully in my temples.

A motor started up, howling, and then a car raced past the house. Countless pebbles crashed furiously against the boarded-up windows.

Alex got on his feet in a flash. "I'll be right back. Stay here."

He ran out of the stable. For a moment I heard his footsteps fading… and then, nothing.

My anxiety threatened to crush me. I had to do something to free myself and get ready, in case Alex did not return, but what?

The dead Russian's gun! Quick! I let myself fall on my rear, bending my legs. I ignored the almost unbearable burning and stinging in my wrists and forced my bound arms below my buttocks, along the back of my thighs, and around my feet.

My hands were in front of me again.

Staggering, I got up, rushed to the dead man's weapon, and picked it up.

Footfalls in the corridor.

Trembling, I raised the firearm. My finger on the trigger.

"It's me, Evelin," sounded a voice. Alex.

He entered the room, took a quick glance at the pistol in my hand, and nodded.

I let my arms sink. Tears came to my eyes. I blinked them away.

"And?" I asked with a cracked voice.

"There was at least one more," Alex said. "He got away."

My tension eased a little. All of a sudden, I noticed that I had a severe headache from the blow.

I pulled myself together. "Should we follow him?"

"He's long gone." Alex secured his pistol and put it in the holster he wore on his back.

"Did you get the plate number?"

"No. Not a chance. It was a gray Toyota," he said.

I suppressed a shiver.

He came to me, put his arm around me, and held me tight. It was not necessary, but it was just right at that moment.

"Now show me the damn cable ties so I can finally free you up," he eventually said.

55

Alex and I used the back exit of the stable and stepped outside. The distant burble of the water could be heard as dark clouds swept above us, headed toward the coast.

My wrists burned like fire. They were sore. The cable binders had cut deep into the skin. The vicious pain on the side of my head came in waves. I ignored both as best I could.

The barn door was wide open. I tried to see something inside, but the distance was too great and the room itself too dark.

"I have to inform our colleagues," Alex said.

"Of course," I replied.

Alex took his cell phone out of his pocket, and I listened to him talking without paying attention to his words. Eventually, he got off. The conversation had probably only lasted a minute but seemed to take forever.

"Strobelsohn and Henrik are on the way with an investigation unit," he said.

I nodded and stared at the barn. Out of the corner of my eye, I noticed that he too was concentrating on the building.

"They must have been hiding in there the entire time," Alex said after a while.

"I assume you're right," I acknowledged.

We continued to stare at the barn.

He took a deep breath. "Forensics will come and investigate the scene thoroughly."

I remained silent.

"That's the procedure," he continued. "We're involved. We cannot and should not…" He broke off.

I kept still.

He cleared his throat. "You think we should have a look now?"

I nodded again and turned to him.

He opened his mouth to answer, then closed it. Then he said, "OK."

Together we walked over the neglected gravel. My heels half sank between the small stones. They crunched with every step we took.

While walking, Alex pulled his gun out of its holster and let it hang loosely at his side.

"Stay behind me," he murmured as we approached the barn in a sweeping motion.

We had reached the left edge of the weathered wooden door. Carefully, Alex peered around the corner.

"A mobile home," he said softly.

He gave me an unequivocal signal not to move, brought his pistol to the ready. With straightened elbows, he quietly drew back the hammer and crept in.

I waited briefly and followed him.

Slightly stooped, we stalked toward the trailer. It was filthy, covered with dust, and looked old. It had been standing there for a long time.

Alex positioned himself at the side of the narrow entrance. I pressed myself behind him against the camper. In a flash, Alex ripped open the door and paused.

We listened attentively. Nothing.

He pushed himself forward, inch by inch, with the pistol raised until he could see the interior. He looked to the left, and then to the right, exhaled in relief, and let the gun drop.

"No one here," he said.

I stepped up to him and also peered into the mobile home. Two beds with rumpled blankets, beer cans and liquor bottles, packaging, dirty dishes in the small sink. Several pots stacked one inside the other on the hotplate.

There were photographs hanging on the wall opposite me. Full sheets of paper, like out of a printer.

I pointed. "What's that there? Can you see them?"

Instead of answering, Alex pulled out his cell phone and turned on the flashlight.

Pictures of various people. Some had been crossed out with a red felt-tip marker. A man and a woman.

"Who are they?" I asked Alex.

He bit his lower lip. "The two victims from the Easter fire. The van carrier driver and the customs agent."

But these were not the only pictures on the wall. The killers had pinned four more up. And they were unmarked.

"Oh my god!" I gasped. "That is Suzanne Carstens in those photos. You have to notify Strobelsohn immediately!"

Alex already had the phone to his ear. The light from the flashlight danced through the dark room. "The guy we rousted up out of here, that murderous pig, is on his way to her," he said to me, waiting for Strobelsohn to pick up. "Suzanne Carstens is the last on the list. She is supposed to die as well."

56

Alex spun the car around backward in one fluid sweep. He slid the shifter into drive. Evelin grabbed the dashboard and supported herself with one hand to catch her balance, lost by the sudden change of direction.

They quickly pulled away from the old farmhouse. The car seemed to take the potholes of Klabautermann Stieg much better at top speed. Still, Alex worried momentarily about ripping off the oil pan, because it would bring their pursuit to a sudden end.

He cleared his voice and said distinctly, "Call Strobelsohn."

The dial tone sounded. The connection was made. After the second beep, the speakers cracked loudly, and Alex felt transported into a squad car as its siren came screaming over the sound system.

"Captain Strobelsohn?" Alex said with a loud voice. "Are you on the way to Miss Carstens's Hotel?"

"Yes," Strobelsohn replied. "Mr. Breiter immediately changed course when you first informed us. We called in back-up. Two officers entered the Hotel Atlantic some minutes before, but we have not had contact with the guard at the door. We are preparing for the worst. I..."

"231, 231, shots have been exchanged—we have a hostage situation. Requesting more back-up. Officer in danger." The police band could be heard over Strobelsohn's telephone. "I repeat: We have a hostage situation at the downtown Kempinski; Police officer is in danger, all able bodies respond, that's a 230 Helicopter deployment. 231 Downtown Kempinski. All able bodies, 230—standby." Another voice came over the channel. "The suspect and his hostage are descending in a rear service elevator—Over."

"Shit," Strobelsohn cursed. "Did you catch that, Mr. Gutenberg?"

"I did." Alex bit his lower lip. He reached the highway and pressed down harder on the accelerator. The car lunged forward.

"And, where are you?" Strobelsohn asked at the same time.

The sudden burst of speed shifted Evelin deeper into her seat. "We are still twenty, maybe fifteen minutes away," she said compellingly.

The police band came over the sedan's Harman Kardon sound system. "Suspect has left building in black C-Class Mercedes four-door sedan, 031, 107. Officer in critical condition, additional fatality in the garage. Repeat—suspect entering the street *Alsterwiete* in a black four-door Mercedes sedan."

Alex did not bother to ask if the reinforcements had arrived in time. It seemed like it all had happened in a matter of seconds. But these few moments were more than enough for the perpetrator to take out the guard, enter Suzanne Carstens's suite, and kill her...

"Oh my God! Suzanne!" Evelin murmured next to him. Apparently, she had come to the same conclusion as he.

But from what he had heard over the radio, only one fatality had been reported. He at first thought it would be better to not give Evelin any false hope. Yet then said, "It sounds like there have only been two victims and just one of them killed."

"Maybe they haven't had a chance to check inside her hotel suite. With all the action around freeing their colleague," Evelin replied. His reassuring words had failed to comfort her.

Alex tried anew. "The fact that the officer was taken hostage is more likely to indicate that the perp had to have changed his plans." He had to admit that did not sound convincing, even to himself.

Evelin did not pay him any mind. "Captain Strobelsohn, are you still there?" she asked instead.

Alex pursed his lips and looked sidelong for an answer.

"Yes ma'am," Strobelsohn replied. "I'm afraid to say that even with the helicopter dispatched, a black Mercedes sedan disappears in this city in a matter of two sharp turns."

Henrik's voice came over the sound system. "The APB has just gone out. The description is notably lacking in detail. Male, approximately six feet tall, slender build, Russian accent." He muttered a suppressed curse followed by, "Get out of the way, you idiot!"

A long pause, and then he came back markedly calmer. "The officer who was taken hostage might be able to give more details. She'll have been moved to the hospital. Evidently, she is concussed and shows signs of having had her jaw broken."

Alex waited for Henrik to finish. "Well," he said, with an effort to give his voice a serene tone, "is there any news on Suzanne Carstens?"

No answer.

Alex turned his head enough to meet Evelin's terrified eyes.

"We have not heard yet." Strobelsohn broke the stiff, dead air. "But we are approaching the hotel now and will let you know in a few moments. I'm hanging up; we are here."

They lost the connection. The speakers squelched.

Silence. Nothing but the noise from the BMW's engine.

Alex decided to hold his tongue and instead maneuvered his car aggressively through traffic. Evelin also remained reticent; her face pointed rigidly forward.

Finally, the Atlantic Kempinski rose in front of them. Alex braked and slid into the easement. He pulled up and parked behind a line of police cars that strung up to the entrance of the Hotel. Hastily, he and Evelin climbed out.

Captain Strobelsohn and Henrik were standing in a group of uniformed officers. Blue lights flickered. When they saw the two approaching, they came and met up halfway.

Henrik was the first to speak. "Suzanne Carstens is fine. There are two patrolmen with her now."

Evelin grasped Alex's forearm with both hands. "I should go to her." She looked him straight on and continued, "Do you think you can fill out the report about the shooting at the farmhouse on your own? I'll come after in a taxi and sign it."

Alex glanced over at Strobelsohn who shrugged his shoulders and simultaneously nodded his head in accordance.

"I don't see why not. I'll have to turn my firearm in, to ballistics. That won't go quickly so take your time," Alex said running his hand over hers with a slight smile.

She studied the lines of his mouth and returned his smile.

57

Henrik flipped through his file folder to a scale photograph of the gun case found in the Carstens's vault. He laid it on a table in the LKA with an exposed upward palm, welcoming Alex Gutenberg to compare it with the ornamentation on the P38 he carried from the stable in a large Ziploc bag.

Alex held the plastic-encased handgun above the photo. Moving it back and forth, he said, "It is an exact match. They shouldn't need much time to confirm whether or not it was the weapon used in the basement massacre at the Carstens's villa. I have to leave my SIG downstairs anyway, so I'll go ahead and take the P38 with me."

Henrik cleared his throat. "Sir, I'd be happy to do that for you."

"That is awfully nice of you Henrik," Alex said sincerely, "but I am afraid they might have some questions that only I could answer. But thanks anyway."

He stood up, nodded to Henrik and Strobelsohn, and then stepped out of the room. He hurried along the corridor. The bustle of the environment contributed to his pace.

Two floors down to the third—considering the stairs, he thought he might not want to be too sweaty when he turned in his handgun and answered questions about the necessary use of fatal force. He made himself slow down.

In the furthest corner, he found the ballistics lab. Everything went smoothly. A routine process: Fill in a three-layered multicolored carbon copy form, which eventually would be transcribed into the system and accompany his report of the incident. As commonplace as it was, it occurred to Alex that this was the first time since he left Afghanistan that he has had to relinquish his handgun.

They might even offer him counseling. He smiled, with the flitting thought that he would take them up on that if Evelin would be his shrink.

Heading back up to the fifth floor, he took the stairs two steps at a time. He felt liberated.

"Well, that went quickly," Henrik said as Alex entered Strobelsohn's office.

Alex smiled. "It clearly isn't the first time they've had to investigate the use of a firearm." He exhaled, and noticed at the same moment that the fear—no, the feeling of insecurity had returned. "I guess most of it will come down to my affidavit."

The weight of the report suddenly hit him heavily. The perp had intended to cause harm and fired a shot. It was self-defense, but maybe he really should change the ordering of events, just a touch, to avoid an unnecessary investigation. The thought of lying on a sworn testimony was making him feel physically sick, deep down in his stomach. He suddenly wished Evelin were back. She would not have any doubt about the succession of events. Or at least about the sequence they would communicate to the authorities.

"I'm going to get on a laptop," he said to Henrik.

Henrik nodded eagerly. "Sure. Make yourself at home." With an inviting motion of the hand toward a desk, he pulled out the chair.

Alex took a seat at the computer and toggled to the dropdown box with all the available forms of the LKA. There, he would find the document he needed to fill out. This part, he had done on several occasions, albeit for other reasons.

Date. Serial number. Type of report. Use of fatal force…

Seeing the choices made Alex think about the event. He had not questioned whether his shots were necessary. That never crossed his mind. It was all mechanical. Should he type in, for the reason, that it was hard-wired in his military training, he had no other choice but to follow his instincts? Certainly not. That would give the know-it-alls down in Internal Affairs just the fodder they have been waiting for. Without batting an eye, they would tear him apart, twisting every word he wrote. They would start a formal investigation, and he would have to spend precious time defending himself…

No. Alex shook his head almost imperceptibly. He was fired upon; his and Dr. Wolf's lives had been in danger. Short and sweet.

He swiveled on the axis of his chair. Strobelsohn's office came into focus. The captain and Henrik looked at him expectantly.

"I suppose Dr. Wolf will have to submit her own report. Maybe I should wait for her in case she remembers something I have forgotten. Or do you think I should send this now?" Alex asked, and immediately questioned himself as to whether that did not sound too suspicious.

Strobelsohn seemed to have caught on to his anxiety. "Mr. Gutenberg, don't worry yourself. In the words of Chief Bolsen himself, *less is more*."

Alex cleared his throat. "I suppose you're right." In all actuality it was Mies van der Rohe, one of the most important architects of the modern age, who made the old aphorism popular. When he said it, he was referring to architecture and not to police work. But it was fitting in this situation.

Alex turned back around to the computer. He read his sentence through. Then he decided to explain why he and Evelin were on the property, why they had separated, and how he had come into the badly lit stable where he found Evelin bound. How the armed assailant made a step toward him, and fired as he entered. He left out the exchange of words. If Evelin included them, it would not be a blundering omission, or would it? Alex stopped and reread the entire entry.

"I should wait on Dr. Wolf," Alex admitted. "What could it hurt?"

"Do that if it makes you feel better, Mr. Gutenberg," Henrik said helpfully.

The young detective was smiling. Alex had to wonder if Henrik had ever been in a similar situation. Probably not, Henrik would not have been able to keep a story like that to himself. But Alex was not completely satisfied with this. He knew he would never share these details with a colleague. Maybe Henrik had?

"Detective Breiter, have you ever had to fill out such a report?" Alex asked.

"No, sir," Henrik replied immediately. "I do know Captain Strobelsohn has. If he can answer any thing about the process, I'm sure he would."

"Henrik," Gert Strobelsohn shook his head in disbelief. "The process is not what is in question here."

"I'm not concerned about the formalities," Alex confirmed.

Strobelsohn puckered his mouth. "That is right, sir. You know, nobody is interested in a witch hunt. It is just a necessary evil, the bureaucracy as well… as well as the need for fatal force sometimes."

Alex nodded. He turned back to the monitor, went through the paragraph one more time, and clicked the three-dimensional looking button that read: *Submit Report*.

Done. The weight now seemed to move from his stomach to his knees. He pushed through to the bottom of his feet and used the impetus to spin his seat until he was once again facing his colleagues.

"Let's say, for matter of argument, that the ornate weapon I took off of the dead Russian is the 9mm from the vault, and that it was used in the murder in Carstens's basement." Alex said with conviction.

"The two corpses we recovered from the Easter fire today were also shot with a 9mm," Strobelsohn interjected. "We could tentatively assume it was the same weapon."

"Isn't that *assuming* too much?" Henrik fired back.

Is Henrik just playing the devil's advocate? Alex thought.

Strobelsohn frowned. "Henrik, what are the chances that we are not dealing with the same gun?" He raised his large hand and began counting. "First of all, the gun we got off the dead Russian is no ordinary firearm. It is a collector's item, and the ornamentation matches the stains in the velvet of the empty display box left in Carstens's wall safe. Second…" He looked at Alex. "This you do not know yet, Mr. Gutenberg. Our colleagues on the evidence collection team found diamonds in the trailer the Russians were using in the barn. The stones are of a similar quality as the two we discovered in the vault at Carstens's villa."

Alex pricked up his ears. "You don't say?"

Strobelsohn nodded. "Yeah, twenty-one rocks. A hefty chunk of change." He paused, furrowed his brow, and then continued, "Thirdly—this will also be news to you, Mr. Gutenberg—in the camper, they discovered an empty file-folder labeled Dmitri Ivanov. It is the exact same type of binder as the other dossiers from the safe. And last but not least, there is a lot of blood on the floor of the stable. It is only a matter of time until we have the lab results and can say with certainty that the two Russians killed our two missing dockworkers there, before they deposited the bodies in the wood piled for the Easter fire."

Strobelsohn paused momentarily and turned to Henrik. "So no, I don't think we are going too far with our speculations."

Henrik blinked once, then nodded reluctantly. "When you put it like that, I have to agree with you."

"I will go one further," Strobelsohn continued. "I would argue that our three cases—the massacre at the villa, the dead women in the container on the Burchardkai docks, and the murdered port workers in the Easter fire—are all connected. And that Dmitri Ivanov is behind it all. He is the one who sent the Russians."

Alex hesitated. "It seems hard to dispute that," he said slowly.

"But…" Henrik began. He threw a cautious glance Strobelsohn's way before he continued with fraught shoulders. "Assuming all this is true, it still doesn't fit."

"What doesn't fit?" Strobelsohn asked.

"Why, or how, did the gun get back in the vault?"

"Now you're thinking, Henrik," Alex encouraged the young detective to continue.

A slight blush of joy passed over Henrik's cheeks. But then he failed to go on.

"What else are we missing?" Alex inquired.

"Well, if we wanted the answer that the same man killed everyone, and that Dmitri Ivanov is behind all of it…" It was Strobelsohn who had to propose the conundrum. "How could that come about?"

"OK, let's say"—Henrik took the floor—"the killers invaded Carstens's villa. Removed the gun from the vault. They used it to shoot one of the victims in the rec room. They massacred the rest by other means. Then they went upstairs, put the gun back in the safe, and returned a few days later to get it for good. And they had to blow the safe? That doesn't make any sense."

Right, Alex thought, and said aloud, "Are we sure the gun was in the vault? If the P38 is Björn Carstens's personal weapon, we cannot disregard the fact that he could have been carrying it on him in the basement."

"Why would he do such a thing?" asked Henrik.

"Maybe, he did not trust his friends all that well." Strobelsohn replied.

"Exactly," Alex said. "Theoretically speaking, it would be feasible that the two Russians do not only have our two dock workers on their consciences. They could also be the assailants from the Carstens's massacre. We can safely say they entered the villa a few days later and blasted into the vault to get the diamonds and Ivanov's file. They had both on them, even if the dossier for Dmitri Ivanov was empty."

"They probably destroyed the contents," Strobelsohn quibbled.

"OK. OK." Henrik Breiter nodded hastily. "But why didn't they eliminate Suzanne Carstens straight off in the cellar when they had the chance? They were in the process of killing anyway… and Suzanne Carstens was obviously part of their assignment."

"For that, there are only two explanations," Alex replied. "What if Suzanne Carstens wasn't in the parlor at all during the massacre?"

"But that is very unlikely," Henrik threw in. "She was covered in the blood of three of the victims, and she had been beaten badly."

"Right," Alex confirmed. "That's why I rather suspect that the Russians, if they are our perpetrators, were interrupted. By something or other…" Alex took a deep breath and let it flow out audibly. "There are still far too many unanswered questions for my liking. I am not one hundred percent satis…"

The door flew open. Bolsen waltzed in. In all actuality, it was more like he was floating. Judging from the expression on his face, he was in the best of moods.

"Good afternoon, gentlemen," he said, smiling broadly. "So, you've found the murder weapon. What else have you got for me?"

"Excuse me, sir. We are not yet sure it is the murder weapon. We can only surmise that it was taken from the scene of the original crime." Strobelsohn hurried to clear up the discrepancy.

Bolsen stepped right up to Strobelsohn and patted him patronizingly on the shoulder. At the same time, eying him insistently from the side. "You're always searching for reasons not to succeed, aren't you, Captain Strobelsohn? Take a note from Mr. Gutenberg's playbook." He lifted a printed page that he had carried in with him to his nose. "This is his report on the shootings at the abandoned farmhouse. And I quote: *The assailant had fired a 9mm that looked surprisingly similar to the presumed missing weapon from the Carstens's massacre.*"

"We should know any time," Henrik added. "We are waiting on the ballistics report now. We can't say much more at the present. We have clues, yes. But the quadruple murder in the basement of the villa, the dead women in the container on the Burchardkai docks, and the two victims who were supposed to be burned in the Easter fire… none of that has been resolved yet."

Bolsen turned to Henrik with much too wide of a grin. "Mr. Breiter, you need to realize when to make problems and when to go along with what the evidence is telling you. If forensics confirms that the engraved P38 is the murder weapon from the Carstens's villa and that it was used in the execution of the two port employees… If a single fingerprint can be assigned to the dead Russian, then for God's sake! Call it a day! Case closed." Bolsen rapped on the desk with his large gold signet ring. "Once you have those reports, you let me know. I will call a big press conference—newspaper, radio, television. And under my auspices, the three of you and Dr. Wolf can explain how we got our man."

58

I knocked on the nondescript office door. The sign on the wall said: *Dirk Hollensen, Department of Internal Affairs.*

"Yes, please?" I heard a man say incoherently.

I opened the door and took a step into the room.

A young man in a fashionably cut jacket behind a meticulously tidy desk looked up from an open file. "Ms. Wolf?"

I nodded and was about to answer.

"Please wait outside. I need another minute here," he said before I could reply. He concentrated on his reading again. I was nothing to him.

I returned to the hallway, closed the door, and sat down on the only visitor's stool. Plastic, uncomfortable, and placed so that anyone who happened to pass by could see me from a distance. I suppressed a smile. The whole thing had a deeper purpose. Anyone who had to wait here was publicly outed to his colleagues as an employee who was at least possibly corrupt or had abused his authority in some other way. At the same time, the internal investigator demonstrated his quasi limitless power. The message was: *You are nothing, I am in charge here, and I will get you.*

I crossed my legs and made myself comfortable. The short breather did me good. I recalled my conversation with Suzanne Carstens in the hotel. Fortunately, she was not very aware of the attempt on her life. Actually, not at all. When the officer posted in front of her suite had been taken hostage, she was sound asleep. She had been woken by the two patrolmen who stormed into her room a quarter of an hour later to check on her. I explained what had happened as gently as I could, and she reacted surprisingly calmly. We had arranged a new meeting in two days. Then we would discuss everything again, thoroughly. Before this, nothing could happen to her. A second officer had been placed in front of her door, and there was a patrol car parked on the street.

Then I had gone back to the LKA with the intention of meeting Alex. When I entered my office, I found a blinking voicemail there. I played it while I freshened up a little and combed my hair so that the distinct bulge on my temple was not immediately noticeable.

Several rather unimportant messages, and then an urgent, concise request from a Mr. Hollensen to report to him immediately after returning. And now I was waiting there.

Five… Ten minutes…

I'd had enough. I got up, knocked on the door again, and immediately opened it.

Hollensen looked up, irritated.

"I have another appointment," I said. "If it's not possible for you to meet now, we can make other arrangements for tomorrow."

He cleared his throat, forcing something similar to a smile. "No, no. Please." He pointed to a chair by his desk.

There was a comfortable meeting corner in the left half of the office. I did not seem to be good enough for that. Another demonstration of power.

I took a seat and studied my counterpart. Hollensen was perhaps in his late twenties. Modern haircut. Short on the sides, longer at the top. Carefully trimmed beard. Strikingly full lips, green-brown eyes. And not a hint of kindness in his face.

"Ms. Wolf?" he began.

"Yes," I responded.

"*Dr.* Wolf." He emphasized my title as if it was something indecent.

"Yes," I said again.

He looked at the file that lay in front of him, leafed through it, and continued talking. "You've been with us a short time, but you're already involved in a lot of things. And in the space of only a few days, you've even managed to get in my office's line of fire." He paused, then glanced up and examined me thoroughly. "That is certainly a record."

"If you say so," I replied.

His stare grew more intense. I did not avert my eyes.

He licked his lower lip. A clear sign of uncertainty. "Now, this district attorney…"

"Mr. Gutenberg," I added.

"Correct. How do the two of you get along?"

"Very well, now," I said.

"*Now*," he repeated with a creepy accentuation. "Meaning the cooperation wasn't that easy at first?"

I shrugged my shoulders. "It always takes a bit of time to grow together as a team."

He laughed artificially and wagged his raised forefinger in rebuke. "How quickly she counters! One notes the psychologist!"

I did not take the bait. "I think I'm supposed to share the truth here. And that's exactly what I'm doing."

"Of course." That came off very patronizingly. "But this Mr. Gutenberg, let me tell you, is unfortunately not without controversy in this office."

"Really?"

"Indeed." He nodded. "He is ambitious. Wants to go places. And that's when someone begins to go over… *dead bodies.*"

He described himself. How revealing.

I did not answer him, but slowly raised my arm and looked calmly at my watch. When I turned back to him, his face had flushed crimson.

"Am I boring you?"

"No." I shook my head. "As I explained to you at the beginning, and as I'm sure you are well aware, I'm involved in several ongoing investigations as part of a special task force set up by Mr. Bolsen. I am busy."

His full mouth narrowed. "Of course, I know that. Do you think I walk into a conversation like this unprepared?" He faltered. "Then let's get straight to the essential point."

"Yes, please," I said.

A distinct crease appeared on his brow. Again, he flipped through the file. "I have a report here from Mr. Gutenberg on the unfortunate use of deadly force at the Mellingburg Locks. And now I would like to hear your side of the story."

"Is this usual?"

His eyelids twitched briefly. "What do you mean?"

"Until right now, I had always assumed that such reports would have been submitted in writing, as Mr. Gutenberg has apparently done."

An imperceptible shake of the head. "You let me worry about that. You will, of course, put your statement in writing. But I'll determine in which order."

"Fine," I said and smiled briefly. "Then I'll start straight off: Mr. Gutenberg and I returned from the scene of the body find at the Blankenese Easter fires. There, the doctor had told us that the victims had been tortured and killed elsewhere, after which they were brought to the beach and hidden in the woodpile. Mr. Gutenberg and I exchanged views and considered where a person unfamiliar with Hamburg would detain and question two people without being observed…"

"Let's skip that," he snapped. "You can write it down later. In detail… What happened when you arrived at the abandoned farm?"

"Okay," I said dramatically. "You don't want to know why we were there or how Mr. Gutenberg and I came to the conclusion that the criminals might be there?"

"No."

"Very well," I continued. "We got out…"

He raised his hand. "One moment. I want to record this."

He opened a drawer and pulled out a dictation device.

"Is that the normal procedure as well?" I asked.

A gleam came into his eye. "Do you have something to hide?"

"You didn't answer my question," I stated dryly.

He took a deep breath, grabbed the Dictaphone, and returned it to its place in his desk. "Fine. Then we'll leave that out."

"Great." I nodded once. "Mr. Gutenberg and I got out of the car and entered the farmhouse. The door was unlocked. The building itself was empty. There was a thick coat of dust on the floor. We had the impression that nobody had been there for quite some time."

"I see. And yet you still saw the need to look around?"

"Well, we were already there. We thought we might as well."

"OK, that's debatable."

"I stayed downstairs," I continued. "Mr. Gutenberg went up on the second floor."

He leaned forward. "Why didn't you go with him?"

"The stairs," I said. "They were dilapidated. I was simply concerned. I didn't think they looked safe."

"And then?"

"In the kitchen, I discovered another door which opened directly into the stable. I walked through it. The barn was dark. I wanted to turn on my cell phone's flashlight when I was attacked from behind and overpowered."

"Why didn't you call for Mr. Gutenberg?" He stared at me again. "Wouldn't that have been the most obvious thing to do?"

I snorted. "I wish I had thought of that. But the attacker knocked me down and gagged and bound me." I turned my head to the side, pushed my hair back and showed Hollensen my bump. Then I raised both hands. The marks the cable ties left were clearly visible on my wrists.

"Yes, of course." He leaned back.

"After a short time, I heard Mr. Gutenberg coming down the stairs."

"Stop," he interrupted me. "What about the assailant, the unfortunate victim?"

He was slowly getting on my nerves. "Your *unfortunate victim* had previously tortured and shot two people in cold blood."

"Don't try to distract me," he said curtly. "What did the consequently dead man do?"

"He stood next to the door, with his gun drawn, and waited for Mr. Gutenberg."

"Now I'm really curious."

"Why?" I asked.

He made a vague gesture with his hand. "Just keep going. We'll talk about that later."

"Mr. Gutenberg came into the stable. The attacker took a step forward. Mr. Gutenberg must have heard that, because he turned to face him."

"Mhmm."

"The assailant fired at Mr. Gutenberg. Mr. Gutenberg drew his gun. The assailant aimed at him again and Mr. Gutenberg discharged his firearm."

"Twice."

"Correct," I confirmed.

"Hmm…" He pursed his lips. "That's the crux of the matter."

"The crux of the matter? I do not understand you."

"According to your account, the men were facing each other at a distance of no more than ten feet. You have just explained that the man who was later killed shot first. How can you miss your target at such close range?"

I shrugged my shoulders. "I don't know. I'm a psychologist. I'm not familiar with the use of firearms."

"But common sense. You have common sense." An impatient expression spread over his face. "You must admit, it's a little unbelievable that a professional criminal not only misses at such a close range but misses by so much. The bullet hit the back wall just above the floor."

I widened my eyes. "It did?" I forced myself to look down and back up again. A little present for Mr. Hollensen. I was sure he had taken a course in non-verbal communication in his training. And he had certainly been instructed there to watch out for signals during an interrogation. The involuntary looking down was a clear indication that the respondent was telling the truth.

"I'm waiting, Mrs. Wolf," he badgered.

"For the life of me, I can't explain that to you." I pulled my shoulders up at a loss. "I can only tell you what happened. The assailant fired at Mr. Gutenberg. Mr. Gutenberg drew his pistol. The assailant wanted to shoot again. Mr. Gutenberg discharged his gun… What else should Mr. Gutenberg have done?"

"That's not the issue right now." He picked up a pen and started scribbling away in the documents with ticking movements. Then he threw the pen angrily on the desk. "You stand by your statement? You have nothing more to add?"

I smiled slightly. "I repeat: I can only tell you what happened. I can't help it if you don't like it."

"*Like! Like!*" He took a deep breath. "It has nothing to do with liking anything! The whole affair is completely unsatisfactory for me."

I leaned forward. "Unsatisfactory for you? I have been attacked. I was knocked down. The criminal intended to kill Mr. Gutenberg and then kill me."

"Conjecture!"

"Nonsense! Following this incident, Mr. Gutenberg and I raced through half the city because our key witness in the multiple murders in Blankenese, which is being heavily covered by the media, was in grave danger of her life."

"Yes, but…"

I did not let him interrupt me. "There was another shooting at the hotel. The second perpetrator, the accomplice of your *unfortunate victim*, tried to force his way to our eyewitness. When that failed, he took a female police officer hostage. He severely injured the officer on his way out and then killed a hotel employee. I had to have a long therapy session with our witness, who is extremely traumatized. Afterward, I hurried straight here. I didn't even have time to have myself examined by a doctor for concussion. And then you come and attack me?"

His mouth fell open for a moment. He closed it and swallowed. "I do not understand why you are getting so excited. I'm just doing my job."

"That's exactly what you're not doing! And we both know it. You've done everything in your power to hang something on Mr. Gutenberg."

A vehement shake of the head. "Well, you're dead wrong. I…"

"No. I will discuss this with Mr. Bolsen. I will ask him if he is aware of how the Internal Affairs department deals with the employees, whether that happens with his approval or not."

Red spots formed on Hollensen's cheeks. "You seem to be taking this personally. After all, a man has died. This must be investigated thoroughly. We live in a state based on the rule of law, and you can't…"

I rose without any sign of haste. "Mr. Hollensen, we are finished here."

I walked out of the office.

March

29

Monday

59

The ringing of a bell. Maybe I just imagined it. But then a second time, and after a short pause, again. I opened my eyes. The clock on my bedside table said 9:37.

Shit! I sat up abruptly.

Alex and I had a 9:30 appointment for a late breakfast. I had overslept.

When was the last time that happened to me? I could not remember.

I swung out of bed, slipped into my dressing gown, and went to the window to have a look, just in case. Alex, indeed. In a trench coat that I had never seen before. With two paper bags in hand.

I ran my fingers through my hair, skipped looking in the mirror, and hurried down .

The ringing repeated. I took a deep breath and opened the door.

"Hello!" I greeted him in the most casual of ways. "Sorry, I actually slept through my alarm."

He smiled. He wore it well. "It's no problem. I, uh…" He broke off.

"Why don't you go on in? You know your way around," I hurried to say. "I'll jump in the shower, put on some clothes, and be right back."

I left him standing there and made my way up the stairs.

"There is no rush," he called after me. "Today is a holiday. We don't have any appointments."

I went to the closet and got fresh clothes out.

Noises from below. The rattle of porcelain and cutlery. The sound of water. Of course, the kitchen. I hadn't had time to clean it up last night. The dirty dishes from our breakfast yesterday were still piled up. And now he was doing them for me… I sighed. Too late. There was nothing I could do about it. So that's the way it would have to stay.

A quarter of an hour later, I came down the stairs, this time in a much more presentable condition. I stopped in my tracks. The dining room table was set for two people. And the kitchen was unrecognizable. Sparkling clean.

Alex was facing the other direction. With his shirt sleeves rolled up, he stood at the stove and fried something in the skillet. The holster at the small of his back was clearly visible. His pistol was in it.

He turned and smiled at me. "That was quick. And you're just in time. The scrambled eggs are nearly done." He stopped a beat. "You don't mind that I raided your fridge, do you?"

I shook my head. "No. Not at all. I haven't eaten since yesterday afternoon, and I'm starving."

"Then it was a good idea," he said, visibly satisfied.

"You got it back?" I pointed at his pistol.

"Yes." He grinned. "Can you imagine? A Mr. Hollensen surprisingly dropped it off personally by Strobelsohn's office last night, just before I was going to leave."

"Really?"

"Mhmm. He's a nice guy, that Hollensen."

"I wouldn't put my money on that. He's not exactly one of your biggest fans." The coffee was ready. I took the pot and carried it into the dining room.

Alex followed me with the skillet. He spooned the eggs onto our plates. We sat.

Rolls, several Danishes, orange juice, butter, cheese, and cold cuts. Even small dishes filled with jam. He had thought of everything. Hence, the two big bags he had brought along.

"Mmm. Heavenly," I said with a full mouth.

"It should be. It comes from the *gourmet baker* at the gas station," he replied.

We both laughed.

The rest of breakfast, we did not say much. Not a word about work or any other unnecessary, forced, small talk. The sun shined in through the window and bathed the room in a bright yellow, warm light. I enjoyed it.

Alex got up, carried our plates into the kitchen, came back, and poured us each another cup of coffee. He sat down again.

"There is a new development in our case," he said.

"Okay," I replied, and at the same time, felt a distinct tinge of disappointment that the brief idyll of a carefree Easter Monday had come to an end.

"I got a call from Strobelsohn this morning," he continued. "The ballistics results are in. The slugs from the bodies found in the Easter pyre and the bullet from the Carstens's villa were fired from the same weapon... the one we recovered from the farmhouse by the lock."

Recovered, a nice way to put it, I thought and then said, "According to this, the two Russians committed the massacre in the villa and also have the people from the Easter fire on their conscience?"

Alex played with his cup, lost in thought. He held it by the handle and indecisively turned it back and forth on the saucer. "At least that's how Bolsen sees it. And he has a culprit for the massacre in the container."

"I don't like it," I replied truthfully.

"Neither do I," he agreed.

"Just because the bullets were fired from the same gun doesn't prove anything. There is no motive. Then we have the nicotine that was used to poison the victims in the villa. The broken safe a few days later. And Suzanne... Why didn't the killers get her when they had a chance? It was obviously part of their contract. It doesn't add up."

Alex pushed the cup away. "I tried to convince Bolsen to reconsider, to no avail. He told us that he felt it was clearly a feud in the red-light district..."

"What about Carstens?" I interrupted him.

"Whew." Alex puffed up his cheeks and let the air out audibly. "According to Bolsen, Björn Carstens had nothing to do with any of it. He had had some lamentable human weaknesses of the sexual nature. And kept the wrong company. Unfortunately, everything got out of control."

I couldn't believe it. "It almost sounds as if Bolsen is trying to cover up for Carstens's involvement altogether."

"I was under the same impression."

"Did they know each other? Bolsen and Carstens?"

Alex moved his mouth. "Bolsen knows all the important people in town. Or he wouldn't be in the position he's in."

"In short, Bolsen wants the case closed?"

"Yes," Alex nodded. "He has put it in motion."

"And Strobelsohn and Henrik?"

"They are anything but happy about it. But they do what they are told. You know how it works."

"Of course, I do."

We fell silent.

"Bolsen has called a big press conference," Alex broke the silence. "Regional and national news. We have all been invited to attend."

I snorted. "I would be happy to skip that!" I made another attempt. "How does he explain Dmitri Ivanov and his involvement in the matter?"

"Not at all. They're just rumors. There is no proof that this phantom actually exists." He paused. "Bolsen has a point there, though. Not even the BND has any concrete information about this man."

"OK," I said. "Or rather, not OK."

Alex looked at me searchingly.

"What I have gotten out of Suzanne Carstens… then Peter Westphal. There is a lot more to this than we know so far."

"Correct. But that is no use to us. We will have to let Peter go. And Suzanne Carstens can do whatever she wants. Find another psychotherapist. She has enough money."

I got up, went into the hall, and came back with a slightly yellowed file folder.

"What is that?" Alex asked me.

"These are the records of the suicide of Peter Westphal's father," I said. "Henrik sent them to me by internal mail. They were in my box when I returned from Suzanne's."

Alex frowned. He did not seem convinced. "We are supposed to get something out of that?"

"I don't know," I replied. "But I think it would at least help me to let go."

"Then pull them out," he said. "It might turn out to be interesting."

"Thanks," I said. I moved my chair to his side of the table and took a seat next to him. I put the file between us and opened it.

60

Several 8 × 12 glossy photos. A man in his fifties slumped over in a recliner. Eyes half closed, mouth open. Elbows on the armrests, palms up, and fingers slightly curled. He was wearing a white shirt. A bullet hole on the left side. The upper edges scorched brown-black. There was a lot of blood everywhere.

Close-ups of various objects: an open old-fashioned-looking laptop on a desk, A blood-soaked towel on the floor, a pistol next to it.

The photograph of a teenager. It was apparently Peter Westphal. He was standing with a female police officer in uniform. She held a pad and pencil and seemed to be taking his statement. Peter had his eyes wide open, and his bloody hands clenched into fists in front of his chest.

Then the police report. Alex and I read it together: On the afternoon of March 20, at 3:11, an emergency call came in to the dispatch switchboard from Peter Westphal. He stated that he had come home and found his father seriously injured in his study. He did not know what to do. His father was bleeding badly, and he could not stop the bleeding. And he found a pistol there as well.

The dispatch sent out an ambulance and a patrol car. Both arrived at the scene of the crime at almost the same time: 3:27 and 3:28, respectively. Peter's father, Sören Westphal, was still alive, but unconscious. Apart from him and Peter, there was no one else in the tract house. There were no signs of a break-in and no evidence of struggle. On the father's laptop, the officers found a succinct suicide note: *Ever since my wife passed, my life no longer has any meaning. I really tried. Peter, I hope you can forgive me.*

The severely injured man died on the way to the hospital, without regaining consciousness.

The authorities ruled the case a suicide. Peter Westphal began psychotherapy with a police psychologist, but stopped the treatment shortly thereafter, when he turned eighteen.

I leaned back and looked at Alex. "I've never heard of a suicide where someone shot themselves in the heart."

"It's rare," he said. "But it does happen now and then."

"Did the deceased have gunpowder residue on his hands?"

Alex furrowed his brow, looking over the report. "There's nothing about that here. But this was clearly a suicide." He put his finger on one part of the page. "The shirt is singed. The muzzle of the gun was pressed against the body. And in view of the lack of any signs of struggle or forced entry…"

"Did the gun belonged to Sören Westphal?" I asked.

"I suppose. A P38. However, unregistered."

I sighed. "Poor Peter Westphal. Comes home to find his father dying. He had already lost his mother, he told us; she suffered from cancer. All these fateful blows at such a young age, they inevitably lead to trauma."

"I'm sure," Alex agreed with me.

"And still, Peter was able to finish high school, and a short time after, went to Australia to study."

"Carstens paid for his schooling."

"Peter's father worked for Carstens. It says it here again in the report. As tax advisor and bookkeeper."

"Well," Alex snorted, "maybe old Carstens decided to do something good for a change."

I shook my head frantically. "No. I don't mean to rob you of your illusions, but people like Carstens don't suddenly discover a taste for charity overnight."

We fell silent.

I leafed through the folder. "A P38," I repeated.

"Yes," Alex replied. "Unregistered. The numbers had been filed away."

"It says here, in Peter's statement, that he had never seen his father with the gun."

"That doesn't have to mean anything. If I had a son, I wouldn't let him near my gun, either."

"Of course," I nodded. "P38… Isn't that the same model as Carstens's handgun, to which the murders have now been traced?"

"Yes."

"Could it be possible that the gun found at the Westphal's also belonged to Carstens?"

Alex made a dismissive gesture with his hand. "That's a bit far-fetched, not to say a bold accusation. This model of pistol is a dime a dozen. Especially the standard version, which is what they discovered on Westphal. Peter Westphal's father probably bought it on the black market."

I looked out the window into the garden, without really perceiving it.

"Help me out here," Alex said. "Why did you want the file in the first place? To get a better understanding of Peter Westphal?"

"Of course," I confirmed, and turned back from the window. "Because he reacted so strongly during our interrogation when his father's death came up. Do you remember that?"

He began to smile. "Sure."

"But," I added, "I wanted to go through the file mainly because of the remnants of blood found on the cufflink."

"Oh! The lab report!"

"Exactly," I confirmed. "On the cufflink that Björn Carstens was holding in his hand when he died, they found blood."

"That came from a close male relative of Peter Westphal."

"And there's only his father."

"Who has been dead a long time." Alex tapped the file with his finger. "Suicide."

"If it was one."

Alex sat upright. "You think it was murder?"

"I don't know," I said truthfully. "Let's take a closer look at the cufflink in Carstens's hand."

"OK."

"The blood was found under the diamond in the setting. How did it get there?"

A shrug. "There are a thousand possibilities."

"One of those possibilities, is that it could have happened while Peter's father was dying. He was bleeding profusely."

"That could be an indication that Björn Carstens might have been present. But nothing more."

"Granted," I admitted. "But why did Björn Carstens have this cufflink in his hand when he died?"

Alex puffed out his cheeks. "You pose questions…"

"Carstens was wearing other cufflinks that evening, right?"

"That's true. Similar style. Expensive, flashy bling. I guess those things were his trademark."

I nodded. "So… why would Björn Carstens, on the night he was killed of all times, be holding this cufflink in his hand that had blood from Peter Westphal's father on it?"

"Well." Alex thought for a moment. "It is highly unlikely that he was going to carry it around at an orgy. That doesn't make sense."

"What if someone put the thing in his hand?"

Alex looked me once over. "By someone, you mean the *murderer*?"

"Exactly."

"For what? Why would the murderer have wanted to do that?"

I pursed my lips. "It would have to be a very personal motive, coupled with a message."

"And that is? *This is why I'm killing you*?"

"Yes," I said. "Revenge."

"Revenge for Sören Westphal," muttered Alex. "Revenge for his father's death." He took a deep breath. "Peter Westphal… Could he have known from the start that Carstens killed his father because the cufflink was on his dying father's body? Did he hide it from the police and instead use it to blackmail Carstens? And is that why Carstens paid for his studies?"

"Excuse me," I said. "I don't think so. Look at the photo of young Peter Westphal in the file. He's completely distraught and upset. In shock. Even now, we've seen him. He is anything but cold-blooded. He is purposeful and focused, but not calculating. Otherwise, he wouldn't have freaked out like that in front of Suzanne Carstens's hospital room and tried to take you hostage."

Alex spread his hands in an inquisitive gesture. "Then what?"

"I don't know. One thing is certain: Peter Westphal's father worked for Björn Carstens as a tax consultant and accountant. It's easy to imagine what his job consisted of. Then there is the pistol that was found with him, the same model as Carstens's personal weapon. It was unregistered, with the serial number filed off."

"Then there is the cufflink."

"Exactly," I said. "With the blood of his dead father and Carstens holding the link in his hand when he died."

Alex leaned forward, pulled the file toward him, and flipped through it.

"March twentieth," he said softly, more to himself.

"What about it?" I asked.

"Sören Westphal died on March 20." He looked up. "We were called to the massacre at the villa on March 21. The murders themselves took place the night before. Also on March 20."

"That is not a coincidence," I said.

Alex's mouth narrowed. "I think we need to talk to Peter Westphal while we still can. He'll be released from custody tomorrow."

61

During the drive along Stadtpark, Alex had contemplated all the reasons he had to keep Peter Westphal in jail, but unfortunately none of them were substantiated. Westphal's assault in the hospital would not be enough.

Now Alex and Evelin needed to coerce a confession out of the man sitting in front of them in the slate gray interrogation room. As previously agreed, Alex would lead the inquiry, while Evelin paid attention to Westphal's nonverbal tells.

"Dr. Wolf and I wanted another chance to talk with you," Alex began and laid a manila file folder on the table.

Peter Westphal leaned back and calmly ran his fingers through his hair. "Oh, yeah?" He looked better than he did the last time Alex had seen him. He seemed much more relaxed and not nearly as pale.

"My attorney told me you'll be letting me out tomorrow," the young man added.

Alex scooted his chair away from Evelin's corner of the table to position himself directly across from Peter. "That's right."

"He did not say much. Just that there was an attempt to kill Suzi that was prevented."

Alex nodded slowly. "That is correct."

Peter continued unabashed, "And the assailants are purported to be the murderers from the Carstens's villa. Which means the case is closed and I can go."

Alex took his time to respond.

"I know… of course," Peter said, hurrying to fill the void of silence. "I'll have to answer for my conduct at the clinic."

"You're right there, too." Alex remained stone-faced.

"I'm really sorry. I was so freaked out about Suzi. What I did was inexcusable. I could apologize until I am blue in the face. But Suzi and I…" Peter contorted his mouth and seemed to be making a conscious effort to hold his tongue.

"Are in love," Evelin finished his sentence.

Peter bobbed his head. "Yes, we became very close. I never expected that sort of thing would happen to me."

"How much do you love her? What are you willing to do for Miss Carstens?" Alex asked.

"I don't understand what you mean," Peter replied hesitantly.

Instead of answering, Alex pulled an 8 × 12 glossy picture of a gold cufflink out of the file and placed it on the table.

Peter blinked several times.

Alex tapped on the photograph. "How do you explain this?"

Peter leaned farther forward, raised his chin, and made a display of looking the photo over. Then he lifted his head, turned to Evelin with a shrug, and looked back to Alex. "A cufflink?"

"Hahaha!" Alex panned and smirked wittingly. "Don't get smart. You know exactly what that is."

Peter reclined back in his chair. "Please, Mr. Prosecutor, what do you want to show me."

"I'll tell you what it is. This cufflink belonged to Björn Carstens. We found it in his hand, and we are certain that his murderer put it there."

"Oh yeah?"

"Under the diamond"—Alex pointed at the stone encrusted in the hunk of shiny metal—"in the crevices of the prongs, we discovered traces of blood. Blood from your father."

Peter's head twitched once.

"When you were seventeen, you found your father dying in his office," Alex continued. "You discovered this cufflink. You never told anyone about it. Who shoots themself in the heart? You knew there was something wrong with your father's supposed suicide."

"No… no there wasn't."

"But there is more," Evelin started in. "A few days ago, Suzanne took me sailing on the Ad Astra."

Peter remained silent.

"Miss Carstens showed me a photograph of her deceased mother there. She is in the arms of a man who has been cut out of the photo. It is Björn Carstens."

Peter crooked his hand on his wrist to form an inquisitive gesture. "And?"

"And you were also on that yacht." Alex intervened. "You met Suzanne Carstens on that boat. You were often out on the water with her."

"Sure!" Peter said. "I told you all that."

"So, you know what picture we are talking about."

Peter looked at the two incredulously. "Of course, it is the photograph of Suzi's mother. But Suzi never told me it was her grandfather that was cut out of it."

"The cufflink is clearly visible in the photo," Evelin said.

"You saw the picture and realized that it was exactly the same cufflink you found in your father's study on the day he died," Alex said. "All of a sudden, the connections became clear to you."

"What are you talking about?" Peter's voice sounded croaky. "What connections?"

"Carstens? Björn Carstens murdered your father and made it look like a suicide."

Peter bit his lower lip.

"But it doesn't end there," Alex continued. "You decided to exact revenge."

"You're crazy! You are just saying this because I trounced you in the clinic. That's why you want to frame me for the Carstens's murders? I told you I was sorry!"

Alex shook his head. "That has nothing to do with it. You got even."

"What?" Peter practically jumped up. Then he paused, took a deep breath, and sat back down. "I entered Carstens's villa and murdered four people? Endangering Suzi. Me, by myself? Are you mad?"

Evelin stepped up the inquiry. "Suzanne Carstens helped you."

"Why in the world would she do that? She is… She is the kindest, gentlest person I know. She would never…"

"Yes, she would," Evelin interrupted. "She also wanted to inflict vengeance on her grandfather."

"Suzi? No way!"

"She told you what her grandfather had done to her mother time and again."

Peter's face lost all expression. "She never said anything to me about that. All I know is that her mother died a long time ago."

"You're lying," Alex stated nonchalantly.

"You're both convinced of this?" Peter asked dumbfounded.

An uncomfortable silence fell over the table.

"You got your revenge," Alex continued. "On March 20, you murdered Björn Carstens. On the exact same date your father died."

Peter at first grew tense, then he started to laugh. "That is your proof? A date that repeats every year. And a photo of a cufflink on a boat? From this you want to paint the picture that I, along with Miss Carstens who is not able to harm a fly… that we have committed these horrendous crimes? That we massacred four grown men?"

Alex looked him straight on. "Or you could just confess to it."

"And I would, too! If I had done it." Peter did not divert his eyes. "But I didn't do it. And if you could prove it was me, I wouldn't be getting out of here tomorrow, and you wouldn't be sitting across from me right now, on a sunny Easter Monday. Instead, you'd be enjoying a nice day off."

62

Peter Westphal had been escorted back to his cell. Alex and Evelin stepped out of the interrogation room into the empty corridor. Alex bent his knee and propped up his foot against the wall. Hands in his trouser pockets, he puffed up his cheeks and exhaled audibly.

Evelin sized him up. "Frustrated?"

"Frustration doesn't begin to cover it. This is real crap, with a capital C."

"You can say that again."

"We can't get this little bastard! He'll walk out of here tomorrow with a shit-eating grin on his face. And he'll have washed his hands clean of this, because he is right. We can't prove a thing."

"Flimsy clues, no substantial evidence—that's all we have," she stated plainly. "Those and our theory."

"It is convincing, cogent, yet full of holes. I wouldn't need to show up in court with that case. The defense would blow me out of the water."

She sighed. "Crap with a capital C."

"That's the one; it's a lost cause," he said grimly.

They remained silent for a while.

She was the first one to speak. "It doesn't necessarily have to be that way."

"What are you getting at?"

Evelin hesitated. Then she shrugged her shoulders. "I am sure we have some other options available to us."

Alex cleared his throat. "Oh yeah? Like what?"

"Well, we won't exactly be playing by the book."

"Ok?" he said without being able to hide his curiosity. "I'm beginning to think that is overrated, anyway."

Evelin took her time with her response. The next words she articulated carefully. "Criminals always put the blame on others when they are given the chance."

Alex waited for her to continue, but when she did not, he did. "True. That goes without saying."

"It is only human," she replied.

"What are you suggesting?"

"All right, I'll tell you."

Back in the interrogation room, Alex fidgeted with the cuticles of his thumbnails. He was uncertain about the plan, but they were desperate, and that called for drastic actions.

A few minutes later, the door swung open, and a female guard led Peter Westphal to the threshold. Peter stopped in his tracks. "I came here in person to tell you in the most direct way, I don't care to talk to you anymore. You are trying to bamboozle me. I want to see my lawyer. He'll put an end to this. This is harassment!"

"All right, you do not need to speak with us. Please just listen," Alex said.

Peter stood indecisively still.

"*Please*, Mr. Westphal. Just one moment." Alex made a gesture to the chair across from him.

Peter hesitated, then tensed his shoulders, came into the room, and sat down.

The female guard gave Alex an inquiring glance. He nodded slightly. She returned his with her own silent nod and left. The door fell into the lock.

Peter peered at the exit and back again. "Why have you brought me here? What's wrong now?"

"Actually, I am not sure how to say this to you," Alex started and then turned to Evelin. "Maybe, Dr. Wolf, you would know the proper way to… inform Mr. Westphal."

Evelin sat upright. "It is not easy for me to tell you this, Peter," she said in a quiet tone.

Peter Westphal looked, bewildered, from her to Alex, who was staring down at the desktop. "What is going on?"

"This is a very difficult situation for us too," Evelin continued.

Alex cleared his throat. "We were not completely honest with you earlier."

"I don't understand." Peter furrowed his brow.

Alex folded his fingers into one another, resting his elbows on the table. "Your lawyer spoke to you about the incident in the Hotel Atlantic yesterday."

"Yes, that you stopped an attack on Suzi, and you got the guys who were responsible for the massacre last weekend in Björn Carstens's basement."

"Sort of. However…"

"*However* what?" Peter retorted.

Evelin started again. "I think you need to understand that we do not always share information with the public, especially if it might disrupt an ongoing investigation."

"OK, obviously. But what has this got to do with anything?"

"For instance, Miss Carstens's assailants yesterday, were not apprehended," Evelin said and threw a sidelong glance at Alex. "And Miss Carstens herself…"

Peter leaned forward. "What about Suzi?"

Alex said, "We didn't want to tell you, but she was injured in the attack yesterday."

"She is back in the hospital?" Peter asked with a rising voice.

Alex patted the table, with the intention to calm Peter.

Peter grew pasty white as he rotated his head abruptly from Alex to Evelin.

"Miss Carstens was taken to the clinic," Evelin said. "At first, it did not seem so bad… but then… I just received a phone call ten minutes ago." She stared at him blankly.

"And? She is not feeling well?"

Evelin and Alex turned to one another before looking at Peter.

"She is dead? Suzi is dead?" Peter whispered.

Evelin shook her head in dismay. "We are never immune from complications. Even with the best doctors, doing everything in their power, still, you can't stop the inevitable."

Peter remained silent. He ran his hands over his face, and then he let them sink. They fell lifeless to his side.

"I know this situation is hard for you. You have our deepest sympathy," Evelin said.

Peter did not utter a word.

"If it would make you feel better," Alex began saying, "you could tell us what really happened. We know you have been keeping quiet in order to protect Miss Carstens. But that is unfortunately no longer necessary."

Peter blinked several times. "What do you mean?"

"Miss Carstens's involvement in the deaths of her grandfather and his three guests."

"You want to hear what she had to do with the murders?" Peter asked.

"That's right." Alex nodded once. "You can speak freely now. It won't hurt her anymore. I can't put a dead man on trial."

Peter audibly exhaled twice.

"Mr. Westphal." Evelin's voice took on a pleading tone. "Tell us what Suzi had to do with the whole thing."

"Suzi?" Peter's face turned rock hard. "She had nothing to do with it. Nothing at all."

"Peter," Alex took over, "think about it. See, you can change your statement, without any consequences for yourself."

"Good." Peter's stone mien turned into a genuine smile.

Now we've got him, Alex thought.

Peter cleared his throat. "Suzi and I had an early date to go jogging. I arrived at the villa. No one answered the door. I checked around the back. The service entrance was ajar. I went inside and eventually found her in the cellar." He paused.

Alex leaned forward. "And then?"

"Suzi was sitting amongst the bodies. There was blood everywhere. She'd been beaten. And she was holding part of her grandfather's skull in her hands. She was unresponsive. I tried to talk to her. She did not reply. That is when I called the police."

Alex exhaled sharply. "Is this your final statement?"

The same bizarre smile danced around the edges of Peter's mouth. "Yes, that is what happened."

63

Peter Westphal had left. The guard had picked him up again and led him away. Alex and I were alone in the prison's dreary interrogation room.

"That didn't work," he said after a long pause.

"I have to admit, that surprised me," I replied. "We were mistaken. We misjudged Mr. Westphal."

"No," came his short answer.

"Of course," I insisted. "He loves her. He will never say anything bad about her. No matter if she is dead or alive."

"OK maybe. But she… she doesn't love him."

"I'm not so sure about that."

"I am. Suzanne Carstens is as cold-blooded as her grandfather. She found a fool, trapped him, and then used him." He hesitated. "As soon as she realized that Westphal believed her grandfather had killed his father, she pulled out all the stops on him. She manipulated him. In a big way… And everything she had, or pretends to have, these spells, the reaction when someone whistles, all this crap, is merely her claims. It's not supported by anything, nothing at all. She has led us all on and manipulated us like she did Peter Westphal."

I shook my head. "Never, ever. I don't believe it."

"Sure!" He snorted. "You're a psychologist. You presume everyone is disturbed." He leaned over. "But some people are just plain evil. No one can confirm that it's even true about old man Carstens raping her mother. The girl probably takes after her grandfather and is simply a rotten bitch. And those orgies in the cellar, who knows what went on down there. She might have been in on them too."

"Are you crazy?" I could not believe my ears. "If she is really such a depraved case like you just described, why would she want to kill her grandfather?"

"Why?" He laughed mockingly. "Have you ever looked through the file and seen how many millions Carstens was worth? It's nine figures. That's more than enough valid reasons for a sole heir to help someone around the corner."

I eyed him. His face appeared closed. Any kind of intimacy that had developed between us seemed to have dissipated all at once. There was no point in discussing it any further with him.

"Then we don't agree on this point." I tried to build a bridge. "We'll never know."

"Unfortunately." He took a deep breath. His eyes narrowed. "Unless we put little Carstens under pressure."

"And how?"

He pointed to the door through which Peter Westphal had disappeared a few minutes before. "Like we did with him. Same tactics."

"You want to suggest to her that Westphal is dead?" I was stunned. "No… Not that way. Absolutely not. That was pushing the envelope with Peter. This is… I'll never give you my consent. I won't have any part in this."

That fierce smile again. "Because you're assuming the wrong things. Suzanne Carstens is much, much colder and shrewder than the stupid idiot with whom we have just wasted our time. She'll turn him over to us the minute she gets a chance and wash her hands of the whole ordeal."

A complete stranger was sitting in front of me. Cynical and… I took a deep breath, forcing myself to stay calm. "I'm telling you again, I'm not participating. Your assessment of Suzanne Carstens is entirely wrong. I have spent a lot of time with her. I know what she's like. And I'm not mistaken about that."

"Hmm," he said, untowardly. "That's what Peter Westphal thought. Dear, sweet girl… innocent angel… You just don't want to admit that you've been played by her. That grates on your professional vanity. The great psychologist is being taken for a ride by a little rich girl."

OK. I'd had enough. "*Professional vanity*? Which one of us is pathologically vain and can't accept failure?"

His dark eyes flashed briefly. "I don't have time for this crap right now."

"Fine!" I replied and got up. "Because I don't either."

I turned around and left him sitting.

64

With the help of a walker, my father was able to move relatively safely. He held on to the padded handles and pushed the walker slowly but steadily along the stone-paved path. I walked closely beside him.

The park of the retirement home was almost deserted. Only one other couple made their rounds: a nurse dressed in white and a woman with a cane. They were surely fifty yards away from us.

My father and I were silent. The afternoon sun was shining. Birds were in a chirping competition, and the purple crocuses in the meadow blossomed more abundantly than in the previous week.

It was sad. Despite the holiday, I was apparently the only one visiting her relative. Poor old souls, pushed away and forgotten.

My father suddenly stumbled. He buckled over on the left side. I gave him a hand and steered him gently to a bench. We took a seat.

He looked at me gratefully. We remained silent.

Two squirrels jumped from a tree, chased each other across the yard, and climbed up a maple. They made that typical clicking noise as if they were scolding us. Cute. I smiled.

"Your mother is a hardworking woman," my father suddenly said.

I looked at him and suppressed the melancholic feeling that wanted to rise up in me. "That she is."

He pointed at the crocuses. "Look how beautifully she has arranged the garden. All the pretty flowers. I don't even know what they're called. But Rosie does."

"Mother likes working outside," I said.

He nodded. "Yes. That's how we're different." He frowned. "I enjoy the plants. But with my job, I'm so busy…" He pointed to the old remote control, which lay alone in the empty net of the walker. "I wouldn't know how to begin with the flowers. How much water they need, or fertilizer." He held up his hands in a helpless gesture.

"You complement each other really well," I remarked.

"That we do, Evi." He patted my knee.

"And you have a great marriage."

"Yes. I am a happy man."

The squirrels were still chasing each other. They had reached the treetop and were climbing over the mostly bare branches. I had to think about my argument with Alex in the prison.

"How come you and Mom never fight?" I asked my father. "Especially since you are so different."

He gave me an irritated look. "We don't argue?"

"Anyway, I never noticed."

"This is something that is not for children to witness either. Rosie and I do have our conflicts." His smile was mischievous. "And how!"

That was news to me. "Really?"

"Mhmm." He nodded. "The trick is to make up afterward. Forgive each other." He paused. "That's the best thing about our marriage."

My phone rang. I decided to ignore it.

The ringing did not stop.

He pointed at my jacket pocket. "Your phone. Answer it."

"Oh, no," I said. "I'm sure it's just work."

He shook his head sternly. "Evi, your job is important!"

I sighed and pulled out the smartphone. A number I did not know.

"Yes?" I answered.

"Dr. Wolf?" a young female voice spoke reluctantly. "It's me, Suzanne Carstens."

"Hello, Miss Carstens."

"You said I could call you if I needed to."

Maybe it was the connection, but she sounded strange.

"Of course," I replied. "What is it?"

"I need to speak with you. In person."

I frowned. "I can stop by tonight if you'd like."

A short silence. Then, "It would be better if you came right away."

I bit my lower lip and glanced at my father. He had taken the broken remote control from the net of the walker and was tapping on it.

"OK fine," I said reluctantly. "I'll be there in half an hour."

"That works well. I will listen to music until then. An opera."

"Good idea."

"I'm trying out my new headphones. To be on the safe side, I'll give the guard in front of the door my key card so that you don't have to knock."

"All right," I said.

"Thank you very much." The connection broke off.

I put my hand on my father's forearm. He looked at me.

"Sorry, I have to go," I said.

"Of course." He gave me a nice but noncommittal smile. "Mrs…" He paused, his expression became inquisitive. "Please excuse me. What was your name again?"

65

It was getting dark when I reached the Hotel Atlantic. The first yellow lights shone behind the divided windows in the façade. The rays of the setting sun bathed the white building with its lush adornment in delicate purplish orange hues.

I found a parking spot less than twenty yards away on the side of the road and hurried to the entrance. The porter in his dark suit, whose coat resembled the wide cape of an old-timey coachman, tapped his top hat and smiled at me.

I climbed the stone steps lined with massive columns, went through the glass door, crossed the foyer, and took the lift to Suzanne Carstens's suite.

One of the two officers assigned to the guard post knew me. We exchanged a few nice, but trivial words, and he handed me the key card.

Nevertheless, I knocked first before I used it.

I entered the suite. I was greeted by dim light. A single floor lamp was burning in the living room next to the couch. Suzanne Carstens was lying there. Her eyes were closed. But she was not wearing headphones.

My eyes fell on the floor. I discovered an overturned water bottle, next to it a glass and all around various torn open medicine boxes.

My heart skipped a beat. I ran to her, shaking her by the shoulders.

She opened her eyes and smiled at me.

"Miss Carstens!" I said.

She did not respond.

I bent down and picked up one of the pill bottles. Empty. I read the print and turned to her.

"Did you swallow all of these?"

She nodded her head silently.

I tossed the bottle to the side, hurried to the next room we used for our talks. The door was ajar. And inside… my file cart had been pushed into the middle of the carpet; its drawers broken open.

I returned to Suzanne Carstens and looked down at her. "Did you get the pills from in there?"

"Yes," she said softly. "Please don't call an ambulance. Please! It's too late anyway. I checked it on the internet. The time has passed, the drugs are already in the blood. You can't help me anymore."

I took a deep breath. Then I nodded. "OK." I sat down next to her on the coffee table and leaned forward a little.

"Miss Carstens," I began "What happened? Why do you want to kill yourself?"

Her dark brown eyes glowed almost unearthly in the dim light. "There's no reason to go on any longer."

I frowned. "I don't understand."

"The public prosecutor… Mr. Gutenberg was here."

A terrible premonition came over me. I clenched my teeth trying to keep the clammy feeling at bay.

"Uh-huh," I said.

"He told me."

"What did he tell you?"

Her expression remained relaxed but expressionless. "About Peter. That he is dead."

"Really?"

Alex, that idiot. That career-obsessed bastard, I thought. *What has he done? I had explained it to him. I made it absolutely clear!*

"You don't need to protect me anymore," Suzanne Carstens continued. "I know everything. There was a fight in the prison. Peter was beaten, took a bad fall and…" She broke off.

"If Mr. Gutenberg told you that," I said softly.

"I am grateful to him for his honesty." She paused. "Peter was the only person besides my mother who ever cared about me. I can't go through that again. I just can't go on."

I kept quiet.

"My grandfather," she began; her voice sounded hoarse and toneless. "Honorable on the surface. In reality, he was a monster. I told you on the Ad Astra. He always called my mother. He whistled. She had to go to him. His own daughter… She suffered so much. He hurt her… a lot. As a child, I didn't understand. And I was terribly afraid… I hid under the stairs. But I still heard everything. Every detail." She looked right at me. "And I'll tell you this. He deserved to die. I would do it again."

She *was* the murderer. I forced myself to remain objective.

"How did you do it?" I asked. "Four grown men and you by yourself?"

She shrugged her shoulders. "With fentanyl. And nicotine—I soaked one of my grandfather's cigars in water. I made ice cubes out of the solution."

I nodded.

"I always had to serve them downstairs while they excitedly waited for the women. I simply used the ice cubes and mixed the opiates into their drinks."

"But only one died from the poison in the adjoining bathroom," I said. "Alistair Grauel."

"Unfortunately." She shook her head. "The others… Grauel was out in the restroom. Big Karl, that fat pig, noticed that something was wrong. I don't know how… Maybe he tasted the poison… He downed his drink in one go." She laughed. "That son of a bitch. He at first thought it was his buddy Schilling."

"The gynecologist?"

She snorted. "Right! Gynecologist—butcher is closer to the truth. Schilling would have had no trouble getting drugs. It seemed obvious. Karl pulled out his knife. He liked to use that knife, especially on women's faces… He went for Schilling, screaming at him that he wanted to poison everybody…"

"Big Karl cut Schilling's throat," I clarified.

"With a single slash. It went quick."

She pressed her lips together. I waited, and when she said nothing more, I asked, "And your grandfather? He didn't intervene?"

"At first, he was confused. Startled. He hadn't expected that. He wanted to have a *nice evening*… Then his eyes fell on me. He knew it immediately."

"He attacked you?"

"He started hitting me. Hard. Like when he broke my nose. *You freak! You, hideous monstrosity*, he screamed. Over and over. And Big Karl came to his aid. They threw me against the cabinet. The glass broke."

"And then what happened?"

"One of the cutlasses fell out. I took it. I got momentum. A lot of momentum. My grandfather backed away from me, stumbled… The top of his skull simply… flew off."

"Then you stabbed him."

"He was suddenly sitting back in the chair…" The corners of her mouth rose.

"And Big Karl? What did he do in the meantime? Just watch?"

She looked the other way.

"Let's go back to the point where you were thrown against the display case," I tried again after a while. "You were lying on the ground, two strong men in front of you."

She still wouldn't look at me.

"Then, I'll tell you what really happened," I said. "You could never have committed the murders alone. You had help. From Peter Westphal."

"No!" She gasped.

"Yes," I insisted. "Peter was hiding upstairs in the house. He was the one who turned out the exterior lights so that the prostitutes didn't come into the villa. You and he wanted to work undisturbed."

"No," she repeated.

I did not respond to her. "Peter took the engraved pistol from the safe. You had given him the combination. When he heard the screaming in the basement, he realized your plan wasn't working. He ran down the stairs and shot Big Karl. And then you killed your grandfather."

"That's not true," she whispered.

"Unfortunately, it is the truth," I replied. "You and Peter Westphal planned it together. You showed him your mother's photo on the Ad Astra. And he recognized the cufflink."

She licked her lips. "My grandfather murdered Peter's father and made it look like a suicide. That much is true. The rest isn't."

"And the cufflink in your grandfather's hand? Peter put that there, didn't he? That link only had meaning for Peter. Not for you. So, Peter was at the scene of the crime when the murders took place."

Suzanne Carstens kept silent.

"You have four people on your conscience," I continued. "What your grandfather did to your mother is terrible. But the others had nothing to do with that. And as for Björn Carstens… You can't just take the law into your own hands. That's not right."

"You have no idea," she hissed suddenly.

I did not understand. "What do you mean?"

"I had every right in the world to do that. Schilling, the so-called gynecologist. He alone deserved to die a thousand times over."

"He took care of Big Karl's prostitutes."

"Exactly. *Took care of!*" she uttered. "He saw to it that they could go on turning tricks. And my mother…"

"What about your mother?"

"She was pregnant. Grandfather didn't want it. Not again… One day he dragged her by the hair. She screamed, crying and begging him to let her go. He showed no mercy." She paused. "Schilling cut the baby out of her belly. In the basement bathroom. Unfortunately, as always, they were all drunk and stoned. The bleeding wouldn't stop…"

I was stunned. I couldn't believe what I was hearing. "Your mother died down there?"

"She died a wretched death."

"Do you know that for a fact?"

A compassionate expression came over her. "Grandpa brought me in the restroom. He showed me what happens when you disobey. I had to wipe up the blood. I was ten at the time… The four men stood by and laughed. They just laughed…" A single tear ran down her cheek.

"I've read the report. Your mother died of a ruptured appendix."

"My grandfather arranged that. Schilling issued the death certificate. It wasn't the first time they did something like this."

Outside in front of the windows, dusk fell. Suzanne dozed off.

I tapped her. She ripped her eyelids open.

"I can't tell you how appalled I am. But there is one thing I don't understand," I said.

"What is it?" she replied softly, and the look on her face showed me that she was ready to let go.

"Your mother was pregnant. Where was the father-to-be? Why didn't she go to him with you?"

"To the father?"

I nodded. "Yes."

"She was with the father."

"You're misunderstanding me. I don't mean Björn Carstens, your mother's father. I mean the father of the unborn child. She could have gone to him."

"That's exactly where she was."

"What?"

"Björn Carstens was the father. My mother's father, the father of the unborn baby and my father."

"Oh, my God," slipped out of me. "I… It's… It's unthinkable how you and your mother must have suffered."

"You think that's unimaginable?" Her face resembled a death mask. "After she died… a few weeks later… it started. He whistled again. This time it was for me. And he did with me what he wanted, where he wanted, when he wanted. When he got tired of me, it was his three friends' turn. They liked it. I was something new. A child, you understand?"

Words failed me. I stretched out my hand and stroked her hair gently. She cowered into herself and closed her eyes.

"Can you stay with me?" she whispered.

"Of course," I said.

Her breathing became calmer. "Peter had nothing to do with any of this," she murmured. "It was me. All alone."

It wasn't long before she fell asleep. I stayed seated, studied her smooth face, the thick eyelashes, the delicate, light skin, and the broken and slightly crooked nose. At some point I got up and left the suite. I closed the door behind me.

The two officers looked at me. And the policeman from earlier said, "Dr. Wolf? Is everything okay with Miss Carstens? You look… faint?"

I squared my shoulders. "Miss Carstens is sleeping."

The policeman smiled. "That's nice! She is usually quite nervous. We can always hear her roaming the rooms. I'm sure you gave her a sedative."

"No." I shook my head. "There is not a single pill in Miss Carstens's suite. Only placebos."

66

Alex was sitting in his kitchen, thinking more and more about mixing a stiff drink. Instead, he decided to make himself a sandwich. Searching the refrigerator, he found a jar of pickles in the door and a Hungarian salami on the bottom shelf. He pulled them out and checked the bread box.

It occurred to him that the conversation with Suzanne Carstens had gone about as well as their first meeting a week before. Although she was evidently more aware of his presence, she had not uttered a word. But he simply had to try it. Now, Bolsen would get his way. He would have his damned press conference and declare the case has been resolved. Then it would be stored away in the archives.

And Evelin? What would come of it when she learned he went to see Suzanne Carstens? Evelin had already been upset. Alex supposed she would get over it. Besides, she should not have made such a fuss. But he had to confess he felt sorry. And more than he wanted to admit.

The doorbell rang, startling Alex, who almost sent the opened pickle jar across the room. He snatched it at the last second and secured the top when the ringing started anew. And this time it did not stop.

"OK, OK! I'm coming," he said vociferously and hurried to the entrance.

He opened the door.

Evelin.

At first sight, Alex could tell he was in trouble. Evelin was bounding forward, her neck muscles flexed for a fight. Eyes pinched tight. If looks could kill, he was going to need a mortician.

"You went ahead and did it all the same! I had explained to you why I would never do that! And you damned well knew that I didn't want you to do it. And yet you waltzed straight over to Suzanne Carstens's and pressured her!"

"Maybe you should come in," Alex suggested.

"I don't see how that would help!" Evelin responded loudly.

Alex took a step to the side. "This can't be discussed in passing. Come on in."

Evelin inhaled audibly. "Fine."

She stormed past him into the living room.

"Don't you want to take a load off and sit down? I'm in the middle of making something to eat." Alex pointed haphazardly over his shoulder in the direction of the kitchen.

"I'm not staying long," Evelin said, opened her coat and sat on the edge of an armchair.

Alex chose the sofa across from her.

"Suzanne Carstens…"

Alex ran his tongue between his lips. "Yes. I can't deny it. Naturally, I visited her. And yes, I confronted her."

"You told her Peter Westphal was dead."

Alex crossed his arms in front of his chest. "Otherwise, it wouldn't have worked. But you don't have to worry. She didn't have a breakdown or anything, she just packed it away. She is as undeniably insensitive and callous as her grandfather."

"You idiot!" Evelin exploded again. "You don't have a lick of common sense! You hadn't been gone five minutes before she broke open my medical cart, took all the sedatives I had stored in the adjacent room, and swallowed every last one of them."

Alex dropped his jaw. "Oh, my God. Is she dead?"

"No, of course not! I don't leave sedatives with depressed clients. I'm not crazy! They were all placebos."

"Really!" Alex raised an eyebrow. "I hadn't thought you were capable of such deceit."

"Don't change the topic! You have put Suzanne Carstens's life in danger by your thoughtless, egotistical, absolutely pointless actions, by giving her this fictitious account of Peter Westphal. And it brought you nothing at all!"

"You have to understand," Alex pleaded, "I am sorry, but I had to try. It was our last chance. We will have our final meeting on this case tomorrow with Bolsen. If I do not have anything on Suzanne Carstens or Peter Westphal, they'll be set free."

"Oh yeah?" Evelin smirked, "But it is not all about you! Do you have any idea what you have done to Suzanne Carstens? She was already severely traumatized! I do not know if she will ever be able to cope with this again, or if she won't actually try to kill herself the next opportunity she gets!"

Alex took a deep breath and ran a palm over his face. "How is Suzanne Carstens now?"

"She is sleeping. I requested that an officer sit next to her so that someone is there when she wakes up."

"Thank…" Alex began, then cut himself off, creasing his brow. "How did you know I was with Suzanne Carstens? And how do you know that she took the placebos? And how she is doing now? Were you there too?"

Evelin turned to him in disbelief. "*Naturally*, I was with her! Someone had to sweep up the mess you left behind in your asininity."

"This whole thing was your idea," Alex retorted.

"Mine?"

"You are the one who started it. *But we won't exactly be playing by the book.*"

She bent forward. "I can't believe that you are actually so arrogant and brazen as to say that now! And to say it right to my face! When we both know for certain that this statement of mine was only referring to Peter Westphal!"

"Yeah, and it didn't work out with him! The logical next step for me was to try it on Suzanne Carstens."

"Even though I told you not to!"

"You could have given me more support. Could have gone with me, but *no*, you left me all alone!"

"Oh, I see! Now it's my fault!" Evelin laughed contemptuously. "Yeah, right. Of course, it is. The infallible Alex Gutenberg? It couldn't have been him. So, let's put the blame on the psychologist."

Alex grimaced. "I didn't mean it like that…"

"No! You know? I've had enough of you, once and for all! Never again as long as I live… even if you were the last person on Earth… I would not work or talk with you, ever. I never want to see you again. Do you hear me?" Evelin was practically screaming. "That's it. Now, it's over, finished and done with. You are a sad, broken man. You radiate a highly toxic vortex that drags everyone around down to your level."

"Fine!" Alex felt the blood rush to his cheeks and tried to get his rising anger in check. "I've had enough too. For all I care, I may be broken. But this is about justice. About justice and the law. There has been a brutal, quadruple murder. I cannot stand around and hope that my banal kid gloves and psychological frills will bring the perpetrator to one day have the generosity to confess his guilt. I had to take matters into my own hands…"

Alex's phone began to vibrate.

He pulled it out of his pocket, looked at the display and furrowed his brow. "Just a moment. It's Henrik." He took the call. "Gutenberg. … Uh-huh. … What? Really? … I'm on my way."

He put the phone away and looked blankly at Evelin.

"What is going on?" she asked.

"There has been an incident with Peter Westphal," Alex responded slowly. "He is lying in the infirmary."

Evelin looked at him alarmed. "Something serious?"

"It sounds pretty bad." Alex stood up. "I'm going there now."

"I'll come with you." Evelin said as she got to her feet.

67

Evelin climbed into Alex's car with him. They drove through the night. Silently.

Alex kept his eyes forward. Then he gave her a clandestine sidelong glance. She was staring out the passenger window.

He started thinking about what he should say to her. But then realized that he could not have acted any differently with Suzanne. He would do it all over again. That is why there was no point in trying to appease Evelin, because she would immediately recognize that he did not honestly mean it and was only saying it for the sake of it. And that would make the situation worse, instead of defusing it.

They drove on, entering the overpass and running into evening traffic. They rolled along at a constant, albeit moderate, speed, getting there, but not quickly.

Evelin broke her reticence. "She confessed."

Holy shit, I knew it! Alex thought, but out loud he just said, "Uh-huh."

"She called me and asked me to come to her, without telling me why," Evelin continued. "I immediately left my father's side and went to her. She was lying on the sofa, had swallowed all the placebos, and was absolutely convinced that she was about to die. She was also really sleepy, which happens to highly sensitive people. They believe it so much that the body follows the patient's expectations."

"Did she act alone?" Alex got straight to the point.

Evelin replied, "No. Peter Westphal was definitely with her. But she denied it until the end."

"How did she do it?"

"As we suspected, with nicotine and fentanyl in their drinks. It worked on Grauel. The rest of them noticed something, went after each other at first, and when they turned on her it got completely out of control."

"Did she say anything else about how it transpired?"

"She confessed to me that she killed her grandfather."

"With the cutlass?"

"Yes. With the sword from the broken glass vitrine."

"All for fucking money." Alex shook his head in disgust.

Evelin twisted in her seat to look him straight on. "No. It wasn't about the money at all."

He threw her a quick glance, before he returned his concentration to the road again. "OK. Peter had another motive. The cufflink he found on his father. And she for her grandfather abusing her mother. That is also part of it."

"That's just the tip of the iceberg."

Something in her voice made him take notice. "What do you mean?"

They came to a red light. He stopped.

"Carstens killed her mother, too."

"Uh-uh, she died from a ruptured appendix."

"That's not true. She died from a botched abortion, which Schilling performed in the basement toilet."

He stared at her. "Oh, dear God."

"Her mother bled to death, and Suzanne had to clean it up."

Alex did not respond. *Heaven's sakes! How can someone do that to a child? The poor girl.*

The car behind him honked. He pulled himself out of his thoughts and looked forward. Green. He moved on.

Evelin continued, "Shortly after her mother's death, the grandfather started abusing Suzanne regularly, and he also shared her with his three friends."

Alex remembered the basement and how it was furnished. He did not even want to imagine what they did to the girl down there. He remained quiet but then said, "Why didn't the mother just leave?"

"I suppose she was already psychologically debilitated and no longer capable of doing that."

"Because of the abuse from Björn?"

"Björn Carstens was not only the father of the unborn child Schilling had aborted, he was Suzanne's father, as well."

"What a disgusting, inhumane, filthy pig," Alex mumbled, and bit down hard on his back teeth.

"That is your motive. It was not about money. Absolutely not."

68

Evelin led the way down the starkly lit hall of the jail's infirmary.

The floor had been recently mopped. It was still wet here and there, but relatively clean. The walls were covered up to Alex's shoulder with beige tiles. The only things that suggested they were in a basement, or still in lockup, were the bars across the high squat windows.

Up ahead, Alex could see Strobelsohn talking with a doctor outside of a closed door. The captain saw them, said something to the physician, and walked down the corridor toward them.

Alex shook Strobelsohn's broad hand and immediately asked, "So what exactly happened?"

Strobelsohn looked up at the low ceiling, probably in recollection, and then began. "The prisoners in the cells on either side of Peter Westphal heard strange noises and called for help. The guards came in a few seconds later and found that he had hung himself from the bars in his cell with a bed sheet. They got there just in time, resuscitated him, and brought him down here to the infirmary. They have him under isolation for the next twenty-four hours, so he won't try it again."

"Have you been able to speak with him?" Evelin asked.

"I was inside with him. He is conscious. He can talk, too. But he's not saying a word. He wouldn't even look at me." Strobelsohn paused shortly before continuing. "I knew this case wasn't over yet. I knew there was more to it. I really tried my best to get him to say something. And now… tomorrow, Westphal will be released. And Bolsen had to call this premature press conference."

"Then let's give it another go," Alex said.

"I can't imagine that it will be any different for you," Strobelsohn grumbled.

"Still, it's worth a try."

Strobelsohn shrugged. "Go on then. I think it is better if I don't join you."

"OK," Alex agreed. "I'll let you know how it goes. We'll see each other tomorrow in Bolsen's office for the debriefing anyway."

Strobelsohn nodded and left Alex and Evelin in the corridor.

As Alex and Evelin entered the hospital room, he thought it looked like the inside of every other clinic. Except very empty. Peter was lying in the only bed. He didn't pay them any attention. He was staring out the curtainless window instead, a nurse's bell at his fingertips. There was no other furniture, no other objects. Nothing.

Alex pushed the door closed. The handle on the inside had been removed.

Evelin looked around. Her gaze stopped at the upper right-hand corner above the entrance. "Camera," she whispered to Alex.

"Yes. Because he is a danger to himself. But there is no microphone," Alex responded quietly.

"Are you certain?" Evelin confirmed.

"I'm positive."

They walked closer to the bed. Peter turned his head and looked at them. Pasty. Bandaged around his neck.

Evelin began, "Mr. Westphal, Mr. Gutenberg and I are so terribly sorry."

Peter did not say a thing.

"Today, in the interrogation room… we made you think by our vague statements that Miss Carstens was dead. But that is not true. She is alive."

Peter stared at her blankly.

"She's not even in the hospital."

"You expect me to believe that?" Peter asked. His voice sounded rough, croaky.

"I just came from her."

Peter sneered unbelievably.

"She told me everything."

Now his facial expression changed, became angrier. "You're trying to manipulate me. You must think I'm dim. She is dead and that is not enough for you. You can't respect that. Now you're trying to extort a confession out of me. You haven't even been to see her."

"We had a long talk. She told me about her mother's abuse."

"You knew that already," Peter said.

Alex took a step back, leaned against the wall and let Evelin work her magic.

"She told me how her mother died. Downstairs in the bathroom. She told me about her own abuse by her grandfather and by the other three men."

Peter inhaled sharply.

"And she told me that Björn was her father. And that Björn also killed your father and made it look like a suicide."

Peter's contemptuous expression changed. A faint glimmer of hope spread across his face. "She's really alive. Isn't she?"

"Yes."

"And... she is well?" Peter carried on without waiting a beat.

"Yes. She is asleep at this moment; tomorrow is another day."

Peter started to breathe more easily, relaxed.

"She explained to me what happened the night of the murders," Evelin continued, "down in the basement."

Peter grew cautious again. "So?"

"We know how she wanted to poison the four men with a mixture of nicotine and fentanyl. That went wrong, they attacked her, and she killed her grandfather and all the others."

Peter shook his head rapidly. "She did not tell you anything about the night of the murders. She wouldn't do that."

"She told me," Evelin started again, "that Big Karl and her grandfather beat her up and repeatedly called her a hideous monstrosity."

"*Hideous monstrosity*," Peter mumbled. His face turned bright red, and he started to shake a little. He pointed a trembling finger at her and at Alex. "That is not what happened."

Alex stepped forward. "Set it straight, make a statement."

"A statement." Peter bit his lip. He nodded, hesitantly at first, and then visibly. He sat up in his bed, "Good. Miss Carstens had nothing to do with it. It was all my idea. Regarding the poison. She wasn't even there. She was at the movies, alone. I snuck into her house, went down to the basement, cut the alcohol with a mixture of fentanyl and nicotine. Then I hid upstairs, turned on the lights, so the prostitutes wouldn't come in. And I simply waited."

Alex grimaced, "That can't be. Miss Carstens was assaulted and brutally beaten."

"She came much later, slipped in the blood and had an unfortunate fall."

"She did not get beaten up?" Alex said.

"No. Nothing, like that."

"You killed all four of them?" Evelin asked.

"Yes. I noticed that it wasn't going well. I heard screaming. So, I opened the safe, I had the combination. I grabbed the gun, ran downstairs. Big Karl had killed Dr. Schilling. I shot him."

Alex raised his chin and looked through squinted eyes down at Peter. "Just like that?"

Peter nodded in response. "Then Björn Carstens came at me. I broke the display case, took a saber, and killed him, too."

"You walked through the room, smashed the display case, and grabbed the cutlass? Why didn't you shoot again?"

Alex watched Peter closely. His eyes rolled to their upper left pinnacle, a clear sign. Alex knew what it meant. Peter was ensuring that his story fit the evidence. "The gun misfired."

Alex shook his head in disbelief. "Aha. And then?"

Peter hesitated again. He ran his tongue over his lower lip. "Then I pressed the cufflink into Björn Carstens's hand and closed his fingers around it."

"Just like your dying father had put the link in your hand when you found him?" Evelin surmised.

"He was guilty of killing my father… Then I hoisted the dead pimp onto his chair, wiped the gun down and put it back in the safe. I wanted to clean up the basement too, but Suzi returned. She had gone downstairs without me noticing. Screaming, she slipped and hurt herself. By the time I got to her, she was sitting there with her grandfather's skull in her hand." Peter fell silent.

"So that is your statement?" Alex inquired.

"Yes. It was me. By myself."

"Apart from the fact that some things don't fit together and are illogical, you have just confessed to a quadruple homicide," Alex said, "and we are going to hold you responsible."

Peter shrugged. "I realize that. I don't care."

"And Miss Carstens will walk free? Are you aware of that?"

"Of course. She'll be released, she has nothing to do with any of it."

"Is there something you would like to add?" Evelin took over. "Think carefully now. This is your last chance."

A slight yet decisive shake of his head. "What I told you is the truth. Now leave me alone."

As Alex and Evelin went to the door and pushed a button to call the orderly. Peter's voice stopped them. "Excuse me, Dr. Wolf?"

Alex and Evelin turned to the young man.

"Are you going to see Suzi tomorrow?" he asked.

"Most definitely," Evelin confirmed.

Peter smiled.

Evelin raised her shoulders, inquiring, "Should I give her a message from you?"

"That won't be necessary."

69

The Hamburg pretrial holding jail on Holstenglacis Street was a bulky building about one hundred and fifty years old. Several stories high, made of red brick, surrounded by a puissant stone wall with rolled barbed wire—imposing and depressing at the same time.

Alex and I had returned to his BMW from the infirmary in silence. There we sat and stared through the windshield at the illuminated building. Still, neither of us spoke a word.

No matter how hard I tried, what Peter Westphal and earlier Suzanne Carstens had reported would not leave me in peace. Although I did not want them to, my thoughts wandered to the murders on that night.

How did it go down exactly? Suzanne was in the basement. And Peter? I furrowed my brow. Upstairs. In Suzanne's room? No, too far away. He must have stayed nearby. To protect her if something went wrong. Where then? In the living room. He must have been sitting in the living room. In one of the armchairs or on the couch. Had he turned on a lamp? Certainly not. He waited in the dark. He did not want to be discovered.

Suzanne Carstens had told me her part of the story in detail. In comparison, Peter Westphal had been much more reserved with his words to Alex and me. Was I able to combine their two statements into one? Imagine the role Peter had played in this? I closed my eyes and concentrated on him. And suddenly I saw it clearly:

The room in front of him was large. It seemed to have no end. The moon, which shone alabastrine from outside, offered only scant light. It gave the furniture unearthly, strange contours that moved and seemed to come alive whenever a cloud passed over the sky.

Peter waited; absolute tranquility reigned—heavy and oppressive, it announced an ominous event that would change everything. Death would come quietly, stealthily, and yet conclusively.

Peter was extremely tense, yet strangely relieved, at the same time.

From far away, sounds penetrated his ear. He sat bolt upright, listened. He did not even dare to breathe.

Nothing. He was mistaken.

Suddenly the sounds came back. This time, louder.

Voices. Incoherent fragments of words were shouted. He concentrated, leaned farther forward.

And then he heard it. Crystal clear: "You freak! You hideous monstrosity!"

Over and over and over…

Peter looked at the table in front of him. At the pistol he had ready to go. He grabbed it, jumped up and ran.

His footsteps echoed through the living room. He reached the servants' stairway that led down. No light here either. He took two or three steps at a time. And still those screams, that roar.

You filthy freak…

He rounded a corner.

Suddenly, everything in front of him is light. The big party room. Schilling is sitting on one of the chairs. His throat is slit. Blood pulsates out of the gaping wound. Suzi is hunched over near the glass vitrine where the nautical cutlasses and swords are displayed. She protects her head with both arms. Big Karl and Björn Carstens take turns punching her. She does not fight back. They are going to kill Suzi.

Peter is catatonic. Unable to move. Unable to act.

Björn grabs Suzi. He picks her up effortlessly and throws her into the cabinet. The glass breaks. A couple of sabers fall out.

Peter's rigidity dissolves. "Quit it!" He yells. "Stop!"

The two men freeze in their tracks, turn to Peter. Without hesitating, Big Karl runs at him. Fast. He is carrying a bloody knife in his left hand.

Peter raises the gun. It is automatic. As if by itself, his finger bends around the trigger. The roar of a gunshot. The large-caliber bullet slaps the pimp's upper body, he goes down.

Peter points the gun at Björn Carstens. Their eyes meet. Carstens is not afraid. He does not show the slightest sign of fear. Only hatred, violence and thirst for the kill play on his visage.

A movement next to Carstens. Peter looks away for a second.

It is Suzi. She is back on her feet, her face swollen and covered in blood. Staggering, she holds one of the big sabers in both hands.

Carstens notices her too. He stares at her.

Suzi straightens herself, groans and swings with all her might. The broad blade of the cutlass whizzes through the air.

Carstens retreats, his foot trips over the coffee table. He stumbles and falls backwards into one of the empty chairs. He sits up, wants to use the armrest to lift himself, to go and attack Suzi again.

The cutting edge of the saber hits him at the temple, slices effortlessly through his head. A piece of his skull flies away. Blood sprays.

Suzi, who has almost fallen over because of the swing, finds her balance again. She raises the cutlass and rams it with an inhuman scream right through her grandfather's chest…

I opened my eyes. Shivering, I rubbed my arms and glanced at Alex. Judging from the look on his face, he had similar thoughts to mine.

"Not exactly your typical murderers," I said.

"Peter Westphal and Suzanne Carstens?" Alex sighed. "Definitely not."

"They did not accuse one another."

He shook his head. "On the contrary. They each took the blame themselves. In order to let the other one… What? To let the other off?"

"Exactly."

"And yet there are four premeditated, cold-blooded murders."

"Premeditated," I admitted. "But not in cold blood."

"Whatever." He shrugged his shoulders. "Murder is murder. They'll have to answer for that."

"In a court of law?"

"Where else should it be carried out?"

I did not answer him and instead looked out of the side window. It began to rain.

"What is it?" he asked me.

"This is all very disappointing and highly unfair."

"Why is it unfair?"

I turned to him. "In particular for Suzanne Carstens, but even Peter suffered excessively because of these men. They are traumatized. Their lives are in shambles." I paused. "Of course, it was wrong what they did. There is no question. But what was done to them… What about that? It was worse than death, especially for Suzanne."

He hesitated. "Yes," he said finally.

"And now? Now you want to punish her again."

He frowned. "What are you getting at? What are you trying to suggest? Should I just let them go?"

"For the time being, apart from these two, we are the only ones who know the truth."

His mouth narrowed. "And tomorrow at the debriefing, I'm going to tell Bolsen and Strobelsohn. All of the circumstances will be taken into account at the trial and in the assessment of their sentences."

"You can look yourself in the mirror after that?" I asked.

"Yes. It's the only way."

I felt myself getting angry. Ice-cold, impotent anger rose up in me. "You're adamant about that. With them, you show no mercy. But... you." I bit my lip.

"But?" His eyes flashed. "Speak your mind!"

"No." I shook my head.

"Yes. Yes! Now it's time to put everything on the table."

"All right," I said. "You are more generous with yourself."

"What does that mean?"

I did not want to say it. But now it flew out of me. "What you did in Afghanistan. With your friend."

He eyed me in disbelief. "It's impossible to compare the two! That was something completely different!"

"No. You did what you thought you had to do, too. You acted according to your own rules."

He was silent for a long while. Then he asked quietly, "Seriously?"

"There is no difference."

He exhaled audibly. "But yes, there is! A huge one!"

"No, there isn't," I insisted. "Keep on lying to yourself."

"Nonsense," he said.

"Just because you can't forgive yourself doesn't mean that other people don't deserve forgiveness."

The look in his eyes became expressionless. "I will inform Bolsen, Strobelsohn, and Breiter about everything tomorrow."

"You can't be dissuaded?" I asked, although I already knew his answer.

"No."

"OK. Then I'd better take a taxi." I turned away from him and opened the passenger door.

"Maybe that would be best," he said to my back.

In the meantime, it had started raining cats and dogs. I got out, took a few steps, and dug out my cell phone.

While I was searching for the number of the taxi company, I heard Alex start the engine of his BMW and drive away.

March

30

Tuesday

70

Bolsen roosted on the top floor of the LKA building. His private conference room, directly adjacent to his office, was functional and yet furnished with a certain elegance. An oval, light-colored wooden table in the middle could seat around fifteen to twenty people. On it stood hot and cold drinks in jugs and bottles, including glasses, cups, spoons, and milk and sugar for coffee.

Large windows offered an expansive view of the city. The chairs were comfortably upholstered and equipped with armrests. A floor-to-ceiling cupboard had been fitted into one of the walls. A video projector, a flip chart in the corner, two modern paintings, and three oversized potted plants completed the picture.

I sat on the right, at the head of the table. Henrik and Strobelsohn were on the left, leaving a chair empty. Presumably for Alex.

The two police officers had folders in front of them. Bolsen was still missing. His secretary had informed us that he was hurrying to finish an important phone call.

Alex had not yet arrived.

Henrik had provided Strobelsohn and me with drinks. We waited.

I'd had a restless night. My thoughts were constantly revolving around Suzanne Carstens and Peter Westphal. I could not find any peace. In a few minutes, their fate would be sealed forever. They had taken three people's lives. There was no way around this. According to the law, they had to be held accountable for their deeds. And yet… the stale taste in my mouth would not go away.

The connecting door to Bolsen's office opened, and he entered in a new, no doubt ridiculously expensive suit, fresh from the hairdresser and in the best of moods.

"A very good morning to you all," he greeted us. "Please remain seated." He pranced around the table and shook our hands one by one. Naturally, each of us stood up.

"I see you've already helped yourselves," he said and grabbed a bottle of water.

The door to the conference room gave way. Alex was standing in the hall. He walked in, heavily laden with four files. He put them on the table.

I looked him up and down. Like Bolsen, he was clean-shaven and freshly coiffed. And like me, he seemed to have not slept much. He gave me an impersonal glower.

"Wonderful," Bolsen said. "Mr. Gutenberg is here. Now we are complete."

The two men shook hands.

Alex sat down directly opposite me. And the expression on his face revealed that he was going to go through with his plan. He was determined to inform everyone about Suzanne Carstens and Peter Westphal's involvement in the murders at the villa.

"The press conference starts in an hour," Bolsen began. "The large hall downstairs is being prepared. This is our final meeting. We should use it to update each other and discuss who will say what later." He glanced around. "Agreed?"

A general nod accompanied by an approving growl from Strobelsohn.

"Good." Bolsen also nodded. "The direction I want to take for the press conference: several high-profile murders, stemming out of the red-light district. Hamburg is a port city, so everything to do with prostitution cannot be completely prevented. However, we at the LKA are very much on top of these things and have achieved outstanding successes in the past in our fight against organized crime…" He deliberated shortly. "At this point, I'll give a few examples that the populace remembers, and put up two slides presenting our statistics on the wall." He paused. "Of course, crimes like this will keep springing up. There's nothing you can do to eliminate them. But thanks to all of you…" He looked at each of us. "This time we succeeded in solving the murders with incredible expediency. That means both incidents at the Carstens's villa and the dead prostitutes from Burchardkai, as well as the two dock workers whose bodies we found in the Easter fire." He turned to Strobelsohn. "Isn't it true that all the cases are linked?"

"Sure," Strobelsohn said. "The pimp Big Karl Marten organized the human trafficking. With certain connections to Russia…"

"We'll skip that part downstairs," Bolsen interrupted him. "No talk about Vladimir Ivanich or whatever his name is."

"Dmitri Ivanov," Henrik said.

"Anyway," Bolsen said and frowned, "this adventurous story of a Russian oligarch… or Russian mafia boss… it's just distracting. We don't have any solid evidence… But Captain Strobelsohn, please go on."

The commissioner briefly bit his lower lip. "Well. We have concluded that Björn Carstens was also entangled in the ring carrying out human trafficking…"

"Hold on," Bolsen raised his hand. "We're lacking evidence for that proposition. Mr. Carstens had a weakness when it came to the female gender. And now he's dead. You see…" He leaned forward and lowered his voice confidentially. "We're not going to make a big deal out of this. We do not want to supply any of the tabloids with sensational speculations."

"OK," Strobelsohn said reluctantly. "Dr. Schilling, the third victim in the mansion, was a gynecologist, but was no longer licensed to practice. That did not stop him from providing medical care under a false name, in particular for Karl Marten's brothels. He was undoubtedly involved. So was Alistair Grauel, who handled the pimp's finances."

"The prostitutes from the Burchardkai docks were without question intended for Big Karl's establishments," Bolsen took over. "Since he had been murdered, he couldn't ensure that the young women would be met at the docks. This led to the scandalous discovery in the container. And the two dockworkers were part of this dirty business all the time and collected their just rewards." Bolsen drank from his water. "To recap: A dispute in the red-light district. Competing factions. We managed to track down one of the killers immediately. He resisted arrest and even shot at Mr. Gutenberg, our chief prosecutor. Unfortunately, the perpetrator died. A manhunt is underway for his accomplice. We are more than confident that we will find him in the shortest possible time and bring him to justice… The cases are closed. And the city can sleep soundly once again." He took another look around. "Do we agree on this?"

While Bolsen was speaking, I had been watching Alex. He had repeatedly sat up in his chair, restlessly. Now he cleared his throat and said, "Well…"

This was as far as he got.

"Yes, I know!" Bolsen waved Alex's interruption aside. "You wanted to see me last night. Please forgive me, Mr. Gutenberg, for not returning your call. I was at a reception, and it got rather late." He smiled dreamily. "But don't worry. Captain Strobelsohn had reached me before and told me about Mr. Westphal's attempted suicide." Bolsen sighed. "It is most unfortunate that it has come to this. And yesterday, of all days… Of course, we won't want to make a big deal about it later, either. The damage to the image of our penal system would be immense. It would distract from our success in solving the murders. And it would also be unfair to Mr. Westphal." Bolsen hesitated. "I don't want you to think I'm trivializing his attempt on his life. It's always very bad when someone commits suicide…" He turned to me. "But we have a specialist among us. Dr. Wolf, perhaps you would like to say a few words so that we can put this incident behind us in good conscience? Fortunately, nothing serious happened… You spoke with both Mr. Westphal and Miss Carstens several times during the investigation."

I could see Alex's mouth squeezing into a furious line. He worked his jaw.

"What makes a person want to kill himself?" I began. "That is an enormously important and extraordinarily complex question. Every single case is unique. But what they all have in common: There is always an exceptional situation. A subjective hopelessness and despair. Otherwise, they wouldn't do that, and it is easily prevented when we're given a chance. In this respect, Mr. Bolsen, what you have just stated is correct: It is very bad when someone commits suicide."

Bolsen beamed. "Thank you. I have always had a great ability to put myself in other people's shoes. It's one of my strengths."

Exactly, I thought but continued. "Hopelessness. That's what Peter Westphal felt last night when he wanted to hang himself in his cell. And that is how he still feels. The entire situation, the murders, the pitiful condition of Miss Carstens, whom he loves. Coupled with the things they both experienced in the basement of the villa. The developments of the past few days…" I looked directly at Alex. He didn't avoid my gaze. "All of these circumstances led him to this sudden reaction."

"Terrible," muttered Bolsen. "Peter Westphal is now being looked after. How is Miss Carstens? Just a little information for us. For me. That will stay in this room, of course."

"Miss Carstens has been through unimaginably horrific things. She is severely traumatized. And what you don't know yet, Mr. Bolsen, is that she also tried to commit suicide herself last night."

"What?" Bolsen jerked his head up. "Why didn't anybody inform me of this?" He turned to Alex. "Or is that what you wanted to tell me, Mr. Gutenberg?"

"Yes," Alex replied. He sat up straighter and pulled his file in front of him "And…"

I did not let him continue. "Fortunately, Miss Carstens escaped harm's way. I had a long talk with her. An officer spent the night with her and was replaced by another this morning."

"Exemplary crisis management," Bolsen praised. His expression took on a thoughtful note. "Twenty-four-hour police protection, therapy sessions with you… The taxpayer can't bear these costs indefinitely. The question is, what is going to happen to them?"

"Honestly, I don't know," I replied truthfully. "Suzanne Carstens and Peter Westphal worry me entirely. They are in a position… in such a tense situation…" I shook my head. "These two cannot and will not cope with this psychologically." My next words were aimed directly at Alex. He wouldn't be swayed. But he should at least know how I felt about it. "The hopelessness remains. I can't imagine that they will find the strength to survive this."

"Um…" Bolsen's mouth twisted as if he had bitten into a sour lemon. "That sounds… cruel. So… serious."

I nodded. "Exactly. Especially when you consider that both got into these circumstances through no fault of their own. They ultimately only reacted to what came at them. The one way out they could see at that moment was death."

Strobelsohn and Henrik looked at the ground. Alex continued to hold my gaze.

"Well…" Bolsen sighed again, though it did not seem genuine to me. "Dr. Wolf, I wouldn't want to have to do your job. I am really affected." He paused. "My thinking is always solution-oriented. Therefore, what has to happen for these two to find the courage to face life? Suzanne Carstens and Peter Westphal are still so young."

"They must be shown a way out," I said.

"Way out?" Bolsen frowned.

"Someone would have to make a leap of faith and give them an opportunity to start over."

An irritated head shake from Bolsen. He looked at his wristwatch. "How time flies! Twenty minutes left. We let ourselves ramble on a bit too long." He turned his attention to Alex. "Mr. Gutenberg. Quickly, what do you have to contribute?" He raised a finger cautiously. "Only what we have to clarify before the press corps arrives. Everything else can be postponed until after the conference. I'll take you all out to lunch."

The corner of Alex's mouth twitched. His gaze bored through mine. Then he looked into his open file, flipped through it. After a little while he took a deep breath, closed the folder, and concentrated his attention on Bolsen. "I have nothing more to add. Dr. Wolf has said everything that needed saying."

I couldn't believe what I was hearing.

"Excellent! Very nice!" Bolsen knocked on the table with his signet ring. "We'll even get out of here early! I have two more points before we go down to the large meeting hall." He lifted a finger. "First of all, you have worked together so outstandingly well as a team. That gave me this vision. I would like to declare the four of you as a permanent special task force for particularly difficult and complicated cases with high public exposure, as a kind of elite response squad. Together with our press office, I'll come up with a more amiable name that'll be catchier." He leaned over to me. "And, as you are the lady of the team, I will ask you first. Could you imagine that, Dr. Wolf?"

"To work with Mr. Strobelsohn and Mr. Breiter along with Mr. Gutenberg in a permanent team?" I repeated his question and looked at Alex. His dark eyes would not let go of mine, though his face remained expressionless.

"Uh-huh. With these three nice gentlemen," Bolsen replied.

I had to smile. "Honestly?"

"Yes of course!"

"It would be a privilege," I said.

Bolsen gave me muted applause. "Bravo! Great! A *privilege*… May I quote you at the press conference?"

"Sure," I said.

Alex grinned unabashedly at me. And Strobelsohn and Henrik too.

"Judging by the expressions on these three gentlemen's faces, I don't even have to ask them," Bolsen continued. "And now my second point." He raised the next finger. "It's regarding the proceedings of the press conference. We are optimally prepared. But please, just take one of those horrible-looking files with you, or…" He frowned. "Better if we leave them all here. I have fake ones in my closet in different colors. We'll match them to your outfits. New folders, moderately filled. A little more TV-friendly than those old, bulky things that are bursting at the seams… I'll run the conference. That means most of the time I'll have to speak." He swung his head back and forth affectedly. "But I'll find a place for each of you to make a statement or two. Especially for Dr Wolf. It is always important and good for a lady to articulate her thoughts. In times of equal rights and these gender battles, we have to show our colors, and we do. Don't we, Dr. Wolf?"

"Of course," I said. "Thank you."

"With pleasure." Bolsen bent over even farther and patted my hand.

April

05

Monday

71

I had taken a chair with a view of the Alster in front of the Poseidon. Shortly after ten o'clock in the morning, the entire open-air seating area was mine. The sun was shining. A gentle breeze brushed against my face. It carried the smell of the river and spring with it.

I was warm, so I took off my jacket and hung it on the back of my chair.

Georgios's young waitress was busy wiping down the rest of the tables and setting them for the noon rush. At this time of day, during the week, there was not much going on. A couple of rowers and small sailboats were scattered across the Alster. Only a few people strolled along the river promenade, most of them tourists or dog owners walking their four-legged friends.

Georgios, with his ever so tight black vest stretched over his white shirt, stepped outside, saw me, and rushed to my table.

"Evi, my dear," he greeted me. "It's nice to see you. So early today?"

"By necessity," I replied. "I had to skip breakfast because I didn't have any more food in the house. I got hungry at the office. And then I thought you could surely throw together a nice brunch."

Georgios beamed. "You bet!" He eyed me briefly but intensely. "For you alone, or is your team coming too?"

His choice of words—*your team*—made me smile. "No, today I'm riding solo."

"It doesn't matter at all. I'll personally whip something up right away…" He hesitated, narrowed his eyes, and looked down the street. "Ah! There's Alex now! You won't have to stay solo after all."

I twisted over the corner of my seat and followed his gaze. Alex, in a suit without an overcoat, was walking toward us.

"Good morning," he said when he reached the table.

"Good morning," I replied.

"A *beautiful* good morning," said Georgios.

Alex made no attempt to join me. And he was not smiling.

Georgios looked from Alex to me and back again. He sighed, grabbed a chair, and invitingly pulled it out a little. "Please, Mr. Presiding President of the Courts. Have a seat with Evi. In the sun. It is good for the mind. Helps to put you in the right mood."

Alex frowned, but sat down.

"There we go," Georgios said. He turned to Alex. "I'm preparing a phenomenal brunch for Evi right now. I'm sure you want to eat something as well. Do you have any special requests?"

"No." Alex smiled slightly. "Surprise me. I put my complete trust in you."

"It's better that way." Georgios straightened his vest, nodded at us both, and disappeared into the restaurant.

Alex and I looked toward the river. We remained silent.

After a while, he cleared his throat. "We haven't had the opportunity to speak privately since the press conference."

"That's right," I said. "How did you find me here?"

"Wasn't hard. I called your office. Your secretary told me you went out for breakfast. The Poseidon seemed obvious."

"No secrets," I said.

"No secrets." He paused. "It was wrong of me to visit Suzanne Carstens. I shouldn't have convinced her that Peter Westphal had died. That was a big mistake and could have ended badly."

I brushed a lock of hair from my forehead. "And I should've known that you wouldn't give up and would try everything to crack this case. I should've stayed with you."

The waitress brought us mineral water and coffee. We kept quiet until we were alone again.

Alex picked up his coffee and took a sip.

"What made you change your mind?" I asked him. "Why didn't you disclose their involvement?"

"Why?" He put his cup down. "Honestly, I don't know. The moment Bolsen asked me for my update… I just didn't have it in me. I couldn't bring myself to do it."

"Because Suzanne Carstens and Peter Westphal deserve to be forgiven," I said.

"Yeah. Maybe that was it." He was playing around with a packet of sugar that had been lying on the saucer. "What are Suzanne and Peter doing now? Westphal has been released. He'll have to answer for what happened at the clinic, but we'll keep that to a minimum."

"Right now, they're both staying at the Hotel Atlantic."

"Suzanne did not want to return to the villa in Blankenese?"

"No." I shook my head. "She told me she's going to sell the property. She's looking for a developer to tear down the house and build something new there."

"It's probably for the better," Alex said.

"I think so."

"Do you know what else they've got planned?"

"Not really." I pursed my lips. "I suggested a good therapist to them. They want to move to the Danish border eventually. Close to the water. They can sail there, and he can continue to work as an underwater welder… What their future holds remains to be seen."

"Are the two of them going to make it?"

I cocked my head. "At least now they have a chance. It's up to them from here on."

"One thing still bothers me," said Alex.

"What's that?"

"The sitting pimp. Remember Peter Westphal told us he put Big Karl back in his chair after he shot him?" Alex furrowed his brow. "Why in the world would he have done that? I do not get it. Why didn't he just leave him lying on the ground?"

"Phew," I exhaled audibly. "We will never know for sure. However, I do have a theory."

"And what would that be?"

"The room was full of blood, death, and destruction. The gynecologist was sitting in a chair with his throat slit. Carstens died sitting in an armchair… By placing the pimp on one as well, Peter Westphal brought a certain kind of order into the chaos."

"Like he was… tidying up?"

I nodded. "At least subconsciously. In doing so, he proved to himself that he was still in control of the derailed situation."

"Which he wasn't."

"The illusion helped Peter Westphal think about what he still had to do."

"Cleaning the gun and returning it to the safe."

"For example." I nodded again. "As well as putting the glasses with the poison residue in the dishwasher and calling the police… And the whole time, he had to take care of Suzanne. Trying to get her out of her shock."

"Her shock was real?"

"It was. Most definitely."

Georgios and his waitress brought us two large platters lavishly laden with zucchini omelets, fava bean pâté, stuffed peppers, grape leaves, a cream cheese spread with garlic and basil, homemade pita bread, and sesame rings. Georgios had even thought of my beloved honey rolls.

He quietly took note of our compliments, wished us bon appétit, and left us to our brunch.

Alex was hungry too. We remained silent for a while and ate.

My coffee was empty. Alex looked at me, I bowed my head, and he poured me another cup.

"The murders in the villa caused a massive avalanche," he said.

"Mhmm," I replied. "At least that part Bolsen got right."

Alex snorted. "Even though he played down Björn Carstens's involvement."

"Bolsen is practically a politician," I said. "We all know that Carstens was pulling the strings. He was the boss. He had contact with this Ivanov in Russia."

"Sure," Alex agreed with me. He dipped a piece of his sesame ring into the fava.

"The two Russians we roused out of the farmhouse were clearly working for Ivanov," I said.

"He dispatched them after the goods in the containers *went bad*. The goons were sent to check it out. That's why they kidnapped the two dockworkers and tortured them. And when they found out that Carstens and company were all dead, Ivanov ordered them to *clean up*."

"That's what I think too. Ivanov must have known that Carstens had created a dossier on him. He definitely didn't want that to get into the wrong hands." I concentrated on my honey roll. Super sweet, super crispy. Simply wonderful.

"That's why they broke into the villa," Alex continued. "And that's how come they were after Suzanne Carstens. The BND man told us that this is Ivanov's trademark. He always cleans up very thoroughly and takes revenge on all of his opponents' living relatives."

I grabbed a napkin and wiped my fingers. "No sign from the fugitive Russian yet?"

Alex twisted his mouth. "It's like he disappeared from the face of the Earth. I assume he snuck onto some ship and is already back in Russia."

"You don't like that," I stated.

"No."

"The same as it goes against your grain that we couldn't put a stop to Dmitri Ivanov's operation."

Alex lifted a finger. "Not *yet*. Criminals like that won't quit. One of these days he's going to get caught."

"Let's hope so," I said.

DMITRI IVANOV

Mikhail had not even managed to set foot on land. No sooner had the ship reached the port in Kaliningrad than they overpowered him. Three or four men—he could not tell. They put a sack over his head, cuffed his hands behind his back, and threw him into the trunk of a car.

A few hours later, tied to a chair in some warehouse, the torture began. They alternately beat him, strangled him, and tormented him with electric cattle prods. Over and over again, without uttering a single word. In complete silence.

At first, he screamed, asserted his innocence, and wailed. Then he begged them to stop and promised them money. Without success. Finally, he gave up and accepted whatever they were going to do to him. Time had no meaning anymore—there was only the pain.

"That's enough!" A voice reached him from a distance.

His tormentors let up on him.

Mikhail slowly raised his head. His left eye was swollen shut. He blinked to clear the other eye of the drops of sweat and blood that were further clouding his vision.

There was a man in the doorway that he did not recognize. Expensive suit, tie.

Mikhail's heart pounded wildly. It had to be Dmitri Ivanov. He would explain everything to Ivanov, and then this nightmare would end.

The man did not come any closer. He stayed where he was.

"All of you out! Now!" he said. "Ivanov is here."

Mikhail's torturers obeyed immediately. They grabbed their jackets and left the room. The man in the suit followed them and closed the door behind him. Shortly thereafter, Mikhail could make out motors starting. The vehicles drove away. Silence returned.

Mikhail heard a repetitive scratching sound. His breath. That was all.

And suddenly, footsteps.

Mikhail began to wheeze.

The door opened. A person approached, paused, and looked down at him.

"Where is Ivanov?" Mikhail managed to get out.

A slow smile spread across the face of his counterpart. And Mikhail understood.

"*You?*"

The smile deepened. Ivanov pulled up a chair, sat down and put a pistol on one knee. A Stechkin decorated with golden trim.

"Where's the dossier?" Ivanov asked.

Mikhail swallowed. "I don't have it."

"The file that Carstens kept on me. Where is it?"

"I don't know," Mikhail muttered.

Ivanov's tongue clicked disapprovingly. "You removed it from the safe, as you were contracted to do?"

Mikhail wanted to nod vehemently but broke off suddenly due to the abrupt pain in his neck. "It was there. We took it with us," he said hastily. "There is no longer any danger. It is gone."

"Gone? Where?"

"Sergei. Sergei hid it. He didn't tell me where he put it."

Ivanov frowned. "Sergei—that was your partner? The one who was shot by the prosecutor? By this Gutenberg?"

"Yes."

"And what about Suzanne Carstens?"

This is not going well. It's not going well at all, Mikhail thought to himself. He had to try to turn everything around for the better.

"Believe me," he stammered. "I did my utmost. As soon as the prosecutor tracked us down, I went straight to the hotel where they kept the granddaughter under police protection. I got to her room. But then more cops showed up and I…"

Ivanov waved him off. "I'm not interested. Did you kill her?"

"No," Mikhail whimpered.

"Well." Ivanov sighed. "This is a most unfortunate development."

"But *I* am not to blame," Mikhail pleaded desperately. "I followed all your instructions without exception. We procured the file. We snatched the two employees from the port and left them as a message in the Easter fire in Blankenese. No one will even dare to think of doing something against you!"

"Uh-huh," Ivanov said, nodding slowly. "That's right. You have given it your best."

"I did! I really did! It was not my fault. We didn't have any support, didn't know our way around…"

Ivanov raised a hand. "Hush now. I can understand that. And I am under the same impression."

Ivanov understood. Mikhail's relief was immense.

"If you want something done…" Ivanov continued. "Especially when what has to be done is a more demanding undertaking… You have to do it yourself."

"Exactly," Mikhail rushed to agree. "I will help you with it. You can count on me. I've proven that I am loyal and one hundred percent on your side."

"Yes. You have."

Ivanov got up. "You have been a good soldier."

"The…" Mikhail began.

Ivanov raised the gun and shot him in the abdomen. Once, twice.

Mikhail's body writhed on the chair from the shock of the impact. He felt something warm run down his thigh. Then the pain came. Explosive. He began to scream.

Ivanov stood in front of him and watched him with slightly tilted head and pursed lips. After a while, Ivanov raised the Stechkin again, aimed at Mikhail's chest, and pulled the trigger.

Fading, Mikhail heard Ivanov sigh, "Hamburg. I haven't been there for quite some time. A beautiful city. Let's see how it has changed."

Dear Reader,

We hope you have enjoyed MOONSLAUGHTER, and you were able to spend some exciting hours with Dr. Evelin Wolf and Alex Gutenberg.

On the next page is a list of our English novels.

Sincerely
Yours

Roxann Hill and Paul Wagle

PS: Dr. Evelin Wolf and Alex Gutenberg will return in DARK SCAR!

ENGLISH NOVELS BY ROXANN HILL AND PAUL WAGLE

Roxann Hill and Paul Wagle

<u>Wolf and Gutenberg Psychological Thrillers</u>

- MOONSLAUGHTER
  Dr. Evelin Wolf and Alex Gutenberg, vol. 1
- DARK SCAR
  Dr. Evelin Wolf and Alex Gutenberg, vol. 2
- TAINTED MIND
  Dr. Evelin Wolf and Alex Gutenberg, vol 3

Dr. Evelin Wolf und Alex Gutenberg will return!

Roxann Hill – translated by Paul Wagle

<u>Misfit Girl Suspense Thriller Series</u>

- MISFIT GIRL: DEATH OF THE BLUE FLOWER
  Misfit Girl, vol. 1
  (First published by AmazonCrossing in 2015. Revised, updated, newly edited, and republished by Roxann Hill and Paul Wagle in 2024).

THE AUTHORS

Roxann Hill

Roxann Hill is one of the most successful thriller authors in the German-speaking world. Her novels have delighted millions of readers and are regularly among the top titles on the bestseller lists. Her books have been translated into multiple languages.
Born in Brno/Czech Republic, the author lives with her family and two large dogs in Middle Franconia.

Paul Wagle

© Frank Peters

Paul Wagle was born the youngest of twelve children in Wichita Kansas. After graduating with a Philosophy degree from the University of Kansas he served in the United States Peace Corps in Ecuador. He moved from South America to Europe where he resides in Berlin with his three children.

Copyright Moonslaughter
© 2024 Roxann Hill and Paul Wagle
Roxann Hill, Schenkstr. 122, 91052 Erlangen, Germany

Printed in Great Britain
by Amazon